GREED

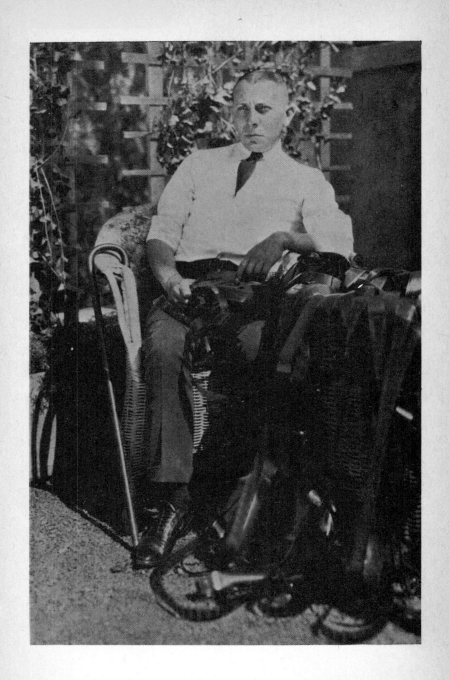

Greed

ERICH VON STROHEIM

faber and faber

LONDON · BOSTON

First published in 1972
by Lorrimer Publishing Limited
Reissued in 1989
by Faber and Faber Limited
3 Queen Square London WC1N 3AU

Printed in Great Britain by
Richard Clay Ltd, Bungay, Suffolk
All rights reserved

British Library Cataloguing in Publication Data is available

ISBN 0-571-12581-6

CONTENTS

A NOTE ON THE SCRIPT OF *GREED*

This volume contains Erich von Stroheim's original ten hour shooting script for the film *Greed*. This film has only been seen by the public in a severely mutilated version, and it is hoped that this publication will allow the reader to visualise the film as it was originally intended by Stroheim. The history of the film and Stroheim's problems with his producers and distributors are well known, and are fully discussed in the introductory articles.

The original script was first published by the Belgian Cinémathèque in 1958 in conjunction with their presentation of *Greed* as one of the Twelve Best Films of All Time. The text was that of Erich von Stroheim's personal copy, preserved after his death by Mme. Denise Vernac. For the present publication the original script was carefully checked against the release version of the film by Joel W. Finler and any additional material incorporated into the text. Significant divergences between the two versions are indicated in the following ways :

1. All scenes contained in the original script but missing from the film are enclosed in square brackets.

2. In many cases whole sequences were removed and new title cards inserted by MGM to fill the breaks in the plot. These are indicated by footnotes.

3. Other alterations in the transition from script to film are indicated by footnotes and/or square brackets.

Stroheim's text is reproduced as closely as possible; however much of his technical description was in semi-note form, and this has been expanded and clarified wherever possible without impairing the flavour of his highly individual and idiosyncratic style. It might be noted in this context that the use of American slang terms and pseudo-German phraseology in describing the Sieppe family was in fact derived from Frank Norris's novel.

Acknowledgements and thanks are due to MGM, L'Avant-Scène du Cinéma and Joel W. Finler for providing stills; special thanks to Herman G. Weinberg for making available his entire unique collection of stills; also to Thorold Dickinson of the Slade Film School and to Andrew Birkin. Grateful thanks are further due to Nicholas Fry, Nicola Hayden and Herman G. Weinberg for their extensive editorial work and helpful suggestions in the preparation of this volume.

S.W.

The entire cast and crew of *Greed* assembled outside the main San Francisco location.

DREAMS OF REALISM . . .

I had graduated from the D. W. Griffith school of film making and intended to go the Master one better as regards film realism. In real cities, not corners of them designed by Cedric Gibbons or Richard Days, but in real tree-bordered boulevards, with real street-cars, buses and automobiles, through real winding alleys, with real dirt and foulness, in the gutters as well as in real castles and palaces. I was going to people my scenes with real men, women and children, as we meet them every day in real life. I was going to dress them as they actually dressed in life, in bad as well as in good taste, clean and dirty, faultless and ragged, but without exaggeration, without modification, and without the then currently popular concession to the conventions of the stage and screen. I was going to film stories which would be believable, life-like, even if I had to make them realistic to the Nth degree. I intended to show men and women as they are all over the world, none of them perfect, with their good and bad qualities, their noble and idealistic sides and their jealous, vicious, mean and greedy sides. I was not going to compromise. I felt that after the last war, the motion picture going public had tired of the cinematographic ' chocolate eclairs ' which had been stuffed down their throats, and which had in a large degree figuratively ruined their stomachs with this overdose of saccharose in pictures. Now, I felt, they were ready for a large bowl of plebeian but honest ' corned beef and cabbage '. I felt that they had become weary of insipid Pollyanna stories with their peroxide-blonde, doll-like heroines, steeped in eternal virginity, and their hairless flat-chested sterile heroes, who were as lily-white as the heroines. I thought

7

they could no longer bear to see the stock villains, dyed-in-the wool, 100 per cent black, armed with moustache, mortgage and riding crop.

I believed audiences were ready to witness real drama and real tragedy, as it happens every day in every land; real love and real hatred of real men and women who were proud of their passions. I felt that the time was ripe to present screen stories about men and women who defied with written and unwritten codes, and who took the consequence of their defiance gallantly, like many people do in real life. People who defied prejudice and jealousies, conventions and the social mores of a hypocritical society, who fought for their passions, conquered them or were conquered by them.

I knew that everything could be done with film, the only medium with which one could reproduce life as it actually was. I knew also that an entertainment that mirrored life would be more entertainment than one which distorted it. The sky was the limit! Whatever man could dream of, I could and would reproduce it in my films. I was going to metamorphose the ' movies ' into an art — a composite of all arts. Fight for it! and die for it, if need be! . . . Well, fight I did. . . . And die . . . I almost did, too!

ERICH VON STROHEIM
Extracts from an unpublished article.

INTRODUCING *GREED*

by Joel W. Finler

Erich von Stroheim was born in Vienna, and emigrated to the United States in about 1906. After trying his hand at a wide variety of jobs, he arrived in Hollywood in 1914. He was hired as an extra for *Birth of a Nation,* and remained with the Griffith Organization for a number of years, working on many films either produced or directed by D. W. Griffith. Stroheim gained more important acting roles and also served as art director, military advisor and assistant director during those years.

Such experience provided the ideal background for Stroheim's debut as director, and star, of *Blind Husbands* in 1918, which was based on his own story and script. The immediate success of *Blind Husbands* gave him the opportunity to direct *The Devil's Passkey* in 1919, and this was followed by his spectacular production of *Foolish Wives.* During the 1918-22 period Stroheim emerged as the leading director of Carl Laemmle's Universal Studios. He helped to establish Universal as one of the leading Hollywood production companies in spite of the gradual deterioration in his personal relations with the studio executives including the young Irving Thalberg.

Stroheim's conflict with the studio began during the production of *Foolish Wives* which was meant to run for about four hours, with an interval. But the film was released in a substantially shortened version, mutilated by the releasing studio (Universal) and the censor. Yet *Foolish Wives* was a great international success and made Stroheim's name as a director. Stroheim's disputes with the studio, however, continued during the production of his following film, *Merry-Go-Round,* and he was replaced by another director before filming was completed.

All of Stroheim's early films enjoyed considerable success with contemporary audiences. He became known for his sophisticated approach to characterisation and sexual intrigue and for the kind of subtle, witty and ironic touches that only a European director could bring to such subjects. (Stroheim began a Hollywood tradition which was continued by such Viennese directors as Ernst Lubitsch and Billy Wilder.) Although filmed in and around Hollywood, all of Stroheim's films were remarkable for the authenticity of their European atmosphere.

Although Stroheim first distinguished himself as a director of films

9

with a distinctly Continental flavour and setting, his cherished project for many years had been to adapt Frank Norris's novel *McTeague,* which was set in California at the turn of the century. He was convinced of the exceptional cinematic potential of the story, but such a powerful example of ' naturalistic ' writing was generally considered to have little commercial appeal. Stroheim had been unable to find the necessary financing until 1923, when he finally was given the opportunity to begin shooting the story, retitled *Greed,* for the Goldwyn Picture Corporation.

The powerful and fantastic elements in Norris's novel probably attracted Stroheim as much as the visual or dramatic qualities of the story. Stroheim's ' cinematic naturalism ' represented an attempt, following Norris's lead, to probe beneath the surface of life and human behaviour. And he saw the use of actual locations as a means of lending added force to the grotesque or unbelievable aspects of the story. In this he discovered a principle which has been of lasting importance in the cinema.

During the period that he was shooting and editing *Greed,* Goldwyn Pictures was involved in a merger, which resulted in the formation of Metro-Goldwyn-Mayer, headed by Louis B. Mayer. Irving Thalberg, Stroheim's arch-enemy from Universal, was hired by Mayer to serve as his executive producer. Both men were less than sympathetic to the *Greed* project, which was far from their ideal of screen entertainment. So when Stroheim presented them with a film of 42 reels (about ten hours), it confirmed their worst fears. They insisted that he should reduce it, and he cut it to 24 reels. The studio regarded even this as excessive, and still refused to accept it. Stroheim gave the film to his friend and fellow-director, Rex Ingram, who collaborated with his regular editor, Grant Whytock, in reducing the film to 18 reels, which he regarded as the bare minimum. These two shortened versions, designed to be exhibited in two parts, separated by an interval, probably represented the ideal compromise between Stroheim's original conception and the demands of the releasing studio. But then the film was taken away from him by the studio and given to an anonymous cutter unfamiliar with the novel, and with Stroheim's style. He reduced *Greed* to a mere ten reels, and this mutilated version was released late in 1924.

During the following years Stroheim returned to the Continental subjects with which he had first made his name. His free interpretation of *The Merry Widow* in 1926 was a great box-office success for M-G-M and earned the company far more money than had been lost on *Greed.* And this was followed by Stroheim's most accomplished

10

and original work (aside from *Greed*) — *The Wedding March*. But again, as with *Foolish Wives* and *Greed*, Stroheim's ambitious plans to complete the film in two parts were thwarted by the releasing studio (Paramount). And his last two films as a director, *Queen Kelly* (1928) and *Walking Down Broadway* (1932) provide a sad epilogue to his career, for both were taken from him and released in a mutilated form.

In filming *Greed*, however, Stroheim fulfilled his stated ambition to put the Norris novel on the screen in its complete form, without that adulteration of the original which often takes place. One can gain a fairly accurate idea of Stroheim's full version of the film from the Norris book. The film was cut down mainly by the elimination of entire subplots and complete sequences, rather than the cutting or rearranging of shots within a sequence. And the order of the sequences was not altered, except for the pub fight between McTeague and Marcus. But many of the titles were crudely altered from those carefully composed by Stroheim or quoted from Norris, and new titles were hastily composed to fill in the substantial gaps in the plot.

A ten-minute fragment of the prologue is all which remains of the opening section of the film, most of which is original Stroheim material not found in the novel. Based on a brief flashback from the book, the prologue was meant to give a full picture of McTeague's early life in the mining camp where his father is shift boss and his mother is the company cook. The character of McTeague Sr. has been entirely eliminated from the film, including an extraordinary sequence in the saloon-brothel where he drinks himself into a stupor and dies of alcohol poisoning.

Also missing from the film are the scenes of McTeague's apprenticeship to the travelling dentist and his arrival in San Francisco. And this was meant to be followed by a long sequence introducing all the important characters in San Francisco on a typical Saturday afternoon. Here Stroheim blended plot and subplot, realistic and fantasy sequences setting the tone for the rest of the film. In addition to introducing the two main subplots, this opening sequence in San Francisco included the first of many scenes at the home of the Sieppe family in suburban

Oakland, all of which were cut as well.

The main subplot was meant to depict the relationship between Maria, the charlady, and Zerkow, the old junk dealer. Maria sells Trina the fateful lottery ticket and steals pieces of dental gold from McTeague which she sells to old Zerkow. Her tales of a solid gold dinner service stimulate the old man's vivid imagination. And at one point he dreams of unearthing the gold in a cemetery amid twisted crosses and open graves. This subplot appeared as a grotesque parody of the McTeague's marriage, and the two stories were linked by a series of symbolic shots of emaciated hands fondling gold coins and a gold dinner service. A few of these shots remain in the film, but have been inserted haphazardly and not in accordance with Stroheim's precise plan, while the character of Zerkow has been entirely eliminated.

The second subplot told the romantic story of a nice little old lady and gentleman who fall in love. Their romance flourishes at the same time and in the same house where the marriage between McTeague and Trina begins to decline. Presented in typical ' naturalist ' fashion, as in Norris's novel, the two missing subplots thus provided an ironic counterpoint to the relationship between McTeague and Trina throughout the film.

The severe mutilation of *Greed* meant many cuts in the main story as well. The development of McTeague's early relationship with Trina, is missing all the shots of him brooding alone in his room or seeking advice from Marcus or visiting the Sieppe's home in Oakland. And after his fight with Marcus in the pub he was meant to return home to find the giant gilt tooth awaiting him, a surprise gift from Trina. But the central portion of the film after their marriage is the most severely cut of all, with every other aspect of the story neglected in favour of Trina's developing obsession with gold. We see very little of their happily married life together and the beneficial influence which Trina has had upon McTeague's slovenly ' bachelor habits '. The long picnic sequence when McTeague fights with Marcus and almost kills him has been entirely eliminated, and the pub fight transposed to this point from earlier in the film.

In accordance with ' naturalist ' principles, the rise and fall of the McTeagues was meant to be closely related to their economic circumstances. When Mac loses his dental practice, they move from their apartment into a small back room in the same house. And towards the end of the film they occupy that same squalid shack in the back yard which had formerly been the home of Maria and Zerkow. Whereas Trina's potential obsession is kept well under control during the years of happy married life and is meant to emerge only gradually, in the mutilated film her transformation is telescoped into a few dramatic scenes. The concluding portion of the film, detailing McTeague's murder of Trina and subsequent departure from San Francisco in the direction of Death Valley, has suffered less from cutting. But Mac's return to the mine where he grew up and success as a prospector with old Cribbens has been cut, while the reduction of the Death Valley sequence means that one loses the feeling of the gradual deterioration in Mac's spirit as he sets out across the desert.

The mutilation has destroyed the original balance of the work, for, like Norris's novel, *Greed* was meant to present a counterpoint between the 'realistic' main plot, and the grotesque or subjective sequences. These were largely concentrated in the subplots and prologue which were entirely eliminated from the released film. Since all that remains is the bare bones of the central plot, *Greed* has gained a reputation as Stroheim's one, uncompromisingly realistic film. In fact, it originally had much more in common with his other films than is generally realised. For Stroheim, as for Norris, the goal was not 'realism' but 'naturalism'. In other words, the aspiration towards a certain objectivity and authenticity of situation and setting, was balanced by the frequently exceptional, even pathological, nature of many of the characters. These are the extraordinary creations of a vivid imagination and have only a slight connection with the objective observation of the life of the time.

Although the opening sections of *Greed* consist largely of original Stroheim material, they are fully integrated with the rest of the film. This material draws attention to Stroheim's artistic affinity with Norris and the 'naturalistic' literary movement of the nineteenth century, of which Norris was a leading American exponent. Although Norris died shortly after the turn of the century and is regarded as a nineteenth century figure, he and Stroheim were born only 15 years apart. Stroheim's *Greed* screenplay suggests that his style of writing is related to that of the 'naturalists', and this was later reaffirmed by his own novels of the thirties, which were strongly 'naturalistic' in style and conception.

Stroheim naturally disowned the version of the film as it was released in 1924, and was extremely bitter about the ruin of a project to which he had devoted so much time and creative effort. Even in this shortened version, however, *Greed* has earned much critical praise, and it has been widely shown and appreciated throughout the world. *Greed* has become one of the most celebrated *films maudits* in the history of the cinema, and it is one of the few silent films which lives up to its reputation as a true film classic.

13

STROHEIM'S *GREED*

by Herman G. Weinberg

One late evening in 1924, three men (accompanied by a silent and brooding fourth) staggered from a projection room where they had been viewing a single film for the previous eight hours, and unanimously declared that they had just seen not only the greatest motion picture ever made, but one that would probably never again be equalled, let alone surpassed. The three men who made this statement were Idwal Jones, a San Francisco journalist (who still contributes occasionally to *The New York Times* and who has since written several books on California), Harry Carr, ex-foreign correspondent and scenarist, and Rex Ingram, director of *The Four Horsemen of The Apocalypse, Mare Nostrum,* etc. The fourth was Erich von Stroheim, the director of the film they had just seen. The film was *Greed* in its entirety, some forty-odd reels.

This film was the realization of a vow Stroheim had made many years before, shortly after he arrived in the U.S. He was living, practically destitute, in a ramshackle hotel in New York and happened to find a copy of a book called *McTeague* by Frank Norris on the dresser in his dingy room, probably left there by the preceding tenant. What a thing is chance! In such an accidental way the seed of *Greed* began to germinate in Stroheim's mind. He read the book that night only because it was there and he had nothing better to do. As the book advertisements are fond of saying, ' He couldn't put it down.' He read the thing through at white heat and it was this story, after he had finished reading it, that decided him on a career in motion pictures. This was before the First World War when films were still little more than a novelty for the penny arcade and the nickelodeon trade. To have such a vision then, of filming this great naturalistic novel by one of America's then foremost writers (frequently referred to as ' the American Zola '), was to have vision indeed, and a remarkable sense of prophesy, unconscious or not. That the movies could ever grow up to become a medium wherein such a story could be filmed — and what is even more, that he, a young penniless immigrant lately come from a stint in the Austrian army to seek his fortune in a new world, could make such a film himself without even any training in the theatre, let alone what little training anyone could have had in those

14

days in the film — was to have a vision for which 'daring' is too mild a word. It was, perhaps, unprecedented. When intellectuals and anyone with the slightest artistic pretence had contempt for this ingenious toy, the 'kinetoscope,' here was a man with a wonderful vision of what this contemptible gadget could do. (It is, perhaps, not without irony that we can observe today how this has been completely reversed : how the ' gadget ' has now become such a miraculous instrument and the films turned out by it so frequently contemptible.)

But the dream to film *McTeague* was put aside, and lay dormant for the decade ahead, in which the necessity to earn a living at any kind of a job was always pressing. A singer of German lieder in a New York rathskeller, a flypaper salesman in the Southwest ('where it was so hot the flies didn't have the energy to fly high enough to reach the kind of flypaper I was selling — the long spiral kind that hung down from chandeliers — so I had to find something else '), a lifeguard at Lake Tahoe who couldn't swim, a riding master (he could ride), a rail-worker — all of this doubtless was to give him a good insight into the seamy side of life on which he was to draw when he actually did become a film director. He also served for a while in the American army in the Mexican campaign.

His early years in Hollywood as extra, assistant director, technical consultant, etc., are too well known to detail here. He sold Carl Laemmle the idea of letting him make his first picture, *Blind Husbands,* which was such a success that Laemmle let him make a second directly afterwards, *The Devil's Passkey.* This, too, was a success and by this time Stroheim could have anything he wanted. He embarked on a spectacular production, *Foolish Wives,* the film which made him internationally famous and of which Renoir said that it had induced him to abandon his career in ceramics for that of the cinema. ' If such a thing were possible in films, then I wanted to work in that medium, too,' said Renoir in 1922. With three hits behind him (including considerable controversy over moral aspects of his last picture which sent the censors, official and self-appointed, scurrying for their scissors), Stroheim was riding the crest of the wave and could film any subject he wanted to under his own terms and conditions. In Hollywood there were then only two others with the same power : Chaplin and Griffith. Most other directors in such a position would not have jeopardized this position of wealth, power, and fame. They would have played it safe. Not Stroheim. When he felt himself psychologically ready to obtain his demands (even after the abortive *Merry Go Round* which followed *Foolish Wives* and which was taken from him early in its production and turned over to another director, because of a difference of opinion

15

between him and Laemmle's production chief, Irving Thalberg), Stroheim felt that now was the time to realize the ambition of his first precarious days in America — to film *McTeague*.

He was out of Laemmle's company, Universal, so he approached the Goldwyn Company and sold them the idea. That they let him embark on it at all must be set down as a first miracle, since it was in direct opposition to everything movies had been up to that time, at least in America. The story of five people destroyed by greed was hardly the kind of story people would rush to the box office for. Movies were very much an escape medium (as they still are, of course), and only Stroheim's powers of persuasion could have overcome any producer's natural resistance to such a pessimistic work.

What was the movie world like at the time Stroheim began to make *Greed*? He had nothing to draw from, no precedent for what he was about to do; he was like a lone explorer setting out into an arid waste. It could cost him his professional life, but he didn't care. Armed with just a 'compass,' Norris' book, he wrote his own script (June Mathis, credited with the script in the ten-reel version now shown was on contract to Metro-Goldwyn-Mayer which had taken over the Goldwyn company in mid-production, and her contract stated that she was to get credit for the script on all MGM pictures, as she was technically head of their script department), he cast it himself (no casting director was ever on a Stroheim-directed film), and, with Captain Richard Day, chose the sets himself. One uses the word 'chose' aptly for no sets were built for the film. All exteriors were shot in the streets and suburbs of San Francisco and the final sequence, in Death Valley; all interiors were shot in actual houses in San Francisco and its suburbs, which the film company rented. Since Frank Norris' book was based on an actual murder case that had taken place in San Francisco, Stroheim went out of his way to rent the very building in which the murder had taken place. To add still more realism, Stroheim had his actors stay in these same buildings during the shooting period, 'to get into the feel of it.' Cedric Gibbons got credit for the 'sets' for the same reason Miss Mathis got credit for the script, namely, that he was head set designer at MGM and his contract, too, stated that he was to be credited with the sets of all MGM pictures. Although Stroheim only got paid for actual shooting time, and was not given any extra salary for all the other activities mentioned here, he was so set on having this film turn out just the way he wanted it, that he was ready to forego the financial returns which by right were due to him. He felt that true realism could not otherwise be achieved. His fanatical quest for more realistic portrayals sometimes led him to extremes, and

16

Erich von Stroheim (centre) with Zasu Pitts, Gibson Gowland and other principal actors of Greed.

Jean Hersholt tells the story of the filming at Death Valley, where Stroheim actually drove his actors frantic until they were in such a state of wrath that they had no difficulty in playing the scenes of the fight at the end of the picture.

Cesare Gravina, who already had appeared in two films under Stroheim (*Foolish Wives* and *Merry Go Round*), was recalled by Stroheim from South America, where he was accompanying his wife, a singer, on an opera tour, to return to Hollywood for the role of Zerkow, the junkman. Unfortunately, all his scenes were later cut out by MGM. Dale Fuller, who had also served under Stroheim in *Foolish Wives* and *Merry Go Round,* was recruited again for the half-demented Maria Macapa. Gibson Gowland, who was in Stroheim's first picture, *Blind Husbands,* was to play McTeague (and was called from England to do so), and Zasu Pitts was rescued from idiotic comedies in which she was then appearing to make her debut as a tragic actress as Trina — another of Stroheim's daring innovations. Jean Hersholt, an anonymous screen extra at the time, was chosen as Marcus. They were all part of the 'Stroheim Stock Company,' as they

17

were facetiously called, all, with the exception of Hersholt, having appeared in two or more Stroheim films. Other members of this 'stock company' were Maude George, Mae Busch, George Nichols, George Fawcett, Sidney Bracey, and Hughie Mack.

When Stroheim sought an insurance policy to cover the players and crew who were to go to Death Valley, it was refused him, but he went anyway. It must be remembered that the Death Valley of 1923 was not what it is today — there were no sleek automobile roads, no hotels or inns, no gasoline stations, no water — just a lot of the most desolate, hot, miserable nothing on the whole continent. There were tarantulas, scorpions, snakes and other such fauna. It was so hot, and there was so little water, that a shuttle of trucks was instituted between the locations in Death Valley and the nearest town, one hundred miles away, carrying out members of the crew who collapsed daily. When the shooting was finished in Death Valley, which are the final scenes in the film, Jean Hersholt spent weeks in a hospital suffering from an internal haemorrhage induced by the heat.

The picture was finally completed at a total cost of under $500,000, which by standards then or today was a low budget. Since Stroheim's contract called for him to be paid only while directing, he had to cut the film without salary. This he would have been only too glad to do, had they let him cut it, but they didn't. The original version he showed his friends, Idwal Jones, Harry Carr (with whom he was later to collaborate on the script of *The Wedding March*) and Rex Ingram, was the complete first rough cut. Stroheim, realizing that no film could run that long, cut it himself to twenty-four reels (four hours), beyond which he said he could not take out another foot. When MGM threatened to cut it down themselves to marketable length, he sent it to his very close friend, Rex Ingram, to reduce further. The latter cut it down to eighteen reels and warned him that he would never speak to him again if he cut out another foot. By this time, MGM lost patience and took the film away from Stroheim to cut themselves. ('It was cut by a hack cutter who had nothing on his mind but his hat,' was the way Stroheim refers to that painful episode.) When it emerged from the MGM cutting room, it was down to ten reels, which is the version the world knows as *Greed*. Here was, perhaps, the only film in history in which more was missing than was contained in it. The version you see today is about one-quarter of the first rough cut version and less than half of the one Stroheim was satisfied to compromise with the twenty-four reel one. So even of this 'compromise' version, there is more missing than you see.

What is missing? Those who have read Norris' book and have seen

18

Greed, needn't be told. They know, for everything that was in the book was originally in the film. For those who have not read Norris' book, the following are the principal scenes missing :

(a) The entire secondary story between Maria Macapa and Zerkow the junkman. Maria Macapa is seen only in a few brief scenes as the Spanish-American servant girl who sells Trina the lottery ticket which starts the woeful chain of events that destroys them all. But her relation to Zerkow, the Polish junkman, to whom she relates fabulous tales of golden service plate her family used to have and who drives the little man, greedy with lust for the golden vessels, until he kills her when she can't produce them and then throws himself into San Francisco Bay — all this is out. Not a foot of film showing Cesare Gravina in the role of Zerkow is left in the film.

(b) A third parallel story, the romance between the nice little old lady and the nice old gentleman, which flourishes in the same house where McTeague had his dental parlours, and where another romance, that between McTeague and Trina, begins to decay with the acquisition by Trina of the $5,000 won in the lottery.

(c) All the scenes of the Sieppe family, of Trina's parents and little brothers, in their home in the suburbs.

(d) The transition of Trina from McTeague's sweet and loving wife to a miserly shrew after she wins the $5,000 from the lottery. Innumerable details are missing, like the scene where Trina goes to the bank to cash her $5,000 cheque and asks to be given it in gold pieces. The character of Trina's uncle is omitted entirely, too. He kept Trina's money for her and let her draw on it whenever she wished. This explains why McTeague knew Trina had all her gold pieces with her that night at the children's school, because he went first to her uncle who told him she had drawn the entire balance.

(e) The entire sequence after the murder of Trina by McTeague between the time he kills her and until his arrival in Death Valley, where he goes to escape with the gold pieces, including his wanderings around San Francisco and Placer County.

(f) Innumerable scenes of long, bony hands voluptuously fondling gold coins and gold vessels (only a few remain, inserted haphazardly and not as a refrain as originally intended). All the nightmare scenes of Zerkow dreaming of unearthing Maria Macapa's golden service plate in a cemetery where she said they were buried, amid twisted crosses and open graves. The hallucinations of Trina in which the bloodied Maria Macapa, after she has been knifed to death by Zerkow, comes to haunt her with ' Wanna buy a lottery ticket? ' The smiling corpse of Maria Macapa twines itself around Trina. ' Wanna buy a lottery ticket?' This happens at a time when the pitiful Trina realizes her life has been ruined by the lottery ticket, but she is helpless against her own lust for her beautiful, shining gold pieces.

(g) Many close-ups and other shots characterizing McTeague's attitude towards Trina and Trina's attitude towards her husband in the first months of their marriage — scenes of real tenderness.

(h) All the scenes of McTeague's father, a foreman at the mine, and a congenital alcoholic. Every Saturday night he turned into a drunken, raging beast in the miners' saloon, with its blowzy 'hostesses,' who took whatever was left of the miners' pay that didn't go for drinks. In this version there are no scenes of McTeague's father at all, and all scenes of the saloon are missing. There was a terrific scene of delirium tremens in this sequence, where McTeague's father sees a snake slowly coming out of a whiskey bottle at him. It is because McTeague's mother doesn't want her son to become a drunkard among the miners like his father, that she persuades him to take up a profession like dentistry, actuated by the chance arrival in town of Dr. 'Painless' Potter, an itinerant dentist-charlatan.

(i) Many shots of Death Valley which gave the sense of the day-by-day, slow, inexorable breakdown of McTeague's spirit as he realizes he has trapped himself in this desolate waste — long before Marcus catches up with him.

It should be stated in closing that the actual incident on which Frank Norris' book is based, took place in San Francisco just before the turn of the century. It should further be stated that Stroheim has disowned the butchered version of *Greed* you see, and that although despite its mutilation it still remains an uncommonly powerful work, he feels towards it as one would feel toward a man lacking one leg, an arm and one eye. He is still a man and can still function, after a fashion. *Greed* (the name given the film by June Mathis, it was originally to be named *McTeague*) is still a film and can still function in that respect, also after a fashion. But a man is born whole, as *Greed* was also born whole. Would anyone attempt to justify the mutilation of a man by saying 'War is War'? As well attempt to justify the mutilation of *Greed* by saying 'Business is Business.'

Even if it were a case of 'Business is Business,' it is shameful and inexcusable on any grounds that the negative of the original *Greed* was not saved for posterity. (Hope springs eternal in the true archivist's breast and a print of the complete *Greed* is the holy grail in his life. . .) This would have harmed no one, as saving the complete negative of Eisenstein's *Que Viva Mexico* would have harmed no one. It would have enabled us to see the full extent of the genius of these two great masters of the film, like nothing else they had ever done. That is the irreparable loss. The world can afford to lose some of its 'businessmen' — it cannot afford the loss of a single artist or work of art. How idiotic is Joyce Kilmer's 'Poems are made by fools like me, but only God can make a tree.' There are billions of trees in the world — there is scarcely a handful of great poems.

(Reprinted from *Saint Cinema* by Herman G. Weinberg, by permission of the publishers, Drama Book Specialists, New York.)

MY EXPERIENCES WITH STROHEIM DURING THE MAKING OF GREED

by Jean Hersholt

I was working with Mae Murray when I was informed that Stroheim wanted me to play the part of Marcus Schouler in *Greed*. I had already read the novel and knew what a wonderful opportunity the role would afford me, so I signed a contract with Goldwyn then and there to make the picture at 250 dollars a week. In February, 1923, Stroheim returned to Hollywood with the script in his pocket and his principals signed up and ready to go to work.

I shall never forget my first sight of ' Von ', as his friends always called him. I was standing just inside the gates of the Culver City Studios, when he drove up in his huge car, a liveried chauffeur at the wheel. With him was his assistant and business manager, Eddie Sowders, whom I happened to know. As Von got out of the car, Eddie came up to me and shook hands. He turned to his chief — massive, erect, groomed to perfection, with the famous haircut and smoking a cigarette in a long holder. ' I don't think you have met Jean Hersholt,' said Eddie, ' whom you have signed for the part of Marcus Schouler.'

Stroheim took the cigarette holder from between his lips and stared at me.

' Are you Jean Hersholt? ' he queried finally in his guttural voice. ' You are not the type I want at all.'

It was my turn to stare this time. Eddie looked rather confused as Von turned to him.

' Is Mr. Hersholt actually signed for the part? '

Eddie assured him that both my signature and that of the studios were on the dotted line.

' Come into my office,' said Von, ' perhaps I can find you another part.'

I followed him to his bungalow office and he sank into a chair, still staring at me.

' You're not Marcus Schouler,' he insisted. ' Your eyes are much too kind.'

I told him that I could make my eyes as evil as he wished and reminded him that his eyes were kind, too, but that in *Hearts of the World*, *Foolish Wives* and other pictures he had himself played sinister roles with very great success.

'But Schouler is a helper in a dog hospital,' he pursued. 'A greasy, smartalick type in a loud suit and derby hat, a cigar always between his lips. Your haircut is wrong, too. His neck is shaved, his hair is smarmed down. I am sorry, but maybe we can find you something else!'

I arrived back home, completely desperate, but next day I went to Zan's in Los Angeles, and spent a long session there. One of the finest make-up artists in the U.S.A. worked on me. I had my moustache shaved off and was given a Bowery haircut. I then dressed myself in a loud check suit, with trimmings to match. My hair was dressed differently, my whole personality was changed. The next morning, with a cheap cigar clenched between my teeth, I went and saw Stroheim again.

He stared at me, and for the moment could not believe that I was the same actor that he had interviewed the previous day. Finally he clicked his heels and bowed.

'I apologise, Mr. Hersholt,' he said with Austrian dignity. 'You *are* Marcus Schouler. I am glad — and only sorry that I did not realize this before.'

I do not know how much *Greed* cost to make, but we worked on it steadily for nine months. Stroheim spent six more months cutting it down to thirty reels (not one of which was made in a film studio); he then reduced it to twenty reels, but refused to cut it any more. It was eventually edited in the studio cutting room and ten reels only were released. Even so it made film history.

For seven months we lived in the Fairmont Hotel in San Francisco without going home once, and for two months more we worked in Death Valley. Out of forty-one men, fourteen fell ill and had to be sent back. When the picture was finished I had lost twenty-seven pounds, and was ill in hospital, delirious with fever.

We made the San Francisco scenes of *Greed* in the actual house and on the sites described by Frank Norris, the author, who had written *McTeague* based on an actual and horrible murder in San Francisco some years previously. We rented the house where the murder had been committed, and most of the film was shot there. At the end of that time we all returned home, and then began the most terrible experience any of us has ever gone through, shooting the scenes in Death Valley. Seven car-loads went on the trip. Myself, Gibson Gowland and forty-one technicians. During the two weeks that we were in the worst part of the valley the highest temperature was 161 degrees and the lowest 91. The scorching air seared our blistered bodies, making sleep impossible. After a few days and nights not one of us spoke to the others unless we had to. It was so hot that an egg had only to be broken on a pan to be fried at once!

Two of the seven cars were kept in use all the time, going back and forth across the valley to Baker, the nearest railroad point to take sick men to the town and bring us back water, water, water. . . .

Every day Gibson Gowland and myself would crawl across those miles of sunbaked salt, the hunted murderer pursued by the man who had sworn vengeance on him. I swear that murder must have been in both our hearts as we crawled and gasped, bare to the waist, unshaven, blackened and blistered and bleeding, while Stroheim dragged every bit of realism out of us.

The day that we staged our death fight I barely recollect at all. Stroheim had made our hot tired brains grasp that this scene was to be the finish. The blisters on my body, instead of breaking outwards, had burst inwards. The pain was intense. Gowland and I crawled over the crusted earth. I reached him, dragged him to his feet. With real blood-lust in our hearts we fought and rolled and slugged each other. Stroheim yelled at us, 'Fight, fight! Try to hate each other as you both hate me!'

And that typified Von. In order to get realism he really *would* make you hate him. When he was making a film everything else was subservient to the picture, all personal feelings came last. No matter what one felt about him while under his direction, the results justified the means. When, months later I saw *Greed*, I realized that Stroheim had got out of me possibly my best performance in my many years on the screen.

(Extracts from *Hollywood Scapegoat: The Biography of Erich von Stroheim* by Peter Noble.)

SHOOTING *GREED*

by William Daniels

Von Stroheim came back for *Greed;* we were seven months on that.
Much of it was very hard going. We were six weeks in Death Valley
during the summer — July and August. It was 132 degrees under the
shade of an umbrella. Of course, being a realist he really *had* to have
it hot! Luckily it was dry heat, and we were all young, and could
stand it. The only water was at Furnace Creek Ranch, which the
English Borage Company kept supposedly for agricultural purposes.
There was a lake with palm trees and we lived on little army cots
in the open air. It was too hot for tents. I remember the beautiful
stars through the palm trees at night. The food was horrible. We had

Erich von Stroheim (right) with his cameramen Ben Reynolds and William
Daniels, during the shooting of *Greed*.

a camp cook. And ice was a problem : it had to be brought down in burlap bags in a case covered with sawdust. The trucks weren't much good in those days. The cast stood up well except for Jean Hersholt, who became hysterical at one stage with the bad sunburn. At that time Death Valley was considered truly to be Death Valley; so many men had lost their lives there. The mountains on each side are so high and the distance so great that you lose all perspective : you look across the valley and you think you can walk it easily, but actually it's twenty-five to thirty-five miles to the foothills.

We used natural interiors in the scenes in San Francisco. It was one of the first times they had been used. The company rented one whole building. We had a big scene they still talk about : the wedding of McTeague and the girl, and during the wedding procession you see a funeral cortege going by, through the window. In other scenes you see the streetcar passing. It was done without process. There was a problem of getting a correct balance of light between interior and exterior so that it looked as though all the scenes were lit by daylight only, and getting enough light on the people to balance the exposure was hell.

We used for the very first time some incandescent lights for that film. A problem with the arcs was that they would smoke, and that made it all very hard. Realism got us into trouble in the gold-mining scenes at the start. Von Stroheim insisted we went into the mine to a depth of 3,000 feet — it was at Colefax, Northern California, I remember — instead of at 100 feet, which would have got us exactly the same effects !

Of course, so much of my best work was cut from the picture. Originally it had a lot about a junk-man and his wife, and they were completely — no, *almost* completely — taken out. We spent months lighting their shack so carefully, to make it real, and it was all wasted. Months, for instance, colouring each *candle flame* with a one-hair brush ! On every print ! It was shown that way in New York, I guess, but never again. It wasn't too successful, anyway, and you can imagine the way we felt after all those months with magnifying glasses colouring the flames, day after day after day. . . . And all the flames did was jiggle. . . .

(Reprinted from *Hollywood Cameramen: Sources of Light* by Charles Higham, by permission of the publishers, Secker & Warburg, London.)

STROHEIM WRITES ABOUT
THE MAKING OF *GREED*

I always used the same actors and actresses whenever possible [in my films]. Gibson Gowland happened to be in Scotland. I sent for him because there was no other man known to me who came as close to the description of McTeague by Frank Norris, both in extraordinary appearance and character. When I wanted Cesare Gravina I found out that he had gone with his opera-singer wife to the Argentine. I sent for him, and the most heart-breaking story in motion picture history concerns this man in this particular film. For nine months he worked extremely hard, as he had one of the most important parts in *Greed* — in the counter-plot. He contracted double pneumonia while having to be submerged in the cold waters of the San Francisco Bay

Erich von Stroheim on the set of *Greed* with Cesare Gravina (Zerkow) and Dale Fuller (Maria).

for two nights in succession during the filming of a scene, but at the end of the production, after June Mathis, and subsequently a cutter, had completely eliminated the counter-plot, there was not one single scene of Gravina's left in the picture! Of Dale Fuller who played in all the scenes with him, as well as in many other scenes, only two or three flashes are left. Both the above constituted tragedies in the careers of two extremely fine players.

At the time when I began my work on *Greed* the slogan of the Goldwyn Company was 'the author and the play are the thing', and I was given *plein pouvoir* to make the picture as the author might have wanted it. However, when — during the time I was cutting the film — the Goldwyn Company became Metro-Goldwyn-Mayer, with Irving Thalberg as the new General Manager, their new slogan became 'The producer is the thing'. I soon realised that the change boded no good for me, as Thalberg and I had often crossed swords at Universal. Thalberg and Louis B. Mayer, the head of M.G.M., did not care a hoop about what the author or I, or the former Goldwyn Company had wanted. Mayer, in fact, made it his business to impress upon me that I was only a small employee in a very large pants factory (pants that, incidentally, have had to fit grandfather, father and child!)

With *Greed* I had again set out with the idea of making the film in two parts, ten or twelve reels each, with time for a dinner interval in between — this was still a long time before Eugene O'Neill 'got away' with the idea with *Strange Interlude*. When I was through making the film as written and passed by Goldwyn, I found myself with forty-two reels. Even if I wanted the film to be shown in two parts, it was necessary to cut half of it. This I accomplished myself. When I arrived at twenty-four reels I could not, to save my soul, cut another foot. But Mayer and Thalberg insisted on cutting it down to what they described as a 'commercial length'. Unknown to them I sent one print to my friend Rex Ingram, who worked at that time in New York, begging him to cut it, if he could. Ingram returned it in eighteen reels, having eliminated six reels, thus accomplishing what had been to me impossible. He sent me a telegram: 'If you cut one more foot I shall never speak to you again'. I showed the telegram to Mayer who told me that he didn't give a damn about Rex Ingram *or* me, and that the picture must be cut to ten reels. He added that it would be a total loss to the company anyway!

Mayer thereupon gave it to a cutter, a man earning thirty dollars a week, a man who had never read the book nor the script, and on whose mind was nothing but a hat. He ruined the whole of my two years' work. During that time I had mortgaged my house, my car and my life insurance to be able to work, as I was neither paid for writing nor for cutting the picture. In fact all I received was a certain sum of money which would have been the same had I taken only two weeks to make *Greed* instead of nine months.

At a time when M.G.M. was making slapstick comedies and farces of fourteen reels in length, *my* picture, a serious work was arbitrarily cut down to nine or ten reels. The rest of the negative was burned to get the forty-three cents-worth of silver out. Only twelve men saw the picture in its original forty-two reels. Two of them well-known writers, Idwal Jones of the *San Francisco Call* and author of many books, and Harry Carr of the *Los Angeles Times,* war correspondent and author, wrote often about the strong impression *Greed* had made on them. Nevertheless the film, which had cost 470,000 dollars, was a comparative flop at the box office because M.G.M. did not advertise it and having written it off in their books as a total loss — for income tax purposes — did not care to exploit it properly.

Greed was, up to that time, the only film in which not one studio set was used. I had rented a house on Laguna Street in San Francisco, furnished the rooms in the exact way in which the author had described them, and photographed the scenes with only very few lamps, making full use of the daylight which penetrated through the windows. Of course this was not always to the cameraman's liking, but I insisted — and we got some very good photographic results. In order to make the actors really feel ' inside ' the characters they were to portray I made them live in these rooms (a move which was favourably received at the studio since it saved the company some hotel expenses !). When I came to the desert sequences which were laid in Death Valley the company suggested that I take my actors to Oxnard, near Los Angeles, where traditionally all desert scenes were — and still are — shot. But having read the marvellous descriptions of the real Death Valley as Norris had depicted them. I knew that it did not look like Oxnard. I insisted on the real Death Valley in California and Death Valley it was.

This was in 1923 when there were no roads and no hotels as there are today. We were the only white people (forty-one men and one woman) who had penetrated into the lowest point on earth (below sea level) since the days of the pioneers. We worked in 142 degrees Fahrenheit in the shade, and *no* shade. I believe the results I achieved through the actual heat and the physical strain were worth the trouble we had all gone to. When I meet you I can tell you more if it would interest you, but not knowing how much space you have for such unessential details I have limited myself to the foregoing. If I talked

29

to you, however, for three weeks steadily I could not possibly describe, even to a small degree, the heartache I suffered through the mutilation of my sincere work at the hands of the M.G.M. executives.

(From a letter written by Erich von Stroheim to Peter Noble, author of *Hollywood Scapegoat: The Biography of Erich von Stroheim*.)

TWO CONTEMPORARY REVIEWS OF *GREED*

Greed, the screen adaptation of the Frank Norris story, *McTeague,* opened at the Cosmopolitan last Thursday night for a run. Metro-Goldwyn presented the picture with Louis B. Mayer acting as sponsor for the production.

It was directed by Erich von Stroheim, and the possibilities are that the director himself selected the story. Nothing more morbid and senseless, from a commercial picture standpoint, has been seen on the screen in a long time than this picture. Long awaited, von Stroheim having utilized two years and over $700,000 of Goldwyn and possibly some Metro money in its making, it came as a distinct shock to those viewing it.

Never has there been a more out-and-out box-office flop shown on the screen than this picture. Even D. W. Griffith's rather depressing *Isn't Life Wonderful?* is a howling comedy success when compared to *Greed.* Metro-Goldwyn will never get the money that was put in this picture out of it, and the exhibitors that play it will have a heck of a time to get back via the box-office route what they pay out in rentals for the picture.

On this picture von Stroheim shot 130 reels of stuff in two years. He finally cut it to 26 reels and told the Metro-Goldwn executives that was the best he could do. It was then taken into hand and cut to ten reels, and as such registered a decisive and distinct flop at the Cosmopolitan Thursday night.

It is a cinch that there isn't going to be a mob clamouring at the door of the Cosmopolitan comprising mothers and fathers who are taking their children to the theatre to give them a good time. After all, the province of the theatre is to provide amusement and entertainment, but *Greed* provides neither.

True, there may be a moral, but it applies to wives only, to the effect wives should not be miserly, greedy, or money-crazed, and with it consequently intolerant of a husband's welfare.

That is another count against it, that the women won't like it. Imagine any girl keeping company with a young fellow urging him to take her to see *Greed* when she knows the night that she sits through it he is going to sour on every thought that has to do with marriage!

As for the men? Well, take this reviewer as an average human, possibly a little more hard-boiled than the average man that one would

31

meet in the average small city. He had to violate the Volstead act to the extent of three shots before starting this story.

From the artistic angle, there is no question but that at directing von Stroheim is a wizard as to detail. His little intimate touches are little short of remarkable, but what of it if the story in which they are employed is such that it offends rather than entertains?

(In ' Variety Weekly ', New York, December 10, 1924.)

Greed, the much talked of picturization of Frank Norris' *McTeague,* is a picture of undeniable power. Erich von Stroheim has let himself go and has produced a picture which by virtue of choice of subject, treatment and emphasis represents a logical development in the work of the creator of *Blind Husbands, The Devil's Pass Key* and *Foolish Wives.* Mr. von Stroheim is one of the great stylists of the screen whose touch is recognizable in everything he does. He has always been the realist as Rex Ingram is the romanticist and Griffith the sentimentalist of the screen, and in *Greed* he has given us an example of realism at its starkest.

Like the novel from which the plot was taken *Greed* is a terrible and wonderful thing. *McTeague* is one of the most savage, uncompromising, ugliest novels ever written. It achieved fame and continues to be read as an example of the horrible. It must be considered in any survey of the development of the American novel.

In judging the picture which Mr. Stroheim has made from it we must use the widest possible perspective. For motion picture art has by this time attained its majority. It is entitled to experiment in any form from the ultra-sentimental to the latest fad in symbolism. The days of censorship in that sense, the feeling that motion pictures must always be pretty pictures, are over. The time has come when we can invite the spirit of Matthew Arnold to the screen to see what he saw in literature, namely a criticism of life.

Most emphatically there is and should be a place for a picture like *Greed.* It is undoubtedly one of the most uncompromising films ever shown on the screen. There have already been many criticisms of its brutality, its stark realism, its sordidness. But the point is that it was never intended to be a pleasant picture. It is a picture that is grown up with a vengeance, a theme for just those adults who have been complaining most about the sickening sentimentality of the average film. Nobody can complain of being deceived when he goes to see it; Zola did not compete with Gautier and Frank Norris would never have sent any story of his to *True Romance.*

(In ' Exceptional Photoplays, New York, December-January 1925)

LOUIS B. MAYER PRESENTS

AN ERICH VON STROHEIM PRODUCTION

GREED

from the American Classic, *McTeague*, by Frank Norris

Personally directed by Erich von Stroheim

*' I never truckled; I never took off the
hat to Fashion and held it out for pennies.
By God, I told them the truth. They liked
it or they didn't like it. What had that
to do with me? I told them the truth, I
knew it for the truth then and I know it
for the truth now ' — Frank Norris*

Dedicated to my mother

CAST:

Characters in the prologue:
McTeague Sr., Shift Boss at the
Big Dipper Mine   Jack Curtis
Mrs. McTeague   Tempe Piggott
McTeague, their son   Gibson Gowland
Dr. 'Painless' Potter, the travelling dentist   Erich von Ritzau

Main characters:
'Doctor' John McTeague, a dentist   Gibson Gowland
Marcus Schouler, his pal   Jean Hersholt
Trina Sieppe   Zasu Pitts

Members of the Sieppe family:
Mr. Hans Sieppe   Chester Conklin
Mrs. Sieppe   Sylvia Ashton
August, Trina's kid brother   Austin Jewell
Max and Moritz, the Sieppe twins   Oscar and Otto Gotell
Selina, their cousin   Joan Standing
Uncle Rudolph Oelbermann   Max Tryon

Characters in the subplots:
Charles W. Grannis, Proprietor of
'The Modern Dog Hospital'   Frank Hayes
Miss Anastasia Baker   Fanny Midgeley
Maria Miranda Macapa   Dale Fuller
Zerkow, the junkman   Cesare Gravina

Friends and neighbours in Polk Street:
Mr. Heise, the harness-maker   Hughie Mack
Mrs. Heise   E. 'Tiny' Jones
Mr. Ryer   J. Aldrich Libbey
Mrs. Ryer   Rita Revela
Joe Frenna   S. S. Simon
The Photographer   Hugh J. McCauley
The Palmist   William Mollemhauer

Others:

The Minister	William Barlow
The Man from the Lottery Company	Lon Poff
The Sheriff of Placer County	Jack McDonald
Cribbens, a prospector	James Fulton

CREDITS:

Screenplay by	Erich von Stroheim based on the novel *McTeague* by Frank Norris
Directed by	Erich von Stroheim
Presented by	Louis B. Mayer
Production Company	The Goldwyn Company/Metro-Goldwyn-Mayer
Directors of Photography	Ben F. Reynolds and William H. Daniels
Assistant directors	Eddie Sowders and Louis Germonprez
Art directors	Richard Day, Erich von Stroheim and Cedric Gibbons*
Edited by	Erich von Stroheim, Rex Ingram, June Mathis and Jos W. Farnham
Settings by	Cedric Gibbons
Made on location in	San Francisco and Death Valley
Process	Black and white (originally gold tinting was used throughout for gold, brass beds, gold teeth, gilt frames, and the canary cage. This tinting is absent from any of the prints available now.)
Length	Original length edited by Stroheim : about 42 reels; then cut by Stroheim to about 24 reels; cut by Rex Ingram to 18 reels; finally cut to 10 reels, the version in existence today
Released by	Metro-Goldwyn-Mayer Distribution Corp.
Shot during	1923-24
First shown	December 1924

* Cedric Gibbons was given an official credit although he was not connected with Stroheim's production.

GREED

Part One

PROLOGUE : The Big Dipper Gold Mine, Placer County, California,
A.D. 1908.

Fade in.

TITLE : ' Gold, gold, gold, gold,
      Bright and yellow, hard and cold,
      Molten, graven, hammered, rolled,
      Hard to get and light to hold,
      Stolen, borrowed, squandered, doled.' [1]

Fade out.

[TITLE : ' Oh cursed lust of Gold! When for thy sake the fool throws
up his interest in both worlds. First, starves in this, then damn'd in that
to come.'] [2]

Iris in on a tree-covered mountain setting with the mine building in the
distance.
Medium shot of the mine building with its chimney smoking.
Medium long shot, inside the building, of a giant ore-crushing machine
in operation. One or two men can be seen working beside it.
Close-up of one section of the machine working.
Close-up of hands shovelling a muddy-looking substance with a trowel.
Medium shot of a miner pushing a rail-car along the track towards
camera, passed by a group of miners headed in the opposite direction.
Medium long shot of various men working in the mine.
[Iris in on a large hand holding a big chunk of quartz gold with a
strong gold vein through it. (Natural colours or hand coloured?) The
hand plays with the stone, weighing it.
Short lap dissolve into close-up of the face of McTeague, then about

---

[1] Thomas Hood (1799–1845), *Miss Kilmansegg: Her Moral.* This title does not
appear in Erich von Stroheim's original script.
[2] Robert Blair (1699–1746), *The Grave* (published in 1743).

twenty years of age with neither beard nor moustache. He is looking down, apparently at the stone in his hand, which is not in the picture.]
Medium close-up of McTeague working.
Close-up of his hand holding up a large chunk of quartz.
Back to medium close-up of McTeague. He puts the rock onto the full car beside him.[1]
[Camera moves back on perambulator while iris opens simultaneously on the complete scene, revealing a tunnel in the Big Dipper Mine. Miners in the background are drilling. McTeague is still weighing the quartz in his hand when his father, the shift boss, comes up to him from the rear and stops.
Close-up of Father McTeague with brutish expression, looking at his son. Camera moves back again on perambulator until both men can be seen from the waist up. Father McTeague pushes his son with his fist against his shoulder. Young McTeague turns, sees his father, grins stupidly and holds out the quartz towards his father, who takes the stone and, without looking at it, throws it carelessly on the car standing next to him. Camera moves back on the track until it reveals the whole scene with McTeague standing full figure next to a train of cars loaded with ore, miners drilling in the background coming and going. Father McTeague in a very rough way spurs his son to continue his work, and as young McTeague continues to grin stupidly, his father kicks him with his knee in the behind. Young McTeague starts to push out the cars while his father goes towards the background, where he busies himself with a waterpump.]
Medium shot from perambulator, moving back on track ahead of McTeague as he begins to push the car. Slowly, cumbersomely, like a heavy draft horse, he ploughs along [gazing without expression at the ore in the car]. A line of miners pass him with their backs to camera.
[Shot from behind towards the mouth of the tunnel. Silhouetted, McTeague passes camera with the cars; he moves in the same tempo along the track with bent knees, pushing along towards the mill, which is seen in daylight not far from the mouth of the tunnel.]
Medium shot, ahead of McTeague, at the mouth of the tunnel in complete daylight. McTeague enters until in the scene from the waist up. He cravingly inhales the fresh air; [he extracts a pipe with a porcelain head from his overalls, extracts some sulphur matches and lights one on the seat of his pants. While he waits for the sulphur vapours to fade, he turns in the direction of the tunnel for a second, then lights his pipe, spits elaborately and, puffing two or three times, ploughs on.]

---

[1] While these three shots duplicate Stroheim's description to a certain extent, they are repeated here for the sake of clarity.

Shot from behind him along the narrow gauge track towards the mill.
Medium shot of McTeague. He hears the squeaking of a little bird
and looks around until he discovers the bird on the rail. [The camera
moves back on the narrow gauge track ahead of him to include the
bird in the foreground on the rail as well as McTeague.]
Cut to close-up of the little bird sitting on the rail. It is apparently
lame as it cannot fly away in spite of its attempts to do so.
Back to medium shot of McTeague. The camera pans slightly as he
leaves the car, walks cumbersomely but carefully towards the bird,
bends down and picks it up.
Close-up of McTeague holding the bird up to his face.
Extreme close-up of him kissing the bird.

Medium close-up of McTeague with the bird in his hand, examining
it closely, but very tenderly.
Medium long shot. Not finding anything wrong, he retraces his steps
to the car, which he then pushes with his right arm while holding
the bird with his left [showing enormous strength through his feat
of pushing four car-loads of ore with one arm].[1] As he starts moving,

---

[1] In the film, he is only pushing one car.

camera again moves ahead of him on the narrow gauge track for a few feet only.

Cut to long shot, reverse angle, from behind McTeague, pushing towards the entrance of the mill : his car approaches another one being pushed by a miner in the opposite direction.

[Medium shot, inside the mill. McTeague pushes the first car in from right to left; he takes the body of the car and lifts it with one arm into such a position that the ore rolls out through a chute into the stamps. Close-up of a miner's face, very ugly and mean. He looks in the direction of the bird in McTeague's hand.

Shot from the miner's angle of McTeague's hand holding the bird.]

Medium shot of McTeague and the other miner as they meet. The miner maliciously slaps McTeague's hand with such force that McTeague drops the bird. [With his right hand he is holding up the second car-load at an angle of forty-five degrees.]

Close-up of McTeague. The look on his face slowly changes from a dumbfounded, questioning, expression to a terrible grimace of anger.

Medium shot getting both in. McTeague lets go of his car, grabs the miner around his chest and lifts him up like a child. [He turns towards the entrance of the mill.

Shot from behind him with the entrance of the mill in the foreground.]

Long shot of the scene. McTeague throws the miner high up in the air and over the edge of a precipice.

Medium shot of the ravine as the miner slides down. Being stunned by the fall he cannot grab hold of the brush near him quickly enough to stop his slide.

Shot from the top of the precipice towards the stream of water at the bottom. The miner tumbles over the rocks in the stream.

Close-up of McTeague snarling with rage.

Medium close-up of the miner at the bottom of the ravine feeling his bones, wiping the blood off his face and starting to climb up again cumbersomely.

Close-up of McTeague again.

TITLE : 'Such was McTeague.' [1]

[Medium shot towards the entrance of the mill. McTeague, walking quickly towards the camera, is apparently looking down into the ravine. He stops with his face in extreme close-up. The expression on McTeague's face changes again slowly from that of uncontrollable rage to one of stupid helplessness.

---

[1] This title does not appear in Stroheim's original script.

Close-up of a steam whistle blowing three times.

Medium shot in front of the mill with McTeague still standing at the edge of the precipice. He turns, spits elaborately and wipes his hands on his pants. Then, remembering the bird on the ground behind him, he retraces his steps and picks up the bird quickly and tenderly. Miners appear from inside the mill; they walk out and stop by McTeague, asking him what has happened; he gestures at the bird in his hand and then in the direction in which he has thrown the miner; they follow his indications with their eyes.

Medium close-up of the miner with a blood-smeared face, crawling back over the edge of the precipice.

Back to the scene as the miners look in his direction, laugh, kid him and josh McTeague about the bird, but with a certain respect for his strength. They start walking on.

Medium shot of the mouth of the tunnel leading to the mine; some miners, Father McTeague among them, appear from the tunnel with tools; they lay them down, blow out the lamps on their caps, and walk away while the night shift files in. Fade out.]

Fade in on a long shot of the cook house through a clump of trees. Smoke curls up from the chimney.

Medium shot of the cook house porch. A Chinaman with his jaw bandaged appears and walks over to replace the dirty towels used by the miners coming off the shift; [he fills some tin pitchers, and puts them on a bench next to some tin basins. Dissolve out.]

Medium long shot of the kitchen interior; Mrs. McTeague is just finishing work and looks over towards the clock on the wall.

Close-up of the clock showing 6:30.

Medium shot of her walking over to a chair and dropping into it exhausted.

Close-up of Mrs. McTeague gazing into the distance.

TITLE : 'Such was Mother McTeague.' [1]

[Dissolve in to the interior of the kitchen with Mrs. McTeague over-worked and overheated. She opens the doors in the big stove, takes out some pans and examines their contents, then puts them back. She is responsible for the food as company cook. The Chinaman appears with the dirty towels. Mrs. McTeague glances at the clock, then indicates to the Chinaman that he should take the platters which are on the

---

[1] This title does not appear in Stroheim's original script.

table, filled with bread and lettuce, into the dining room. He picks them up and exits. Mrs. McTeague once more looks at the clock and realizes that she has a little time with nothing she can do right now. She drops exhausted into a chair that happens to be standing near. Fanning herself with her hands, she looks around and spies an old magazine; she picks it up and fans herself for a second, then drops it into her lap.

Medium close-up of Mother McTeague casually fingering the pages with a distracted expression; her expression slowly changes to one of concentration.

Insert of an advertisement of some correspondence school with fat black letters saying : ' Earn from $2,000 to $10,000 a year. Others have done it, why can't you? Send your coupon today.'

Close-up of Mrs. McTeague reading interestedly. Then she looks into space. Dissolve out.

Dissolve in to an elegantly furnished office with one solitary desk in the centre. Her son McTeague, as we have seen him, only with an entirely different bearing — self-possessed, self-confident and full of energy — is apparently signing an important document, while an employee stands waiting at a respectful distance. As McTeague hands the paper to him, the man takes it, bowing very deferentially. The employee asks a question which McTeague answers brusquely yet importantly; the man bows again. Dissolve out.

Dissolve in to medium close-up of Mother McTeague holding the magazine, apparently coming out of her trance. Looking again at the advertisement, she continues to dream. The Chinaman appears and tells her that the miners are at the pay office; she rises, looks very quickly at the stove and a pot or two, and gives him an order. The Chinaman leaves. She looks down at her dirty apron, takes it off quickly, takes a clean one from the peg on the wall, ties it and flattens the folds as she exits quickly.

Interior of the dining room. Mother McTeague enters from the kitchen, walks quickly over to the table, gives it a final inspection and runs over to the screen door.

On the front of the cook house porch, the Chinaman sounds the gong. Mother McTeague steps to the screen door and looks over in the direction of the office.

Shot from behind her back, showing her in silhouette; through the screen door the men can be seen turning in the direction of the cook house. Those that have lingered about after having received their pay run as fast as they can towards the cook house, kidding each other and laughing as they go.

42

Medium shot of the entrance to the cook house. Mother McTeague appears from inside and looks searchingly in the direction of the office. The front of the office : the men are filing out and disappearing towards the right at a run. ' Old Man ' McTeague is just going in.

The front of the cook house : the miners run towards the cook house and ' storm ' it as Mother McTeague quickly descends the steps and walks as fast as she can towards the office. Men greet her as they pass. The front of the office : Old Man McTeague appears from inside, pay cheques in hand, as young McTeague goes in. Old Man McTeague stops for a second to read his cheques.

Close-up of his hands holding two pay cheques, showing one marked ' McTeague Sr., Shift Boss '.

Medium shot showing a bush near the gate in the fence in front of the office. Mother McTeague arrives at the same speed as she left the cook house. She hides behind the bush and looks through the branches towards Father McTeague. Men pass in front of her in the direction of the cook house, but don't see her.

Close-up of the second cheque in Father McTeague's hands, marked ' Mrs. McTeague, Cook '.

Medium close-up of Father McTeague. He finishes reading the cheques and puts them into his pocket as he walks towards the gate in the fence.

Medium shot of the gate and bush with Mother McTeague hiding behind it. Father McTeague appears through the gate. He looks towards the cook house and does not see her; then he turns towards the road leading up to the camp saloon. Mother McTeague realizes where her husband intends to go and, with mixed feelings of fear and wifely instinct, she quickly steps from behind the bush and runs after him.

Medium shot of Father McTeague and his wife. She touches his sleeve and he turns.

Close-up of Mother McTeague with a pitiful expression on her face. Without a word she hesitantly holds out one hand, apparently asking for her earnings.

Close-up of Father McTeague. He looks at her, then at her hand, then back at her. Then a diabolical grin comes over his face and he bends down, out of shot.

Medium shot of both. He bends to the ground, picks up a stone, rises and laughingly puts it in her outstretched hand.

Close-up of Mother McTeague. She looks at the stone in her hand, then up at her husband; tears come into her eyes and roll slowly down her cheek. She begs him with a few words not to go and get drunk as

43

usual.

Close-up of Father McTeague. He sneers indescribably and brutally at the pleadings of his wife.

Medium shot of both. He turns to go; she keeps on begging and takes hold of his arm. With his right hand he takes her hands off his sleeve and pushes her away from him. He walks out of frame to the left.

Close-up of Mrs. McTeague. She looks after him, cries, and stands there for a second meditatively.

Medium close-up inside the office. The paymaster is talking to the bookkeeper. McTeague Jr. stands at the railing still holding the bird in his left hand. The paymaster turns, and sees him there. He walks quickly over and hands McTeague Jr. his cheque. He looks at it.

Close-up of his big hairy hand holding the cheque, showing the name ' McTeague Jr.'

Back to the scene. He turns and exits.

Medium shot of the outside of the office. McTeague Jr. appears from inside and bangs the screen door behind him.

Close-up of Mother McTeague. She hears the screen door bang, turns quickly, takes out a handkerchief and starts to dry her eyes.

Medium shot of Mother McTeague standing near the gate. Young McTeague appears through the gate. He looks up, sees his mother and steps up to her; she is just then blowing her nose, and tries to smile up at him.

Close-up of Mother McTeague smiling through tear-dimmed eyes.

Close-up of McTeague Jr., looking down at his mother questioningly.

Medium close-up of both. Mother McTeague looks involuntarily in the direction in which her husband left. McTeague follows her look.

Shot from his angle of the road with Father McTeague walking along.

Medium shot of mother and son. McTeague Jr. turns and looks back towards his mother, then he looks accidentally at the pay cheque which he holds in his right hand. He holds out the cheque to his mother, who sweetly takes the cheque, pressing her son's hand with her other work-worn one. McTeague pats her kindly on the back, and she sighs deeply. Then they both start to exit towards the cook house.

Medium shot of both as they go off towards the right.

Medium shot from perambulator moving ahead of Father McTeague. A hag is trying to catch up with him. Father McTeague walks towards camera. The hag (Mrs. Kroll) catches up with him. He stops, turns and talks to her. Her vile facial expression reflects a great intimacy with Father McTeague and also indicates that she has witnessed the scene with his wife. She points in the direction of his wife and son, then punches him insinuatingly in the ribs. Out of the pocket of her skirt she takes a pint flask containing a white liquid, apparently moonshine. She holds it out to him. He takes it, takes two or three shots in quick succession and starts to put the bottle in his own pocket when the hag grabs it, and also takes a few shots. They start to walk off past the camera.

Medium shot of the porch of the cook house. McTeague and his mother appear. His mother goes into the house; McTeague has a pipe in his mouth and the bird in his hand. At the top of the steps, he takes the pipe out of his mouth, spits and wipes his mouth with the back of his hand. He knocks out the pipe, puts it in his pocket and then disappears into the house.

Medium shot of the front of the camp saloon. Father McTeague and the hag appear and look up towards the right.

Shot from their angle of the road with a green-painted gypsy wagon driving towards them. Above the driver's seat there is a gilded tooth dangling down from an iron rod; also crudely painted signs on all four sides of the wagon making known what the owner is. [Back to medium shot of Father McTeague and the hag, who look up towards the stranger, make fun of him, then enter the saloon.]

Long shot of Mike's Saloon in the background with the dentist's buggy just appearing in frame in the foreground.

Close-up of the saloon tarts looking out of the upstairs window and pointing at the dentist.

Medium shot of the buggy approaching.

Medium close-up of people at the front of the saloon looking off at the dentist.

Medium close-up as the dentist gets down. The giant tooth dangles just above the driver's seat of the buggy.

Medium long shot of the dentist approaching people at the entrance to the saloon. He bows elaborately as he hands out leaflets.

Close-up of a leaflet which reads: ' Dr. " Painless " Potter, Dental Surgeon, extraction and fillings guaranteed free of pain — 50c to $2.00. Have your teeth attended to now.' Fade out.

Medium shot of the interior of the cook house dining room. The miners are eating, stuffing it away. The Chinaman brings in coffee pots and places them on the table. McTeague Jr. sits down.

Close-up of McTeague seated at the table. He looks at the platters.

Shot from his angle of the table with the platters almost empty.

Back to close-up of McTeague looking stupidly from one platter to the other; then he realizes that he still has the bird in his hand.

Medium close-up taking in the top of the table; McTeague takes a spoon, dips it into a water glass and holds the spoon full of water so the little bird can drink.

Close-up of his hands holding the bird and the spoon filled with water. The bird drinks.

Medium shot of the whole table. The other miners look up from their plates at McTeague, nudge each other, then laugh good-naturedly. Mother McTeague enters with two smaller platters, walks over to her son's chair and places the platters in front of him.

Medium close-up of McTeague and his mother behind him bending down a little. He turns to his mother while he is gurgling noodle soup, sucking in long strings of noodles. His mother looks at the bird, which she notices for the first time, and which he holds out to her with his left hand. He points with the spoon in the direction of where he found it. Mother McTeague takes the bird out of his hand while he heaps the plate with meat and starts eating with tremendous appetite. His mother sighs, puts the little bird close to her cheek, then exits.

Medium shot of the front of the saloon with Dr. Potter's wagon in shot. Potter climbs down, takes a hammer, some tacks, and half a dozen printed hand-bills from underneath the seat, and enters the saloon.

The interior of the saloon. Father McTeague and the hag are sitting at a little table opposite the bar. The bartender puts down two drinks of whisky, while Father McTeague takes the last draught from the hag's flask. He pays with one cheque, getting back some change. The dentist walks from the door over towards their table. Bills in hand, he greets them profusely and deferentially, introducing himself with great pomp, more like an actor than a dentist.

Medium close-up of the dentist introducing himself pompously, handing out bills with a stagey manner to each of the three.

Insert of a bill in Father McTeague's hand : ' Dr. " Painless " Potter ' etc.

Medium shot as they finish reading. By this time already a little under the influence of drink, Father McTeague imitates the travelling dentist's manner and, with one hand on his back and one on his abdomen, rising a little from his chair, bows in a kidding way. He gulps down the drink in front of him, after having seated himself again; then, reaching over with his right hand, he grabs the hag by her hair and draws her face close to him, pressing her chin down so as to look into her mouth.

Close-up of the hag's face with a few teeth missing.

Back to the scene. The hag doesn't like this at all and pushes Father McTeague's hands away. She gulps down her drink while Father McTeague becomes menacing. He takes one of the dentist's hand-bills

and tells her, pointing to same, that this is a great chance for her to have her mouth fixed. She resents this. He crumples up the bill and, forcibly opening her mouth, stuffs the bill into it. The bartender laughs, the dentist also. The hag takes the paper wad out and throws it at Father McTeague; then the two make up. Father McTeague orders another round, asking the dentist what he'll have. The dentist tells him with pantomime that he does not drink. He asks the bartender for permission to tack up one of his bills. The bartender says go to it.

Medium shot of the dentist, who nails up a bill on the wall, leaving a dozen or so on the bar.

Medium shot of Father McTeague's table. The bartender appears and puts down the drinks.

Medium close-up of the dentist. He greets them profusely again. Shot from his angle of Father McTeague, the hag and the bartender. Father McTeague and the hag again imitate his graceful manners and bow back laughingly. Father McTeague and the hag gulp down their drinks.

Medium shot at the door. The dentist exits.

The exterior of the saloon. The dentist tacks one bill on the wall near the door, then, putting back the hammer and the rest of the bills under the seat, climbs up and drives off towards the cook house.

The interior of the cook house dining room. The miners finish eating. They start rising one by one; some of them light their pipes, or take a chunk from their battleaxe (tobacco) and start to exit.

Close-up of McTeague, still eating without looking up. In front of him is a dish of suet pudding. He looks around for a butter dish, cuts off an enormous slice and mixes it up with the pudding and adds four or five teaspoons of granulated sugar.

The exterior of the cook house with the miners on the porch; some of them start to go off towards the camp, some of them linger, some of them light their pipes. The dentist's wagon drives up and stops. They all look up. Dr. Potter gets off the wagon. He greets the boys in the same pompous fashion as before and some of the roughnecks nudge each other and laugh. Dr. Potter again has with him a lot of hand-bills which he distributes among the miners, to whom this little diversion is very welcome. They read them and all look towards the miner whom young McTeague had thrown down the precipice. He had been continuously feeling his tooth with his fingers and didn't eat much. They at once start to kid him in a rather rough way and push him from one to the other towards the dentist. He lands on the dentist's breast. He greatly resents his comrades' behaviour and sulkily moves away, followed by their laughter.

Medium shot of the entrance of the cook house. McTeague appears from inside. He wipes his mouth again with the back of his hand in his characteristic way, and takes out his pipe and fills it, all the while watching the dentist and the miners below.

Shot from his angle of the miners below with the dentist in their midst, apparently asking where he can get something to eat. Some of them point to the cook house. He thanks them and tells them that as soon as he has eaten a few bites he will be ready for work, pointing to his wagon. He starts ascending the steps to the cook house.

Medium shot of the front of the cook house with McTeague at the top of the steps. Dr. Potter ascends the last few steps and greets him, and asks whether he could eat. McTeague opens the screen door and calls in.

The interior of the kitchen. The Chink is just entering with the dirty dishes. He puts them down. Mother McTeague hears the call and starts to exit.

Medium shot of McTeague and the dentist in front of the cook house. Mother McTeague appears from inside the house, wiping her hands on her apron. McTeague points with his pipe to the dentist, telling her that he wants something to eat. Mother McTeague looks him over as he gives her a hand-bill and one to McTeague. She reads it and then, with a certain respect for the dentist in her expression and manner, she invites him, with a motion of her hand, to enter the dining room. He steps in, followed by Mother McTeague and her son.

The interior of the dining room. Mrs. McTeague, in her energetic way, clears a space for the dentist at the table while the Chink does a final clean-up. She exits towards the kitchen while McTeague, smoking his pipe, sits down opposite the dentist.

The interior of the saloon. Father McTeague and the hag are pretty well gone. The bartender is just putting down a new round of drinks for which Father McTeague pays. Some of the miners enter, lean against the bar and order drinks.

Medium shot of the miners at the bar turning towards Father McTeague and the hag. They kid him about the hag.

Shot from their angle of Father McTeague and the hag. She sticks out her tongue at them.

Back to the scene. They laugh and call Father McTeague over to them, inviting him to have a drink.

Shot from their angle. Father McTeague gulps down his last drink and starts to rise with more or less difficulty. The hag tries to hold him back. He first slaps her hand which holds him by the coat sleeve, then, as the hag does not let go, he pushes her brutally away and starts to stagger towards the bar.

Medium shot of the miners at the bar. Father McTeague appears, staggering. They order him a drink as they down their own.

Medium shot. One of the miners goes over to the player piano and puts a coin in. The thing starts going.

Medium close-up of the old hag. She is quite intoxicated by now and starts swaying to the rhythm of the music. She rises with difficulty and starts to dance by herself, grinning in a silly way.

Medium shot of the miners at the bar with fresh drinks in their hands. They see her dancing and laugh.

Shot from their angle of the hag. She looks up at the laughter of the miners, sees that she is the object of their jokes and merriment, gets sore and walks over to them.

Medium shot at the bar as the hag walks over to Father McTeague, grabs his sleeve and wants him to dance with her. He pushes her roughly and gulps down his drink.

Medium shot of the stairway leading to the upper storey in the corner of the bar. Three girls, cheaply and flimsily dressed, showing their profession without any doubt, appear from above. They stop on the stairway, looking down.

Shot from their angle of the boys at the bar who look up towards them and, on seeing them, cheer and invite them down.

Medium shot of the stairway as the girls descend, smiling.

Medium shot of the bar. The girls appear and are rushed by the men. They order drinks. Father McTeague is in the centre of the group. Slow fade out.

Fade in to medium shot of the front of the cook house with the dentist, McTeague and his mother, carrying the bird in her hand. McTeague sees the bird, stops, and takes it. They go off in the direction of the wagon.

Medium shot of the rear of the wagon as they arrive. The dentist pulls down the steps, takes out two lanterns with reflectors, lights them and hangs them up at the rear of the wagon. A crowd of about twenty miners close around the wagon. The dentist climbs the stairs into the interior. He pushes some kind of old-fashioned dental or barber's chair to the edge of the wagon along with an old dilapidated handbag, apparently containing tools and instruments, and a small dental engine. He starts to lift the dental chair in order to carry it down the steps when McTeague grabs hold of it with the utmost ease and lifts it down, with one arm. The dentist thanks him profusely and descends the steps.

Medium shot at the rear of the wagon as the bunch of miners back up to give room. The dentist opens his bag and lays out a few instruments on a board attached to the chair.

Medium shot of the crowd of miners looking on. The Chink appears and tries to squeeze himself through. They turn, see him and kid him, laughingly pushing him towards the front. He tries to remonstrate, but without effect.

Shot from the interior of the circle of miners towards the dentist's chair and the McTeagues. The Chink is pushed in from the miners to the dentist.

Shot of the faces of the miners from inside the circle as they yowl and cheer the Chink. To them this is a great diversion.

Close-up of the Chink. He looks at the dental chair, then at the tools, then fingers his tooth.

Shot from his angle of the dental instruments.

Back to close-up as he looks at the dentist, then at the tools.

Medium shot as he tries to slink away. He reaches the inner edge of the circle, but the miners, glad to have a little diversion, don't let him pass, and make a tight ring. The Chink tries to break through at several places but they laughingly stop him, and a couple of tough ones push him more or less roughly back and make him sit in the

chair. Others applaud. Mother McTeague and her son can't help but smile at poor 'Charlie'. Dr. Potter, glad to have a patient, grabs hold of an instrument and a mirror and at once examines the teeth of the Chink before he has another chance to get up. The dentist's touch and action inspire confidence in Charlie and he points with his long nail to the bad tooth.
Medium close-up of Mother McTeague and her son looking on, exceedingly interested.]

TITLE: 'Filled with the idea of having her son enter a profession and rise in life . . . the chance came at last to Mother McTeague.' [1]

Fade in on long shot of the crowd in front of the saloon at night, including tarts and miners.

Medium shot as Potter takes his forceps. [On the pretext of looking once more into Charlie's mouth, he clamps the forceps on the tooth, places his left hand on Charlie's chest, while his knee presses itself against Charlie's lap.] One quick jerk and Charlie's tooth is held up

[1] This title does not appear in Stroheim's original script.

in the forceps.

[Medium shot of the scene including miners and whores, who howl and applaud. This is great fun for them. Potter hands a cup of water to the Chink who doesn't know what to do with it, so he drinks it. Charlie rises, raises his pants leg and takes money from his sock, to the great merriment of the boys; he hands it to Potter, who takes it and puts it away.]

Medium close-up of Mother McTeague approaching [with her son. Mrs. McTeague has great respect for the fact that Potter has made the $1 so easily and whispers something to that effect to her son, who just nods, looking stupidly, smoking and spitting.]

Medium close-up of McTeague smoking his pipe and watching the dentist with interest.

Long shot of the entire scene as the dentist finishes with the Chink.

Return to medium close-up of McTeague Jr.

Medium close-up of Mother McTeague gazing thoughtfully at the scene.[1]

Medium shot of the dentist being paid by the Chink.

Dissolve to McTeague in the same position as the dentist and wearing a similar suit.

Dissolve back to the scene as it was originally.

Return to medium close-up of Mother McTeague.

Long shot of the entire scene. Fade out.

[Medium shot of the scene as, with great pathos and pompous gestures, the dentist asks the next to step up. To their surprise one of the miners really steps forward in spite of the great laughing and kidding of his comrades. He sits down in the chair and with all kinds of comical touches Potter ties a napkin around his neck, while Mrs. McTeague tells him that she will have to go. Potter looks up, bows pompously to her, and tells her that he will see her tomorrow. Followed by McTeague, she walks through the circle of miners who then close in around the chair. Potter starts working.

Long shot of the interior of the saloon with the miners and three girls dancing at the bar, all more or less gone.

Quick lap dissolve to Father McTeague, half-lying over a table with a spilled glass next to him. The hag is leaning back in her chair, pressed against the wall, also paralysed. Father McTeague is apparently dreaming and tries to push something away with his arms, yelling loudly at the same time.

---

[1] Mother McTeague's daydream comes at a later point in the original script. See page 56.

Long shot of the bar. The miners stop and look in his direction and some of them cross over to him.

Medium shot of Father McTeague at the table as some of the miners grab him and lean him back in the chair, trying to wake him up, but without result. Father McTeague keeps on raving, although his eyes are open now, with an absolutely wild and crazy look in them. One of the miners takes a glass of water and throws the contents into Father McTeague's face. He keeps on raving. They keep on trying to revive him.

Medium shot of the McTeagues' shack, with mother and son in front of it, seen from the street in the dim light of a lamp on a nearby tree. McTeague is carrying the little bird.

The interior of the shack. Mrs. McTeague lights a lamp while her son goes to the shelf, takes down a small bird cage made of wood and wire, blows off the dust and puts the little bird into it. He takes a piece of cube sugar and a leaf of lettuce out of his pocket and puts it between the wire uprights, then hangs the cage up in the window near the shelf. He takes down his concertina and goes out.

Medium shot of the front of the shack as McTeague comes out, sits down on the front step and fingers the concertina. He quickly lays the concertina down on the ground, takes off his shoes, pulls the tips of his socks so as to give his toes a little freedom, and stretches his long legs. Then he picks up the concertina and, assuming a comfortable position, he starts to play.

Close-up of McTeague. The slow rhythm and the serious expression on his face indicate that the tune is a mournful one.

Long shot from behind McTeague towards the road leading from the saloon, with McTeague in the background, still playing. A bunch of men with a mysterious load are moving towards the McTeague shack. McTeague casually looks up and stops playing. He looks again, with greater interest, as the men come nearer. He lays down his concertina and half rises. The miners are carrying Father McTeague and are unmistakably coming to the McTeague house.

Close-up of McTeague; he looks dumbfounded.

Shot from his angle of the group of miners, carrying the lifeless body of his father.

Back to close-up of McTeague. He turns and yells to his mother inside the house, through the open screen door.

Medium shot of McTeague by the screen door. His mother looks out. McTeague points to the group below. His mother, frightened to death, quickly disappears through the door.

Medium shot from behind the group, shooting towards the house. The

53

miners carry the body up the steps. Young McTeague and his mother rush to help. They accompany the miners up the steps and Mrs. McTeague opens the door while the others carry the body inside the house.

The interior of the bedroom in the shack. The miners carry the body in, preceded by Mrs. McTeague and her son, who leads the way with a lamp that he has picked up in the living room.

Medium shot in front of the bed. McTeague puts the lamp down on a nearby table. The miners lay Father McTeague on the bed, then, more or less embarrassed, turn and move away from the bed towards the door and exit one by one. Mrs. McTeague takes hold of her husband's hands, trying to revive him.

Medium shot of Father McTeague with his wife and son. Just then Father McTeague has another fit. With staring eyes, he is apparently seeing things crawling all over the bed; with both arms outstretched he pushes everything aside. His son takes hold of him and with all his strength holds him down on the bed.

Close-up of Mother McTeague as she has an idea; pointing in the direction of the dentist's wagon, she gestures that she will fetch the 'doctor'.

Medium shot as she runs out.

Outside, Mother McTeague appears from the house and runs off in the direction of the wagon.

Medium shot of some miners surrounding the dentist's chair in which another miner sits with his mouth wide open. Potter is working on him. Mother McTeague appears, and pushes her way through the crowd until she stands next to the 'doctor'. She grabs his arm and, gesturing in the direction of the house, she tells him in a few words to hurry. The miners come closer and listen attentively, watching Mrs. McTeague. The 'doctor' grabs his satchel, leaving the patient with his mouth wide open, and follows Mrs. McTeague who drags him along by the sleeve. All the miners follow.

Medium shot of the miner in the dentist's chair with a napkin around his neck. He opens his eyes, sees that he is alone, and looks off in the direction in which the miners have left. He realizes that there must be something wrong and, forgetting the white napkin around his neck, he starts to run after them.

Medium shot of the exterior of the McTeague shack as the group appears. The dentist and Mrs. McTeague climb up the front steps, followed by the miners. The dentist and Mrs. McTeague enter the house, but the miners hesitate.

Medium shot of the bedroom with Father McTeague on the bed,

McTeague standing next to him. The dentist enters with Mother McTeague, runs over to the bed, looks at Father McTeague, examines his eyes, feels his pulse, then with an unmistakable gesture indicates that there is no hope. Both wife and son look at the dentist, then at Father McTeague, unable to understand at once; then they realize. Young McTeague shows no emotion whatsoever, but Mrs. McTeague breaks down, crying over Father McTeague while the dentist stands there helplessly. Iris out completely.

Iris in on a long shot of the graveyard at Iowa Hill. In place of a priest, the dentist is reading from a Bible at the foot of the open grave. Mother McTeague and her son are on one side of him facing camera, with miners on both sides of the grave. The coffin is out of sight already, but the ropes are still being let out as it goes down into the grave. The dentist then picks up some earth with a small shovel in his right hand and dumps it down. Right in front of camera, the branches of weeping willows swing rhythmically to and fro, covering most of the scene. Slow iris out.

Iris in on a close-up of a wilted wreath tied with old black crêpe hanging on a front door. Iris opens while the camera moves simultaneously back to reveal the front of the McTeague shack. Mother, son and dentist appear from the left in their funeral clothes and stop for a second. The dentist once more shakes hands with Mrs. McTeague, trying to console her. Some of the miners who also attended the funeral pass by, while young McTeague slowly and cumbersomely ascends the steps, unlocks the door and removes the wreath. He enters the shack as the dentist goes off towards the right and Mrs. McTeague follows her son in.
Interior of the living room in the McTeague shack. McTeague puts the wreath on the shelf and takes down his concertina while his mother takes her hat off and puts her apron on. McTeague exits with the concertina.
Medium shot of the exterior of the McTeague shack. McTeague appears from the house with the concertina; slowly and sluggishly he sits down on the upper step and starts playing.
Medium shot of McTeague with the door behind him. His mother comes out from the house and stops by her son. She puts her hand lovingly into his big shock of hair, grabs hold of his curls and presses his head against her body.
Close-up of Mother McTeague with tear-dimmed eyes, gazing into space.
Medium shot of both. She indicates with her arm that she is going to

55

the cook house and that he had better change and get ready. He nods stupidly without interrupting his playing as she walks off.

Medium close-up of McTeague playing his concertina. From the slow rhythm one realizes that he is playing a mournful tune. Iris out.

Iris in on the front of the cook house with Mother McTeague and the Chink on the porch, handing out dinner pails to the miners who are all dressed in rubber boots ready for work. They take their pails and walk off. There are about three or four men left as young McTeague appears in rubbers and working clothes. He is the last one. Mother McTeague hands him a dinner pail.

Medium close-up of McTeague with the dinner pail. He opens the top and looks in.

Close-up of the contents of the pail, including suet pudding and immense slices of apple pie with chunks of butter.

Close-up of McTeague's lips; his tongue wets them.

Medium shot as the dentist appears, walks up the steps and stands next to Mother McTeague. He looks at McTeague with a friendly smile. Mother McTeague nods to her son.

Close-up, in iris, of a whistle blowing.

Back to the scene as McTeague leaves.

Medium close-up of Mother McTeague and the dentist looking after him.

Shot from their angle of McTeague walking slowly with the dinner pail in his hand.

Back to the scene as Mother McTeague turns from her son towards the dentist, who is next to her; she gestures in her son's direction, apparently indicating the drudgery and hard life her son has ahead of him as a miner; then she looks off into space. The dentist, having listened, apparently asks her why she doesn't influence her son to go out into the world and try his luck at something else, indicating the wide, wide world and the many chances open to him. He finally suggests through gestures that he might be willing to take young McTeague along and teach him his profession. Mother McTeague listens, never looking at the dentist, but still staring into space with wide eyes.

Close-up of Mother McTeague still looking into space; then her gaze falls accidentally on the dental chair at the rear of the dentist's wagon near by. Her look becomes more concentrated.

Shot from her angle of the dental chair, at first empty with no one around. Suddenly, into the dental chair dissolves the figure of a patient — one of the miners perhaps — with the dentist working on him so that his face can be seen from Mother McTeague's angle. Some miners look on from either side. The figure of the dentist slowly dissolves into the figure of her son, McTeague, wearing a similar suit to the dentist.

Quick lap dissolve into a medium shot of the patient in the chair and McTeague as the dentist. He seems to have finished his work and removes the napkin from the patient's neck; the patient rises and asks the price. McTeague answers with a gesture of two fingers, indicating $2. The patient extracts two silver dollars and lays them one by one in McTeague's palm. McTeague bows gracefully but slightly comically, as he would in Mother McTeague's imagination, one hand on his abdomen and the other on his back. The patient starts to leave. Dissolve out.

Dissolve in to the empty dental chair with no one around, as it is in reality.

Medium close-up of Mother McTeague and the dentist. Mother McTeague wears the faintest trace of a smile; the dentist seems to understand her thoughts and at once follows up the idea, accompanying his words by gestures. Iris down on the dentist talking. Pan right from him until Mother McTeague is in iris. She is listening, gazing into space. Iris out completely.

Iris in on the interior of the living room in the shack, Mrs. McTeague in shot. With a whimsical smile, and in such a way as only a mother can, she folds up a blanket, socks, shirts, and her son's few pieces of underwear. She opens each one of them, holds them up, looks at buttons, etc., and lets her hands glide into the socks to see whether there might be a hole that has escaped her scrutiny, as she puts these articles together.

Close-up of Mother McTeague. She looks about, thinking, figuring what else she could possibly put in for the boy. Her glance falls on a primitive night table next to the bed in which Father McTeague died. Shot from her angle of the night chest with an old-fashioned silver watch and chain that belonged to her husband, with a large tooth as a locket.

Medium shot of Mother McTeague and the night table. She walks over and picks up the watch, sighs, looks at it and lets the tooth glide through her fingers.

Close-up of the tooth in her fingers.

Close-up of Mother McTeague's face, looking from the tooth up into space as if realizing and understanding its significance. She nods slightly as if to say, it must be so.

Medium shot. She goes to the drawer of the dresser and opens it. She takes out an old cigar box with all kinds of little shells pasted on it, opens same and counts the money inside it. Finally, still thinking of her boy, she extracts a $20 gold piece, then closes the box and puts it back into the drawer. She places the gold piece next to the watch with the other things on the main table, then sits down on the chair next to the table, her arms subconsciously embracing the blanket and things that lie on it, and gazes into space. Slow iris down on her face; hold for a second, then iris out completely.

Iris in on the exterior of the McTeague shack. It is midnight. There is a dim light inside. McTeague, carrying his lunch pail, enters shot with his slow, cumbersome gait, ascends the steps and goes into the house.
Medium shot of the living room. Mrs. McTeague is sitting at the table, her arms in the same position as last seen, subconsciously embracing the blanket and the things belonging to her son. Her head lies on the blanket; she is apparently asleep. McTeague enters and at the sound of his steps she awakens, looks up, rubs her eyes and looks at the clock.
Shot from her angle of the clock, which says ten past twelve.
Back to the scene. McTeague yawns and starts to take off his rubbers and coat. Mother McTeague looks up at her son as he stands near by and stretches. She says : ' Mac,' and points to the second chair, indicating that she has something to say. Mac looks at her for a second, then his glance casually falls on the blanket, etc., which doesn't mean anything to him as yet. Then he obediently sits down, looking at her questioningly.
Medium close-up of both, with the top of the table in shot. Mother McTeague starts to tell him in pantomime that his future here does not amount to anything and is not worthy of a man; that she has great ambitions for him and great hopes for his future; that the coming of the dentist seems to her a great intervention of Fate; that she has talked to the dentist and that he suggested that Mac should go with him; that she agreed with him and that she has packed all his things. She points to them.
Close-up of Mac looking at her without any emotion, then following the movement of her hand, looking at the things laid out on the table; he thinks for a second to let the proposition sink in, then without any sign of emotion he nods.
Back to the scene. Mother McTeague takes the watch and $20 gold piece from amongst the things and holds them out to him. He takes them.
Close-up of Mac with the top of the table in shot. He lays the watch down on the table and lets the chain glide through the fingers of his

left hand until the tooth comes to lie between his thumb, forefinger and middle finger, while his right hand holds the $20 gold piece. He nods with a primitive little smile. Iris down on his hand holding the gold piece. Pan up until the hand with the tooth is seen in the iris. Pan to McTeague's face in iris, and hold for a second as he nods stupidly. Iris out completely.

Iris in on the front of the McTeagues' shack with the dentist's wagon all packed up. McTeague, his mother and the dentist are on the porch. McTeague carries the blanket roll, a lunch basket, the little bird cage containing the bird he saved, and his concertina. The dentist says goodbye to Mrs. McTeague, then tells her with gestures that he will take good care of Mac and make a big man out of him. Greatly elated over this fact, Mother McTeague shakes hands with him, and he climbs up on the wagon.

Medium close-up as Mother McTeague embraces her son and presses her head close to his body, looking up at him. Still holding the different articles, he puts his arms around the emaciated body of his mother, then stoops and touches her hair with his lips. Just then Mother McTeague moves her head and looks up into the face of her son, then kisses him on both cheeks, while McTeague shows little emotion. They break loose; Mac says goodbye once more and walks towards the wagon while Mother McTeague remains standing on the steps.

Close-up of McTeague as he walks down the steps. He suddenly stops with a worried expression, transfers the objects which he has in his right hand to his left arm and then feels in his pockets with his right hand. He seems very disturbed, but finally he finds what he is looking for in his right vest pocket and takes it out.

Close-up of his hand holding the object; his fingers open the newspaper it is wrapped up in as if to reassure himself that it is still there. It is the $20 gold piece.

Close-up of Mother McTeague on the porch asking him: 'Did you lose anything?'

Medium close-up of Mac. Hearing her question, he turns in her direction and says: 'No. I found it.' He holds up the $20 gold piece, wraps it up again and puts it in his pocket; then, without looking back, he walks off.]

TITLE: 'His mother's ambition was fired . . . and Mac went away with the dentist to learn his profession.'[1]

Long shot of the dentist standing beside his wagon in the background as McTeague and his mother approach along the path, walking away from camera. McTeague climbs up. The dentist has a final word with his mother, shakes her hand, then climbs up beside him. The wagon moves off to the right, and Mother McTeague is left alone. She runs a few steps after it, waving.

Long shot of the road leading out of the camp. The wagon drives away from the camera towards the hill as Mother McTeague waves from the foreground. [Without turning the dentist raises his whip, while Mac turns once more and waves his hand.]

Close-up of Mother McTeague with tear-dimmed eyes [through two layers of veil].

Reverse shot with the road stretched out in front of her and the dentist's buggy in the far distance [just then silhouetted against the sky].

Return to close-up of Mother McTeague. She stuffs her handkerchief, bit by bit, into her mouth [then pulls on the edge of the handkerchief so hard she tears it]. Slow iris down on the wagon and hold for a

---

[1] This title does not appear in Stroheim's original script.

second; then, as the wagon disappears, iris out completely.

[Fade in.

TITLE : ' Ah ! curst ambition ! to thy lures we owe all the great ills that mortals bear below.'

Fade out.
Iris up on McTeague's face; he is apparently watching something with great interest. Camera holds there for a second. Pan right until the face of a patient leaning back with a napkin around his neck comes into iris. The hands of an unseen person are working on a tooth in the patient's mouth. Iris opens completely while camera moves simultaneously back on perambulator to reveal the entire scene. Medium shot shows quite a crowd of village folks standing around the chair with the patient in it, while our friend the travelling dentist is working on him. McTeague stands very close to him. The dentist turns, holds out a hand to Mac, and Mac gives him an instrument from a small table next to him. The scene is taken at Colfax. Slow iris down on McTeague's face watching; hold for a second, then iris out completely.

TITLE : ' At the revolution of every five years we find ourselves another and yet the same. . . .' Sir Walter Scott.

Iris up on McTeague's face silently looking down at something. Pan to the left until the dentist's face is in iris. He is making his spiel. Iris enlarges completely, revealing the dentist and McTeague on a 1913 model truck, with two dentist's chairs. The date is approximately 1913. There are presto light tanks on the four posts of the truck, and quite a number of people are standing around it. The Salvation Army passes with flags and drum in the background. (The scene will be taken on Lower Market Street.[1]) Signs on the truck as before : ' Painless ' Potter, etc. Two bums, a boy of about eighteen and a girl of about sixteen, climb up the steps onto the truck.
High angle medium shot from the truck as the girl steps up to it.
High angle medium shot from the truck as the boy steps up.
Back to the scene; the girl steps up to McTeague's chair while the boy sits down in Potter's chair.
Close-up of the girl looking up at the huge McTeague; she grins.
Close-up of McTeague looking down at her, terribly embarrassed.
Back to close-up of the girl, who smiles even more broadly.
Back to close-up of McTeague, even more helpless than before; he

---

[1] In San Francisco.

looks over towards Potter.

Medium shot of both chairs and both dentists. McTeague slowly and cumbersomely walks over to Potter and whispers something to him; Potter looks over his glasses, resting low down on his nose, sighs comically, then with a very pompous gesture steps forward and invites the young lady bum who has seated herself in McTeague's chair to step over to his.

Close-up of the girl in McTeague's chair, looking at him; she does not understand. She rises, more or less peeved, while Potter also asks the young man in his chair to step over to the other chair. They start walking across.

Close-up of the girl as she passes McTeague and makes a face at him.

Close-up of McTeague, embarrassed.

Back to the scene. The boy sits down in McTeague's chair, the girl in Potter's. Both ' doctors ' put napkins around their patients, and take an instrument with a mirror to examine the tooth in question. McTeague picks up his forceps.

Medium close-up of McTeague and the bum with his mouth open. McTeague tries to put his open forceps over the refractory tooth; the forceps don't fit. He looks a little puzzled for a second, then places the forceps back on the moveable rack.

Close-up of the patient's tooth, with McTeague's thumb and forefinger taking hold of it and pulling it out. He lays it down on the rack, not realizing himself what an extraordinary feat he has just performed. He fills a glass with water and gives it to the boy to rinse his mouth out.

Medium shot as the boy pays and the next man steps up and sits down on McTeague's chair. McTeague puts a napkin around him. Iris down on McTeague's face; hold for a second, then iris out completely.

Iris in on the post office building at Seventh and Market Streets, San Francisco. General traffic. McTeague appears from the left and walks up to the main entrance.

Quick lap dissolve to the general delivery window. McTeague enters and asks for his mail. The clerk gives him one letter; he takes it.

Close-up of McTeague, who weighs the letter and looks at it. It bears a strange handwriting; he looks at the stamp and sees that it is from the Big Dipper Mine, Placer County. He starts opening the letter, then suddenly stops, looking terrified and helpless, as if having an intuition. He looks again at the envelope, starts to open it again, extracts the letter, then again looks terrified as though filled with foreboding of some ill to come. Then finally he forces himself to calmly open the note and read it.

Insert of a section of the note : ' Mrs. McTeague, your mother, passed away yesterday, and asked me to inform you that she had left with me her belongings and the sum of $250, which I will send to you as soon as you let me know . . .'

Close-up of McTeague showing his reaction to the news. He leans mechanically against the wall and gazes into space, then takes up the letter and reads it again. His finger goes up to the date of the letter.

Insert of the top of the letter with the heading of the mining office. It is dated December 24th.

Back to close-up. McTeague looks up and around as if to try to find out what date it is today. His look falls on a calendar, seen through the grating of the window.

Shot from his angle of the calendar behind the grating, showing February 12th.

Back to close-up. He realizes that it is too late to see her buried.

Medium shot. Still with the open letter in his hand, McTeague starts to walk towards the entrance, gazing into space and bumping into people.

Quick lap dissolve to the front of the post office. McTeague comes out, still with the open letter in his hand, not knowing what to do. Then, sighing deeply, he starts to walk over towards the left, in the direction from which he came, bumping into people as he goes. Slow iris out.

Iris in on a small dingy hotel with its lobby windows facing onto the street. McTeague, dressed as in the post office, appears from the right, still carrying the letter in his hand. He enters the lobby. Quick lap dissolve out.

Quick lap dissolve in to the interior of the lobby with the dentist sitting in a chair with his legs on the radiator, heaps of newspaper next to him on the floor. Mac appears from the foreground, sees him, walks over and hands him the letter, then drops into a chair next to him. The dentist reads, then looks up and pats Mac consolingly on the back; Mac just nods, stupidly gazing into his face. Iris down on Mac's face; hold for a second, then iris out completely.

Iris in on the exterior of the dingy hotel. The dentist and Mac emerge from inside. Mac carries an old suitcase tied up with a cord, his concertina wrapped up in a newspaper (*The San Francisco Call*), showing the headline. The dentist shakes hands with Mac, patting him on the back and assuring him of his friendship. Mac nods, then exits towards the right; the dentist looks after him, waving his hand once more in a very pompous fashion. Iris down on the dentist looking after Mac. Pan quickly until the face or head of Mac walking on the sidewalk is caught in iris; it pans with him for a step or two; then iris out completely.

Iris in on a house on the corner of Laguna and Hayes Streets with 'To Let' signs in each of its bay windows. Hold there for a second; then camera moves back to the corner across the street while iris opens up simultaneously, revealing the entire house and the sidewalk, on which we recognize McTeague, carrying his suitcase and concertina. Quick lap dissolve out.

Quick lap dissolve in to McTeague's face, as he looks up towards a window from the sidewalk. He turns and looks up the street.

Flash of the street from his angle.

Back to close-up. He turns slowly to look at the other side of street.

Shot from his angle, panning to show what he can see on the other side of the street, up to the corner.

Back to close-up. His head is turned, looking at the corner behind him. Then he turns to face camera again.

Medium shot of the front entrance of the house. McTeague appears from the left, stops for a second, looks at the signs in the doorway, then opens the door and enters.

Medium shot from inside the doorway, shooting up the steps. On the steps are the owner of the house, McNally, and Marcus Schouler. Marcus has a dog in his arms, which barks at Mac as he appears from the foreground.

Close-up of Marcus with his dog; he looks curiously at the stranger.

Close-up of Mac from Marcus's angle, looking down the steps. Mac looks from Marcus to McNally questioningly, asking whether he can see the corner room.

Shot from Mac's angle, shooting up the steps, with McNally pointing to himself, saying yes, he will show it to him.

Medium shot of all three. Marcus descends the steps as Mac starts to ascend. They meet on the steps, while McNally waits for Mac a little ahead of them. Mac and Marcus look at each other as they pass.

Close-up of Marcus from behind as he steps into frame and turns, looking back at Mac.

Shot from his angle of McTeague and McNally taking one step higher. Mac turns and looks back after Marcus.

Shot of Marcus from Mac's angle as he turns away, opens the door and exits into the street.

Medium shot from the stair landing. McTeague and McNally enter from the left. McNally points down the hallway, away from the camera, and they both start walking towards the end of the hallway in the background.

Medium shot of the lower end of the hallway; there is a door on the left with a ' To Let ' sign on it. McTeague and McNally appear in the foreground. McNally opens the door with a key. McTeague enters and McNally follows.

Shot from the extreme left corner of the room, with the door on the right and the bay window in the background on the left. McTeague and McNally enter.

Close-up of McTeague as he looks around. Camera moves back on perambulator to include McNally. They are both seen from the waist up. McTeague asks him the price; McNally tells him; McTeague nods. Camera moves back on perambulator until both are full in. McTeague puts down the suitcase and concertina. He takes out his pocketbook, extracts a banknote from it and hands it to McNally. Iris down on McTeague's face as he looks around; hold for a second, then iris out completely.

TITLE : ' Then five more years passed — McTeague felt that his life was a success, that he could hope for nothing better.' [1]

Vertical barn door in on medium shot of McTeague's bay window.[2] The camera is on a platform at the same height as the window. Hold barn door on the edges of the window. On the window the words ' Dr. McTeague, Dental Parlours, Extractions and Fillings, Gas Given ' are written in gold leaf. Through it can be seen the dental chair with a male patient in it and ' Dr.' McTeague working on him with the dental engine.

Quick lap dissolve to a shot from inside the window, in the same direction. McTeague puts away the dental engine and starts to put in a temporary filling. In the background, on one of the three chairs which are against the wall, another male patient can be seen. Fade out. Fade in.

TITLE : ' The poor man's inspiration — Saturday ! '

Barn door down horizontally on a sign which reads : ' The Modern Dog Hospital — Chas. W. Grannis — established 1895 '. Hold long enough for the words to be read, then barn door down completely,

---

[1] Stroheim adds the note ' from book ' indicating that this is a quotation from the novel *McTeague*.
[2] ' Barn door ': a method of opening a shot by means of a shutter drawn horizontally or vertically across the frame.

revealing the front of the house, with the dog hospital in the background.

Quick lap dissolve to the lower end of the garage through which one has to pass in order to reach the dog hospital, which is in the back yard. A door opens into a narrow, filthy little alleyway with a water faucet outside.

Quick lap dissolve out and into a shot from the rear of the garage in the alleyway, showing the actual entrance of the dog hospital with all kinds of signs. The door into the yard is open.

Quick lap dissolve out and into the interior of the back yard, more or less filthy, with dog cages all along the walls. Old Grannis is crouched in front of a little dog cage, watching something.

Quick lap dissolve to medium close-up of him, with a dozen tiny mongrel puppies squirming in the straw at the bottom of the cage. Old Grannis takes the cute little puppies up in his hands. They are still blind and his kind face shows his enjoyment of their cuteness and their youth. They lick his hands instinctively. He puts them back in the straw and with a deep sigh rises out of shot.

Medium shot of Old Grannis as he continues to rise, his whole figure coming into shot. A man enters the scene from the left, wearing a very loud black-and-white-striped shirt, college-cut pants from a pepper-and-salt suit and bulldog-tipped tan button shoes. His shirt sleeves are rolled up, his waistcoat open and he has a loud red, white and red watch fob with the name 'Marcus' in brass letters across it. Also a red bow tie with white dots and stripes, underneath which is a horse-shoe fake diamond necktie pin stuck into his shirt. A brown derby with a black band sits at a cocky angle on the back of his head. He has the stump of a dead cigar, with the belly band still on, in his mouth.

Quick lap dissolve to show his arms : in one hand he carries an empty gunny-sack, in the other a large bottle.

Close-up of the label on the bottle which reads : 'Reese's Pharmacy Chloroform.'

Back to close-up of Marcus, whom we recognize as the man who had been so curiously attracted to McTeague when he entered the house five years ago. With a cold-blooded manner, Marcus points his thumb over his shoulder towards the puppies in the cage, asking Old Grannis a question. Camera moves quickly back on perambulator to include Old Grannis. He hears the question and looks at Marcus, then turns away from him and only then nods faintly. Marcus smiles cynically over the foolish sentiment of his boss, turns towards the cage, opens the wire door that Old Grannis has closed, crouches down and lays down the bottle.

Close-up of Old Grannis. He turns towards the cage again, then quickly turns back, covering his eyes for a second with his hand, then he goes off towards the entrance.

Shot from the rear of the garage towards the entrance of the dog yard. Old Grannis steps out of the yard, turns for a second, looking back, then quickly turns again and walks on past camera.

Shot from the rear of the garage towards the front of it, with the street in the background, seen through the open door. Old Grannis walks with his back to camera towards the background.

Shot of the front of the garage from the other side of the street with the dog hospital sign above it. Old Grannis appears from the house as a small covered cart comes up with a dirty, greasy, mean-looking individual driving an emaciated horse. It is the kind of wagon that is used to carry refuse away. The driver stops and asks Old Grannis a question. Old Grannis nods, motioning with his head towards the back yard, while the driver ties up the reins and cumbersomely descends from the cart. Marcus arrives, all dolled up, with his coat on, carrying the gunny-sack with something in the bottom of it. As he sees the driver he hands him the sack, rather carelessly, while Old Grannis

extracts a coin and gives it to the driver, who puts the gunny-sack inside the cart, climbs up, and drives off.

Medium shot of Marcus and Grannis. Marcus brushes his hands off, pulls at his coat, jigs a couple of buck-and-wing steps and cocks his derby; he takes hold of the watch fob, swings his watch out like a vaudeville artist and catches it in his hand, looks at it, then swings the watch on the end of the fob so that it lands in his waistcoat pocket; he seems very satisfied with himself. Old Grannis meanwhile counts some notes from his pocket, then hands them to Marcus, who counts them, folds them up, tells Grannis he needs a shave and beats it from right to left, while Old Grannis slowly follows towards the left.

Shot from the front of the dog hospital towards Laguna Street with Marcus walking away from camera, followed by Grannis.

Cut to medium long shot from Laguna Street towards the alley, from which Marcus and Grannis emerge on the right. Marcus comes towards camera while Old Grannis stops for a second, then walks up the street in the opposite direction, away from camera.

Medium shot of the front of a second-hand book shop, with old pamphlets and magazines stacked in the front door. There are all kinds of signs in the window. The bookseller sits on a chair in front of the open door, reading a newspaper. Old Grannis enters from the right and greets the bookseller; the latter returns the greeting and rises, putting his newspaper on the chair. Old Grannis tells him what he wants. The bookseller picks up a stack of about twenty-four unbound pamphlets of the *Nation* and *The Breeder & Sportsman* (or something similar), all of medium size and tied up with a cord. He holds it out to Grannis. Grannis pays for it, picks up the bundle and puts it under his arm, then says: 'So long,' and goes off, crossing the street diagonally towards the right.

Medium shot of McTeague's house from the sidewalk opposite, showing the main entrance. Old Grannis finishes crossing the street from the right of camera, and goes towards the main entrance. At the same time an old maid with false curls approaches, carrying a geranium pot and a large net bag containing a few small packages, a couple of apples and three bananas.

Medium shot of the two of them. Neither of them sees the other, and they arrive simultaneously at the door. Flushed with embarrassment, they both start for the door knob at the same time; they both pull their hands back; then, realizing how foolish they are, they both start simultaneously for the knob again. This time Old Grannis takes it and, though unable to look at the old maid, he courteously opens the door, trembling visibly. The old lady with her false curls enters, trembling,

and whispers an embarrassed 'Thank you' under her breath. Old Grannis himself follows, intentionally stalling.

Medium shot looking up the steps from inside the door as the old maid — Miss Baker — quickly runs upstairs.

Reverse angle medium shot of Old Grannis stalling at the bottom of the stairs; he listens.

Medium shot of the top of the stairs from the left of the lower hallway. Miss Baker enters quickly, stops, turns, listens, sighs, then walks very fast towards camera. As she passes the bathroom, Maria Macapa comes out in shabby working clothes, with her skirt pinned up, and carrying a bucket, scrubbing brush and rags.

Close-up of Maria. She looks after Miss Baker for a second, and shakes her head.

Medium shot from the right of the stairway in the hall so that the bathroom door is on the left with Maria standing in front of it, while Miss Baker is seen in the background, tripping as fast as she can down the lower hall towards her room. Maria Macapa turns away from Miss Baker towards the stairway and starts to walk quickly in that direction with her bucket in her hand.

Close-up of Maria looking down the stairway.

Shot from her angle of Old Grannis standing at the foot of the stairs, still stalling and listening. As he sees Maria he is embarrassed and starts to ascend the steps.

Close-up of Maria. She grins at Grannis, then turns in the direction of Miss Baker's room, grinning still more, and walks towards camera.

Medium shot of Miss Baker in front of her door. Wedged in the door is a copy of the *Christian Science Monitor* with the wording visible at the top, in a paper wrapping with a typewritten name and address. The old maid looks in every pocket for her keys, finally finds it and quickly unlocks and opens the door. As it opens the newspaper falls down to the floor. Thoroughly fussed, she picks it up quickly and steps inside.

Medium shot of the interior of Miss Baker's room, looking towards the door. She closes the door, locks it from the inside and stands leaning against it panting and listening. Then she leans back against the door, completely exhausted, with her hand over her heart and her eyes closed, reliving in her imagination the terribly exciting adventure she has just had.

Shot of the top of the stairway, seen as before from the left side of the hallway. Old Grannis sneaks up, listening in the direction in which Miss Baker and the maid have gone. When he sees that they have disappeared, he removes his hat, takes out his handkerchief and wipes his brow excitedly. Then he tiptoes past camera in the direction taken by Miss Baker.

Medium shot of the interior of Miss Baker's room, with her still standing at the door. She takes the newspaper and starts to read it.

Insert from her angle: '*Christian Science Monitor*, Miss Anastasia Baker, Laguna Street, San Francisco.'

Medium shot in front of the door adjoining Miss Baker's. Old Grannis appears from the right, very carefully inserts his key into the keyhole, turns it with as little noise as possible and steps into the room.

Medium shot from inside the room as he closes the door, locks it and puts down the pamphlets on the table near the door. Then he walks towards the wall on the right which separates his room from Miss Baker's.

Medium shot looking towards the separating wall. Old Grannis enters shot from the left, steps close to the wall and listens with one ear against it.

Close-up of Grannis. He closes his eyes as if reliving in his imagination the terribly exciting adventure he has just had.

Medium shot in Miss Baker's room, looking towards the separating wall. Miss Baker enters shot from the right, taking off her bonnet and fingerless silk gloves. She also steps up to the wall.

Close-up as she listens with closed eyes.

Close-up, from a baby tripod, of Old Grannis's shoes on the floor. A loose board moves as he moves his foot and apparently creaks.

Close-up of Miss Baker; she hears it, smiles, then quickly goes out of shot.

Close-up of Old Grannis; he hears her move, smiles faintly and also goes out of shot.

Shot of McTeague's room from the extreme left including the door on the right as well as the bay window with the dental chair. The coke stove is going. The last patient, a street-car conductor in uniform, steps down from the chair and puts on his collar and necktie. He asks McTeague when he wants him to come again. McTeague takes out a little black cardboard imitation slate, with a piece of chalk and a sponge attached to it. Two or three names with hours and dates are written on it. McTeague looks at the slate and then tells the conductor the next appointment. The conductor says : ' All right,' and Mac puts it down. The door opens.

Close-up of the bell on top of the door which rings automatically when the door opens.

Back to the scene. In comes Marcus Schouler with the *Saturday Evening Post* folded up under his left arm, carrying a little package wrapped with haberdashery paper. He greets Mac noisily with a wave of his right hand. The conductor says : ' Goodbye,' and leaves; the door closes. Marcus walks up to Mac, who is cleaning up his instruments. With a very jovial and nonchalant air Marcus unwraps the package, after assuring Mac that he is going to give him a surprise. Mac stops his work and looks more or less interested, while Marcus opens the package, takes out a tie and holds it up in the last rays of sun shining through the bay window.

Close-up of his hand holding the necktie; it is a beauty, decorated with stars, stripes and handpainted forget-me-nots.

Close-up of Marcus; he looks at Mac expectantly and says :

TITLE : ' Just look at that — Just look at that — ain't she a pip? — Huh — Ain't she a pip? '

Close-up of Mac looking at it. He really seems to like it. He says :

TITLE : ' Sure is a pip — that's the word ! '

Medium shot of both. Marcus is glad his friend likes the necktie and looks on proudly while Mac fingers it. Then, looking preoccupied, he extracts his watch in the same way as before and looks at it.

Close-up of the watch, showing five o'clock.
Back to the scene. He flips it back and says:

TITLE: 'By damn, I'll be late. I'm supposed to meet my cousin Trina at the ferry at half past six and I got to doll up yet. Steppin' out a little — I got to beat it.'

Back to the scene. He takes the paper sack and the necktie and goes out of shot.
Close-up of McTeague as he looks in a friendly way towards Marcus, his fashionable friend who has such high social obligations, and says: 'Yes.'
Medium shot of the door. Marcus appears from the left, opens the door, turns and looks back, raising his hand, and says:

TITLE: 'So long Mac. Don't do anything I wouldn't do. You know.'

Close-up of Mac looking in his direction. We see him say: 'So long Marcus.'
Back to medium shot of the door as Marcus closes it from the outside.
Medium shot of McTeague, who has finished cleaning up his tools. He takes off his coat, descends from the platform and walks towards camera.
Reverse shot of the far corner where there is a bed-lounge and a clothes closet. He hangs his old coat in the closet.
Medium shot outside Marcus Schouler's room. Marcus appears from the right, swinging his necktie. He unlocks the door, opens it with his foot, then steps into the room, and kicks it closed behind him.
Quick lap dissolve to close-up of a visiting card fixed to the outside of the door with four thumb-tacks. On the visiting card, in the most wonderful scroll writing, is written: 'Marcus Schouler.' There is a little pigeon with a wreath of forget-me-nots in the corner, evidently done by hand.
Medium close-up of McTeague slipping on two detached cuffs over his enormous hands. He slips into his other coat, takes his hat and goes off towards the door.
Medium shot of McTeague's door from the hallway with a sign painted on it: 'Dr. McTeague, Dental Parlours, Gas Given, Walk In.' The door opens from inside; he comes out, closes the door, locks it and walks off towards the left.
Medium shot in Marcus Schouler's room. Marcus, without collar or necktie, takes off his jacket and waistcoat and his shoes.
Medium shot of the front of the house with the main entrance. McTeague comes out from inside and walks towards the left.

Medium shot in front of the 'Car Conductor's Coffee Joint'. McTeague appears from the right and enters the café as a couple of motor men and one conductor come out. He is seen through the windows as he sits down at a table inside.

Medium shot of the interior of Miss Baker's room. She goes to the washstand, picks up a towel and soap and goes out of shot.

Medium shot of the door to Miss Baker's room. Miss Baker appears, listens, opens the door and exits.

Medium shot of the hallway outside her door. She comes out of her room and goes off in the foreground.

Medium shot of the interior of Marcus's room. He is in athletic B.V.D.s and socks. With a towel over his arm and soap in his hand, he steps up to the door. Before he opens it, he remembers something and runs quickly back.

Medium shot of the hallway with Marcus's door on the right and the bathroom door opposite on the left. Miss Baker appears in the background, heading towards the bathroom; she puts her hand on the door-knob just as the door opens on the right and Marcus comes out in his B.V.D.s with his towel and soap, the *Saturday Evening Post*, and a bathrobe over his arm. Miss Baker turns, sees him and, nearly fainting, runs back towards her room as fast as she possibly can. Marcus laughs as hard as he can.

Medium shot from the hallway outside Miss Baker's room. She comes into shot, opens the door and runs in.

Reverse shot from inside. She closes the door and locks it, then runs, highly agitated, over to the wall separating her room from Grannis's, where she stops and listens.

Medium shot outside the bathroom. Marcus goes in, still laughing, and closes the door.

Medium shot of the interior of Old Grannis's room. He hears Marcus laughing and goes over to the wall, where he listens, wondering.

Medium shot inside the bathroom. Marcus lights the instant water heater, then lights a cigar stump with the belly-band still on it. He sits down on a chair, puts his feet on top of the bathtub, opens the *Saturday Evening Post* and looks through the pages. Finally he finds the story which he wants to read, with illustrations of cowboys in chaps and with lassoes.

Insert of the page with the title of the story, author's name and one illustration. Marcus turns to the next page, which shows an illustration of two cowboys, one with two guns, and the other with his hands up.

Medium close-up of McTeague sitting at a table in the Car Conductor's Coffee Joint. He is eating the last two or three spoonfuls of a very heavy thick grey soup. He scrapes out the plate and lifts it up, pouring the last drops of soup into his spoon. He cuts off a piece of bread, wipes the soup plate and puts a chunk into his mouth. Then he takes a whole slice of bread, smears butter on it, cuts it with a knife and starts to eat. The hasher comes up to him with her hand on her hip. She looks flirtatiously at him and plays coyly with her chewing gum, pulling it out and letting it snap back with a zip. She scratches her scalp with a pencil that is in her hair. With gestures, he orders a very heavy thick steak, rare and hot on a cold plate. She takes a little pad that is suspended from her belt and notes down the order with her pencil, then walks leisurely back to the stove in the background and gives the order.

TITLE : (Some slang expression for rare steak).[1]

Medium shot of the bathroom with Marcus smoking and reading. He leans over and turns on the water. Boiling hot water comes out steaming; he keeps on reading.

Medium shot of the interior of Old Grannis's room. He walks over to the washstand, picks up a towel and soap, then goes over to the wall and listens.

Medium shot of the interior of Miss Baker's room. She is greatly upset over the terrible adventure she has had. She fusses around with a teacup and saucer, strikes a match, lights the oil stove and puts on the teapot. Then she goes to the wall and listens. She sits down in a chair beside the wall and folds her hands in her lap, listening and waiting.

Medium shot of the interior of Grannis's room. He steps over from the wall, looks at the alarm clock on the table, then goes to the door, opens it and exits.

Medium shot of the hallway, with Grannis's door on the right. He comes out of the room and starts to walk towards camera.

Medium close-up in the bathroom, looking down into the bathtub full of hot water. The whole room is full of steam. One foot is seen stepping into the bathtub, then another; then the figure jumps from one foot to the other as the water is very hot. All that can be seen are the feet and legs up to the knee; a hand appears and turns on the cold water. The cold water starts running.

Medium shot outside the bathroom. Old Grannis arrives with his towel and soap, puts his hand on the knob and tries to open the door; it doesn't give; he listens.

Same close-up as before with the cold water running and the two feet

---

[1] Stroheim's note in the original script.

74

that were standing changing to the horizontal position of a person sitting.

Medium shot outside the bathroom. Greatly disappointed, Mr. Grannis starts to walk back towards his room.

Medium shot of McTeague in the coffee joint. The hasher approaches very slowly, swinging her body. Taking her time, she brings up the steak and other food on a plate and sets it before McTeague. McTeague picks up a knife, sharpens it on the marble table, then starts to eat.

Medium shot in the hallway outside the photographer's laboratory, which is identified by a sign on the door. The door opens and the photographer comes out with a towel and some soap and starts walking towards the bathroom.

Medium shot outside the palmist's room. The palmist also appears with a towel and some soap.

Shot from the photographer's angle of the palmist going towards the bathroom.

Shot from the palmist's angle of the photographer going towards the bathroom. Seeing the palmist, he stops in his tracks and turns to go back.

Close-up of the palmist with terrible ' muff ' (whiskers) all over his face and the menu cards of three past generations on the lapels of his Prince Albert coat. He calls to the photographer.

Shot of the photographer from the palmist's angle. He stops, turns, looks and listens.

Close-up of the palmist. With extraordinary grace he gives a deep and courteous bow, touching his heart with his right hand, and invites the photographer to have his bath first, as it isn't so very urgent with him.

Medium shot from up the hallway, with the bathroom in the foreground, the palmist's room on the right and the photographer standing in the background on the left. The palmist disappears into his room and closes the door, while the photographer walks towards the bathroom door in the foreground.

Medium shot in front of the bathroom door. The photographer puts his hand on the knob, turns it and is greatly surprised to find the door locked.

Medium close-up of the interior of the bathroom with Marcus sitting in the bathtub. All that can be seen are the upper part of his body and the cover of the *Saturday Evening Post*, which he is reading with great interest. He is still puffing on his cigar stump with the belly-band still on, half burned through.

Back to medium shot of the bathroom door. The photographer tries again; then, very disappointed, he retraces his steps and goes out of shot. Fade out.

Fade in on the exterior of Rudolph Oelbermann's Toy Store, between Third and Fourth Streets on Mission Street. Trina Sieppe appears from the left and walks to the entrance carrying a large basket, covered up with a shawl. She enters the store.

Quick lap dissolve to medium shot of the front of the counter. Trina puts down her basket and takes off her shawl.

Close-up of the contents of the basket. It contains small figures cut in soft wood, painted in three or four different colours. Ahead of her is another girl, the contents of whose basket a man on the other side of the counter is taking out and counting. When this scene starts, he is almost finished. He gives the first girl a receipt, whereupon she leaves, going towards the cashier's window. He then steps up to Trina, greets her in a more friendly way than the other girl, says a few pleasant words while he counts Trina's dolls, then writes her a receipt. She thanks him and exits.

Medium shot in front of the cashier's window. Trina appears and hands the receipt to the cashier, who also greets her in a very friendly manner, saying a few pleasant words while he hands her the pen to sign the receipt. She takes the pen.

Close-up of her hand writing her name on the receipt, which now reads : ' $4.50 Value received — Trina Sieppe.'

Back to the scene. She hands back the pen and receipt to the cashier, who gives her the money in coin.

Close-up of Trina, her hand held out, the cashier's hand putting the $4.50 into her palm. Trina gives a slight smile, indicating satisfaction at her own industriousness.

Back to the scene. She thanks the cashier and puts her money into her pocketbook, holding the pocketbook carefully in her hand together with a handkerchief. She takes a few steps away then remembers something, retraces a step or two and asks the cashier a question. He nods reassuringly, pointing to a door with frosted glass on it, bearing a name in black letters : ' Mr. R. Oelbermann, Private.' Trina thanks him and goes off towards the door.

Medium shot outside Oelbermann's office. Trina appears and knocks.

Interior of the office. Mr. Oelbermann is sitting at his desk, an old book-keeper standing next to him. Oelbermann hears the knock, turns in the direction of the door and says come in. The door opens and Trina looks in.

Close-up of Trina who says :

Title : ' Hello, Uncle.'

Close-up of Mr. Oelbermann. He smiles a little, says : ' Hello, Trina,' and motions her to come in.

Back to close-up of Trina who says :

Title : ' Just wanted to say hello, because I'm in a hurry. I have an appointment with Marcus at the Ferry and I got to shop yet.'

Back to medium shot of both, together with the book-keeper. Oelbermann asks his niece how her family is. She answers that they are all right, then with a gesture says : ' Well, goodbye.' Her uncle does the same and adds : ' Greet the folks.' Trina says she will and exits. The door closes.

Medium shot of Oelbermann and the book-keeper. The book-keeper says :

Title : ' My but Miss Trina is getting to be some girl.'

Oelbermann looks at him, nods and says : ' Yes, she sure is.'

Cut to medium shot of the front of the store on the street. Trina comes out of the store and looks up Mission Street, as if looking for a street-car. Right in front of her uncle's store there happens to be a sign indicating a street-car stop. A car appears from the right and stops.

Medium shot, reverse angle, showing Trina getting into the street-car. The car starts and leaves.

Medium long shot of the coffee joint. Mac is still at table, just finishing some suet pudding and a cup of coffee, which he drinks holding the spoon in the cup with his forefinger.

Medium shot outside the bathroom door. The door opens and Marcus, in a flowered flannel bathrobe of terrible taste, steps out carrying the *Saturday Evening Post* and his soap. He walks towards camera, remembers something, stops and steps back, still facing camera but looking to the right, in the direction of Miss Baker's room. Using his hands as a megaphone he calls out something, laughing to himself, then comes towards camera and goes off.

Medium shot of the interior of Miss Baker's room. She is sitting in a chair, listening, holding a tea-cup and saucer, the cup held very gingerly with her little finger crooked. She puts the tea-cup and saucer on the little table next to her, all very much according to Hoyle.

Medium shot of the interior of Old Grannis's room. He is sitting at a little pine table alongside the wall and sewing a number of pamphlets together with a large upholsterer's needle. He looks up and listens at the wall.

Medium shot of the interior of Miss Baker's room. She rises very carefully so as not to make any noise. She picks up a towel and soap from the table, then steps in front of the mirror and gingerly touches her false curls.

Medium shot of the interior of Old Grannis's room. He looks at the alarm clock, picks up a towel and soap and walks towards the door.

Medium shot in the hallway showing the doors of Miss Baker's and Old Grannis's rooms. Both doors open simultaneously. Miss Baker and Old Grannis, each with a towel and a piece of soap, carefully poke their heads out, looking in each other's direction. On seeing each other, they both withdraw quick-as-lightning and close their doors.

Close-up of Miss Baker with her hand over her heart and her eyes closed, leaning against the door.

Medium shot of the interior of the coffee joint. Mac is at the counter. He receives his change, takes a handful of matches and puts them in his pocket, takes half a dozen toothpicks and puts them in his pocket too, except for one which he puts between his teeth. Then he goes off towards the door.

Medium shot of the exterior of the coffee joint. Mac comes out and stands on the sidewalk facing camera. He looks up and down until his eyes fall on a certain point across the street.

Shot from his angle of a bird store opposite with bird cages on both sides of the entrance and hanging from above it.

Quick lap dissolve to a gilded cage just above the entrance with one male and one female canary hopping around inside.

Medium close-up of McTeague still looking in the direction of the store. Almost mechanically he takes a few coins out of his pants pocket. He looks at them, replaces them in his pocket while he looks over towards the bird store again and starts walking towards it.

Reverse shot towards the bird store, from the restaurant. McTeague continues walking.

Medium shot of the front of the bird store as McTeague appears. Mrs. Beckman, the owner, a stout, elderly woman, is busy putting some bird seed in the cages. She looks up, sees McTeague and says: 'Good evening, Doc.' Mac says: 'Good evening.' She continues her work for a second, then, pointing to the bird cage in question, turns back to McTeague and says: 'Going to buy it today, Doc?'

Close-up of Mac looking up at the gilded cage with two canaries in it. He points to it.

Close-up of Mac as he says:

TITLE: 'Ain't got enough to buy both. I take the male and the cage.'

Back to the scene. Mrs. Beckman kids him about not being able to afford the other. With a gesture, she offers him both birds at a reduced price but Mac dully shakes his head and says: 'No, I'll take just the one,' also with a gesture. She agrees and fetches a step-ladder that is leaning against the door. While Mac looks on stupidly she climbs up, takes down the cage and opens the door. She puts her hand in, catches the female and puts it in a little empty wooden cage while Mac takes hold of the bird cage and pokes his finger between the uprights, talking to the male bird. He also asks for a package of bird seed, takes it with the other hand, then remembers that he hasn't paid yet. He puts the bird cage down on the sidewalk, makes as if to put the package down too, then changes his mind and puts it under his arm. He takes out some money and pays — he has about 60c left — then picks up the bird cage again and says: 'Goodbye.' He goes off in the direction of his house across the street, while Mrs. Beckman looks after him, shaking her head to herself, then goes back to her work.

Medium shot in front of the house. McTeague appears from the right with the bird cage and package, and walks towards the door. The door opens and Marcus comes out in a great hurry, all dolled up with his new necktie and swinging a little bamboo cane. He sees Mac, stops for a second, and smiling superciliously says: 'So you did buy your bird after all.' Mac nods, and just then Marcus hears the noise of an

79

approaching street-car on Hayes Street.

Medium shot of the street-car on the corner of Hayes and Laguna Streets, just starting to leave.

Back to medium shot of McTeague and Marcus. Marcus waves at him with his cane and starts running. Mac looks after him.

Shot from Laguna towards the intersection of Hayes as the street-car passes with Marcus running after it.

Medium shot of the front door as McTeague, preoccupied with his bird cage and seed, enters the house.

Medium shot of the rear of the packed street-car from a moving automobile. Marcus is running after it, waving to the conductor; he finally makes it. As he climbs up on the platform he starts an argument with the conductor, pointing in the direction of the corner, where the car should have stopped longer. Marcus is as sore as a boil. The conductor has troubles of his own and doesn't answer back. That gets Marcus sore and he picks at the conductor's sleeve, telling him with broad gestures to take off his coat and fight it out like a man. He starts pulling off his coat. The automobile stops and the street-car goes on.

Cut to medium shot of the meat market at the foot of Market Street. A lot of people with packages are going in and out in a great hurry. Trina enters, also in a hurry. She squeezes through a mob to get to the sausage counter.

Medium close-up of a big stock of frankfurters lying stacked up on a marble slab. Trina appears and puts her face close to the frankfurters as if to smell them, touching with her hand and squeezing them to see if they are fresh. A big fat German butcher comes into shot and asks Trina what he can do for her. She points to the frankfurters and he asks how many she wants; she tells him and he picks up quite a large quantity — about two dozen — and goes off.

Medium shot of a scale further down the counter.

Close-up of Trina, seen from behind the counter, looking at the scale. Shot of the scale from her angle showing that the frankfurters are a little bit underweight. The butcher is about to take the sausages off and wrap them up.

Shot from his angle of Trina pointing to the hand of the scale and telling him that it is underweight.

Shot of the butcher from her angle. He gives her a significant glance; although it is very hurried it expresses a lot. He takes one pair of frankfurters and dumps them on the scale, which now shows overweight. He takes the pair of frankfurters off, breaks it in half and throws the single one back, giving her a sarcastic glance.

Shot from his angle of Trina, quite undisturbed, yet satisfied with herself and her business ability.

Shot from her angle of the butcher putting the last touch to the package.

Medium shot of both. He hands it to her, she pays him. He looks at the money while she takes the package and, to make her sore, takes one of the coins and slaps it on the counter to hear it ring. She goes off quickly.

Shot at the foot of Market Street with the ferry building in the background and the market on the left. Trina appears from the left carrying some packages; she looks up towards the clock as a lot of people run past, then walks very fast towards the ferry building.

Medium shot of McTeague's office including the bay window. McTeague is standing on the dental chair with a hammer in his hand; the bird cage is hanging in the centre of the room and he has attached a piece of wire, the end of which he hooks over the head of a nail on the wall so that he can pull the cage up and down from below without having to climb up every time. He stands looking up at the cage, very much satisfied with himself and his work, then replaces the hammer behind the screen, takes a cloth, climbs up again, ties a napkin around the bird cage, and goes off, looking back.

Medium shot of the hallway outside McTeague's door. He comes out and locks the door behind him, then goes off towards the stairway.

Interior of the ferry building with a line of people at the ticket office. The entrance to the Oakland ferry : Trina walks up and down carrying her package, apparently waiting for someone.

Medium shot in front of McTeague's house. McTeague comes out of the house again and looks up and down the street, then exits in the direction of the sign-painter's shop.

Medium long shot of the end of the street-car line, in front of the ferry building. A street-car stops.

Medium shot at the rear of the car. People try to get off in a hurry. Marcus is among them; he takes his time in getting off. A big, heavy-set fellow behind him pushes him out of the way. Marcus gets sore again and is just about ready for a fight, but the big fellow is in a hurry and ignores him entirely and runs for his boat. Marcus follows in the same direction, swinging his little bamboo cane.

Medium shot of Trina, waiting. Marcus appears, tips his hat and tells her all about the fight. Trina looks at the clock above her.

Shot of the clock from her angle; they are just in time.

Back to the scene. People are running past them. With a gesture she asks Marcus whether he has any tickets. He says : 'No, haven't you got some?' He is suddenly in a great hurry also. She says : 'Yes.'

81

They both go off quickly.

Medium shot of the gate with people running through. The couple run into shot. Trina hands Marcus the tickets and they run towards the gate, dropping their tickets.

Medium shot in front of the gate, which the gate man is just about to close when Marcus and Trina run into shot, last of all, Marcus waving at him and yelling. Marcus pushes Trina through.

Medium shot of the gangplank with the boatman just taking up the ropes. Marcus pushes Trina across by the elbow. Once they are over, the boatman takes up the gangplank.

Close-up of the steam-whistle blowing.

Back to medium shot as the boat starts to leave.

Long shot from the bay, looking towards the ferry building. The boat starts to move slowly towards camera, which is on the other ferry.

Medium shot of the hallway in McTeague's house. On the landing is Maria Macapa, more or less cleaned up, with an old shawl around her head and neck, and an old box under her arm. Out of this box stick the necks of old bottles of different shapes — whisky flasks, quart bottles, beer bottles, etc. — a couple of old, terribly worn-out shoes, a busted and broken umbrella with all the spokes sticking out, a couple of old newspapers and a couple of old *Saturday Evening Posts*. She turns on the electric light in the hallway and starts to descend the steps.

Medium long shot from the corner of the alley and Laguna Street, looking towards the alley and including the wooden fence of the junk yard. Zerkow's house is in the background and a corrugated sheet iron sign on the left bears the words : 'Zerkow the Junk Dealer.' From the opposite side in the background, the junk wagon appears with Zerkow on the box holding the reins of a terribly emaciated horse; the wagon stops in front of the gate in the wooden fence.

Quick lap dissolve to medium shot in which Zerkow stops the wagon near the gate, gets off and starts with great difficulty to unload some unusually heavy pieces of junk.

Close-up of Zerkow working extremely hard, half-lifting, half-dragging the heavy pieces of junk; the sweat is rolling off him. He cuts his hand and stops for a second and looks at it; it is bleeding; he licks it, then goes back to work.

Back to medium shot as Maria Macapa enters from the right, carrying her box of old junk. She stops for a second and watches Zerkow.

Close-up of Maria as she watches him.

Back to medium shot of Zerkow. He finishes unloading the junk.

Medium shot from the sidewalk across the street. Maria appears from the right and walks up to him; he sees her.

Medium close-up of both. She shows him the box and he looks into it for a second with the eyes of a connoisseur. A sarcastic smile plays around his thin lips and he shakes his head. Maria looks at him for a second, then looks around carefully to right and left, to make sure that no one is watching. Then she goes very close to him while she digs something wrapped up in an old handkerchief out of her skirt pocket and holds it in the hollow of her hand. She opens it carefully and lets him look at it.

Close-up of Zerkow. His eyes grow bigger. He wets his lips and his fingers start playing nervously.

Shot from his angle of non-cohesive gold tape and some gold fillings in the handkerchief in Maria's hand.

Close-up of Maria. She smiles sarcastically as she realizes that her trick has worked again.

Back to medium shot of both. He indicates with a gesture that he is willing to buy the gold alone. She shakes her head and says no, the box and the gold or nothing at all. He tries to take hold of the gold fillings and the tape, not to take them away, but to look at them a little closer, but Maria quickly closes her hand over them and puts it behind her back. They look at each other threateningly, then Zerkow's expression relaxes. He gives in to her and points towards his shack. Maria enters through the gate, while Zerkow starts back for the wagon.

Medium shot from the other side of the street, showing not only the wagon, but also the back yard, where Maria can be seen walking towards the shack. Zerkow meanwhile takes a feedbag from underneath the seat of the wagon, then takes two handfuls of feed from a small wooden box under the seat and puts them in the bag. He walks to the horse's head and puts the feedbag on him. Then he goes through the gate, closing it from inside, and walks with dragging feet towards the shack.

Medium shot of Maria at the entrance to Zerkow's shack. Zerkow appears, carefully unlocks the door and enters first, followed by Maria. Shot of the rear of the room towards the entrance, with Zerkow closing the door. He lights a short candle stump, then motions to Maria to follow him. They start walking towards camera.

Reverse shot. They walk away from camera and disappear behind a curtained partition.

Quick lap dissolve to a shot inside the curtained partition. Zerkow takes off his hat and sits down, apparently exhausted. Immediately remembering the objects in Maria's hand, he nods to her and motions to her to sit down next to him.

Medium shot of the two. He asks her to let him see again. She opens her hand and lets him look once more. He then takes each object out of the box, looks at it, puts it on the table, thinks for a second, then with a gesture says : ' 50c.'

Close-up of Maria. She says : ' What — 50c? You're crazy.' She starts grabbing hold of the things and putting them back in the box.

Close-up of Zerkow. He watches her, but lets her do it.

Close-up of Maria, who now has the last object back in the box.

Medium shot of both. She takes the box under her arm and, with the handkerchief containing the fillings in her right hand, starts to move towards the curtain.

Close-up of Zerkow watching her out of the corner of his eye, wordless.

Close-up of Maria taking one step towards camera, indicating with her eyes that she anticipates his calling her back.

Back to close-up of Zerkow.

Shot from his angle of Maria taking hold of the curtain and walking through; only part of her arm remains visible.

Close-up of Zerkow. He yells : ' Come back, you,' very much excited and half-rising in his seat.

Shot from his angle of Maria poking her head through the curtain.

Close-up of Maria. She asks him: 'How much?' with a sarcastic smile in her expression, realizing that she has won.

Close-up of Zerkow, who thinks for a second with shifty and greedy eyes and then says: '65c.'

Medium shot of both. Maria retraces her steps and puts the box back on the table. She opens the handkerchief in her right hand, looks once more at the shiny gold, then takes it gingerly out of the handkerchief and puts it on the table.

Medium shot of both. He tries to take hold of the gold, but she is faster than he and covers it up with one hand. They look at each other threateningly. He takes an old and worn leather pouch from inside his coat pocket, opens it slowly and extracts 65c, including a shiny 50c piece.

Close-up of Zerkow. He looks at the money on the table.

Shot from his angle of the shiny 50c piece.

Back to the scene. He grabs the coin quickly, looks into the bag and picks out another one that is not so shiny, but dullish-looking and dirty. He lays it on the table, putting the shiny one back into the box. Maria quickly grabs the 65c, puts it in a corner of her handkerchief and ties it up, holding the handkerchief in her hand, then turns with the intention of going.

Close-up of Zerkow. He looks at Maria, sees that she wants to go and quickly glances over to the cupboard on the wall.

Shot from his angle of a whisky bottle and tumbler on the cupboard.

Back to close-up of Zerkow. He calls Maria back.

Shot from his angle as Maria turns, looking at him expectantly.

Medium shot of both. He waves to her to come back and points to the whisky bottle on the cupboard. She follows his look, thinks for a second, then nods, retraces her steps and sits down at the table. Zerkow goes off.

Medium shot of the cupboard. Zerkow appears, takes down the whisky bottle and broken tumbler, looks at the bottle against the light, and goes off towards the table.

Medium shot of Maria sitting at the table. Zerkow appears with the whisky bottle, takes the paper stopper off and shoves the bottle and tumbler over to Maria. He tells her to help herself, then takes the gold that he has just bought and goes off to the right.

Medium shot of an old wooden closet in a corner of the room. Zerkow appears. He looks carefully back to see whether Maria is looking, then opens the wooden door of the closet, which is apparently filled with old coats and pants hanging down low. He lifts them up to reveal a small safe. He looks back towards Maria again, then starts opening the combination.

Close-up of Maria, who has filled her glass. She looks in the direction of Zerkow.

Shot from her angle of Zerkow just opening the steel door of the safe. Back to close-up of Maria. She squints her eyes and watches him with a calculating look.

Medium close-up of Zerkow at the safe. He puts the non-cohesive gold tape and fillings into a heavy glass candy jar, then puts the jar quickly back into the safe, closes the door and quickly turns the combination. Suddenly he remembers Maria and looks quickly round with a suspicious and distrustful expression.

Shot of Maria from his angle. She is caught looking at him, but quickly glances away and tries to look unconcerned.

Medium shot of Zerkow. He goes off.

Medium shot of Maria at the table. Zerkow appears; Maria picks up the glass to drink and asks him if he is going to have one himself. He sits down, much exhausted, takes the bottle, raises it towards Maria, then takes a good swig out of it while Maria empties her glass. They put the bottle and glass back on the table. Zerkow looks at Maria with a calculating look. He has something on his mind but he doesn't know exactly how to put it. Maria starts to rise but Zerkow quickly stops her.

Close-up of Zerkow who says : ' Maria isn't your only name, is it? '

Back to close-up. He watches out of the corner of his eye with great anxiety.

Close-up of Maria. She looks at him and, shaking her head, says : ' No.'

Medium shot of both. Zerkow thinks for a second, then pushes over the whisky bottle; as she hesitates, he fills her glass halfway up again. Maria glances at him, takes the whisky glass, empties it quickly, then settles back in her chair, satisfied.

Big close-up of Maria with her chin in her hand, filling the whole screen. Her eyes start to gaze into space and, with a slight shaking of her head, she speaks :

Title : ' Name is " Maria — Miranda — Macapa ".'

Back to close-up of her still gazing into space, still shaking her head. Suddenly she has an after-thought and starts speaking again :

Title : ' Had a flying squirrel and let him go ! '

Close-up of Zerkow. He looks at her with a little satisfied smile on his thin lips. He says :

86

TITLE : 'Say, how about those gold dishes you told me about the last time you were here?'

Close-up of Maria, puzzled. She speaks :

TITLE : 'What gold dishes?'

Close-up of Zerkow looking at her. He speaks :

TITLE : 'You know — the plate your father owned in Central America a long time ago — don't you know — it rang like so many bells? Red, gold — you know — like oranges?'

Close-up of Maria, her eyes wide, gazing into space. She throws her chin in the air and says : 'Oh, that.'
Medium shot of both. Zerkow nods, his claw-like fingers feeling his mouth and chin. Then he says : 'Tell us about it, go on' — urging her. Maria refuses and makes a move as if to go. Zerkow holds her back. Again he takes the bottle and, although it hurts him terribly, he fills the tumbler full. She takes it, swallows it, then breathing deeply settles her elbows on the table, looking straight in front of her.
Close-up of her eyes, which see nothing as she speaks :

TITLE : 'It was when I was little. My folks must have been rich, oh, rich in . . . into the millions — coffee, I guess — and there was a large house, but I can only remember the plate. Oh, that service of plate! It was wonderful.'

Close-up of Zerkow listening, his eyes glued on Maria.
Close-up of Maria speaking, seeing nothing. She continues to speak :

TITLE : 'There were more than a hundred pieces, and every one of them gold. You should have seen the sight when the leather trunk was opened. It fair dazzled your eyes.'

Back to close-up of Zerkow listening, beside himself.
Back to close-up of Maria. She continues speaking. Dissolve out.
Dissolve in to a large leather trunk of weird, unnatural form, against a mysterious background, one side curved, the other straight, indicating that it is only a hallucination. White, ghost-like hands ending in a will-o'-the-wisp, with nobody whatsoever attached to them, open the top. There is a dazzling light coming from the trunk. The hands take out the dishes so that each one of them can be seen — soup tureens, pitchers, great big platters, cream jugs and bowls with handles carved like vines, drinking mugs and gravy dishes. Dissolve out.
Dissolve in to medium close-up of Maria talking. She says : 'And a

great big punch bowl,' making a gesture with her arms to show its shape, indicating that it was very heavy.

Close-up of Zerkow; his eyes are popping out of his head.

Back to close-up of Maria. She finishes her mimed description of the punch bowl. Dissolve out.

Dissolve back to the scene with the trunk. Four hands lift the punch bowl just described out of the trunk, indicating its weight. It is heavily carved and of an odd shape to indicate its unrealness. There is a ladle hanging from it. Lap dissolve out.

Dissolve in to a large, oddly shaped black table against a mysterious background with every piece of the service of plate standing on it. Four hands lift the punch bowl into the centre of it, then disappear. Dissolve out.

Dissolve in to close-up of Maria, still talking, her eyes seeing nothing. She strikes at an imaginary object with the knuckle of her right middle finger. Dissolve out.

Dissolve in to one hand holding the immense punch bowl from above so that it does not touch the table; another hand strikes the punch bowl in the centre with its knuckle, three times. Dissolve out.

Dissolve in to a tremendously large church bell with a rope attached to it, seen against the sky with fantastic clouds in the background, swinging rhythmically but apparently not suspended from anything. The bell swings slowly to and fro three times. Dissolve out.

Dissolve in to Maria's face with wide open eyes, listening to the imaginary ringing of the bell.

Cut to close-up of Zerkow. He looks at her with wide eyes, moves his head just for a fraction so as to get his ear in the right direction and puts his hand behind his ear to hear better. Then he seems to see something on the wall opposite him; his eyes never move, but they seem to pop out. Lap dissolve out.

Dissolve in to a shot from his angle of the wall opposite with all the junk standing and hanging against it. Dissolve out.

Dissolve in to a tremendously large table with a mirror top standing on a black floor with a real wall in the background. On it is piled the gold plate service, this time of a realistic shape, unlike that which Maria imagined. A vision of Zerkow comes into shot, dressed exactly the same as he appeared when seated at the table, with even his hat on. Standing on the other side of the table, facing camera, he looks over the gold plate. A vision of Maria appears, dressed as she was when sitting in the chair. She looks at Zerkow who turns, sees her and makes a gesture as if to say : 'This is all yours?' Maria nods 'Yes' with wide open eyes. Zerkow seems to appreciate the fact. Dissolve out.

Dissolve in to the wall of Zerkow's shack as it was before with junk standing and hanging around it.

Cut to close-up of Zerkow still looking in the direction of the wall with extraordinary light from a spotlight shining brightly on his face. He comes out of his trance and looks towards Maria and the light disappears.

Medium shot of both. Maria's eyes are wide open; her stare becomes less fixed as she slowly comes back to earth. Maria rises and Zerkow, still under the influence of the imaginary vision, rises also. He offers her another drink but she refuses; then he accompanies her to the curtain and they both go out.

Medium shot looking from inside towards the front door. They both appear with their backs to camera. He unbolts the door and lets her out.

Medium close-up of both. Zerkow speaks :

TITLE : 'Come again, come again — don't wait until you've got junk — come any time you feel like it and tell me more about the plate.'

Back to the scene. Maria nods slightly.

Medium shot from ahead of them (on perambulator) as Maria steps down off the stoop, with him following close behind. He speaks :

TITLE : 'How much do you think it was worth?'

Back to the scene. Maria looks at him and says vaguely :

TITLE : 'Oh, a million dollars.'

Back to the scene. He nods, looking into space, while she keeps on walking.

Medium shot of the wooden fence as seen from the sidewalk. The gate opens from inside and Maria appears. She comes out and closes the gate. Then she unties the knot in her handkerchief to make sure that the 65c is still in it. She ties it up again and goes off to the right, holding it tightly in her hand.

Quick lap dissolve to medium shot of Zerkow still standing in the middle of the yard where we left him. He is still deep in thought as he turns his back to camera and walks back towards the shack and in through the open door.

Medium shot from inside the house, looking towards the door. He bolts it with three big gas pipes and walks towards camera.

Reverse shot as he walks towards the curtained partition.

Medium shot from inside the curtained partition. Zerkow enters

89

through the curtain and goes to the alcohol stove on the little table. He picks up a dirty coffee can, takes the lid off, looks in and puts it back, then lights the stove with block matches. Then he takes the remainder of some dry, almost mildewed rye bread, cuts off a chunk and leans against the stove with the bread in his hand.

Close-up of Zerkow looking into space, preoccupied and thoughtful, muttering to himself.

TITLE : ' A million dollars, a gold service worth a million dollars. A punch bowl worth a fortune, red gold plate, heaps and piles — God ! '

Fade out.

Fade in to long shot from a boat in the bay looking towards Oakland shore. The ferry boat is just standing at the slip. Quick lap dissolve out. Lap dissolve in to medium shot of the gangplank. Marcus pushes Trina across it ahead of everyone else. By now he is carrying the package of frankfurters while Trina is carrying the basket covered with a shawl.

Quick lap dissolve in to medium shot of a street-car with a crowd of people rushing towards it. Marcus is in the lead and he pushes Trina in first.

Medium shot of McTeague's office. McTeague is seen putting lettuce-leaf and cube sugar between the wire uprights of the bird cage. He also fills a little basin with water. He takes a towel and wraps it around the cage, then raises the cage. He goes off.

Medium shot of the door of McTeague's office. He takes a hat from the stand and opens the door.

Medium shot from the hallway looking towards McTeague's door. He comes out, closes it, locks it and goes off towards the stairs.

Medium long shot of Thirty-Fourth Street Station. A street-car comes up and stops. Marcus and Trina get off followed by one or two other people and the car moves off again.

Medium shot of Owgooste and ' der Tervins ',[1] who have wooden toy guns and newspaper soldier-hats with newspaper feathers. Owgooste himself is ' der ' Field-Marshal. He also has a bandolier made out of newspaper fringes and a toy sword. The greyhound is also in line. As Trina and Marcus arrive, Owgooste raises his sword and gives a command.

TITLE : ' Attention — Salute ! '

Back to the scene. The two kids present arms, each in a different way.

---

[1] The twins. Stroheim's method of using his characters' speech and attitudes in the description of the action is particularly evident here. See the Note on this Edition, page 6.

Marcus, who is still carrying the frankfurters, salutes back with his cane, as he is also militarily inclined. Trina laughs, puts the basket down on the ground and stoops to kiss the two ' Tervins ' and Owgooste. The two ' Tervins ' hang on to her skirt while the Field-Marshal puts his sword into his scabbard and walks with Uncle Marcus towards their house.

Medium shot of the front of McTeague's house. McTeague comes out, looks up and down the street and finally walks off towards the right.

Medium long shot showing the whole of the Sieppes' house as Marcus, Trina, Owgooste and the ' Tervins ' appear. Owgooste is trying to tear the paper off the frankfurter package, very anxious to see what is inside. The Papa is standing outside watering the flowers with a green sprinkling can with flowers painted on it. He looks up.

Close-up of him, angled to include the sign on the house which reads : ' Hans Sieppe.' He sees Marcus, waves and says : ' Hello there.'

Back to the scene. Marcus waves back with his cane. Trina goes up to the Papa and kisses him. They all walk into the house, Papa having first hooked up ' der ' sprinkling can on a chain, locked it, and put the key in his pocket.

Medium shot from the main entrance looking into dining room with the kitchen in the background .The dining room table is set. There are two children's chairs for ' der Tervins '. They appear in the foreground; ' der Mama ' looks out of ' der ' kitchen, and on seeing the guest she waves. She is all heated and perspiring as she has been making pies and bread.

Medium shot of the kitchen. Trina enters with the package of frankfurters and dumps them down on the table. Then she goes through the kitchen door into her parents' bedroom.

Medium shot of her as she takes off her hat and coat and gloves and puts them down on her parents' bed.

Medium shot of the Mama who has produced a big tin pot filled with water, of the kind that they use to boil laundry in. She opens the package, takes the lid off the pot and puts in the frankfurters with a large wooden spoon; then she opens the top of a second pot.

Close-up of the pot filled to the top with sauerkraut, steam pouring from it.

Back to the scene. Mrs. Sieppe covers up the pot and goes on with her cooking.

Medium shot of Trina in front of the mirror on her mother's dressing table. She takes a cardboard box of rice powder and powders her nose with a little sterilized piece of cotton. She also does her hair.

Medium shot of the front parlour next to the dining room. Marcus is telling Mr. Sieppe with dramatic gestures about the fights that he had with the street-car conductor and the guy who pushed him out of his way.

Medium shot. Trina enters the kitchen from the bedroom. She steps up close to her mother, opens her pocket book and takes out the $4.50 which she has earned. She gives her mother $2 and puts the other $2.50 back into her pocket book. Her mother thanks her, then goes to the door of the kitchen and yells out :

TITLE : ' Papa setz der children. The food is coming.'

Medium shot of the front parlour. Mr. Sieppe hears her and immediately interrupts Marcus's story. He stands at attention and yells :

TITLE : ' Attention — Vorwarts ! '

Back to the scene. The two twins, led by Owgooste, march in goose-step out of the front parlour, followed by their father and Marcus.

Medium shot from the door of the front parlour looking into the dining room. The group enter and march in a circle around the table until the kids arrive at their seats.

Close-up of Mr. Sieppe who yells :

TITLE : ' Ground der rifles.'

Back to the scene. ' Der Tervins ' lay down their toy guns, while Owgooste puts his sword into its scabbard.

Back to close-up of Mr. Sieppe who yells :

TITLE : ' Down setzen.'

Back to the scene. The ' Tervins ' climb up into their chairs, as does Owgooste. Marcus and Papa sit down also. Trina and the Mama carry in soup tureens with steaming frankfurters, which they put in the centre of the table along with a dish of sauerkraut. The Mama and Trina sit down also. The Papa dishes out the frankfurters.

Close-up of Owgooste, who draws his sword and tries to cut a frankfurter with it.

Medium shot of the Papa and Owgooste. The Papa reaches over and gives Owgooste a slap in the face, whereupon Owgooste starts crying.

Close-up of ' der Tervins '. They are looking over at Owgooste and at once join the orchestra.

Close-up of Mr. Sieppe. He bangs ' der ' fist on the table and says :

TITLE : ' Attention — the child vot ist not good vill not to the pignick go tomorrow.'

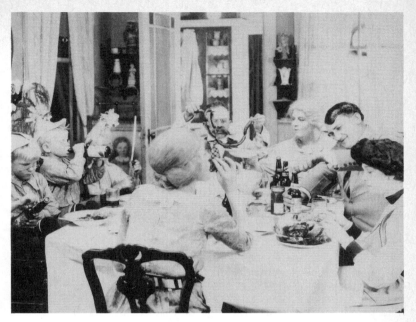

Close-up of Marcus. He makes funny faces at the 'Tervins'.
Close-up of the 'Tervins' crying. They look over at Marcus.
Shot from their angle of Marcus still making faces.
Back to shot of the 'Tervins'. They stop crying, smile through their tears and start eating frankfurters.
Medium shot of the whole table. Owgooste is still crying but much more softly. The Papa eats the sauerkraut; everybody is gay and happy. Iris down on part of the soup tureen with steam coming out and a couple of frankfurters sticking out of it; hold for a second, then iris out completely.

Iris in on a gilded tooth; hold for a second, then camera moves back on perambulator while the iris opens up simultaneously to reveal a sign shop at night with all kinds of signs, among them two gilded teeth, one larger than the other. McTeague stops in front of the display window and looks at the tooth.
Close-up of McTeague from inside the shop window with traffic passing in the street behind him. It is dark by now.
Cut to shot from his angle of the gilded teeth in the window.
Back to the scene. McTeague walks a bit closer, looks a bit, walks two

steps to the left, looks, takes three steps backwards, looks, and stands lost in utter ecstasy. The owner of the sign store comes out smoking his pipe. He sees McTeague and says : ' Hello, Doc.' McTeague sees him, greets him back and walks slowly over to him. The two lean against the door-sash of the entrance.

Medium close-up of both. The sign-painter asks :

TITLE : ' Did you want that tooth tonight, Doc? '

Back to the scene as he finishes speaking.

TITLE : ' Ain't got enough yet. Just came to look at it.'

Back to the scene. The sign-painter says :

TITLE : ' Yep, sure is a dandy.'

Back to the scene. McTeague nods and says :

TITLE : ' Huh-huh, that's the word.'

Medium shot of Miss Baker's room. She is sitting close to the wall, with an old novel in her hands.

Insert of a page of the book, with the title : ' Chapter 4 — In which the Fair Young Viscount, falsely betrayed by the treacherous Baron, is thrust from his Ancestral Home by the Cruel Unrelenting Earl.'

Back to the scene. She lets the book sink into her lap, bends her head slightly towards the wall and listens.

Quick lap dissolve to medium shot of the interior of Old Grannis's room. He is sitting on the other side of the wall close to the pine table with some bookbinding apparatus on it, binding copies of the *Breeder & Sportsman*. He stops in his work, puts his head close to the wall and listens.

Close-up of Old Grannis, with a dreamy expression and a faint smile on his lips.

Quick lap dissolve to close-up of Miss Baker on the other side of the wall, in an almost identical position, with her head a little closer to the wall. She also listens, with a sweet, dreamy smile on her lips.

Medium shot of the front of the sign-painter's shop. McTeague and the sign-painter are still talking. Another customer enters and the sign-painter has to go inside, leaving McTeague alone. McTeague stands there, still gazing longingly at the tooth.

Close-up of a church clock striking nine o'clock.

Back to the scene. McTeague looks up, takes out a heavy, old-fashioned nickel watch, winds it, puts it back and starts to walk off. Just before he leaves, he looks back longingly once more, then goes off. Iris down on the gold tooth; hold for a second, then iris out completely.

Iris in on the Sieppes' dining room. The frankfurters are all gone, the sauerkraut too. The Mama and Trina are picking up the dishes; everybody rises.
Close-up of Mr. Sieppe who speaks :

TITLE : ' Now ve shell put der beer into der bottles. Attention.'

Back to the scene. The kids clap their hands; Marcus is greatly elated. They all go off into the kitchen.
Medium shot of the kitchen. They all enter. The Papa and Marcus start filling bottles with the help of a rubber tube or something similar (whatever is used in making home brew), while the Mama and Trina start washing the dishes. Owgooste breaks a bottle; the Papa slaps him and he starts crying. Marcus makes a funny face. While drying a plate, Trina walks over to Marcus, puts an arm through his and leans against him, then whispers something. Marcus looks at her and says : ' All right.' Trina lets go of him, goes over to her mother and whispers something to her. Her mother says : ' All right.' Trina goes towards the door, where she turns and waits for Marcus. Marcus tells the Papa that he is going out on the front stoop; the Papa says all right. The two go out. Medium shot of the two of them as they come out of the house and sit down on the front stoop.
Medium close-up of both. Trina sits with her elbows on her knees and her chin in her hands, gazing into space. Marcus speaks :

TITLE : ' Well, Trina, take a look at me, take a look at me.'

Back to the scene. She turns slowly and looks at him questioningly. He continues to speak :

TITLE : ' They made me Secretary of the Polk Street Improvement Club.'

Back to the scene. She looks at him and says : ' Is that so? Isn't that wonderful.' Speaking condescendingly, he says :

TITLE : ' They wished it on me, wouldn't have nobody else, it's a fact.'

Back to the scene. He nudges her with his elbow, looking at her significantly, and says :

TITLE : ' Won't be long now — won't be long now.'

Back to the scene. Trina is glad and also just a bit embarrassed over the insinuation that ' it won't be long now ', whatever that means. She goes back to her original position with her chin in her hands and her elbows on her knees, and looks into space while Marcus keeps on bragging about himself. Iris down on his face as he talks. Pan from him to her until her head is in iris.

Shot from her angle of the full moon on the horizon over the marshes; a cloud is just moving across it.

Back to her face in iris, then iris out completely.

Iris in on McTeague's house. McTeague appears on the right of camera and walks up to the main entrance. He has his hand almost on the doorknob when he thinks of something, steps out again and walks towards the left.

Medium shot of the corner of the building showing the bay window of his office. McTeague appears from the right, thinking; he looks up at the bay window and stops.

Close-up of McTeague looking up.

Shot of the bay window from his angle. The large gilded tooth dissolves in, suspended from an iron rod and hanging between the two windows.

Back to close-up of McTeague. He smiles a little.

Back to shot of the window from his angle with the gilded tooth still visible. It dissolves out.

Medium shot of McTeague as he comes out of his reverie, slowly turns and starts to walk off. A girl passes and, seeing a big husky man, stops for a second, turns and looks at him flirtatiously. Not understanding, McTeague looks around on the ground, thinking the girl has dropped something.

Medium shot in front of the entrance as he appears from the left and enters the house. Iris out.

Iris in on a clock showing 2:30 in the afternoon. Quick lap dissolve out.

Quick lap dissolve in to the exterior of the Car Conductor's Coffee Joint.

Quick lap dissolve in to medium shot of the interior. McTeague is at the counter. The owner rings up the bill on the cash register and gives him back his change. McTeague takes some matches and toothpicks, puts one between his teeth and starts to leave.

Medium shot of the exterior of the coffee joint. McTeague appears from inside with his toothpick, gorged with food. He belches slightly and fingers the toothpick, then looks over towards the saloon.

Shot from his angle of Joe Frenna's saloon.

Back to the scene as he walks in the direction of the saloon.

Medium shot of the entrance of the saloon. McTeague enters, walks

96

through the cigar store vestibule and starts to push the swing doors.

Shot from the interior of the saloon towards the swing doors. McTeague enters.

Medium shot from the door of the private room towards the bar showing the bartender and three or four other men. McTeague appears from the left and goes up to the bar; the bartender greets him. McTeague looks around and sees no one he knows. Without any prompting, the bartender takes a small tin bucket with a handle in such a way as to indicate that McTeague regularly has the same thing.

Medium close-up of the bartender behind the bar. More or less secretly, he starts pumping steam beer into a pitcher.

Close-up of the bartender's face to indicate that he is doing it secretly. He looks furtively around.

Medium shot of the bar and the door. A tough guy enters very quickly and says : ' The copper ! '

Medium close-up from behind the bar. The bartender quickly turns off the faucet, puts a tin top over it with one hand while he grabs a bottle of coca-cola with the other.

Close-up of his hand holding the bottle of coca-cola.

Back to the scene as the bartender shoves glasses to all the men at the bar and starts pouring in coca-cola. The cop enters and looks around. The bartender gives him a salute. The cop returns it and, looking around with a casual air, passes the bar and goes to the back door.

Close-up of the copper's hand taking a key with a wooden tag on it down from the wall.

Medium shot of the cop as he disappears through the door.

Shot from behind the bar. The bartender takes the tin cover away and continues to let steam beer in.

Shot from behind the bar of the men, including McTeague, all leaning against the bar, looking at each other with slightly insinuating smiles.

Close-up of the bartender's hands behind the bar. Holding a tumbler in his left hand, he takes a bottle of Haig and Haig from underneath the counter, fills the tumbler and puts the bottle back again.

Medium shot towards the bar. The bartender puts the hand in which he is holding the tumbler under his apron and walks towards the door through which the copper disappeared. He opens the door and goes out.

Medium shot of a small hallway with a gas jet and a little shelf. The bartender puts the full tumbler on the shelf, and goes off in the direction he came from.

Medium shot of the bar. The bartender enters from the right.

Close-up from behind the bar. The bartender shuts off the steam beer faucet as the pitcher is full; he takes a newspaper and covers it crudely. Medium shot towards the bar including McTeague and the bartender. The bartender hands the pitcher to McTeague; McTeague puts some money into his hand, thanks him and goes off towards the left.

Medium shot of the swing doors from outside. McTeague comes out holding the pitcher covered with newspaper and starts to walk across the street towards the house.

Medium shot towards the bar. The copper comes in through the back door, hangs up the key, greets the bartender casually and saunters out. The bartender leaves the bar and goes out through the back door into the hallway.

Close-up of the shelf with the tumbler, now empty. The bartender's hands appear and take down the tumbler.

Medium shot of the bartender with a little sarcastic smile on his face as he goes off towards the bar.

Medium shot towards the bar. The bartender appears from the right and goes behind the bar. The men who have coca-cola glasses in front of them pick them up and pour the coca-cola into the spittoon. They then shove the glasses towards the bartender who says: 'What'll yi have?'

Medium shot in front of McTeague's office. McTeague is just unlocking the door.

Medium shot from inside. McTeague enters with his pitcher, closes the door, walks over to the dentist's chair and puts the pitcher down on the platform.

Medium shot of the stove, which is already alight. McTeague takes brickette after brickette and crams the stove full to the top. Then he takes the Sunday paper from the unmade bed-lounge, looks for the page with the funnies and goes off towards the dentist's chair.

Medium shot of the dentist's chair. McTeague takes off his coat after extracting from it a leaf of lettuce and a piece of cube sugar. He then opens his waistcoat, lets down the bird cage and puts the lettuce leaf and sugar between the uprights. He talks to the bird for a second, then raises the cage and takes down an enormous porcelain-head pipe that is hanging on the wall and a tin can of the cheapest pipe tobacco.

Close-up of the can with the brand name on it.

Back to the scene. He fills the pipe and lights it. Then he loosens his suspenders, opens the top button of his trousers and, puffing on his pipe, sits down in the dentist's chair.

Close-up of McTeague peacefully smoking. He turns his back towards the stove.

Shot from his angle of the stove, which is white hot.

Medium shot of the dentist's chair. McTeague turns his back to camera as he reaches down to pick up the pitcher. He drops the newspaper in which it is wrapped on the floor, then takes the water glass from the dental spittoon on the left of the chair and fills it with steam beer. He drinks the glass down in one draught, fills it again and places it next to him. Then he puts the pitcher on top of the dental spittoon, picks up the funnies page and leans back in his chair. As he puffs on his pipe big clouds of smoke envelop him. Suddenly he sits up again; something is annoying him. He leans forward and takes off his shoes.

Close-up of his feet and hands. His fingers pull the heavy woollen socks away from his toes to give them freedom. Then he leans back, drinks the other glass of beer, fills it again and puts it back. He picks up the funnies page and starts reading.

Close-up of his face as he puffs on his pipe. He belches very slightly and comfortably.

Close-up of the bird singing.

Back to the scene. McTeague is still looking at the funnies. Iris down on his face and hands holding the funnies page. The sheet slowly drops and he closes his eyes. Iris out completely.

Iris in on Trina sitting in a swing. She and the swing move out of iris, revealing Marcus's face. The iris enlarges to show Marcus pushing the swing, then opens up entirely, revealing 'der Papa' and 'der Mama' with Owgooste and 'der Tervins', lying peacefully on the ground. Trina is flying very high.

Close-up of Marcus. He pushes her ferociously.

Close-up of Trina swinging terribly high, screaming. One of the ropes is seen breaking.

Medium long shot. Trina flies through the air and lands on her face. 'Der Papa' and 'der Mama', Owgooste and 'der Tervins' all scream and run over to her, Marcus also.

Medium close-up of Trina. They pick her up; she is very pale and there is a little blood coming out of her mouth. She is holding her hands to her jaw and mouth. She fingers her teeth and takes one out with her fingers; it is broken at the root. She holds it in her fingers and looks at it, still fingering a second one with her other hand. Then she starts crying and tells them that the other one is loose too. Owgooste wants the tooth to play with; he hops up and down trying to grab it; 'der Papa' reaches over and hands him a good one. Owgooste starts crying and 'der Tervins' follow his example. 'Der Mama' wipes the blood from Trina's chin.

Close-up of Trina crying. Looking at her tooth, she says:

TITLE : ' It's your fault, Marcus, now I'm disfigured for life.'

Close-up of Marcus who says :

TITLE : ' That's nothin' — that's nothin'. My pal, Doc McTeague'll fix that easy — it's a cinch — that's a fact.'

Back to the scene. The kids are still crying; ' der Mama ' is leading Trina back to ' der ' plateau and ' der Papa ' is investigating the rope. ' Der Mama ' sits Trina down.

Iris down on Trina's hand holding her tooth. Tilt up to her face. Still crying, she repeats : ' I'm disfigured for life.' Iris out completely.

Iris in on McTeague's mush; his mouth is wide open, and he is snoring.

Close-up of the stove, which is white hot.

Close-up of the bird singing.

Back to close-up of McTeague. He awakens and yawns terrifically.

Camera moves back on perambulator as McTeague stretches and looks over towards the beer pitcher. He takes the glass and fills it with what is left in the pitcher.

Close-up of the glass, full of stale, warm beer. He drinks it and wipes his lips with the back of his hand, then stretches again and looks up towards the shelf.

Shot from his angle of the seven volumes of *Allen's Practical Dentist*, and his concertina.

Medium shot of McTeague. He rises.

Medium shot of the shelf. He comes into shot, takes down the concertina, blows off the dust and goes off again.

Medium shot of the dentist's chair. McTeague appears and sits down. He wonders for a moment which of the six tunes he knows to play, then starts playing.

Close-up of the canary, singing louder than ever.

Medium shot of the corner of Laguna and Hayes Streets. A street-car appears and stops.

Medium shot of the rear platform. There is ' der Mama ' and ' der Papa ' Sieppe, and Trina and Owgooste and ' der Tervins '. Each of ' der Tervins ' is carrying a big bunch of wilted wild flowers. Trina is holding a handkerchief up to her mouth, looking very pale. Marcus says goodbye to everybody, and steps off the car. ' Der Mama ' Sieppe talks to him until the conductor rings the bell and the car starts. They all wave from the platform. Marcus waves back, turns, and walks towards the main entrance of the house.

Medium shot of the interior of McTeague's office. McTeague is playing to beat the band.

Medium shot of Old Grannis's room. Old Grannis is sitting at the little pine table binding his pamphlets. He stops for a second, listens towards the wall and smiles a little dreamily.

Quick lap dissolve in to medium shot of the interior of Miss Baker's room. Miss Baker is sitting with a cup and saucer in her lap. She sips her tea, then leans over towards the wall and listens. She too smiles, just a little dreamily. As she listens she looks up accidentally towards the ceiling. Her expression is casual at first but then she seems to concentrate on something.

Shot from her angle of a rosette on the ceiling, half of which is covered up.

Back to medium close-up as she looks, thinks and looks again. She seems to realize something terrible.

Medium shot of Miss Baker, who rises, very agitated. She quickly glances up once more, looks at the wall and goes quickly out of shot.

Medium shot of the door. Miss Baker appears, listens at the door, which is ajar, opens it more and steps out.

Medium shot of the two doors opening onto the hallway. Miss Baker appears from the inside and sneaks on tip-toe over to Old Grannis's door, which is also ajar. She stops there with her hand over her heart and looks through the door.

Close-up of Miss Baker from inside, looking through the open door.

Shot from her angle of the ceiling above the partition wall showing a semi-circular rosette identical to the one in her room.

Back to close-up. She closes her eyes; her heart almost stops; she can hardly believe it. She looks at the wallpaper.

Shot from her angle of a section of the wallpaper.

Back to her face. We can see that she is trying to convince herself of something.

Medium shot of both doors again as she sneaks back to her room and disappears, leaving the door open.

Medium shot from the inside as she stops at the door and looks up at the wallpaper.

Close-up of a section of the wallpaper with an identical pattern.

Big close-up of Miss Baker's face as she realizes something. Terribly agitated, she goes out of shot towards the wall.

Medium shot towards the wall. Miss Baker appears, listens, then sits down in her chair with her hands folded in her lap, thinking and thinking.

Medium shot of McTeague's office. McTeague is still playing his concertina when the door opens and Marcus comes in. He fans himself with his hat, indicating that it is terribly hot in the room, and looks over towards the stove.

Shot from his angle of the stove, which is white hot.

Medium shot of McTeague as he stops playing and looks up. He says : 'Hello,' to Marcus, who enters the scene and points in the direction of the stove, then at his wilted collar. He can't understand it. He tells McTeague that he has been out with the Sieppes down at the beach. He talks very fast and excitedly and gestures with his arms as he describes how he was swinging Trina and she fell, breaking one tooth and loosening another.

Close-up of Marcus speaking :

Title : ' It's a wonder she didn't kill herself. It is a wonder, it is for a fact. Ain't it now? Huh? Ain't it? Y'ought t'have seen ! '

Back to medium shot of McTeague listening. Marcus flips out his watch, looks at it and flips it back. He asks McTeague if he wouldn't like to go over to Frenna's. McTeague thinks for a second, says : 'Yes,' and buttons up.

Medium shot as he puts on his coat and hat.

Medium shot of the door as the two exit. Iris out.

Iris in on Marcus's face. He is talking and talking. Iris enlarges as he bangs the table with his fist. Camera moves back on perambulator, revealing the parties to whom he is talking; among them are McTeague, Heise, the harness-maker, and Mr. Ryer.

Close-up of Marcus speaking :

Title : ' There's where the evil lies — the masses must learn self-control. It stands to reason.'

Back to close-up as he bangs his fist on the table.

Close-up of McTeague, who is awe-struck.

Medium close-up of Heise and Ryer both smoking their pipes and nodding.

Back to close-up of Marcus as he speaks again :

Title : ' Look at the figures. Look at the figures. Decrease the number of wage-earners and you increase wages, don't you? Don't you? '

Close-up of McTeague, smoking. He nods and says :

Title : ' Yes — yes — that's it — self-control — that's the word.'

Close-up of Marcus as he speaks :

Title : ' It's the capitalist that's ruining the cause of labour . . .'

102

Back to close-up of Marcus speaking.

TITLE : '. . . white-livered drones, traitors, with their livers white as snow, eatun the bread of widows and orphuns; there's where the evil lies.'

Close-up of McTeague who nods and says :

TITLE : ' That's it, I think it's their livers.'

Medium shot of Marcus and McTeague. Marcus suddenly becomes calm again, forgetting his pose in an instant as he turns to McTeague and says :

TITLE : ' Say, Mac, I told my cousin Trina to come round and see you about that tooth of hers. She'll be in tomorrow, I guess.'

Back to the scene. McTeague looks at him, puffs, spits, and nods his head. Iris down on McTeague. Hold for a second, then iris out completely.

Iris in on a pad calendar hanging on the wall. The word MONDAY appears in large letters followed by the different appointments for today. At the top is ' Miss Baker ', from ' one to two ', then some other names. Camera moves back on perambulator revealing McTeague working on Miss Baker. He fills a glass with water and lets her rinse her mouth while he goes to a moveable rack to prepare something.
Close-up of Miss Baker as she speaks :

TITLE : ' Something extraordinary has happened, Dr. McTeague.'

Close-up of McTeague. He turns to look at her and listens.
Back to her in close-up as she speaks :

TITLE : ' I found out yesterday that the wallpaper in Mr. Grannis's room is the same as in mine, I declare. I believe at one time that was all one room.'

Back to close-up as she finishes speaking.
Close-up of McTeague. He listens stupidly, but can't make out what she is driving at.
Back to close-up of Miss Baker as she continues speaking :

TITLE : ' It almost amounts to our occupying the same room. I don't know — why, really — do you think I should speak to the landlady about it? '

Close-up of McTeague. First he shakes his head, then nods stupidly, not getting her meaning at all.

Back to close-up of Miss Baker as she continues to speak :

TITLE : 'I know Mr. Grannis would feel very upset about it, too — they say that he's the younger son of a baronet, and was thrust from his ancestral home by the cruel, unrelenting, treacherous earl.'

Close-up of McTeague looking very surprised. He keeps on working.]

TITLE : 'Mac learned dentistry after a fashion, through assisting the charlatan . . . and, years later on Polk St. in San Francisco, "Doc" McTeague was established.' [1]

Vertical barn door in to reveal the house on the corner of Laguna and Hayes Streets in extreme long shot which includes the entire intersection. Two street-cars are just passing in the street below as Mac's white dental jacket can be glimpsed through the bay window on the first floor.

Medium shot of McTeague working on Miss Baker in the dental chair.

Close-up of McTeague, who looks up from his work.

Close-up of the door bell.

Back to close-up of McTeague looking at the door.

Medium shot of the door, which opens. Marcus ushers in Trina. He says : 'Hello,' pointing to his cousin.

Medium close-up of McTeague standing by the dental chair. He nods his head gravely and says : 'In a minute,' and proceeds to go on with his work.

TITLE : 'Have a seat, Marcus.'

Back to medium shot of Marcus and Trina by the door. They walk off towards the right.

Medium shot of the chairs against the wall. Marcus and Trina walk over and sit down.

Medium close-up of both of them. Marcus nudges her, moving his head in the direction of McTeague and then back to her as he says :

TITLE : 'Mac's the strongest duck you ever seen, by damn.'

Back to the scene. Marcus grips his own arm muscle as if demonstrating his point. Trina looks over in the direction of Mac. [Marcus nudges her and says :

TITLE : 'Get on to the size of him. Yes, Mac's all right.']

---

[1] This title does not appear in Stroheim's original script.

Medium shot of Mac working.

Close-up of Trina looking over towards McTeague.

Back to medium shot of the seated couple. Trina continues to look at Mac, while Marcus feels his own tooth.

[Medium shot of the door as it opens and Maria Macapa appears. She stops at the door and asks Mac if she can come in and make the bed.

Shot from her angle as Mac looks up and nods.

Back to medium shot of Maria as she walks towards the bed-lounge.]

Medium shot of McTeague's bed-lounge. Maria is just shaking out the bedclothes.

Medium shot of Marcus and Trina sitting against the wall. Marcus nudges Trina, and Trina looks over at Maria.

TITLE : 'That's Maria. She keeps Mac's place clean. She's cuckoo in the head.' [1]

[Medium close-up of Marcus and Trina as Marcus speaks :

TITLE : 'She's a greaser and she's queer in the head — you ought to

[1] This title does not appear in Stroheim's original script.

hear her go on about a gold dinner service she says her folks used to own.'

Back to the scene as he finishes speaking. Trina looks from him to Maria with much interest. Marcus nudges Trina as if to say : 'Watch,' and says :

Title : 'How do, Maria?'

Shot from his angle of Maria, who nods to him over her shoulder.
Back to close-up of Marcus and Trina. Marcus continues speaking :

Title : 'Didn't always have to work for your livin', though, did you, when you ate offa gold dishes?'

Close-up of Maria. She doesn't answer, but puts her chin in the air, shutting her eyes, as if to say she knows a long story about that if she had a mind to talk.
Back to close-up of Marcus and Trina. Marcus says : 'Can't always start her going,' then continues :

Title : 'Say, Maria, what's your name?'

Close-up of Maria from his angle. She turns, with her hands on her hips, and says : 'Huh?'
Back to close-up of Marcus and Trina. He says : 'Tell us your name.'
Close-up of Maria who says :

Title : 'Name is Maria — Miranda — Macapa.'

Back to close-up of Marcus and Trina. Marcus nudges Trina in a Julius Stern manner and smiles cynically.
Close-up of Maria still thinking, with wide open eyes. She has an after-thought and says :

Title : 'Had a flying squirrel an' let him go.']

Medium close-up of Marcus and Trina.
Medium shot of Maria still making Mac's bed. Suddenly she drops the bedclothes and approaches the couple.
Medium shot of Marcus and Trina still seated against the wall as Maria appears in front of them. She takes a bunch of blue tickets furtively from her pocket, steps over to them, and holds out the tickets towards Trina.
Close-up of Trina looking up at her.
Close-up of Maria as she says :

Title : 'Buy a ticket in the lottery?'

106

Shot from her angle of Trina looking at her.
[Back to the scene as Maria speaks :

Title : ' Just a dollar.']

Close-up of Marcus as he looks quickly down.
Close-up of his hand going into his pocket; it withdraws from it, holding
three dimes. Then it disappears once again into his pocket.
Back to close-up of Marcus.
Close-up of Trina.
Close-up of Maria watching Marcus.
Close-up of Marcus speaking :

Title : ' Go along with you. Lotteries is against the law.'

Back to close-up of Marcus.
Medium close-up of Maria as she looks from Marcus to Trina, then
thrusts her bundle of tickets towards Trina and says :

Title : ' [Buy a ticket — try your luck.] The butcher on the next
block won twenty dollars the last drawing.'

Close-up of Trina looking at her.
Close-up of Marcus with his little finger in his ear. He picks his nose.
Close-up of Trina looking a bit uneasy.
Close-up of Marcus watching her.
Close-up of Trina as she takes a dollar out of her bag and holds it out.
Medium shot of Maria, Marcus and Trina. Maria takes the dollar and
holds out the tickets to Trina. Trina picks one from the bunch. Maria
thanks her and goes off towards the bed-lounge.
Close-up of Trina looking at the ticket.
Back to medium shot of the scene as Maria goes back to the bed, and
Trina shows the ticket to Marcus. Marcus takes the ticket and makes
light of it, saying : ' You might just as well throw it away now,' and
hands it back to her. Trina puts it into her little bag.
Medium close-up of Maria resuming work.
Back to medium shot of Trina and Marcus.
Medium shot of McTeague and Miss Baker. Miss Baker gets out of the
dental chair, makes another appointment and says : ' Goodbye.'
Medium shot of Marcus and Trina as they watch Miss Baker and
McTeague. Miss Baker passes them on her way out.
[Medium shot. Miss Baker appears and goes out through the door.]
Medium shot of McTeague. Marcus brings Trina forward and intro-
duces the two. They shake hands dumbly.

TITLE : ' Mac old pal, I wantcha to shake hands with my cousin, Trina Sieppe. She's my sweetie ! ' [1]

Close-up of Marcus as he finishes speaking.
Close-up of Trina from McTeague's angle. She sizes him up, quite unembarrassed.
Close-up of McTeague acting very embarrassed and nodding his head.
Close-up of McTeague's huge hand shaking Trina's little one.
Close-up of McTeague.
Close-up of Trina.
Close-up of Marcus as he slaps McTeague cordially on the shoulder and says :

TITLE : ' Don't you hurt her too much Mac.'

Back to close-up of Marcus.
Close-up of McTeague nodding.
Close-up of Trina.
Back to close-up of McTeague.
Close-up of Marcus speaking :

TITLE : ' So long, Mac, I got to do some work yet . . . at the dog hospital.'[1]

Back to medium shot of the scene, including all three. Mac and Trina both say : ' Goodbye,' to Marcus, who starts to walk off. [Mac invites Trina over to the dental chair. They both start to walk towards the chair.]
Medium shot of the door as Marcus appears in frame and turns to make a parting remark :

TITLE : ' Don't do anything I wouldn't do . . . you know.' [1]

Back to medium shot as Marcus opens the door and goes out.
Medium close-up of Trina and McTeague as she sits down in the dental chair.
Close-up from reverse angle. She explains with gestures what happened to her [and shows him an ugly hole in her teeth]. He puts a bib on her, then turns and takes a mirror ready to examine her teeth. He sees the hat on her head and asks her to take it off. She takes it off and puts it on her lap. He bends forward to examine further.
Close-up of McTeague examining her teeth.

---

[1] This title does not appear in Stroheim's original script.

Close-up from his angle of Trina's face with Mac's hands working.
Back to close-up of McTeague.
Medium close-up of both. He wipes the mirror on his coat sleeve. Trina looks up and says : ' Well, Doctor, it's dreadful, isn't it? What can you do about it? '
Close-up of McTeague looking vaguely about as he says :

TITLE : ' [The roots of the broken tooth are still in the gum; they'll have to come out.] I guess I'll have to pull them three teeth and make you a bridge.' [1]

Close-up of Trina looking terribly upset, saying :

TITLE : ' Oh, no. That will cost too much, won't it? '

[Close-up of McTeague looking at her uncomfortably. He says : ' Let me look again,' and starts to move off in her direction.
Medium shot as he comes closer to Trina, looks into her mouth again, then straightens up.
Close-up of McTeague as he says :

TITLE : ' I guess that'll have to come out, too.'

Medium shot of both. Trina sits holding her hat in her lap. McTeague leans against the window, his hands in his pockets. Trina absolutely refuses. She says : ' One hole is bad enough.' McTeague reasons with her, tries to explain, but Trina is blindly persistent.]
Close-up of McTeague as he looks at Trina a bit amused, a bit surprised, a bit annoyed.
Shot from his angle of Trina's face, with its tear-dimmed eyes. She points to the hole and indicates that she is not going to have the other one pulled as well.
Close-up of McTeague, looking terribly embarrassed and annoyed. This has never happened to him before. He becomes a little more interested and says : ' Let's look at that again.'
Close-up of Trina's face. She looks very pale and helpless.
Close-up of McTeague. He adjusts his eye-shade and looks again in the mirror.
Extreme close-up of their two faces.
Medium close-up of McTeague and Trina. He studies the case as he has never studied before. He figures out step by step what he could

---

[1] In Stroheim's original script, McTeague says : ' I guess I'll have to pull that other bicuspid,' and the title for Trina's reply does not appear. Trina is merely seen to reply : ' Oh no ! '

possibly do. His expression shows how hard he is at work. Finally he makes up his mind to do it. Fade out.

Title : ' For the first time in his life Mac felt an inkling of ambition to please a woman.' [1]

Fade in on a close-up of Trina and McTeague as he begins to talk.
Medium shot of the two of them. He explains to her with gestures what he intends to do.
Close-up of Trina listening to him intently.
Medium shot of the scene as he assures her that he will do his best not to hurt her. Fade out. [He takes the bayonet forceps and extracts the loose tooth. (This will be taken more or less from back so that we do not have to watch the disagreeable operation.) She shows considerable pain, but just then he holds up the tooth in the forceps. Fade out.]
[Close-up of McTeague as he asks whether it hurt.
Close-up of Trina. She nods.
Close-up of McTeague who is terribly upset that he has hurt her. He fills a glass, and she starts rinsing her mouth.
Medium close-up of McTeague as he takes the tooth out of the forceps and puts it aside on the moveable rack, then turns.
Medium shot of both. As she puts back the water glass, McTeague looks at his calendar, and they set her next appointment. Trina rises and puts on her hat. She says : ' Goodbye,' to him, stretching out her little hand, which he takes, very much embarrassed. She goes off.
Medium shot of the door. She goes out and the door closes behind her.
Medium shot of McTeague still standing between the platform and the door. He unconsciously brings his hand up again as he did when he shook her hand; his big enormous fin closes as it did over her little hand; slowly and unconsciously his hand relaxes and falls to his side. He goes off towards the platform.
Medium shot of McTeague on the platform between the chair and the moveable rack. He stands there and acts helpless, then seems to be trying to find out what has come over him. He looks down at the floor.
Shot from his angle of a hairpin lying there.
Back to medium shot as he bends down and picks it up. He stands there with the hairpin in his hand, realizing that it is hers. Then he seems to realize that it is only a hairpin and has nothing to do with her; it's just a lifeless object. He turns impulsively and throws the hairpin into the waste basket, then turns back towards the moveable rack to straighten out his instruments, and sees Trina's tooth. He picks it up

---

[1] This title does not appear in Stroheim's original script.

110

with the same helpless expression. Then he suddenly gets an idea; he bends down, takes a piece of newspaper which is sticking out of the waste basket and tears it off. He wraps the tooth carefully in the paper and looks around to make sure that no one saw him do something so foolish. He puts the tooth into his waistcoat pocket, then, under the influence of some unseen force, he sits down in the operating chair.

Medium shot of McTeague seated in the operating chair with the head-piece and two arm-braces visible. He fingers the part of the right arm-brace on which Trina's hand has rested, then he turns slightly and looks at the head-rest where her head has rested. He closes his eyes and grits his teeth; with a jerk, he puts his head into the head-rest, gripping both arm-braces with his hands where her hands have lain.

Close-up of his face. He opens his eyes and stares into space. Iris out.

Iris in on the hallway with Old Grannis's and Miss Baker's doors in shot. Both doors are ajar. Maria appears from the right with a very dirty half-filled pillow-slip over one arm; she stops at Old Grannis's door and opens it.

Shot from her angle of Old Grannis sitting near the wall, threading pamphlets with an upholsterer's needle. He looks up.

Shot of Maria from his angle. She speaks :

TITLE : ' Got any junk, Mr. Grannis? '

Shot from her angle of Grannis shaking his head as he says :

TITLE : ' No, nothing, nothing that I can think of, Maria.'

Shot from his angle of Maria as she speaks :

TITLE : ' What you allus sewing up them books for, Mr. Grannis? — They ain't no good to you.'

Shot from her angle of Old Grannis as he rubs his chin timidly and says :

TITLE : ' Well, well, a little habit, you know. I don't smoke; it takes the place of a pipe, perhaps.'

Shot from his angle of Maria as she looks into the closet. She turns towards Grannis, holding an old yellow pitcher with a broken handle. She holds it up, points to the broken handle, and asks him whether she can have it.

Shot from her angle of Old Grannis as he says : ' Oh, Maria, I don't know. I'm afraid — you see — that pitcher — '

111

Shot from his angle of Maria as she says : 'Ah, go 'long — what's the good of it. Ah, go 'long.' She starts walking towards the door and says : 'That's all right, you don't need it.' She walks out.

Medium shot of the hallway with both doors visible. Maria comes out of Grannis's room, closing the door behind her.

Close-up of Old Grannis looking in the direction of the door; he calls out.

Medium shot of both the doors from outside. Maria hears him, opens the door again and looks in.

Close-up of Old Grannis; he says : 'Don't quite shut it; it's a bit close in here at times.'

Close-up of Maria from his angle, as she grins and swings the door wide open.

Medium shot of both the doors in the hallway as Maria comes out again.

Close-up of Old Grannis, who is terribly embarrassed and annoyed.

Medium shot from Miss Baker's room towards the door, which is ajar. It opens to reveal Maria, who calls out :

Title : 'Got any junk?'

Shot from her angle of Miss Baker, sitting in a rocking chair close to the wall, her hands lying idly in her lap. She says : 'You're always after junk — you know I haven't got anything like that.'

Shot from her angle of Maria, who comes further into the room and says, with a gesture : 'Ah, you always say that.' She holds up the pitcher to show it to Miss Baker and says loudly, pointing to the pitcher : 'Look here what Mr. Grannis give me.'

Close-up of Grannis as he hears Maria's voice — he is also terribly confused.

Medium shot of Miss Baker's door from outside. Maria steps back into the doorway, leans out a little and calls out :

Title : 'Ain't that right, Mr. Grannis? Didn't you give me this here pitcher?'

Close-up of Old Grannis. He hears but pretends not to. He half-rises from his chair, not knowing what to do.

Close-up of Miss Baker, terribly upset.

Medium shot of Maria as she goes from the door to Miss Baker's clothes closet and laughingly looks through her things. She finds a pair of shoes and, holding them up, she says : 'What's the matter with these old shoes?'

Close-up of the shoes in her hand, which are by no means old.

112

Close-up of Miss Baker, who is absolutely beside herself and doesn't know what to do. Finally she says : 'Yes, yes, anything — you can have them, but go, go — there's nothing else, not a thing.'

Medium shot from her angle of Maria, who walks towards the door with the shoes in her hand.

Medium shot from the hallway; both doors are open, so that we can see Old Grannis as well as Miss Baker sitting in their respective places. Maria, who has left the pillow-slip in the hall, exits from Miss Baker's room, shoes in hand. She picks up the pillow-case and stores away the old pitcher. As she is about to put the shoes away, Maria says with a sarcastic smile : 'These here are first-rate shoes, Miss Baker. Look here, Mister Grannis, get onto these shoes Miss Baker gi'me.' She walks over to Old Grannis's door, holds the shoes up so that he can see them, and asks him whether he hasn't got something like that to give her. He is seen shaking his head.

Close-up of Maria smiling sarcastically as she says loudly :

TITLE : 'You two people have less junk than anybody.'

Close-up of Grannis looking terribly embarrassed.
Close-up of Miss Baker, also terribly embarrassed.
Close-up of Maria, who smiles and says :

TITLE : 'You two are just alike, you and Mr. Grannis.'

Back to the scene as she turns towards Miss Baker's room and says :

TITLE : 'Ain't you, Miss Baker?'

Medium shot from the hallway including both doors. Both old people are paralysed at having been practically brought face to face with each other through that stupid woman. Maria leaves with the pillow-case.

Medium shot of Old Grannis as he rises, goes to the door and closes it a little. He walks back to his table, listens and then resumes his book-binding.

Medium shot of Miss Baker's room as she rises and lights her alcohol stove.

Medium close-up of Old Grannis. He pricks his finger with the needle.

Medium close-up of Miss Baker, who drops the saucer of her tea service. She picks up the broken pieces and listens towards the wall. Iris out.

Iris in on McTeague sitting on his bed-lounge. It is night. He is wearing a terrible pair of flowered, flannel pyjamas. In his hands he is holding a dingy mirror, and perhaps for the first time in his life he is looking at

113

himself closely from all sides, full face, profile, etc. He lays the mirror down, thinks, and then his eyes fall on his enormous hands. He raises one and looks at it.

Close-up from his angle of his hand, which turns, then starts to move out of shot.

Back to the scene. He drops his hand and thinks. Then, as if in a trance, he reaches over to the chair where his waistcoat is hanging and extracts a bit of newspaper. He holds it in his hand and then unwraps it very carefully. It contains Trina's little white tooth. He holds it between his two fingers, shaking his head over it for a minute; then he nods, sighing deeply. Iris out.]

Fade in.

TITLE : 'During the next two weeks Trina was a daily patient[1] [and passed nearly two and even three hours in McTeague's chair].'

Fade out.

[Fade in to medium shot of McTeague's office. Trina is seated in the dental chair. McTeague is polishing the two false teeth with the buffer on the dental engine. He stops the engine, takes the mirror, looks at the teeth once more, and then says that the job is finished.

Close-up of Trina, who is very happy. She asks him whether he has a mirror.

Close-up of McTeague from her angle. He has now lost all his embarrassment and awkwardness.

Medium shot of both. Mac walks off towards his bed.

Close-up of Trina. She fingers her new teeth, then turns in Mac's direction, looking across at him.

Medium shot of the bed. McTeague appears, takes the dingy mirror which he uses for shaving from the wall and goes off again in the direction from which he came.

Medium shot of Trina. Mac appears and hands her the mirror. She looks at herself, looks at her teeth, then hands the mirror back to him and asks him to examine the rest of her teeth. He takes the dental mirror.

Close-up of Trina's face lying back with her mouth open. McTeague's hands are seen as, holding the mirror, he touches different teeth here and there.

Close-up of McTeague as he concentrates his attention on a certain

---

[1] Stroheim's script has: 'For a fortnight Trina had come nearly every other day,' etc.

114

tooth.]

Medium shot of both. [Pointing to the tooth, he explains to her that there is a cavity which must be enlarged with the drill in order to be filled. She asks him whether it will hurt and he says : ' No.' She says : ' All right.'] He takes the drill and starts to use it.

Close-up of Trina with the drill working; she shows great pain.

Close-up of McTeague, who stops at once and asks her about it.

[Shot of her from his angle. She nods to say that she is in great pain.]

Medium shot of both. Mac feels helpless. He scratches his head; he doesn't know exactly what to do. [He sprays the tooth with glycerite of tannin and then tries to drill again. Trina shows considerable pain. He stops and tells her that the only thing he can do is to give her ether. She asks, with pantomime towards a bottle containing nitrous oxide, whether he can't give her laughing-gas. He looks at the bottle, then back at her, shakes his head and says : ' No, I don't like it.'] He points to the ether bottle and, raising it, says : ' This is much better.'

Title : ' Ether . . . not so dangerous as gas.' [1]

Close-up of Trina agreeing to the ether.

Medium shot as McTeague prepares the ether mask.

Back to close-up of Trina.

Medium shot of McTeague approaching and putting the mask over her face. Fade out.

Title : ' So Mac administered the ether.'[1]

Medium shot of both. McTeague looks terribly nervous as he watches Trina.

Close-up of Trina from his angle as she succumbs slowly to the anaesthetic.

Medium shot of both as McTeague removes the ether mask.

Back to close-up of Trina's face, unconscious and very pretty.

Close-up of McTeague; his eyes are fixed on Trina. He moves his eye-shade back onto the top of his head.

Medium shot of both. Mac bends towards her. [Iris down on her face; camera pans along her body and stops at waist height for a second.

Close-up of McTeague looking at her and breathing hard.

Back to shot from his angle, in iris; camera continues to pan until it comes to her feet with her trim ankles.]

Close-up of McTeague breathing hard.

Medium shot of the two of them as Mac turns, looks about the room

---

[1] This title does not appear in Stroheim's original script.

and then turns back to Trina.

Back to close-up of McTeague's face.

Shot from his angle of Trina, who is unconscious and breathing regularly. She becomes hazy and goes out of focus.

Close-up of McTeague looking at her. There seems to be something the matter with him. His hand goes to his eyes and then his head. He does not understand. His face approaches hers. [Both his arms extend towards Trina.

Medium shot of both as he continues to approach Trina.]

Close-up of Trina's face.

Big close-up of McTeague's face. His eyes are bulging, his nostrils dilated, and his lower lip protrudes, as he leans forward looking at Trina with incomparable lust and desire.

Medium shot of both. McTeague leans forward, extending his arms slowly towards Trina. He hesitates for a moment, then moves forward again, with more lust and desire than before. He comes closer and closer but then stops, as if held back by some invisible force. His arms are still extended, his eyes glued to her face, his hands clenched when, with superhuman strength, he finally draws himself away.

[Close-up of Trina, still unconscious, breathing regularly.]

Close-up of McTeague clenching his fists as he mutters : ' No, by God ! — No, by God ! ' [1]

Shot from his angle of Trina, looking sweet and adorable, lying there unconscious.

Medium shot of McTeague calming down as he stands beside Trina.

Close-up of Trina's face.

Medium shot of both. He quickly forces himself to take the drill and starts to work. He has to bend down close and is still very disturbed.

TITLE : ' But below the fine fabric, bred of his mother, ran the foul stream of hereditary evil . . . the taint of generations given through his father.'

Close-up of their two faces. He seems to smell her hair and the sweet innocent perfume of her body; his nostrils dilate, his eyes grow big again, his lower lip is just a little protruding, his eyelids waver a second, and suddenly he leans over and kisses her, grossly, full on the mouth.

Close-up of the bird hopping about in its cage.

Medium close-up of the conclusion of the kiss. Mac reacts immediately by throwing himself once more into his work with desperate energy.

---

[1] These words are indicated as a title in Stroheim's script but do not appear as such in the film.

Fade out.

TITLE : 'Terrified of his weakness, McTeague threw himself once more into his work with desperate energy . . . until he finished.'[1]

[Fade in to the scene, with Trina and McTeague in shot. Trina slowly comes to herself with a long sigh, a little confused; she lies quiet in the chair.

Close-up of Trina. She looks round and up at Mac.

Close-up of Mac. He looks at her, but he is embarrassed and looks away.

Close-up of Trina. She speaks :

TITLE : ' I never felt a thing.'

Back to the scene as she smiles at him very prettily.

---

[1] Neither this title, nor the previous one, appears in Stroheim's original script, which instead has a different version of the first title at this point :
' But below the fine fabric of all that was good in him ran the foul stream of hereditary evil, like a sewer — Why should it be? He did not desire it. Was he to blame? '

Close-up of McTeague. He suddenly turns and says, with unreasoned simplicity :

TITLE : ' Listen here, Miss Trina, I like you better than any one else; what's the matter with us getting married? '

Close-up of Trina. She sits up quickly and draws back from him, frightened and bewildered.
Close-up of McTeague, as he says : ' Will you? Will you? Say, Miss Trina, will you? '
Close-up of Trina from his angle. Looking confused, she says :

TITLE : ' What do you mean? '

Close-up of McTeague as he repeats : ' Will you? '
Close-up of Trina from his angle. She shakes her head violently : ' No! No! '
Medium shot of both. Mac takes hold of one of her hands and repeats : ' Will you? Will you? '
Big close-up of Trina's face as she looks at Mac's hand, frightened to death; she looks up at his height, his face; shaking her head violently, she cries : ' No! No! '
Back to the scene. Trina holds out her hands, and shrinks away from him into the operating chair. McTeague draws closer and closer to her and repeats : ' Will you? ' She repeats : ' No! No! ' Terrified, she suddenly puts one hand to her stomach and the other to her forehead and says : ' Oh, I'm sick.'
Medium shot from behind, so that only their backs can be seen. She quickly moves towards the spittoon and leans over it, while McTeague quickly steps round from behind her, and holds her head with one hand.
Close-up of McTeague as he says :

TITLE : ' That's the ether.'

Medium shot of both, still from behind. He gives her a napkin, walks quickly to the medicine closet and takes out a graduated glass and bottle.
Close-up of the bottle, which contains bromide of potassium. He pours some into the glass.
Back to the scene. He puts the bottle back, hands her the glass, and says : ' Here, swallow this.' She takes it, drinks it and then rises slowly, drawing away from him a bit.
Iris down on Trina's face, hold for a second as she looks in dreadful fear up at McTeague.

Close-up of the door bell ringing.]

Medium close-up of McTeague and Trina from behind. [They look towards the door.]

Medium shot of the door. Marcus enters with a hop and a skip, closing the door behind him with his foot, and says : 'Hello Mac, hello Trina.' He blows Trina a kiss.

Medium close-up of Mac and Trina from Marcus's angle, looking towards him. They look very embarrassed and neither of them greets him back.

Medium shot of Marcus approaching.

Medium shot of Mac and Trina as Marcus joins them.

Close-up of Marcus as he makes a clownish imitation of Napoleon with his coat closed and his hat sideways, laughing.

Close-up of Trina not reacting.

Close-up of McTeague who also fails to react.

Close-up of Marcus still clowning.

Close-up of Trina smiling weakly.

Close-up of Marcus.

Close-up of Trina.

Close-up of Marcus looking from one to the other, puzzled.

Medium shot of Mac and Trina. Trina is the first one to say anything. She tells Marcus, with gestures, that she has just finished, showing him the two teeth which have been repaired. Marcus approaches.

Close-up of Marcus peering into her mouth to look at her teeth. Then he speaks laughingly :

TITLE : ' [Didun't I tell you — didun't I tell you. Mac's all right.] Oh, Mac's all right . . . by damn.'

Medium close-up of Marcus. He reaches over and playfully punches Mac.

[Close-up of Trina as she smiles, feeling compelled to do so.

Close-up of Mac, busying himself with his instruments. He looks up.]

Medium shot of all three. Marcus says : 'Well, are you ready? ' Trina looks at Mac as if she would ask : ' Is that all right? ' Very embarrassed, Mac nods slightly. [Trina asks him when she is supposed to come again. Mac looks at his calendar and tells her. He writes it down while Trina puts her hat on and takes her basket from a chair near by. We recognize it as the basket in which she had carried the wooden figures to her uncle's store a couple of weeks ago. The day on the calendar is Saturday, and we realize that she must have been at the toy store before visiting McTeague.

Close-up of Marcus as he says : ' I'm taking Trina home now and I'll stay there for dinner. See you later, Mac.']

119

Medium long shot of all three. Fade out.

Title : ' Trina was to come no more.' [1]

Fade in to the scene. McTeague looks up and nods stupidly as Marcus and Trina walk over towards the door.
Shot of their backs from Mac's angle.
Medium shot. Marcus opens the door for Trina, who goes out. Marcus turns and says : ' So long, Mac,' then goes out also.
Shot from his angle as McTeague nods and says : ' So long.'
[Medium shot of McTeague on the platform; he stands there, still looking after Marcus and Trina. Then he slowly turns; his eyes fall on the sponge and ether bottle.
Shot from his angle of the sponge and ether bottle.
Close-up of McTeague. It reminds him. Again he looks in the direction in which they went out. Then he gets an idea; he runs quickly to the bay window and looks out.]

Title : ' His dream was gone.' [1]

Medium close-up of McTeague, from the back, standing at the window.
Shot from his angle of Marcus and Trina waiting for a street-car across the street.
High angle shot including McTeague in the foreground and the street outside.
Shot from his angle of Marcus and Trina as a street-car comes down Hayes Street and stops at Laguna. [One woman and one man get off while] Marcus helps Trina onto the rear platform.
[Close-up of McTeague from outside the window, looking down, motionless. He grits his teeth so hard that his jaw bones stick out.]
Back to shot of Mac in the foreground as the street-car goes off to the left, seen through the window in the background.
Long shot through the window on the left as the street-car travels along Hayes Street into the distance. Fade out.
[Shot from his angle of the street-car starting to move. Marcus takes Trina's arm and whispers something in her ear laughingly; camera pans and follows as the street-car goes down Hayes Street until it disappears.
Close-up of McTeague, looking after it, gritting his teeth, and clenching his fists. Iris out on his face.

Iris in on the Car Conductor's Coffee Joint at about 5:30. McTeague

---

[1] This title does not appear in Stroheim's original script.

enters.

Medium shot of the interior. McTeague comes in and sits down at a table where a couple of conductors, a policeman, and a couple of messenger boys are already sitting. The hasher appears, takes away some dirty dishes from Mac's place, shoves them to the other end of the table and wipes the top. She scratches her scalp with a pencil as she hands him the bill of fare.

Close-up of the hasher, who says :

TITLE : ' Nice big T-bone? '

Close-up of Mac. He looks up at her and thinks for a second in a dazed way, as if not realizing right away what she wants. He makes a motion with his mouth as if to taste the steak, then shakes his head.

Medium shot of both. The waitress makes a few more suggestions. Each time Mac shakes his head. Finally he lays the bill of fare down and says :

TITLE : ' Gi' me a cup of coffee.'

Close-up of the waitress. She can't believe that she has heard right; she looks at him with her eyes bulging and says : ' Cup of coffee? Will that be all? '

Close-up of Mac. He nods, and looks up at her.

TITLE : ' That'll be all.'

Medium shot of both. The hasher looks at him and says :

TITLE : ' You ain't sick, Doc, are you? '

Back to the scene. Mac looks up at her, thinks for a second, then shakes his head. The hasher walks out towards the back to get the coffee, while Mac looks through the glass door in the direction of Hayes Street.

Shot from his angle through the glass door onto Hayes Street.

Lap dissolve to a long shot of the ferry boat halfway across the bay going towards Oakland.

Lap dissolve to Marcus and Trina on deck, sea gulls flying around them. Trina looks unhappily into the water.

Shot from her angle of the waves flashing.

Back to the scene. Marcus is busily engaged in tying two strings crosswise. At the end of each string he has tied small chunks of bread. He looks around, then throws the crossed strings into the water.

Shot from their angle of the water with the string falling into it. The

121

sea gulls snap for it; four of them grab the chunks of bread but cannot swallow them down and have a terrific fight in the water.

Lap dissolve back to a close-up of McTeague's face. He is still looking in the same direction as before. Iris out.

Iris in on a clock showing two o'clock in the morning. Moonlight shines on it.

Lap dissolve in to McTeague's face, lit by the moonlight which falls through the bay window upon his bed-lounge. His eyes are trying to penetrate the darkness. He rubs his forehead with the palms of his hands, then throws the blankets away and sits up, thinking. He takes the bit of newspaper out of the pocket of his waistcoat which is hanging on the chair. He opens the package and holds Trina's tooth between his fingers, nods his head, then rises and walks up and down, stumbling over a stone pug-dog. Fade out on him as he walks.

Iris in on medium shot of the front of the Car Conductor's Coffee Joint. McTeague comes out with a toothpick in his mouth. He stops to watch a party of picnickers who pass by with knapsacks, wearing khaki suits and carrying flowers. Mac looks after them, then he starts for Joe Frenna's saloon; he turns suddenly to the right as he hears someone call.

Shot from his angle of Marcus with four dogs; one of them is 'Alexander', the dog he had on his arm before.[1] He waves to McTeague to come over.

Shot from his angle. McTeague starts to walk across to him.

Medium shot of Marcus in front of the house. Mac appears.

Medium close-up of both. Marcus asks Mac what he intends to do this afternoon. Mac says: 'Nothing,' and shrugs his shoulders. Marcus says:

TITLE: 'I got to take these dogs out for exercise, lets you and I take a walk — Huh?'

Back to the scene. Mac is not very crazy about it and hesitates. Marcus says:

TITLE: 'We'll walk out to the Cliff House — by damn. It'll be out o' sight.'

Back to the scene as Mac finally agrees; Marcus slaps Mac on the back. They walk towards Hayes Street. Iris out.]

---

[1] This would seem to be a reference to the very first occasion on which we saw Marcus, when McTeague first came to rent the room.

TITLE: 'The following Sunday Marcus took McTeague to the Cliff House.' [1]

[Iris in on Seal Rocks, enlarging to show the Cliff House. Marcus and Mac appear from the right.]
Long shot of the boardwalk with the sea in the background.
Medium long shot of the stairway leading down; Mac and Marcus descend; people are coming and going. A large sign overhead reads: 'Seal Rock. Tea Gardens and Grill, etc.'
[Shot from below looking up the stairway as Marcus and Mac descend. There is a nice breeze blowing. The women hold their hats and skirts; two girls and their boys walk past them. The wind blows strongly and the girls laugh while trying to hold their skirts down. Marcus nudges McTeague, but Mac does not notice anything. He is thinking, looking dully ahead of him. Marcus flirts with the girls.

Medium shot of the restaurant door. Marcus suggests a drink; Mac agrees; they go in.

---

[1] This title does not appear in Stroheim's original script.

Medium shot from inside towards the door as they enter.
Medium shot from behind them. They walk to the lower end where the bar and billiard table are.
Medium shot from the window towards the bar. They appear from the left and order a bottle of beer. There are two men playing at billiards. Marcus suggests that they sit down; Mac dully agrees, and they start towards a table in the foreground.
Medium shot from the bar. They come into view and sit down.
Long shot of the breakers.
Medium close-up of them.
Quick dissolve to medium close-up of seals barking.
Quick dissolve to medium close-up of the bartender putting a brass coin into the player piano.]
Medium shot of Marcus and McTeague seated at the table. Marcus says: 'Here's how.' They drink. Marcus says: 'It's good, for a fact.'
Medium close-up of the player piano in action.
Back to the scene. Mac nods slightly, looks glum and drops his hat.
Close-up of Marcus. He looks searchingly at McTeague.
Close-up of McTeague from his angle; he looks stupidly at the floor.
Close-up of Marcus as he says:

TITLE: 'What's the matter with you these days, Mac? Huh. [You got a bean about somethun, hey? Spit ut out.] '

Medium close-up of both. Marcus leans forward on the table; Mac shakes his head and says: 'No, no,' then looks at the floor. [The billiard players go out behind them.
Close-up of Marcus as he says:

TITLE: 'Ah, rats! — Huh — guess you're in love.'

Close-up of McTeague gasping. His feet shuffle.
Close-up of Marcus as he says:

TITLE: 'Maybe I can help you. We're pals, you know. What's the row?'

Close-up of McTeague, terribly agitated.
Close-up of Marcus as he speaks:

TITLE: 'I'll do all I can to help you.']

Medium shot of them both. McTeague can't hold it any longer. He looks at Marcus, then down to the floor, and says:

TITLE: 'It's — it's Miss Sieppe.'

Close-up of Marcus, who looks surprised [then with a gesture says : 'Trina, my cousin? How do you mean?' Mac shrugs his shoulders in pantomime : 'I don't know']. Marcus says :

Title : 'You mean [— that you are —] that you, too.'

Close-up of Mac looking despondent.
Close-up of Marcus reacting to Mac's words.
Close-up of McTeague looking at the walls, then at the floor. He finally breaks out and says :

Title : 'She's been the first girl I've ever known.' [1]

Close-up of Mac. He continues :

Title : 'I couldn't help myself. [It wasn't my fault.]'

Close-up of Marcus. He is dumbfounded, and drops back into the chair.
Close-up of McTeague who speaks again :

Title : 'I was so close to her . . .'
[Title : 'It came on so slow that I was that — that it was done before I knew it, before I could help myself.'

Close-up of Marcus, listening interestedly.]
Close-up of Mac as he continues :

Title : '. . . An' smelled her hair . . .'
[Title : 'I know we're pals, us two, and I knew how — how you and Miss Sieppe, were, I know now, I knew then.'.

Close-up of Marcus, looking at him.]
Close-up of McTeague, his hand to his head as he continues :

Title : '. . . An' felt her breath . . .'
[Title : 'But that wouldn't have made any difference. Before I knew it — it — it — there it was.']

Back to close-up of McTeague with his hand to his mouth. He says : 'I can't help it.'
Close-up of Marcus listening. He shakes his head slowly.
Close-up of McTeague as he continues :

---

[1] This and the following titles which appear in the film do not appear at this point in Stroheim's original script; they are in fact an expanded version of a piece of dialogue which occurs a little later in this scene.

Title : ' [. . . she was the first girl I had ever known — and you don't know ! Why, I was so close to her and smelt her hair and her breath.] Oh, you don't know.'

Close-up of McTeague. He is beside himself, and talks as he never talked before.

Title : ' It's everything. It's — it's — Oh, it's everything — I — I — why, Mark, it's everything — everything ! '

Medium shot of both men looking down at the floor. McTeague looks helpless.
Medium close-up of the player piano in action.
Back to medium shot as Marcus rises, walks towards the window and looks out, with his hands in his pockets.
Close-up of Marcus's anguished face.
Medium shot of people passing on the boardwalk outside.
Long shot of waves.
[Quick lap dissolve to a shot of seals barking.]
Back to medium shot of the boardwalk.
Close-up of Marcus's face as he looks sideways towards Mac.
Back to the scene as Marcus turns and comes back, saying :

Title : ' Well, what are we going to do about it? '

Close-up of McTeague as he says :

Title : ' I don't know. [I don't want anything to come between us, Mark !] '

Close-up of Marcus as he says : [' Well, nothun will, you bet — No, Sir, you bet not, Mac.' He thinks again, then strikes the table with his fist and says :

Title : ' Well, Mac, go ahead ! I guess you — you want her pretty bad. I'll pull out, yes by damn,] I'll give her up to you, old man ! '

Back to close-up of Marcus as he finishes speaking.
Close-up of Mac as he looks up at Marcus, terribly agitated.
Close-up of Marcus as he says, with tears in his eyes :

Title : ' By damn [Mac — I'll give her up to you — I won't stand between you.] '

Back to close-up of Marcus, as he finishes talking.
Close-up of Mac.
Medium close-up of both. Marcus, with tears in his eyes, holds out

126

both hands to Mac, who rises and faces Marcus.
Close-up of the two men shaking hands.
Close-up of Marcus as he says :

TITLE : ' — Friends for life — '

Close-up of Marcus speaking.

TITLE : ' — or — death ! '

Close-up of Marcus as he finishes.
Close-up of McTeague. He is almost sobbing himself.
Medium shot of both.
Close-up of McTeague speaking :

TITLE : ' I'm much obliged ! — I'm much obliged [— much obliged],
Mark.'

Back to the scene. Marcus says : ' That's all right, you'll be happy.'
Close-up of the player piano in action.
Back to the scene. Marcus can't go on talking. He shakes hands with
Mac silently [and turns away. Mac says : ' Let's have a drink.' Marcus
does not answer. Mac calls to the bartender.

127

Medium shot from his angle, as the bartender looks up.

Shot from his angle of Mac, who orders another bottle.

Shot from his angle of the bartender, who goes to get it from behind the bar.

Medium shot of Marcus and Mac. Marcus turns as the bartender appears and puts down the bottle, fills the glasses, then goes off. The two take up their glasses and look at each other; then Marcus rises. Mac imitates him; they touch glasses with great ceremony, then drink. Marcus is much elated after the drink; he slaps Mac on the shoulder and says : 'Let's have another one.' Mac says : 'All right.' Marcus calls the bartender and makes a gesture to him for one more. He walks up and down, passing the billiard table. The bartender appears and fills the glasses anew.

Close-up of McTeague as he holds up his glass. He raises it to Marcus.

Close-up of Marcus at the billiard table; he has a billiard ball in his hand. He goes off, absent-mindedly playing with the ball.

Medium shot of both at the table. Marcus takes his glass and drinks, then puts it down and becomes conscious of the billiard ball. He says :

TITLE : 'Look's here Mac — I know something you can't do. I'll bet you two-bits I'll stump you.'

Back to the scene. They both put a quarter on the table. Marcus says : 'Watch,' and takes the billiard ball in a vaudeville artist's fashion. He touches the end of his sleeves like a magician, shows Mac the inside of his hand, saying : 'Nothun here — nothun here.' Mac looks laughingly at him as Marcus puts the ball into his mouth and closes it.

Close-up of Mac. For a second he is baffled, then he bursts out roaring and slaps his thighs and he laughs and laughs.

Back to the scene. Marcus takes the ball out of his mouth, wipes it on the tablecloth and hands it over to Mac, saying : 'Now you do it.'

Close-up of Mac. He becomes serious, parts his moustache[1] and rolls his eyes. He looks at the ball, then at Marcus, then opens his mouth as wide as he can. He puts the ball into his mouth and closes it.

Medium shot of both. Marcus applauds and shouts. Mac reaches for the money and puts it into his vest pocket. He nods his head with a knowing air.

Close-up of Mac as he tries to take the ball out; he cannot.

Close-up of Marcus who watches, smiling a bit.

Back to close-up of McTeague. He paws his cheeks and tries to force his jaws open; he cannot.

---

[1] In Stroheim's original script, as in Norris's novel, McTeague wears a moustache.

Medium shot of both. Mac runs about among the dogs; Marcus yells and swears.

Close-up of Mac, choking terribly.

Back to the scene as the bartender rushes in, followed by a waiter. The lady of the restaurant arrives. Mac keeps trying; Marcus gives him advice; other guests arrive.

Close-up of Mac. Suddenly the ball slips out of his mouth as easily as it went in.

Medium shot of the entire scene. McTeague drops into a chair, mopping his forehead and gasping for breath. Relieved, Marcus comes and claps him on the shoulder, and on the strength of the occasion orders drinks for the crowd. Iris down on McTeague, still out of breath; hold for a second, then iris out completely.

Iris in on the lock of the dog hospital. Hands unlock it and the iris enlarges to reveal Marcus and Mac with the four dogs. Marcus opens the door, and they enter. Marcus puts three of the dogs quickly into cages, gives them each a biscuit, and walks out again. He closes the door and locks it. They go off. Lap dissolve out.

Lap dissolve in to the tiny back yard behind the house. A water barrel serves as a kennel for Marcus's dog. Marcus and Mac enter with the dog and Marcus puts the dog into the kennel and gives him a biscuit. Then he says :

TITLE : ' What are you going to do about this — about that — about — about my cousin now, Mac? '

Close-up of McTeague. He shakes his head helplessly and says : ' I don't know what to do, Marcus.'

Close-up of Marcus. He looks at Mac and says :

TITLE : ' Well, you must make up to her now. Go and call on her.'

Close-up of McTeague, startled. He never thought he would have so much trouble over a girl. He shakes his head in a frightened way.

Close-up of Marcus who says :

TITLE : ' Of course, that's the proper caper.'

Close-up of Mac, who says : ' I don't know.'

Medium shot of both. Marcus speaks :

TITLE : ' I tell you what, we'll go over there Washington's birthday, next Wednesday, sure, they'll be glad to see you.'

Close-up of Mac. He looks at Marcus in deep appreciation and says :

TITLE : ' Say, Mark, you're all right, anyhow.'

Back to the scene as they shake hands and walk out. They close the door.

Close-up of a collie dog seen through a crack in the fence, sniffing and barking.

Close-up of ' Alexander ', Marcus's dog, in the barrel, eating. He hears it and runs out.

Medium close-up at the fence. Both dogs are seen from above; both of them look at each other and bark ferociously.

Medium shot of a window in the hallway, from outside. Marcus and McTeague appear, open the window and look down.

Shot from their angle of the two dogs barking at each other through the crack in the fence.

Back to medium shot of both. Marcus says :

TITLE : ' By damn ! They don't love each other — Wouldn't that make a fight if the two got together? '

Back to the scene as McTeague looks at Marcus for a second, then nods his head and says :

TITLE : ' Sure would ! That's the word ! '

Back to the scene. They close the window. Iris out.

Iris in on a bust of George Washington, draped with American flags against black velvet. Hold it in iris, then iris out.

Iris in on a little dingy mirror in McTeague's office, in which we see McTeague's face covered in lather; he is shaving. Iris opens up to medium close-up, showing the back of his head, and his face reflected in the mirror. He is singing.

(Music lines with notes and accompanying words appear in animated fashion. That is, each note and the respective word for the note or notes appears one after the other as it is being sung — this only for the first two lines.)

WORDS : ' No one to love, none to caress,
        Left all alone in this world's wilderness.'

Cut to close-up of the door bell.

Medium close-up of McTeague. He hears the bell and looks in the direction of the door. Camera comes back on perambulator until there is room enough to show Marcus entering from the left. He has his flowered pyjamas on. He smiles sarcastically and motions to Mac to come with him; he is going to show him something. Mac does not know what he wants and, with lather on one side of his face, the razor in his hand and a napkin round his neck, he follows Marcus out of shot.

Medium shot of the door. They appear from the right and go out into the hallway.

Medium shot of the top of the stairway. They appear from the background and step towards the banister. Marcus points down to the bottom of the stairway. Mac looks down.

Shot from their angle of Maria sitting on the step next to the bottom, her chin propped in her fists. The junk man, Zerkow, is leaning against the door, talking eagerly. With gestures, he pleads with her to tell him just once more :

TITLE : ' There were more than a hundred pieces and every one of them gold — '

Shot from their angle of Marcus and Mac leaning over the banister, looking down and smiling. Marcus speaks :

TITLE : ' Ain't they a pair for you? '

Back to the scene. Mac nods.

Shot from their angle of Zerkow and Maria. Zerkow speaks :

TITLE : ' Where did it all go to? Where did it go? '

Back to the scene. Maria shakes her head solemnly and speaks :

TITLE : ' It's gone, anyhow.'

Back to the scene as Zerkow speaks, gazing into space :

TITLE : ' Ah, gone, gone ! Think of it ! '

Medium shot from their angle of Marcus and McTeague at the top of the stairs. Marcus laughs, then turns to Mac and slaps him on the back as he says : ' Hurry up.' Mac nods and goes off towards the left while Marcus goes off to the right. Iris out.]

TITLE : ' Then, with unselfish friendship for his " pal," Marcus took McTeague to Oakland the next Sunday . . . that he might again be with Trina and meet her folks.' [1]

[Iris in on] long shot from above of the train from the pier approaching.

Medium shot of the Sieppe family at the station.

---

[1] This title does not appear in Stroheim's original script.

Back to long shot from above as the train stops.

Medium long shot of 'B' Street Station. Marcus and Mac get off and the train goes on.

Medium shot of 'der Mama' and 'der Papa' Sieppe. Trina and Owgooste and 'der Tervins' are there also. Owgooste is holding the dog on a rope and each one of the kids as well as Trina and 'der Mama' carries a large basket covered with a newspaper with the ends of bottles sticking out from it. Trina is dressed in a pleated blue cloth skirt with a striped shirt, and around her waist is an alligator belt. 'Der Papa' has khaki puttees laced diagonally on the sides and a pair of khaki pants; the pants are lighter than the puttees in colour. He also wears a stiff, white-bosom shirt, a red necktie with stripes, and suspenders; his waistcoat is open, and a sack coat hangs over his shoulders, fastened with a piece of cord in dolman fashion over his left shoulder. He has five bronze medals on his chest, wears a green velour Tyrolean hat with a white and black cock-feather in the back, and carries a Winchester rifle and a leather bag with fringes. Marcus introduces McTeague to 'der Papa':

TITLE : 'This is Trina's father.'

132

Back to the scene. Mac shakes hands with Mr. Sieppe.

TITLE : ' Sure glad to know ya, Mr. Sieppe.'

Back to scene. Marcus introduces Mrs. Sieppe :

TITLE : ' Mommer.'

Medium shot of Mac shaking hands with Mrs. Sieppe as Marcus introduces the last of the family :

TITLE : ' Doc . . . shake hands with my cousin, Selina.' [1]

Medium shot of Trina and McTeague. Trina holds out her hand and with a very sweet smile looks at McTeague. He shakes her hand gravely. [She speaks :

TITLE : ' It is so nice to see you again.']

Close-up of Trina as she says : ' Look, see how fine my filling is.' She lifts a corner of her lip and shows him the clumsy gold bridge.

---

[1] Neither this nor the previous three titles appear in Stroheim's original script, where Trina's cousin Selina does not appear until later in the scene.

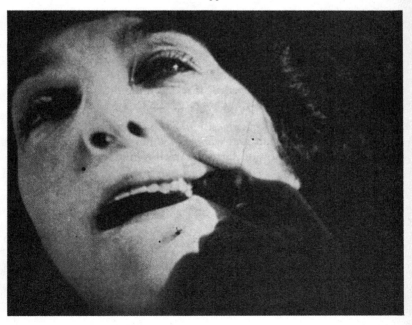

McTeague looks at it and nods gravely.

Medium shot of the group. Camera pans slightly to the right as Owgooste goes to look at a passing train in the background; camera pans back to the left as he is fetched back by 'der Mama'; the rest of them continue talking in the foreground.

Medium long shot of the group. 'Der Papa' gives orders to Owgooste to lead the hound and carry 'der basket No. 3'. (Each basket has a piece of cardboard stuck on the side with a black number on it.) 'Der Papa' calls over 'der Tervins' and they stand at attention. One of them carries a camp stool and the other one basket No. 4. He places Owgooste ahead of 'der Tervins', just behind himself. The rest of them line up on the track behind the kids. Mac and Trina continue talking in the background.

[Medium shot of a girl just arriving; she is slender and unhealthy-looking. She is a cousin of Trina's. She greets everybody. Marcus also presents Dr. McTeague to Selina; McTeague does not say a word; all he does is to nod gravely.

Close-up of Mr. Sieppe. He yells : 'Attention!' with the motion that accompanies this command.]

Back to the scene. Mr. Sieppe assumes the attitude of a lieutenant leading a charge.

Cut to side view of the group as they start down the track, Marcus with Selina towards the rear, followed by McTeague and Trina. 'Der Mama' and 'der Papa' walk together; he leaves her constantly to shout orders up and down the line.

Medium close-up of Trina and McTeague as they walk between the rails along the track; camera tracks back on a hand-car ahead of them. Trina is looking very happy and sweet. [She looks up at McTeague :

TITLE : 'Don't you think picnics are fine fun, Doctor McTeague? You race about in the open air and when lunch time comes, oh, aren't you hungry? And the woods and the grass smell so fine.'

Back to the scene as McTeague looks down at the railroad track, gravely shakes his head and speaks :

TITLE : 'I don't know, Miss Sieppe — I never went on a picnic.'

Back to the scene as Trina looks at him, astonished, and repeats : 'Never went on a picnic? Oh, you will see what fun we'll have.'

Close-up of Mr. Sieppe. He waves his rifle and shouts : 'To one side,' motioning with his arm for them to step off the track.

Medium long shot of a train approaching in the background. They all step off, obeying 'der Papa's' command. Marcus has a splendid idea;

he tells everybody quickly about it and takes a nickle out of his p
and runs over to the rail.
Medium close-up of him as he puts the nickle on the rail.
Back to the scene. He rises and asks whether somebody has got two
pins. Selina, the girl who has been walking with him, says she has. She
takes two pins from the lapel of her coat and he puts them on the
railroad track.
Medium close-up of the two pins crossed on the rail.
Back to the scene as the train passes. Marcus waves his hat, and the
children shout; nobody in the train pays any attention to them. After
the train has passed everyone in the party runs over to the rails to look
at the pins; Marcus picks them up.
Close-up of his hand holding the two pins, which are now stuck together
in a cross.
Back to the scene as Mr. Sieppe takes them. Owgooste vants der pins
and ' der Tervins ' vant them too.
Close-up of Mr. Sieppe holding the pins in his hand. He speaks :

TITLE : ' Attend now. At der end of der day, will it pe adjudged a
reward of merit to him who the best behaves. It is an order. Vorwartz.'

Back to the scene. They all agree. The kids clap their hands and the
party starts off again. Fade out.]
Extreme long shot of the party walking along, seen from a high angle
as an electric train passes. A signboard reads : ' Shell Mound Park —
Shooting Range.'
Medium shot of the entrance to Schutzen Park. The party enters from
the road. ' Der Papa ' waves his rifle to make the party stop.
Medium shot of Marcus as he steps up to Mac and says to him :

TITLE : ' Here's where we shell out — Mac.'

Back to medium shot of both.

TITLE : ' Gimme four bits.'

Close-up of McTeague. Frightened and stiff, he looks down and says :

TITLE : ' I ain't got no money with me . . . only a dime.' [1]

Close-up of his hand extracting a dime from his pants pocket.
[Back to close-up of him as he says in a terrified way : ' I — I — I
only got a quarter.']

---

[1] This title does not appear in Stroheim's original script.

Close-up of Marcus. He looks at Mac for a second, then says : ' Oh, all right,' with accompanying gestures. Then he says :

Title : ' I'll pay for you and you can square with me when we get home.'

Medium long shot of Trina as she joins Mac; Marcus is seen paying at the window in the left background, while Mr. Sieppe is talking to some acquaintances in the far background.
Medium long shot of the group filing into the park while ' der Papa ' counts them off.
[Close-up of ' der Papa '. He yells : ' To der beach,' and accompanies his command with the appropriate motion. Owgooste removes the rope from the dog. The children race ahead, and the others follow.
Lap dissolve to a cosy place under some trees. The party arrives and ' der Papa ' gives a sign with his rifle that this is the place where the camp is going to be pitched. They all put their baskets down and rest for a second.
Medium shot of ' der Papa ' and ' der ' three kids. He gives them orders to take their shoes and stockings off, which they comply with. Then he says :

Title : ' You vill der glams dig.'

Back to the scene. The kids run off with a small coal shovel.
Back to close-up of ' der Papa ' as he says :

Title : ' Mommer make der fire.'

Medium shot of ' der Mama '. Selina and Marcus go about looking for dry wood. Trina and ' der Mama ' start to unpack some of the lunch baskets, making McTeague and Marcus help. They are all laughing and joking.
Close-up of wieners and frankfurter sausages, pretzels, radishes, big pickles, limburger cheese, mustard, chicken and two dozen bottles of beer. Iris down on the limburger cheese; hold for a second, then iris out completely.]

Title : ' What a day that was for McTeague, what a never to be forgotten day — '

[Iris in on McTeague lying on his back; his collar and necktie are open, his coat is off, his waistcoat open and braces down. He is smoking his pipe, and Trina is sitting near him. The collar of her shirtwaister is open, her sleeves are rolled up and her skirt is pinned up with safety pins. She has a handkerchief in her hand and is fighting the flies away as they try to land on McTeague's mush (face). Selina and Marcus are also lying on the ground near by. The place is littered with the remains of the lunch — paper bags, bones, crusts and 'dead soldiers'.

Medium shot of Marcus and Selina; Marcus suggests that they all get up and go to the merry-go-round. Selina is greatly pleased and Marcus calls over to the others.

Medium shot of McTeague and Trina, as they hear him. Trina likes the idea and asks McTeague to come with her. He yawns, stretches, rises, and makes himself presentable.

Long shot of 'der Mama', who stays there to watch the baskets while the others go off with the kids. Fade out.

Fade in on a long shot of the merry-go-round moving.]

Fade in to a medium shot of Trina and Mac on the merry-go-round. Camera is on the platform and revolves with them. The scene is half in darkness, half in sunlight, so that they appear to ride out of the fade. Behind Trina, on two horses riding abreast, are Selina and Marcus. ['Der Tervins' and Owgooste are in a chariot.]

Medium shot of a rifle range : all kinds of Dutchmen, in funny hats, with moustaches, with and without glasses, beer-bellies and mush faces; plenty of tin and brass medals decorate their manly chests. Among them is 'der Papa'.[1]

Medium shot of a white flag marking the target in the distance.

Medium shot of 'der Papa' aiming his rifle and firing.

Back to medium shot of the target.

Medium shot of 'der Papa' looking over for a score.

Shot from his angle of the rifle-stand with a sign coming up saying : 'No hit.'

Medium close-up of 'der Papa', very worked up over this, gesturing wildly to the men standing beside him.

Back to the scene on the merry-go-round. McTeague is happy as never before, rearing, laughing and slapping his thigh. Trina is very gay and is laughing. Marcus is very gay and he hits the horse with his cane as if to make it go a little faster. Fade out.

[Fade in on the front of the Sieppes' house as the party arrives.

Medium shot of 'der Mama' and 'der Papa' urging Marcus and McTeague to stay; they do not accept at once.

Medium shot of Trina as she approaches McTeague and urges him

---

[1] In Stroheim's original script the shooting-range sequence occurs just before Marcus, McTeague and the others go to the merry-go-round.

to stay. McTeague looks at her, very embarrassed, then looks over towards Marcus who appears in shot. The two finally accept; everybody is happy. They enter the house. Fade out.

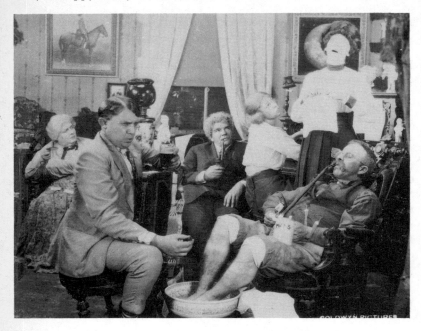

Iris in revealing the Sieppe family with McTeague, Marcus and Selina all sitting in the front parlour. McTeague is sitting on the couch. Selina is playing a small organ. Marcus is sitting on the other end of the couch with McTeague, while Trina stands near the organ. They are all singing. Mr. Sieppe is in the centre of the room, leading the choir.

Close-up of Trina, sweet-faced, as she sings, looking towards McTeague.

Close-up of McTeague, his mouth wide open, eyes closed. He crows.

Close-up of Marcus, as he makes a motion like an opera singer, his left hand on his right breast and his right hand in the air.

Close-up of ' der Mama ', fast asleep.

Close-up of Selina with her eyes raised to heaven, playing with great feeling.

Close-up of the clock on the mantel shelf as it strikes nine o'clock.

Back to the scene as Mr. Sieppe hears it. ' Der Mama ' wakes up and stops the orchestra. They break up at once. Selina takes her hat and coat, says : ' Goodbye,' and leaves. ' Der Mama ' gets a sheet and pillow and a blanket and puts them on the couch in the front parlour, explaining that this is Marcus's bed. They all say: 'Good night,' to each other. Trina lights a candle on the mantel shelf and asks McTeague to follow her. He says: 'Good night,' and they exit through the kitchen and 'der Tervins'' room. 'Der Tervins' and Owgooste are in the room when they pass.

Medium shot of 'der Tervins'' room. Trina, with the lighted candle, points to Owgooste's bed and explains with a gesture that she is going to sleep there with Owgooste tonight. They go out towards the back yard.

Reverse shot from the back yard. Trina and McTeague appear with the lighted candle and walk towards camera.

Shot from behind as they walk towards a little shed which is the 'Villa Trina'. She opens the door and lets him enter, giving him the candle. She stretches out her hand which he shakes and goes off towards camera, while the door of the shed closes.

Medium shot of the inside of Trina's room. Holding the lighted candle, McTeague stands motionless in the middle of the room, looking about. Then he puts the candle down on the bureau and looks down.

Close-up from his angle of a hair brush on the top of the bureau.

Back to the scene as he picks it up and, without knowing why, holds it up to his face, inhaling the odour of Trina's hair; then he puts down the brush.

Long shot of him as he goes softly about the room from one object to another. Finally he stops in front of the closet door.

Medium shot of the closet door, which is ajar. He opens it wide and pauses on the threshold. Inside there are skirts, jackets, stiff white petticoats, etc.

Close-up of McTeague from the angle of the closet as he catches his breath, spellbound.

Back to the scene as he recognizes the black dress that Trina wore when he first met her. He takes the skirt with his left hand and finds the jacket with his right. He closes his eyes, holding the two garments, and seems to recollect. He reaches further into the closet, touching the clothes gingerly and stroking them softly with his huge hands.

Back to close-up of McTeague. His nostrils dilate as he inhales the delicate perfume that comes from the folds.

Back to medium shot of McTeague as, with an unreasoned impulse, he opens his huge arms and gathers the garments close to him, plunging his face deep among them. Iris out.

Fade in.

TITLE : 'What a night that was for McTeague, what a never to be forgotten night.'

Fade out.
Iris in on the upper deck of the ferry boat between Oakland and San Francisco. Marcus and McTeague are in the same suits as they had on at the picnic. There are a lot of commuters on board.
Medium close-up of Marcus and Mac. Marcus looks down into the waves. A deep sigh comes from his manly chest. McTeague looks at Marcus and says : 'What's the matter?' Marcus speaks without looking up from the waves :

TITLE : 'What is my life? What is left for me? Nothing, by damn!'

Back to the scene. McTeague remonstrates with him as much as McTeague can. Marcus looks at him, then says :

TITLE : 'Never mind, old man, never mind me. Go, be happy, I forgive you.'

Back to the scene. McTeague looks harassed with the thought of some injury he had done his friend, and he is terribly sorry. Marcus sighs again and Mac looks at him. Iris out.]

TITLE : 'Weeks passed, and March rains put a stop to their picnics . . . but McTeague saw Trina every Wednesday and Sunday.'[1]

[Iris in on McTeague holding a concertina wrapped up in a news-paper. When the iris is full in, McTeague is seen to be in the front of a moving railcar. 'B' Street Station appears.
Medium long shot of the front of 'B' Street Station. Trina is standing there in an old overcoat, carrying an umbrella. She is apparently looking for someone. The train stops.
Shot from her angle of McTeague stepping out of the car, with the concertina in his hand.]
Medium shot of the station. The train pulls in and the grate slides back. Trina stands waiting, as McTeague descends carrying his con-certina wrapped in newspaper; they greet each other.
Medium close-up of Trina and Mac as the train passes out in the background. Mac is very much surprised to find Trina waiting for him. Trina points off to the right as she says : ['This is the first day it hasn't

---

[1] Stroheim's script has a slightly different title :
'Weeks passed, February went, March came in very rainy, putting a stop to all their picnics and Sunday excursions.'

rained in weeks, I thought it would be nice to walk.' McTeague says : ' Sure — sure.']

TITLE : ' Let's go over and sit on the sewer.' [1]

Medium long shot as they start walking towards camera. She points along the bed of the tracks.
Long shot from behind. They talk animatedly as they walk along the pathway. Fade out.
Iris in on a medium shot of a dead rat and other sewage floating by in the water.
Long shot of them walking up the pathway towards the sewer, approaching camera. A train passes in the background as they stand by the sewer-pipe, talking for a moment. Medium shot as they hop up and seat themselves on it.
Medium shot of them sitting. He takes a newspaper off the concertina and shows it to her. She is very interested. He asks what tune she would like and she replies :

TITLE : ' Hearts and Flowers.' [1]

[1] This title does not appear in Stroheim's original script.

Back to the scene as Mac shakes his head.

TITLE : 'No . . . but : Nearer my God to Thee.' [1]

Medium shot of both, Mac playing as she listens. Iris down on the concertina playing; hold for a second, then iris out completely.

[Iris in. It is much darker. The two are still sitting there, but Mac is not playing any more; he is talking.

TITLE : 'Some day I am going to have a big gilded tooth outside my window for a sign. Those big gold teeth are beautiful — beautiful, only they cost so much I can't afford one just now.'

Back to the scene as Trina holds out her palm and exclaims : 'Oh, it's raining.' He extends his hand also and both of them look up at the sky. It is starting to rain a little.]
Shot of dark clouds in the sky.
Medium long shot. They jump off the sewer. Mac closes his coat over the concertina and Trina opens her umbrella. They start to walk back to the railroad station, coming towards camera. Fade out.
Fade in on medium shot of the station shed as they appear from the left.
Medium shot of the couple seen through the rain. They are silent and embarrassed. McTeague paces about, a bit agitated.
Close-up of Mac as he bends over Trina and says :

TITLE : 'Say, Miss Trina, [what's the good of waiting any longer?] Why can't us two get married? '

Back to the scene as Trina, with an anguished expression on her face, shakes her head and says : 'No.' McTeague replies :

TITLE : 'Why not? Dontcher like me well enough? '

Back to the scene. She nods and says : 'Yes.' He says :

TITLE : 'Then why not? '

Back to the scene. She looks away and says :

TITLE : 'Because.'

[Back to the scene as he speaks :

TITLE : 'Aw — come on.']

Back to the scene. Trina still shakes her head, while McTeague continues to say : 'Aw come on — Aw come on.' Suddenly he takes her

---

[1] This title does not appear in Stroheim's original script.

in his enormous arms, almost crushing her with his immense strength. Trina immediately gives up the struggle and turns her head to his. Close-up of them both. They kiss each other grossly on the mouth. Medium shot of the couple embracing as the Overland train with its flaming headlights (hand-coloured green and red, like the eyes of an evil demon) roars past. Medium close-up of Trina and McTeague. She struggles to free herself. ' Oh please! Please!' she pleads with tear-dimmed eyes. McTeague releases her. Trina draws away from him. [Close-up of Trina. She suddenly puts her face into her hands and begins to sob. Close-up of McTeague. He comes forward a step and says:

TITLE : ' Say — Miss Trina. Listen, listen here, Miss Trina.']

Medium shot of the couple as they come towards the station entrance. McTeague goes to take her in his arms again. Trina gasps and says:

TITLE : ' [I must go home, it's late, Oh! I'm so — so — so —] Let me go alone . . . please.'

Medium shot of the couple. McTeague looks very hurt.

TITLE : ' You may — you may come Sunday.'

Back to the scene as she says: ' Goodbye.' McTeague also. He grabs her hand happily, nodding and talking animatedly:

TITLE : ' Can't I kiss ya again? '

Back to the scene. Trina firmly shakes her head, while she withdraws her body from him and puts some distance between herself and him, as she says: ' No! No! You must not.' She frees herself from his grasp and runs away, opening her umbrella. Close-up of McTeague, stunned and bewildered, gazing stupidly after her as a train roars by behind him. The rain continues to pour down. [Shot from Trina's angle up ' B' Street as she runs through the rain. Medium close-up from a perambulator moving ahead of Trina as she runs. She turns back once in the direction of McTeague.] Medium close-up of McTeague. An enormous smile distends his thick lips and his eyes grow wide and flash as he draws his breath quickly. He strikes his mallet-like fist upon his left palm, exclaiming under his breath:

TITLE : ' I've got her. By God! I've got her. [By God!] '

Back to the scene as he repeats : 'I got her, By God ! I got her. By God ! '

Medium shot of McTeague from behind.

Back to the scene. Mac's self-respect has increased enormously. He hears a train approaching and walks out of shot.

[Medium long shot of the station as the train pulls in.]

Medium long shot from the station as Mac goes to meet the approaching train. He gets in and the train pulls out again.

[Medium shot of the interior of the Sieppes' kitchen. Mrs. Sieppe is busy setting a mouse-trap.

Close-up of the mouse-trap in Mrs. Sieppe's hands as she puts some cheese in it.

Back to the scene as Trina enters from the dining room, crying. She embraces her mother, and puts her head on her chest. Her mother says : 'Ach, what has happened?' Trina tells her. Mrs. Sieppe says : 'So soon?'

TITLE : 'Ach vell, vat you cry for den?'

Close-up of Trina plucking at the end of her handkerchief. Shaking her head, she says : 'I don't know.'

Close-up of 'Mommer' as she speaks :

TITLE : 'You loaf der younge Doktor?'

Medium close-up of both. Trina shakes her head and says : 'I don't know.' 'Mommer' speaks :

TITLE : 'Vell, vhat for you kiss him?'

Back to the scene. Trina shakes her head and says : 'I don't know.'

Close-up of her mother. She looks at Trina and says :

TITLE : 'You don't know! You don't know! Vere haf you sensus gone, Trina? You kissed der Doktor, you cry and you don't know. Is ut Marcus, den?'

Back to the scene. Trina shakes her head and says : 'No, it isn't Marcus.'

Her mother says :

TITLE : 'Den ut must be der Doktor.'

Back to the scene. Trina does not answer and her mother says : 'Eh?' Trina says :

TITLE : 'I — I guess so.'

Back to the scene. Trina shrugs her shoulders and says : ' I don't know.' She puts her right forefinger absent-mindedly into the mouse-trap which is now standing on the sink.

Medium close-up of McTeague with his knees in shot, sitting in the local train going to the pier. He doesn't seem to realize that there are other people sitting around him, and with an enormous smile on his distended lips and wide eyes he strikes his mallet-like fists upon his knees, exclaiming under his breath :

TITLE : ' I got her, by God ! '

Close-up of the mouse-trap with Trina's finger accidentally touching the spring. The mouse-trap closes.

Back to the scene as Trina yells with terrific pain, the mouse-trap hanging on her hand. ' Mommer ' waves 'der ' hands and ' der Papa ' comes in with Owgooste and ' der Tervins '. ' Der Papa ' quickly gets the trap off her finger and Trina holds her sore finger, crying. Iris out.

Iris in on Marcus's door. Mac appears and opens the door.

Medium shot of the bed. Marcus, with drawn-up knees, is reading some ' Zane Gray ' story. He looks in the direction of the door.

Medium shot of them both. Mac walks in, all aflame. Waving his arms, he goes over to Marcus and slaps him on the back and says : ' I got her ! '

Close-up of Marcus as he looks at him and swings his legs down from the bed. He shows his reaction to the news in his face and says :

TITLE : ' You've got her, have you ? '

Back to the scene with both in shot. McTeague says : ' Yes.' Marcus speaks :

TITLE : ' Well, I'm glad of it, old man — for a fact. You'll be happy with her. I would have been. I forgive you, freely by damn ! '

Back to the scene. Marcus gets off the bed and goes over to the dresser. He takes a whisky flask and two water glasses and pours two drinks. McTeague does not like the smell of it and refuses it. Marcus drinks to him and Trina. Iris out.

Iris in on Trina's bedroom (camera on perambulator). Trina is in her nightgown, with her wonderful hair down, brushing and brushing it. She stops, looking into space in a preoccupied way. Camera moves up until Trina is in close-up.

Close-up of her. She stares into space, thinking, imagining McTeague in front of her, looking at her sore finger tied up in a white linen rag. She suddenly but decidedly shakes her head and says : ' No — No.' She almost shivers at the thought. She is very unhappy. Camera slowly moves back and she throws herself on the bed, almost covered by her marvellous hair. Iris out.

Iris in on a medium shot of the Car Conductor's Coffee Joint. Marcus and Mac are seen eating lunch along with conductors, etc. Marcus looks at Mac, who is stuffing the food away, and says :

TITLE : ' Say Mac, now that you got Trina, you ought to take her out to a show or somewhere, that's the racket ! '

Back to the scene. Mac looks up, while he pours coffee from his cup into a saucer, then blows on it a little. He drinks it, then stops and says : ' You think I ought to, Mark ? ' Marcus says :

TITLE : ' Why, of course, that's the proper caper. You'll have to take her mother, too, of course.'

Back to the scene as Mac looks at Marcus, then turns and gazes dully down at the table-top, nodding his head. Iris out.

Iris in on the front of the Sieppes' house. McTeague steps up and knocks on the door.
Medium shot from behind Mac. The door opens and Trina appears, very much surprised to see him.
Shot from behind her looking through the open door. McTeague steps in and Trina closes the door. They go off.
Medium shot of the lounge. They enter from the left. Trina invites him to sit down. She is very much upset. McTeague sits down ; as soon as he is seated, he realizes that he did not greet Trina in the way he felt he should. He moves towards Trina, and Trina rises at once, putting out her hands, and says : ' Don't ! — Wait a minute ! ' McTeague moves one step towards her, then Trina speaks : ' I've got something to say to you.' McTeague doesn't understand.
Close-up of Trina from his angle as she says : ' I don't know what was the matter with me last night.'
Close-up of McTeague. He does not know what she is talking about.
Back to a close-up of Trina ; she continues to speak :

TITLE : ' I've acted like a bad girl — I don't love you well enough to marry you — '

Close-up of McTeague. His face gets that wild, passionate look, and, ignoring her words entirely, he starts to move towards her.

Back to the scene with both of them in shot. She retreats, her hands stretched out before her to fend him off. He approaches and grabs hold of her. She tries to remonstrate, tries to talk, but he embraces her in bear-like fashion and all but smothers her.

Close-up of both their heads. McTeague turns her face to his and kisses her again upon the mouth. She clasps McTeague's huge red neck with both her slender arms, raises her adorable chin and kisses him in return, exclaiming :

TITLE : ' Oh, I do love you, I do ! '

Iris out.

Vertical barn door in on the Orpheum Theatre. McTeague appears from the right. People are coming and going from the ticket window.

Medium close-up of McTeague as he looks up and makes sure that it is the Orpheum. He suddenly feels his pockets, thinking he has lost the money. He dives into one and finds his pocket-book. He is greatly relieved.

Back to the scene as he continues walking towards the ticket window.

Medium shot of the ticket window. McTeague appears and says :

TITLE : ' Is it here you buy your tickets? '

Close-up of the ticket seller through the grating. He looks at the poor boob, and says, very superciliously : ' How many? '

Close-up from his angle of McTeague seen through the grating. McTeague says again :

TITLE : ' Is it here — '

Reverse shot from McTeague's angle of the cashier seen through the grating. In a very mean way, he says : ' Yes.'

Close-up of McTeague seen through the grating from the seller's angle. He speaks, looking very embarrassed :

TITLE : ' I want four seats for Monday night in the fourth row from the front and on the right hand side.'

Shot from his angle of the cashier, who says :

TITLE : ' As you face the house or the stage? '

Back to close-up of McTeague as he says :

TITLE : ' I want to be on the right-hand side to be away from the drums.'

Shot from his angle of the ticket seller. He looks at McTeague in a

147

funny way and says :

Title : 'The drums are on the right, you want the left then.'

Close-up of McTeague as he speaks :

Title : ' I want to be on the right hand side.'

Medium shot of them both. The seller takes four tickets and throws them out without another word. With a magnificent and supercilious gesture he says :

Title : ' Now you're right up against the drums.'

Close-up of McTeague from the seller's angle as he says : ' But I don't want to be near the drums.'
Close-up of the cashier, who thrusts his head at McTeague and says : ' Do you know what you want, at all? ' He takes a house-plan from the wall, shoves it through the window and shows it to McTeague, pointing to four seats. He takes four other tickets from behind him, after having put the first four tickets back. Then he turns and slams the four tickets into McTeague's hand and says :

Title : ' That's away from the drums.'

Close-up of McTeague as he speaks :

Title : ' But I want on the right — No, I want on the left — I want —
I don't know — I don't know — '

Medium shot of both. The cashier roars and McTeague moves away,
gazing stupidly at the blue pasteboard. Two girls take his place at the
window. In another minute McTeague comes back, peering over the
girls' shoulders and calling to the seller :

Title : ' Are these for Monday night? '

Medium close-up of the seller and the two girls in shot. The seller
looks up at McTeague but doesn't pay any attention to him whatsoever. He smiles broadly at the girls, and McTeague walks off.
Medium close-up. McTeague appears, takes out his immense wallet
and puts the tickets in it. Suddenly he becomes enraged. He walks off.
Medium shot of the two girls at the ticket window. McTeague appears
and yells over the girls' shoulders :

Title : ' You can't make small of me. You — You — I'll thump your
head — you little — you little — pup — '

Back to the scene. The ticket seller shrugs his shoulders worriedly, then
smiles at the girls and says : '$1.50.' The girls pay.
Close-up of McTeague as he glares at him, breathing heavily. He
finally decides to let the matter drop and walks off.
Medium shot on the steps. McTeague appears and stops once more.
He turns and wags his head and shakes his fist in the direction of
the ticket office, yelling : ' You can't make small of me. I'll — I'll —
yes — ' He walks off. Iris out.

Iris in on the clock of the Ferry Building showing 7 :30. Iris enlarges
to show the whole Ferry Building.
Quick lap dissolve to the entrance, where we see McTeague in blue
trousers and a Prince Albert coat and white lawn necktie. He looks
around very impatiently. Just then ' der Mommer ' arrives with Trina
and Owgooste. ' Der Mommer ' carries a basket with two bananas and
an orange in it. She has lisle mitts on. They see each other.
Medium close-up of McTeague and Trina shaking hands. She is very
animated and quite beside herself. She looks very pretty in her black
dress. She has a new pair of gloves on.
Back to the scene. Mrs. Sieppe shakes hands with McTeague. Owgooste

149

is crying. McTeague stretches out his hand to Owgooste. Owgooste is rubbing his eyes with his hands. His mother makes him shake hands with the Doctor.

Medium shot of all four. Pointing to Owgooste's torn stockings, Mrs. Sieppe says : ' Voult you pelief, Doktor, dot bube has tore his stockun alreatty.' Trina smiles, and McTeague also. He pats Owgooste on the head. Mrs. Sieppe is anxious that they may be late, so is Trina; McTeague urges them to come and they start to walk off. Iris out.

Barn door in on the front of the Orpheum. There are very few people arriving as yet. McTeague, ' der Mommer ', Trina and Owgooste appear from the left. They enter the theatre.

Medium shot of the entrance from the lobby, with the man at the ticket box. They enter from the left. McTeague puts his hand in his pocket, terrified he has lost his tickets. Trina is terrified; ' der Mommer ' is terrified. McTeagues tears through his pockets and looks through his wallet. He does not find them. A few people are looking on, smiling. McTeague suddenly remembers and, with a gasp of relief, he removes his hat and takes them out from underneath the sweat band, greatly elated. They go in.

Shot from the interior towards the entrance. They come in and the usher takes the tickets. They walk towards camera.

Reverse shot from behind them. Very few people have arrived as yet. The usher brings them to their seats and gives them programmes.

Medium shot as they sit down with much to-do. They read the programme. Trina is greatly excited and very happy. McTeague is very happy also.

Close-up of McTeague's hand holding Trina's hand.

Close-up of Owgooste, who speaks :

TITLE : ' Maw — when are they going to start? '

Back to the scene. ' Mommer ' says : ' Sit down,' and pushes him back into his seat.

Shot from the rear of the theatre with them at the front. More people enter. Iris out with iris set on them.

Iris in on a gloved hand knocking on a door. Hold there for a second. Iris enlarges showing a strange man with a very funny face, in a tan overcoat. He is knocking on Marcus's door. The door opens; Marcus looks out and sees the strange man. The stranger very politely asks a question and Marcus looks at him questioningly and says : ' Yes,' he knows. He goes off towards camera, following the man.

Reverse shot looking towards the bathroom. Marcus appears, followed by the stranger. They pass through the bathroom and turn to the right. Marcus knocks on Maria's door; the door opens. Maria looks at Marcus; Marcus tells her that this gentleman is looking for her. She seems to know him and he seems to know her. Maria asks him to step in. Marcus stays outside. The door closes from the inside. Marcus goes off thoughtfully; his curiosity is awakened.

Medium shot towards Marcus's room. He enters the scene, walks into his room and closes the door.

Medium shot in the bathroom, looking towards Maria's door. The door opens quickly and Maria runs out, beside herself. She is followed by the stranger.

Medium shot from the banister with the bathroom on the left and Marcus's room on the right. Maria and the stranger appear from the bathroom. Maria is very excited. She yells at the top of her voice as she knocks at Marcus's door. He asks what the hell is the matter; before she answers she runs down the hall and knocks on Mr. Grannis's door and yells. Granis opens the door and comes out. Maria runs from his room to Miss Baker's door and yells again. Miss Baker comes out. Meanwhile Grannis has come towards Marcus, who asks the stranger what has happened. The stranger explains without gestures to Marcus, who is joined by Old Grannis, while in the background Maria tells Miss Baker and drags her forwards. There is absolutely no indication of what it is all about — just great excitement and consternation. From the other side of the hallway the palmist and the photographer appear also; when they are all standing in a circle about the stranger and Maria, Maria tells them what has happened. Iris out.

Horizontal barn door up, like a curtain, revealing the stage with two ' knock-abouts ', apparently drunk.

Quick medium close-up of the two doing something.

Shot from their angle of the audience laughing.

Medium shot of McTeague, Trina, 'der Mommer' and Owgooste who is standing in the aisle. McTeague roars, Trina laughs and 'der Mommer' laughs too; she is sitting next to Owgooste.

Close-up of Owgooste's feet. One foot is stepping on the other.

Close-up of 'der Mommer'. Owgooste bends over and whispers something into her ear; she pushes him back into his seat.

Shot from their angle of the 'knock-abouts' on the stage making their last stand. The curtain falls.

Back to a medium shot of McTeague, Trina and 'der Mommer' as they applaud furiously.

Close-up of Owgooste's feet.

151

Long shot from the rear of the Orpheum towards the stage. The whole house is applauding. Some of the people are rising; some are coming towards camera, i.e. to the rear of the theatre, while the two 'knockabouts' take their last bow.

Back to medium shot of all four. They rise with a lot of trouble and McTeague fishes for his hat underneath the seat.

Close-up of McTeague's hat and Mrs. Sieppe's reticule in the aisle on the floor. Feet are walking over them. One foot kicks them and they both disappear out of the picture.

Medium close-up of Mrs. Sieppe and Trina. Mrs. Sieppe bends over to Trina and says :

Title : 'Save der brogaramme for Popper.'

Back to medium shot of all four. Mrs. Sieppe discovers that her basket has gone and McTeague cannot find his hat. They look and look and turn about while the other people file out and look at them smilingly as they pass. McTeague gets out of the row and looks for the two lost things.

Back to close-up of Owgooste's feet stepping on each other.

Medium shot of McTeague as he finds his hat and the reticule above in the aisle. He picks them up, raises them above his head and turns.

Shot from his angle of 'der Mommer', Trina and Owgooste still looking for the two things in their row. Trina sees McTeague with outstretched hands holding the hat and the reticule. She tells 'Mommer', who looks up.

Shot from their angle of McTeague in the midst of the people filing out, waving the hat and the reticule while everybody is giggling at him.

Shot from his angle as they start walking up towards him.

Reverse shot of McTeague. They join him. He gives 'der Mommer' the reticule, then brushes off his hat and puts it on. They file out at the end of the crowd.]

Title : 'Trina and Mac became engaged. The event was celebrated with a theatre party.'[1]

Exterior long shot from above the theatre as the crowd files out. Cabs are rolling up and people are getting in.

Medium shot of McTeague in the crowd approaching Trina and 'Mommer'.

Medium shot of McTeague, 'der Mommer', Trina and Owgooste, all very much elated. [They don't realize that they are the object of

---

[1] This title does not appear in Stroheim's original script.

people's looks. McTeague points to a street-car and they all agree and start to walk off.]
Close-up of Trina as she says :

TITLE : ' I liked the lady best . . who sang those sad songs.' [1]

Close-up of ' Mommer ' as she says :

TITLE : ' I liked pest . . . der yodlers.' [1]

Close-up of Mac as he says :

TITLE : ' I liked best the fellow who played *Nearer my God* on beer bottles.' [1]

Iris out.
Close-up of Owgooste twisting his legs with one foot standing on the other.
Close-up of ' der Mommer ' watching him.
Back to same close-up of Owgooste complaining.
Close-up of ' Mommer ', who bends down to hear him and tells him :

TITLE : ' Pehave ! ' [1]

Long shot of the theatre exterior from above. Fade out.

TITLE : ' And afterwards there was to be something to eat at Mac's dental parlours.' [1]

[Iris in on the Oyster Grotto on Hayes Street, across from McTeague's flat. ' Der Mommer ' and Trina and Owgooste are standing outside. The door opens, and McTeague appears from inside carrying a large package. ' Der Mommer ' asks him :

TITLE : ' You got der tamales? '

Back to the scene. McTeague nods. Trina says she loves tamales. They start to cross the street. Lap dissolve out.
Iris in on a medium shot of the front of McTeague's house as they enter.]
Medium shot in the hallway at the top of the stairs. Maria calls to the others. Miss Baker, Old Grannis, the photographer, the palmist, Marcus and the stranger are assembling at the top of the stairway.
Shot from the top down of ' der Mommer ', Trina, Mac and Owgooste

---

[1] This title does not appear in Stroheim's original script.

as they enter and look up, surprised at the sounds they hear above. [They start walking upstairs.]
Back to medium shot of the group waiting at the top of the stairs.
Medium shot in the hallway from the right of the staircase. They all appear; the new arrivals look a bit baffled. The stranger steps forward to Trina and asks : ' Is your name Trina Sieppe? '
Close-up of Trina, terribly agitated and frightened. She nods.
Close-up of Mac, who does not know what to make of the situation.
Close-up of ' der Mommer ', equally mystified.
Close-up of the agent, who bows formally to Trina.
Close-up of Trina, still frightened.
Back to close-up of the agent, who speaks with the mien of an under-taker :

TITLE : ' Your lottery ticket has won five thousand dollars.'

Close-up of Trina, wide-eyed, turning to ' der Mommer ' and Mac.
Medium close-up of ' der Mommer ' and Mac reacting to the news.
Medium shot of the entire group. Trina, Mac and ' der Mommer ' look at each other, then at the others. The others cheer and applaud.
Close-up of Trina. She looks from one to the other and says : ' What nonsense.'
Close-up of ' der Mommer ' talking excitedly.
Close-up of Mac, who still does not know what to make of the news.
[Back to medium shot. Marcus steps forward, takes Trina's hand and says : ' Let me be the first to congratulate you.' he bows.
Close-up of Trina. She does not know what it is all about. She looks at Mac.
Close-up of Mac. He stammers : ' What — what — what? '
Close-up of Maria as she says : ' Don't you remember the lottery ticket I sold you in Dr. McTeague's office? '
Back to the scene. She points in the direction of the office.
Close-up of ' der Mommer ' as she almost screams :

TITLE : ' Fife tousand thalers — If Popper were only here ! '

Close-up of Marcus as he says :

TITLE : ' What are you going to do with it Trina? '

Close-up of Miss Baker. Her false curls quiver with excitement as she says :

TITLE : ' Let me kiss you — to think I was in the room when you bought the ticket — ']

154

Close-up of Trina shaking her head. She says :

Title : ' Oh, there's a mistake — [Why — why — should I win? It's nonsense.] '

Back to close-up of Trina as she finishes speaking.
Medium shot of the entire group. Maria screams and says : ' No mistake — no mistake — here it is in the list.' She points to the list in her hand and holds it out for them to see.
Medium shot of the group as Trina looks at the list.
Close-up of the stranger as he speaks :

Title : ' On presentation of your ticket, you will receive a cheque [on our bank] for five thousand dollars.'

[Close-up of Trina. She looks at him with consternation.
Back to the scene as the stranger says : ' I congratulate you,' and holds out his hand. Trina shakes it.]
Close-up of Trina. Only now does she realize that it must be true. Thrills of gladness surge up in her. She claps her hands and cries : ' Oh, I've won — I've won.' She turns towards her mother : ' Mama, think of it ! '
Close-up of her mother with tears in her eyes and rolling down her cheek. [She says : ' Kiss your Mommer, Trina.']
Brief close-up of Mac.
Medium shot of Trina and her mother. [Trina bends over and kisses her mother.] ' Der Mommer ' speaks :

Title : ' What efer vill you do mit all dose money, Trina? '

Close-up of Marcus. He smiles cynically in Mac's direction and says :

Title : ' Get married on it for one thing.'

[Medium shot of the group. They all shout with laughter.
Close-up of McTeague grinning and looking about sheepishly.
Close-up of Marcus who shakes his head at the dentist and says :

Title : ' Talk about luck.']

Back to close-up of McTeague. He grins.
Back to close-up of Marcus, who says : ['Well, are we going to stay talking out here in the hall all night? ']

Title : ' Can't we go into your parlours, to celebrate? '

Back to Marcus as he finishes speaking, pointing in the direction of the

155

' parlours '.

Back to close-up of Mac as he says : ' Sure, sure,' and starts to move off in that direction.

Medium shot of the group walking towards McTeague's office. He is leading. Mrs. Sieppe says : ' Everybody gome.' Mac turns and invites everybody as Marcus says : ' We'll celebrate, by damn.'

Medium long shot of the interior of Mac's office, looking towards the door. The door opens and they all enter. [Trina walks over to the chair in which she had been sitting when she bought the ticket and points to it. Miss Baker points to the operating chair and says : ' I was here.' Maria steps into the same position as she was in when she sold the ticket, holding out her hands as if she were holding the tickets.

Close-up of Trina in ecstasy. She says :

TITLE : ' And I didn't want to buy one at first. Think of it.'

Close-up of Maria. She points to Marcus and says : ' And he told me it was against the law.'

Close-up of Marcus. He nods and scratches his head, looking sore.

Medium shot of McTeague in the centre of the floor muttering : ' Think of it; think of it ! ' He walks aimlessly about the room. Fade out.

Fade in.

TITLE : ' The wheel of fortune had come spinning close to all of them. They were near to this great sum of money. It was as though they, too, had won.'

Fade out.

Fade in on three tables in the centre of the room. Some of McTeague's dental napkins are spread on the tables. There are hot tamales, beer . . .[1]

Maria speaks :

TITLE : ' I don't believe that Mr. Grannis and Miss Baker have ever met — and they have been living side by side for years.'

---

[1] At this point there would appear to be a page missing from Stroheim's original script. In Frank Norris's novel, the scene continues with general celebrations and the consumption of the beer and tamales, during which Marcus acts as master of ceremonies. He suddenly notices that Old Grannis has disappeared and goes to get him from his room. Grannis has been preparing for bed and is minus his collar and cravat, and he is thoroughly annoyed and embarrassed at being seen thus by Miss Baker. Marcus introduces him to Mrs. Sieppe and Trina, then Maria Macapa breaks in.

Close-up of Miss Baker looking out of the corner of her eye, trying to appear preoccupied.

Medium shot of Marcus and Old Grannis. Marcus slaps Old Grannis on the back and drags him by the sleeve out of shot.

Medium shot of Miss Baker. Marcus drags in Old Grannis. He introduces Miss Baker to Old Grannis, then Old Grannis to Miss Baker, all with great formality. Miss Baker extends her hand shyly. Old Grannis touches it for an instant, then lets it fall. Maria passes between them with a half-empty bottle of beer in her hand. The two old people fall back from one another. Miss Baker sits down again.

Medium shot of Marcus. He drags Old Grannis into shot, pointing to a place, pushes Old Grannis into the chair and gives him a glass of beer and a tamale. Then he takes a handkerchief out and wipes his forehead.

Close-up of the agent. He knocks on a glass with a knife.

Medium shot of the group. They all stop talking and all look at the agent. Marcus tells them all to be quiet as the agent is going to make a speech.

Close-up of the agent as he speaks :

TITLE : ' I wish all joy and happiness to this happy pair — Happy in the possession of a little fortune and happy in the possession of each other — '

Back to the scene. He picks up his glass, holds it out and speaks again :

TITLE : ' I drink to the health, wealth and happiness of the future bride and groom.'

Back to the scene. He makes a motion with his arms for everybody to rise, and they do so. They all drink.

Close-up of Marcus as he speaks :

TITLE : ' McTeague — speech — speech ! '

Back to the scene. Everybody is clamouring for the dentist to speak.

Close-up of McTeague, terrified. He grips the table with both hands and looks wildly about him.

Close-up of Marcus yelling : ' Speech ! Speech ! ' He runs out of shot.

Medium shot of Marcus as he runs around the table and up to McTeague, endeavouring to drag him up.

Medium shot of Mac and Marcus. Mac refuses.

Back to medium shot of the group. They all rattle on the table with their beer glasses, insisting.

Close-up of McTeague shaking his head.

Medium close-up of Marcus and McTeague. Marcus whispers in his ear and says : ' Aw get up and say something anyhow, it's the proper caper.' Mac looks at him.

Medium shot of them all. McTeague rises and everybody applauds.

Close-up of McTeague. He looks slowly about him.

Back to medium shot. He sits down again, shaking his head hopelessly.

Close-up of Trina looking over at him. She says : ' Oh, go on, Mac.'

Medium close-up of Marcus and Mac. Marcus tugs at his arms and says : ' You got to.'

Medium shot of them all. McTeague rises again. Everybody applauds.

Close-up of McTeague. He looks steadily down at the table and says :

TITLE : ' I don't know what to say. I — I — ain't never made a speech but — but I'm glad Trina won the prize.'

Close-up of Marcus as he says, with a cynical expression :

TITLE : ' Yes, I'll bet you are ! '

Back to close-up of McTeague as he continues speaking :

TITLE : ' — and you're all welcome and drink hearty — and I — and — and — that's about all I got to say.'

Medium shot of the scene. Tremendous applause as McTeague sits down.

Close-up of McTeague. He wipes his forehead.

Back to medium shot of the group. They push their chairs back and rise.

Close-up of the stranger as he says : ' Well, I must be going.']

TITLE : ' The party ended late. McTeague and Marcus gave up their rooms to Trina, " der Mommer " and little " Owgooste ".' [1]

Back to the scene. He shakes hands with everybody [offering a cigar to Marcus], congratulates McTeague and Trina once again, and bows himself out. The others also start to leave.

Medium shot of the guests saying goodnight.

Close-up of Maria near the operating chair where McTeague keeps his gold. She swipes a handful of it.

Back to the scene as the last of the guests leave. Maria is last of all. Trina alone remains.

Medium long shot of Mac and Trina by the door. Maria appears, says goodnight with a characteristic gesture of her arm and goes out through the door, puffing on a cigar. McTeague puffs on his pipe, then

---

[1] This title does not appear in Stroheim's original script.

goes over to Trina.
Medium close-up of them both as Trina says :

TITLE : 'Oh, Mac, think of all this money coming to us . . . just at this moment. [Isn't it wonderful? Don't it kind of scare you?] '

Back to the scene as she looks up and smiles at him. McTeague shakes his head and says : ' Wonderful — wonderful.' He hugs her in a bear-like fashion and kisses her, lifting her up off the floor. She pushes him away. He hears somebody calling him and looks towards the door.
Close-up of Marcus looking through the open door and calling him :

TITLE : ' Come along Mac we've gotta sleep with the dogs tonight, you know.'

Back to the scene as he leaves.
Medium shot of Marcus at the door as Mac appears followed by Trina. Mac and Marcus go out and Trina closes the door behind them.
Medium shot of Trina looking up towards heaven in a gesture of gratitude as she walks over to the bed-lounge.
Medium shot of Owgooste sleeping.
Medium shot of Owgooste with Trina sitting on the bed beside him.
[Medium shot at the top of the stairway. Everyone is just going into their respective rooms. Mrs. Sieppe is standing in front of Marcus's room. Marcus and Mac start to descend the stairway and wave back at Mrs. Sieppe.
Medium shot of the front of the house. Marcus and McTeague walk off in the direction of the dog hospital. Iris out.

Iris in on a medium shot of Miss Baker's room. She is rocking slowly in a chair, holding a tea-cup and saucer, with a sweet smile on her face, as she listens in the direction of Grannis's room.
Quick lap dissolve to a medium shot of Old Grannis's room. Grannis holds his upholstering needle and a half-bound pamphlet in his hand as he stands by the wall with an idealistic smile on his face and listens in to Miss Baker's room. Iris down on his face. Iris out completely.]

Long shot of the front of the dog hospital as Marcus opens the door and puts on the light. They enter.
Close-up of Trina sitting on her bed, contemplating the paper which tells of her winning lottery ticket.
[Medium shot of the dog hospital office. Marcus points to the bed and tells Mac to go on to bed. He points to himself and says : ' I got to look at the dogs before I turn in.' Then he leaves.
Medium shot at the rear door as Marcus opens it and goes out.

159

Medium shot in a little alley as Marcus turns to his right and goes into the yard.
Medium shot from the middle of the yard towards the entrance. Marcus appears.
Medium close-up of a dog cage; the dogs are whimpering.]
Back to the scene. [Marcus pays no attention and walks up and down. Suddenly he stops.] He stands motionless in the yard.
Close-up of Marcus as he speaks :

TITLE : ' What a damn fool I was.'

Back to close-up of Marcus as he continues :

TITLE : ' If I'd a' kept Trina I'd a' had five thousand bucks [— and I played it right into his hands].'

Close-up of Marcus as he says :

TITLE : ' Damn the luck ! '

Back to close-up of Marcus. Fade out.

[Iris in on Zerkow's kitchen. Zerkow is standing and just handing

Maria a tumbler. She takes the glass and he takes the bottle. They drink. They put the glass and bottle down. She takes out her handkerchief with some gold tape in it, uncovers it and holds it out to him.
Close-up of Zerkow looking at it, his eyes popping.
Shot from his angle of the gold tape glittering (in natural colour).
Medium shot of both. They bicker over it but Zerkow wants the gold and he gives her $2. Maria starts talking :

TITLE : ' I sold a lottery ticket to a girl at the flat. How much do you suppose that girl's won? '

Back to the scene. Zerkow shakes his head and says : ' I don't know, how much — how much? ' Maria says : ' Five thousand dollars.'
Close-up of Zerkow. He looks as though a knife has been thrust through him. A physical pain twists his face and his entire body. He raises his clenched fists into the air and, his eyes shut, his teeth gnawing his lip, he whispers : ' Five thousand dollars.' Then he continues :

TITLE : ' For what? For buying a ticket, and I — I have worked so hard for it — '

Back to the scene. He is sobbing as he continues : ' So hard — so hard.' Tears come to his eyes and run down his cheeks as he speaks :

TITLE : ' — To come so close and yet to miss me — me who had worked for it, fought for it, starved for it, and dying for it every day.'

Back to the scene as he cries and says :

TITLE : ' Five thousand dollars, all bright, heavy pieces.'

Close-up of Maria. Her chin propped on her hands, her eyes gazing into space, she says :

TITLE : ' Bright as the sunset.'

Medium shot of both. Zerkow draws his chair closer and shuts his eyes in ecstasy as he says : ' Go on, go on.' Maria starts speaking. Dissolve out.
Dissolve in to a banquet table with imaginary gold service plate on it, but this time we are using a convex mirror instead of a concave one and the imaginary plates will be all drawn out lengthwise, whereas in the former scene they were all drawn out in width. Dissolve out.
Back to the scene. Zerkow digs his nails into his scalp and tears at his hair. He breaks down and puts his head on the table, sobbing. Iris out.
Iris in on some gold coins lying on a black velvet floor, two greedy

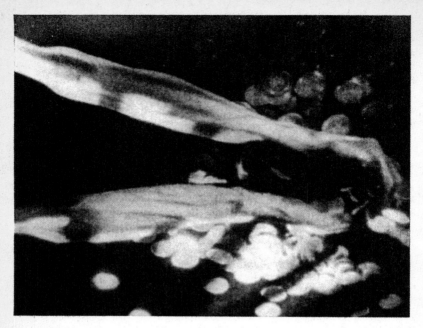

hands playing with them in a miserly fashion (in natural colours). This will be our *leit-motiv* of Gold and Greed. Iris out.

Iris in on the cashier's window at Oelbermann's Toy Store. Trina stands holding her basket with a shawl over it. The cashier takes her receipt and gives her $5. He extends his hand through the window and congratulates her on her win, of which he has heard. She thanks him and puts the $5 very carefully into her little purse, then goes off towards the private office of her uncle.

Medium shot of the door of her uncle's private office. Trina appears and knocks.

Shot of the interior of the office. Her uncle is at his desk. He looks up and says : 'Come in.' The door opens and Trina enters. She puts the basket down on a chair near the door and comes over and kisses her uncle. He asks her to sit down and she does so. She says : 'I got the cheque.' She opens her purse, extracts the cheque and hands it to her uncle, who holds it in his hands and reads it.

Insert of the cheque : 'Mexican Lottery Company to Trina Sieppe, dated May 15, 1918. Signed by the Treasurer and Vice President for Five Thousand Dollars.'

Back to the scene. Her uncle dips his pen into the ink and hands it to her, then turns the cheque around and points to the place where he wants her to sign. She signs and he blots it; then he opens the drawer of his desk, takes out an agreement and hands it to Trina. Trina takes it in her hand and starts to read.

Insert of a section of the agreement stating that Trina invests $4800 in her uncle's business at 5% interest, which will be payable at the rate of $25 per month, on the 1st of every month.

Back to the scene. She agrees to it, takes her pen and signs both copies; he signs also and gives her one. He also takes out his wallet and extracts $200, which he hands to her. She folds the notes up very carefully and puts them into her pocket book. Iris out.]

TITLE : ' In the new order of life, Trina reduced Mac's visits to Frenna's saloon to one night a week.' [1]

Fade in on a long shot of the exterior of Joe Frenna's saloon.

[Iris in on the interior of the Coffee Joint. Marcus is already seated as McTeague enters. McTeague says : ' Hello.' Marcus answers very indifferently while pouring catsup on his plate. Mac sits down at Marcus's table in silence.]

Close-up of Mac drinking, seated near the back of the bar.

Close-up of Marcus drinking whisky at the table.

Close-up of Mac again drinking and belching.

Back to close-up of Marcus; Mr. Ryer can be glimpsed at his table at the extreme left.

Shot of the scene. Marcus is close to camera on the left with an angry look on his face. As Mac, in the background, lights his pipe and begins to puff on it, Marcus begins to twist about in his chair. His emotional state is reflected in the intensity with which he turns a coin over and over on the table. Finally he can contain himself no longer. He speaks :

TITLE : ' Say Mac, when are you gonna pay me that money you owe me? '

Back to the scene as McTeague, very astonished, says :

TITLE : ' Huh, [what I don't — don't —] do I owe you any money? '

Medium shot of the scene as Marcus speaks :

---

[1] This new title and the shots of Trina (see footnote on page 164) reflect the fact that this scene has been transposed to *after* the wedding in the release print. Moreover, in shooting the film Stroheim compressed two separate scenes into one, so that the beginning of the dispute between Marcus and McTeague — originally intended to take place in the Car Conductor's Coffee Joint — now follows straight on to the scene in Joe Frenna's Saloon on page 167.

TITLE : ' Well you owe me four bits. I paid for you and Trina that day
. . . at the picnic.'

Back to the scene as McTeague says apologetically :

TITLE : ' [That's so, that's so —] you oughta have told me before.'

Back to the scene. Mac takes some money out of his pocket and puts a
fifty-cent-piece on the table, saying :

TITLE : ' [Here's your money and] I'm, I'm obliged to you Marcus.'

Back to the scene. Marcus speaks sullenly :

TITLE : ' — and you never paid me for sleeping in my dog hospital the
night you was engaged, either.' [1]

Back to the scene as he pockets the fifty cents and McTeague says :

TITLE : ' Well do you mean I — I shoulda paid for that too? '

Marcus speaks :

TITLE : ' Well you'd a had to sleep somewheres. You'd a had to pay
four bits for a bed anywheres ! '

Back to the scene as McTeague hastily feels in his pockets and says :
' All right, I don't want you should be out anything on my account,
old man. Here.' He angrily slaps down another fifty-cent piece. Marcus
picks up the coin and plays with it.[2]
[Marcus throws the coin back and speaks :

TITLE : ' I ain't no beggar — I don't want your damn money.'

Back to the scene as McTeague pushes the coin back again and pleads
with him to take it. Marcus pushes it back and says : ' I don't want
your money . . .'] Marcus continues speaking :

TITLE : ' I've been played for a sucker long enough.'

Back to the scene as McTeague remonstrates with him, very unhappy.
He says :

---

[1] Stroheim's script has : ' — and I ain't saying nothing about you sleeping,' etc.
[2] A three-shot sequence of Trina is inserted at this point in the release print as
follows :
Medium shot of Trina sitting at the foot of the bed polishing some coins.
Close-up of the coins held up in her hand.
Back to medium shot of scene as she holds the coins so as to catch the light.

Title : ' What's the matter with you lately, Marcus? Is there anythin'
I've done? '

[Back to the scene as Marcus says : ' That's all right, I've been played
for a sucker long enough.' He rises and exits. McTeague looks after
him in consternation. Iris out.

Iris in on a medium shot of the door of McTeague's office. Trina,
with her basket and some bundles, opens the door, and through it we
see McTeague working. There are no patients there; she goes in.
Medium shot of the interior of McTeague's office. She enters and
closes the door. McTeague sees her and walks over.
Medium shot of both. She puts the basket down, and he hugs her in
his bear-like fashion and kisses her. She rests her head for a second on
his breast, then sits down exhausted. She opens her pocket book and
takes out the agreement. She unfolds it and hands it to him. He takes
it and looks at it and reads. His face becomes serious and disappointed
as he says :

Title : ' — well, that's gone and think what we coulda had for it.'

Back to the scene as Trina with a very wise look says :

Title : ' But we could get it back whenever we wanted it.'

Back to the scene as he shakes his head. He doesn't like the idea at all.
She continues speaking and says :

Title : ' But don't you see Mac that that capital is working for us,
the interest alone will pay the rent.'

Back to the scene. She points to the apartment at the back of Mc-
Teague's office. He thinks for a second, then nods his head and says :
' Well, I guess that's right.' She takes the agreement out of his hands,
folds it and puts it back into her pocket book. She takes one of the
bundles and opens it; it contains a pair of chenille portieres. She holds
them up and says : ' Don't you like them? That'll be for the arch
leading into the bedroom.' She points again towards the photographer's
apartment. He looks at the material, touches it with his clumsy hands
and says : ' Very nice.' Trina says :

Title : ' — and think how cheap I got them — $2.50.'

Back to the scene. She puts the curtains back and opens another
bundle. She takes out a pair of Nottingham lace curtains, holds them
up and looks at Mac as she says :

TITLE : 'Forty-nine cents.'

Back to the scene. She opens up another large parcel which she has in her basket. It contains half a dozen or more pots and pans, all of highly polished tin. He looks at them and smiles.
Close-up of Trina's hand holding one pot and turning it. On the bottom of the pan in black writing is '25c'. He points to it.
Back to the scene. McTeague nods and she puts the pots down, rises quickly and with an outburst of affection stretches her hands out towards him and says :

TITLE : 'But never mind all that — Mac — Do you really love me? Love me big?'

Back to the scene. McTeague stammers something, gasping and shaking his head. She grasps him by both ears and, swaying his head from side to side, she holds her face up to be kissed. He kisses her, then she picks at the hair that grows out of his nostrils, laughingly, then she drags his head down towards her and says :

TITLE : 'Do you know you got a bald spot?'

Back to the scene. He nods with his head down, while she holds him. Then she kisses the bald spot and says very seriously :

TITLE : 'That'll make the hair grow.'

Back to the scene. All at once McTeague makes a fearful snorting noise. Trina jumps with a stifled shriek. McTeague bellows with laughter and his eyes water. She says :

TITLE : 'Mac do it again, you scare me so.'

Mac snorts again. She jumps, frightened. Mas bellows with laughter. Iris out.

Iris in on Joe Frenna's saloon. It is night. Marcus enters and walks to the family entrance.
Medium shot from the bar in the private room with the door leading to the street. Heise, three other men and Marcus are visible. Marcus has a whisky tumbler; he takes a pint flask of whisky out of his pocket, fills the glass and gulps it down. McTeague enters. Marcus looks up and says : 'Hello.' McTeague says : 'Hello.' McTeague sits down at the table next to Marcus and, while filling his big porcelain pipe, orders himself a bottle of beer. Marcus, twisting to and fro in his chair, shrugs one shoulder then the other. McTeague lights his pipe

166

and smokes; tobacco smoke drifts into the faces of the adjoining group
where Marcus sits.
Close-up of Marcus. He strangles and coughs; his eyes aflame, he says :

TITLE : ' Say, for God's sake, choke off on that pipe! If you've got to
smoke rope, smoke it in a crowd of muckers. Not among gentlemen.'

Back to the scene. Heise leans forward and says : ' Shut up, Schouler.'
Close-up of McTeague. He takes his pipe out of his mouth and stares
blankly at Marcus.
Close-up of Marcus, who turns his back on him.
Close-up of McTeague, who resumes his pipe.
Medium close-up of Marcus and Heise. Marcus is telling Heise loudly
about some grievance, while the latter is trying to pacify him. Marcus
swings around in his chair and looks in the direction of McTeague.]
Back to the scene. Marcus speaks :[1]

TITLE : ' All I know is that I've been soldiered out of my girl — '[2]

Close-up of McTeague as he gapes at him, bewildered. He removes his
pipe from his mouth and stares at Marcus, his eyes filled with trouble
and perplexity.
Back to the scene as Marcus speaks :

TITLE : ' [Where do I come in — now that you've done me out of my
girl] and out of my money, [you give me the go-by.'

Close-up of McTeague gasping.
Back to the scene. Marcus shouts :

TITLE : ' You'da been plugging teeth at two-bits an hour.'

Back to the scene as Marcus says :

TITLE : ' Ain't you got any gratitude? '

Back to the scene as Marcus continues :

TITLE : ' Ain't you got any sense of decency? ']

Long shot, revealing the entire scene. [Heise tells him to shut up.
Marcus pushes Heise away.]
Medium shot. Marcus looks over to McTeague in the background and

---

[1] At this point, in the film, McTeague's quarrel with Marcus continues from the
scene which Stroheim originally intended to take place in the Car Conductor's
Coffee Joint.
[2] In Stroheim's original script this title has ' $5000 ' in place of ' my girl '.

167

says :

TITLE : 'Do I get any of them 5000 bucks from the lottery? '

Close-up of McTeague. He looks over and says :

TITLE : ' It ain't mine to give.'

Back to long shot of the scene.
Medium shot of Marcus and McTeague as the latter continues speaking :

TITLE : 'You're drunk . . . that's what you are.'

Long shot of the entire scene.
Medium shot of the two men.
Back to long shot of the scene.
Medium close-up of Marcus, who rises unsteadily and says :

TITLE : ' Am I gonna get some of that money? '

Medium shot of both. McTeague shakes his head and says : 'No, you don't get any of it.'
Medium long shot of the scene as Marcus turns to the others as if to say : ' See? ' Then he turns back to McTeague and says :

TITLE : ' I'm through with you.'

[He starts for the door, then comes back and says, shaking his finger : ' Don't you dare speak to me again.' He starts for the door once again, and says :

TITLE : ' You one-horse dentist.'

Back to the scene. He starts for the door and speaks again :

TITLE : ' You ten-cent zinc-plugger — '

Close-up of Marcus as he continues :

TITLE : ' You hoodlum — '

Back to close-up as he says :

TITLE : ' You mucker.']

Back to close medium shot of the scene. Marcus thrusts his angry face close to Mac's. McTeague is pulling hard on his pipe. [Smoke gets into Marcus's face again.] Marcus knocks the pipe from his hand with a sudden flash of his hand.

168

Close-up of the pipe breaking on the floor.

Medium shot of McTeague rising to his feet, his eyes wide, not angry yet, only surprised by the suddenness of Marcus's outburst, as well as by its unreasonableness.

Long shot of Heise restraining Marcus as he steps back.

Close-up of Marcus's hand reaching into his pocket.

Back to the scene as Marcus makes a quick, peculiar motion, swinging his arm upward with a wide and sweeping gesture, his jack-knife open in his palm.

Medium close-up of Marcus throwing the knife.

Close-up of McTeague's head with the wall behind. The knife hits the wall and quivers as it sticks a few inches from McTeague's ear.

Close-up of Marcus's face turning away.

Back to long shot of the scene. Marcus heads for the door and snatches his hat. He exits quickly and the door closes behind him.

Close-up of Joe Frenna's hand withdrawing the knife from the wall.

Medium shot as they all look at it. Heise says :

TITLE : 'Look out he don't stab you in the back, if that's the kind of a man he is — you never can tell.'

169

Close-up of McTeague, who looks stupidly down at the floor. His eye falls on the broken pipe.

Close-up of the broken pipe on the floor.

Medium shot of McTeague, who bends over to pick it up.

Medium shot of the entire group.

Medium close-up of the three men : Heise on the left and Frenna to the right of McTeague.

Medium long shot of the scene.

Back to medium close-up of the three men as McTeague begins to react.

Close-up of McTeague. His huge jaws click together. He clenches his fists and says :

TITLE : ' He broke my pipe.' [1]

Back to shot of the three men as McTeague continues :

TITLE : ' He can't make small of me. [I'll show him — I will —] '

Back to shot of the three men again as McTeague repeats once again :

TITLE : ' He broke my pipe.' [1]

Medium long shot of the scene. McTeague claps on his hat. Heise and Frenna grab him and say : ' Now, listen, don't go and make a fool of yourself.'

Medium close-up as the two men try to restrain him. He holds the fragments of his pipe [and says :

TITLE : ' I'll show him.']

Medium shot as McTeague pushes Heise and Frenna aside as if they were little children. He strides towards the door like a raging elephant.

Long shot of the entire scene.

Medium close-up of McTeague heading for the door.

[Medium shot outside the saloon. McTeague comes out, storming towards his flat.]

Medium shot of the inside of the saloon. Heise rubs his shoulder, as does Frenna; [Heise says :

TITLE : ' Might as well try to stop a locomotive.']

Fade out.

---

[1] This title does not appear in Stroheim's original script.

[Medium shot of the hallway showing the stairway. McTeague rushes in and goes over to Marcus's door. He tries it but the door is locked. The dentist puts one enormous hand on the knob and pushes the door in.

Medium shot from behind McTeague towards Marcus's room; it is dark and empty. McTeague leaves the door open as he goes off towards the right.

Medium shot outside McTeague's office. McTeague appears from the left and stumbles over a big packing box. He opens the door and drags it inside. He examines it.

Close-up of the label on the top, addressed to: 'Dr. McTeague, Dentist, Polk Street, San Francisco, California.'

Close-up of McTeague, joyful and curious. He looks around.

Medium shot of McTeague. He goes over to the stove, gets the fire shovel and comes back and breaks the case open. On top is an envelope. He takes it and looks at it.

Close-up of the letter: 'For my dear Mac, from Trina. P.S. The man will be around tomorrow to put it in place.'

Back to the scene. McTeague tears away the excelsior and suddenly utters an exclamation.

Close-up from his angle. It is the golden molar, his greatest ambition in life.

Close-up of McTeague as he speaks :

Title : ' Ain't she — ain't she just a — just a jewel.'

Back to the scene. He very carefully removes the rest of the excelsior and lifts the ponderous tooth from its box. He sets it upon the marble-top centre table. He circles about the golden wonder, touching it gingerly with his hands. He sits down and gazes at the tooth in ecstasy. Fade out.

Fade in on a medium shot of the top of the stairway and the hall. Marcus comes upstairs and walks towards his door.
Medium shot of the front of Marcus's door. He appears and sees the broken door. He thinks for a second, then yells in the direction of McTeague's room :

Title : ' — and now he breaks into my room, by damn.'

Medium shot of McTeague's room. He is in his pyjamas, folding up his pants while looking at the tooth. He hears Marcus and he starts up with his fists clenched, but immediately drops back upon the bed-lounge with a gesture of indifference.
Medium shot of Marcus as he yells :

Title : ' It's come to stealing from me now, is it? '

Medium shot of McTeague muttering in the direction of the voice :

Title : ' Aw, go to bed.'

Medium shot outside Marcus's room. Marcus goes in, banging his door.
Medium shot of McTeague. He turns out the light and goes to bed, arranging himself so he can see the tooth.
Shot from his angle of the tooth on the top of the table, shining out dimly as if with some mysterious light of its own. Iris out.

Iris in on the fence in the back yard with Alex, the Irish setter, and the collie, snarling their endless hatred at each other, barking and clawing on the boards. Iris out.

Iris in on the Sieppes' house. There is an American Express Company wagon in front. Two men are carrying a box up to the truck.
Close-up of the box, and on it, in large black letters : ' No. 3 ', and the address : ' Hans Sieppe — Los Angeles, California.'

Back to the scene. 'Der Popper' is supervising the carrying of the box. McTeague appears from the left; he nods at 'der Popper' in greeting. Then he enters the house.

Medium shot of the inside of the house. Everything is upside down. Cases and trunks are standing about and there are pieces of furniture in crates. 'Der Mommer', Marcus and Trina are visible. They see Mac, and Trina runs to him and greets him lovingly. 'Der Mommer' greets him too. Marcus turns and walks into the other room.

Medium close-up of 'Mommer' and Trina. They turn in the direction in which Marcus has left, then back to look at Mac.

Close-up of Mac as he makes a gesture with his head as if to say: 'Aw, he's crazy.'

Medium shot of the group. Trina leads Mac out of the room towards the kitchen; 'der Mommer' follows.

Medium shot of the Sieppes' bedroom. They enter from the kitchen. Mac sits down on the bed. This room is also upside down. Trina is worried and, pointing with her head in Marcus's direction, asks Mac what has happened. Mac starts to tell the story.

Medium shot of Mr. Sieppe and Marcus in the dining room. Two Express men carry out another box, marked 'B'. Marcus speaks:

TITLE: 'Well Uncle, if you hear of anybody in Los that wants to go in for ranching just let me know. I'm sick of the city life.'

Back to the scene. Mr. Sieppe slaps Marcus on the back and says: 'Of course.' He tells him about the upholstering business, pointing frequently at himself; Marcus picks up the thread, pointing just as often to himself. They both have a good time.

Back to medium shot of the bedroom with McTeague and Trina sitting on the bed. Mac finishes his story and Trina's mother goes out. Trina, very much aroused, says:

TITLE: 'He threw his knife at you? The coward! He wouldn't have dared to stand up to you like a man.'

Back to the scene. McTeague points about an inch away from his head, smiling rather proudly. Trina continues to speak:

TITLE: ' — and he wanted part of my money, eh? I like his cheek!'

Back to the scene. McTeague smiles and Trina, very much excited, continues:

TITLE: 'Why, it's mine, every single penny of it. Marcus hasn't the least bit of right to it. It's mine — mine.'

173

Back to the scene. Mrs. Sieppe enters, dragging Marcus with her. Trina notices and says :

Title : ' I mean it's ours, Mac dear.'

Back to the scene. McTeague looks at Trina, then down at the floor. When Trina sees Marcus she turns her back on him. Mrs. Sieppe speaks :

Title : ' Now you two fellers, don't be dot foolish. Schake hands and maig ut oop.'

Back to the scene. McTeague gets up, and Marcus mutters an apology and stretches out his hand. Miserably embarrassed, McTeague shakes it and says : ' That's all right — that's all right.' ' Der Mommer ' says : ' — And you will pe der pestman at der vedding.'
Back to the scene. Marcus flares up again and says : ' Oh, no, I've made up with him all right, but I'll not stand up with him.' Then he says :

Title : ' That would be rubbing it in.'

Back to the scene. Marcus goes off and ' der Mommer ' follows, making gestures with her hand to McTeague as if to say : ' Not to worry, he'll be all right.' Trina comes up to McTeague. She has something behind her back and she says to him : ' Close your eyes.' He does so. She puts a box in front of him and says : ' Open.' He opens his eyes and looks down.
Shot from his angle of an imitation orange-blossom wreath.
Back to the scene. He looks from the wreath up to her. She kneels on the bed and embraces him, then kisses him on his bald spot. Iris out.]

Title : ' Trina and Mac were married a month later in the photographer's room that Mac had rented for their future home.' [1]

Close-up, in iris, of a hand holding a wedding ring. Camera moves back on perambulator while lens opens simultaneously to reveal McTeague in his office, with Old Grannis seated near by. [McTeague is in shirt sleeves and is just putting on a collar and necktie.
Close-up of Old Grannis. He speaks :

Title : ' Marriage is a — a noble institution — is it not, Doctor? '

Close-up of McTeague as he nods and says : ' Sure is.'
Back to close-up of Old Grannis as he speaks :

[1] This title does not appear in Stroheim's original script.

TITLE : ' It's the foundation of society.'

Medium shot of them both. McTeague nods gravely.
Medium close-up. Seen against a black velvet background a hand is
holding a piece of hard wood, while the other hand works a saw.]
Medium shot of the dining room, including Marcus, Selina and the
Minister, Miss Baker and Uncle Oelbermann. Selina is sitting in front
of the parlour melodeon and is looking through some music sheets.
Oelbermann is standing alone by the window, looking out. [Heise is
standing with Miss Baker, pulling on his yellow gloves.] The Minister
is reading his book. Mr. Sieppe is measuring the number of steps from
the curtain of the bedroom to the centre of the room. He makes an
abrupt turn in the centre and walks towards the little table in front
of the window where the Minister is standing. He makes two chalk
marks for his feet and two chalk marks for another pair of feet in the
same line. He is very much excited and feels the importance of his
office.
Back to medium shot of Mac and Grannis talking as they get ready.
[Medium shot of Maria and a funny-looking waiter in the kitchen.
The waiter has a dirty shirt front. Maria is perspiring. Smoke is curling
up from the stove. There are pots and pans and platters everywhere.
Everything seems to be cooking.]
Medium shot from the centre of the dining room looking towards the
curtain leading into the bedroom. Mr. Sieppe runs to the curtain,
looking at his watch. He calls through.
Medium close-up. While holding the curtain together, ' der Mommer '
pokes her face through the folds, not letting anything else be seen.
' Der Popper ' asks her whether Trina is ready; ' der Mommer ' nods
very excitedly. Her head disappears. Mr. Sieppe claps his hands for
attention as he walks towards camera.
Medium shot of Selina at the parlour melodeon. Sieppe appears and
explains to her that ' der ' signal for the entrance of the bride ' vill pe
der shaking of der curtains '. Selina nods. Miss Baker, Marcus, Uncle
Oelbermann and the Minister stand near by, talking.
Medium shot of Mac and Grannis excitedly making a last check of
their appearance and of the ring.
Medium shot from the melodeon, including as much of the dining
room as possible. Mr. Sieppe, very serious and important, tells ' der
peeples ' that ' eferything is reatty '. He tells them to take their positions.
They start to do so.
Medium shot in McTeague's office looking towards the door that leads
into the bedroom. McTeague is standing near the door, listening. Old

Grannis is near him. Old Grannis looks at his watch and tells McTeague that the time has come. McTeague nods gravely and they suddenly both look towards the main entrance. They walk off.

High angle long shot towards the main entrance of the room. Old Grannis and McTeague enter. McTeague opens the door, through which one can see Mr. Sieppe standing at attention. [Mr. Sieppe says :

TITLE : 'Are you reatty?'

Back to the scene. McTeague and Old Grannis both nod. McTeague fingers his necktie and his cuffs. He seems to be terrifically excited. Mr. Sieppe then waves to them to come and they step out.

Medium shot of the hallway including the doors to the photographer's former apartment. Mr. Sieppe is followed by Mr. Grannis and Mc-Teague as they appear in the foreground. Mr. Sieppe is walking at a funeral pace. He stops at the centre door leading into the dining room and makes an abrupt turn. He arranges McTeague and Grannis so that they face the door. He gives them a last instruction, then retraces his steps to the door that leads into the bedroom from the hallway. He enters.]

Long shot of the dining room with the guests all arranged in their places. The Minister is standing by the window.

Medium shot of Grannis and McTeague from behind as they enter the room. McTeague trips over the door sill.

Back to long shot of the scene as McTeague and Grannis step up and take their places according to the chalk marks that have been previously pointed out to them by Mr. Sieppe. Marcus helps them find the correct places as both are extremely nervous.

Close-up of the Minister.

Close-up of McTeague.

Shot from the kitchen door including the entire group.

Medium close-up of Selina looking expectantly towards the curtain.

Medium shot of the curtain, which suddenly begins to shake violently.

Medium shot of Selina, who swings around and pulls the stops, then starts playing the melodeon.

Medium long shot. The curtains open and out steps Trina on her father's arm, preceded by 'der Tervins', dressed exactly alike, each carrying an enormous bouquet of cut flowers in lace paper holders. Behind Trina and her father is Mrs. Sieppe, walking alone. She is crying.

Shot from the middle of the bedroom through the arch showing the scene in the dining room. Mr. Sieppe marches Trina up to the centre of the room, makes an abrupt turn and marches towards the Minister,

then steps back three paces.

[Medium shot of a hand sawing wood against a black velvet backdrop.]

Medium close-up of the Minister speaking.

Grainy close-up of McTeague shot through a layer of gauze.

Grainy close-up of Trina also shot through a layer of gauze.

Similar close-up of McTeague again.

Close-up of Marcus scowling.

Close-up of the Minister talking.

Close-up of McTeague nodding : ' Yes.'

Close-up of Trina also nodding.

[Close-up of the keyboard on the melodeon with Selina pulling out the stop labelled ' tremolo ' and playing.

Insert of a title on the music sheet which reads : ' Call Me Thine Own '.

Medium shot of the Minister, McTeague and Trina from a raised platform so that camera can see the street below. The Minister invites the two to kneel down.

Close-up of McTeague. He does not know what to do. Frightened stiff, he looks in the direction of Grannis.]

Close-up of the Minister as he invites them to kneel.

[Close-up of Old Grannis who makes a motion and whispers : ' Kneel down.']

Close-up of Marcus scowling.

High angle medium shot as McTeague and Trina kneel down. McTeague puts the ring on Trina's finger, while in the background a funeral hearse is seen through the window, slowly passing by in the street below.

Quick lap dissolve to a medium shot of the funeral procession and hearse, just long enough to make sure that no one in the audience has missed it.

Quick lap dissolve back as the couple's hands are joined.

[Close-up of Marcus. His eyebrows are knitted and he looks down at the floor.]

Close-up of Mrs. Sieppe crying and sobbing.

[Close-up of Mr. Sieppe. His eyes are shut; not a muscle moves.

Medium shot of the hand sawing wood.

Close-up of Miss Baker looking shyly in the direction of Mr. Grannis.

Close-up of Old Grannis looking in the direction of Miss Baker. He immediately becomes terribly embarrassed and looks down at the floor. Back to a flash of Miss Baker. She too is terribly embarrassed and looks down at the floor.]

Close-up of Owgooste fidgeting.

Close-up of Mrs. Sieppe still crying.

Close-up of Owgooste idiotically turning his head from side to side.

Close-up of ' der Mommer ', who notices him; she stops sobbing and makes a sign to Owgooste.

Close-up of Mr. Sieppe.

Close-up of the Minister.

Medium shot of the couple.

Close-up of Marcus's hands clenched angrily behind his back.

Close-up of Mrs. Sieppe.

Close-up of the Minister.

Medium shot of Mac and Trina. Trina throws back her veil as if she could not believe that they have now been bound together for life. The couple rise and shake the Minister's hand.

Close-up of McTeague, dumbfounded.

[Medium shot of the hand sawing wood.]

Medium shot of Trina kissing her mother.

Back to a medium shot of the group as Marcus steps up to Trina like a man of the world, takes her hand and says : ' Let me be the first to congratulate Mrs. McTeague.' The guests crowd about the pair, shaking hands and all talking at once. Trina kisses Selina, Grannis and her father, and she cries a little herself.

Medium long shot from behind of Mr. and Mrs. Heise approaching the wedding group, having just arrived. Mr. Sieppe is talking animatedly to them and pointing to his watch. Fade out.

TITLE : ' And then they viewed the gifts.' [1]

[Medium shot of Mr. Sieppe, near a small table where the wedding presents are laid. He calls the company's attention and points to the presents. They all flock around to look at them. Mr. Sieppe points to the melodeon and an ice water set.

Close-up of the ice water set.

Back to the scene. He points to a carving knife and set with elk-horn handles.

Close-up of the set.]

Back to the scene [as he points to himself and Mrs. Sieppe]. He points to a polished slice of redwood.

Close-up of the wood, with a view of the Golden Gate handpainted on it.

Close-up of Selina. This is her present.

Back to long shot of the scene. Mr. Sieppe points to a chatelaine watch of German silver.

Close-up of the watch.

Back to the scene. Mr. Sieppe points to Marcus. With a motion of his hand Marcus makes it clear that this gift is for Mrs. McTeague and not Mac.

Close-up of McTeague, who steps forward and whispers in Trina's ear that he also has a wedding present for her. She looks up, astonished and curious, and gestures as if to say : ' You? — for me? '

Back to the scene. McTeague nods, a little embarrassed, and steps over to the table and stoops down. He takes a covered canary cage from underneath the table. They all look at it as he takes off the towel.

Close-up of his gilded cage with not only the male that we saw him buy once before, but also a female bird in it.

[Back to the scene. They all look at each other.]

Close-up of Trina. She is disappointed.

Close-up of McTeague as he looks at her, nodding gravely.

Back to close-up of Trina. She turns and looks at him and forces out a thin smile.

Close-up of Mac smiling happily.

---

[1] This title does not appear in Stroheim's original script.

Close-up of Marcus with a terrible sneer on his face.

Close-up of Trina.

Close-up of Marcus cleaning his ear with the little finger of his gloved hand in a characteristic gesture. He spits.

Back to the scene including the entire group. Miss Baker is the only one who does not seem to think small of Mac's gift. She comes near the cage and talks playfully to the birds. Owgooste and 'der Tervins' crowd around the cage. Owgooste pokes the stick of his 'all-day sucker' (lollipop) through the wires. 'Der Popper' sees it and grabs him by the shoulder and tells him to stop. When Owgooste pokes at the bird again, in a mean way, 'der Popper' lets him have one and Owgooste cries; 'der Tervins' join him. Mr. Sieppe spanks them also. [Then he points to the two cases still to be opened, then at Mr. Oelbermann, who nods gravely.

Medium close-up of Trina and McTeague. Trina is very animated and curious. Holding her hands together and looking very lovely, she says: 'Let's open them.' She turns to Mac and he nods gravely.

Back to the scene. Everyone is in shot. Marcus as usual assumes the office of master of ceremonies, assisted by Mr. Sieppe. They have a hammer ready and start to open the first case.

Medium close-up of the open case. It contains all sorts of toys. Mr. Sieppe holds up a bunch of them.

Medium shot of the group. Trina and McTeague take some of the toys and look at them.

Medium shot of Trina and McTeague. They look at each other and McTeague says : ' But what — what — I don't make it out; we have no need of toys.' Trina looks at him, then laughs modestly.

Medium shot of the entire group. They all laugh and Trina sits down on the chair near by and laughs so hard that she begins to cry into her handkerchief. McTeague is still standing there with the toys in his hand; he still can't make it out.

Close-up of Miss Baker, very embarrassed. She looks in the direction of Grannis, then down at the floor.

Close-up of Old Grannis, who similarly looks in the direction of Miss Baker, then down.

Back to medium shot. The second box is open. Sieppe and Marcus both have a bottle of champagne in each hand and are holding them up.

Close-up of a bottle.

Back to the scene. Trina rises and they all crowd around the box and look at the bottles, as they have never seen champagne before. Mr. Sieppe looks at his watch, then speaks :

TITLE : ' Ve must start der dinner now, as der train leaves at elevun.'

Back to the scene. Trina calls to Maria.

Shot from her angle towards the kitchen. Maria and the waiter poke their heads out. Trina asks whether the dinner is ready. Maria and the waiter both nod.

Back to the scene. With great excitement they all start to prepare the dinner table, draw up chairs, etc. Fade out.

Fade in on medium shot of the hand sawing wood. Fade out.]

TITLE : ' And then for two full hours they gorged themselves.' [1]

[Fade in on the dining room of the McTeague apartment. Everyone is seated at the table; the waiter is just opening a bottle of champagne; he fills the last glasses. Marcus rises and proposes the health of the bride; they all rise and drink.

Close-up of McTeague. With a long breath of satisfaction, he says :

TITLE : ' That's the best beer I ever drank.'

Back to the scene. There is a general roar of laughter.

---

[1] This title does not appear in Stroheim's original script.

Close-up of Marcus. He says: 'Oh Lord! Ain't that a break,' making fun of McTeague.

Close-up of McTeague, dumbfounded, looking in Marcus's direction.

Close-up of Trina who says: 'Now, Mark, you just shut up. That isn't funny any more. He called it beer on purpose. I guess he knows.'

Close-up of Marcus rather slowly giving up the kidding.

Back to the scene. Everyone drinks and eats.]

Camera moves back on perambulator as the iris opens simultaneously from a close-up of McTeague and Trina, to reveal the entire group seated at the dining room table.

Close-up of Mr. Sieppe chewing on a calf's head and using his napkin to mop the sweat from his brow.

Close-up of Mrs. Sieppe similarly gnawing on a calf's head.

Medium close-up of the three children sitting at their own little dining table near by. They begin to fight.

Close-up of Mrs. Sieppe admonishing them.

Medium close-up of the children, who stop fighting.

Close-up of Mr. Heise eating. He stops for a second to belch, then goes on eating.

Close-up of little Uncle Oelbermann eating in a tiny space, cramped by the arms of his large neighbours.

Close-up of the hunchbacked photographer eating a sticky piece of cake, then licking his fingers and taking a drink.

Close-up of the Minister, nibbling on chicken bones, but with his fingers poised in a very refined and dignified manner.

Close-up of the massive back of Mr. Heise and his tiny wife beside him.

Close-up of Marcus, who suddenly rises from his seat.

Close-up of McTeague looking in the direction of Marcus as he talks to Trina.

Close-up of Marcus standing and proposing a toast.

Close-up of Selina clapping.

Back to close-up of Marcus, who finishes speaking.

Close-up of McTeague and Trina watching him.

Back to the general scene as Marcus sits down and calls over the waiter. Everyone continues eating and drinking. Fade out.

[Fade in on the hand sawing wood. Fade out.

Iris in on the table, which looks like a devastated battlefield. The men have their waistcoats and collars open and are all feeling very good. Everyone is standing around the melodeon which Selina is playing. Most of them have their champagne glasses in their hands. They are singing, and Mr. Sieppe is leading with a fork.

Insert of a music sheet : 'Nearer my God to Thee.'

Close-up of Trina singing with closed eyes.

Close-up of McTeague nodding his head.

Back to a shot of the entire group as the song finishes. Uncle Oelbermann starts to put his hat and coat on and says : 'Goodbye.' Marcus helps him on with his coat and he leaves. 'Der Popper' takes out his watch and says : 'Attention ! Der time have arrive, shtop everythink, ve depart.' There is tremendous confusion as 'der Mommer', Owgooste and 'der Tervins' put on their coats and hats. Old Grannis, with his usual delicacy of feeling, realizes that he should depart before the family; Miss Baker and Mr. Heise also leave. As Marcus and Selina go to leave, Marcus says to Mr. Sieppe : 'Don't forget now.'

Close-up of Trina watching them go one by one; she looks over towards Mac.

Close-up of McTeague, looking at her more or less gravely.

Back to a close-up of Trina; she has an increased feeling of uneasiness and vague apprehension.

Close-up of Mr. Sieppe as he speaks :

TITLE : 'Vell Trina, goot py ! '

Close-up of Mrs. Sieppe. She starts to cry again.

Title : ' Ach. Trina, ven schall I efer see you again ? '

Medium shot of Trina and her mother (through double veil). Trina starts to cry and looks into space saying :

Title : ' Oh, some time — Oh, some time — '

Medium shot of them all. Owgooste and ' der Tervins ' cling to Trina's skirt, fretting and whimpering.
Close-up of McTeague aside from the group. He is very much put out.
Close-up of Trina as she speaks :

Title : ' Write to me very often, Mama, and tell me about everything — '

Back to medium shot of them all. ' Mommer ' just nods. ' Der Popper ' takes out his watch and says : ' Mommer, Owgooste, say goot py, den ve must go. Goot py Trina — Goot py Trina.' He reaches over and kisses her, then he lifts Owgooste and ' der Tervins ' up to be kissed by Trina. Then Mr. Sieppe says : ' Come on.' Mrs. Sieppe cries harder and starts to go, then remembers and says : 'Doktor! Vhere is der Doktor? ' She sees him and starts to run over to him.]¹

TITLE : ' Then came the farewells.' ²

Close-up of Trina's and ' Mommer's ' faces framed by darkness. Trina embraces her mother and looks fearfully over towards McTeague off-screen.
Close-up of McTeague by himself, peacefully puffing on his pipe.
Back to close-up of Trina.
Medium close-up of Trina and her mother saying their goodbyes.
Medium shot of Trina and her mother as they finish kissing goodbye. Camera tracks back to reveal ' Popper ' helping the children to put on their hats and coats in the foreground. Then ' Popper ' picks up each of the children for Trina to kiss them goodbye, too, as ' Mommer ' goes towards Mac, who has remained apart from the family group throughout the scene.
Medium close-up of Mrs. Sieppe and McTeague. She speaks to him, in tears :

TITLE : ' Doktor, pe goot to her — [pe goot to her, eh?] pe vairy goot to her, von't you? '

Back to medium shot of both. McTeague nods.
Medium shot at the door. Mr. Sieppe urges : ' Come on — come on.'
Medium shot of ' der Mommer ' leaving and Trina following.
[Reverse shot from McTeague's angle, showing ' der Popper ', ' der Tervins ', Owgooste and ' der Mommer ' and Trina standing at the door. Mrs. Sieppe kisses Trina once more, then they run out. Trina follows.]
Medium close-up of ' der Mommer ' at the top of the stairway.
Close-up of Trina with a heart-breaking expression on her face as she looks over at Mac.
Close-up of Mac holding his pipe with a benign expression on his face.
Close-up of Trina waving goodbye. [She runs off.
Back to the scene. Mrs. Sieppe's head is just disappearing. Trina runs into shot and runs down the stairs.]
Medium shot on the landing of the stairs. Trina catches her mother

¹ Stroheim's original version of the first half of the farewell scene (i.e. the preceding section in square brackets) has been condensed to a short series of shots. For the sake of clarity, this condensed version now follows, over the next half-dozen shots.
² This title does not appear in Stroheim's original script.

around the neck. Very frightened, she looks back in Mac's direction as she whispers something in ' Mommer's ' ear. ' Der Mommer ' speaks :

TITLE : ' [Ach, you preak my heart. Don't cry poor leetle scairt girl.] Der's nuttun to pe 'fraid oaf. Go to your husban'.'

Back to the scene. Both of them are crying.
Medium shot of the main entrance from inside. The door opens and Mr. Sieppe pokes his head back in and yells : ' Mommer, come ! '
Shot from his angle (from below) of Trina and ' Mommer ' on the stair. [Shot through two veils; Trina is straining her eyes after her mother and waving goodbye.]
Medium shot of Mr. Sieppe going out.
Shot from Trina's angle of ' Mommer ' at the door. She turns and waves back once more, then goes out, closing the door behind her. Grind on the closed door for six feet.
Close-up of Trina waving goodbye. [She is leaning against the wall, still looking down into the empty hall. She breaks down and sobs, covering her face with her handkerchief. She makes a pitiful figure with her bridal wreath and veil.
Medium shot of the hand sawing wood.]
Medium shot of the top of the hallway. Trina slowly starts walking up. She passes the open door of the dining room and stops for an instant.
Medium shot of Trina standing in the doorway and McTeague seated at the table. He is dozing with his back to her and the bird cage on the cluttered table in front of him.
Close-up of Trina.
Close-up of McTeague's huge back from her angle.
Back to medium close-up of Trina with a worried expression on her face as she looks over towards the double bed.
Medium shot of the bedroom and bed.
Close-up of Trina.
Close-up of the bird cage and two birds.
Back to close-up of Trina with tears in her eyes.
Back to the bird cage, going out of focus.
Close-up of Trina.
Medium shot of the scene as Trina disappears from the doorway. McTeague is still dozing in his chair.
Long shot of the hallway as Trina goes on to the bedroom door.
Medium shot of the interior of the bedroom. Trina enters and closes the door.
Shot from her angle of McTeague through the arch.
Medium close-up of McTeague reacting to the sound of the bedroom

186

door. He turns and asks : ' Is that you, Trina? '

Medium shot of Trina by the bed, holding her breath and trembling. She gives no answer, her hand over her mouth.

Shot of McTeague as he rises and starts towards the arch.

Close-up of Trina looking frightened.

[Reverse shot from behind him. He walks towards her quickly, making as if to take her in his arms.]

Medium close-up of McTeague arriving in the bedroom.

Medium close-up of Trina.

Medium close-up of McTeague approaching.

Close-up of Trina.

Close-up of McTeague.

Close-up of Trina from his angle, drawing back in fear.

Shot from her angle of McTeague, his eyes alight.

Medium shot of the scene as McTeague approaches her.

[Medium shot of Trina. She cannot back up any further. He appears and sits down on the bed, then puts one arm around her waist and leans his head against her body. She looks curiously into his face and says : ' I'm afraid of you.' She draws back a bit and suddenly he rises.]

Shot of the two of them as McTeague takes her in his huge arms.

Crushing down her struggle with his immense strength, he kisses her full upon the mouth.

Close-up of the two birds in their cage.

Close-up of Trina's feet in satin slippers, standing on McTeague's feet and then slowly coming up on tiptoe until they assume the position of a toe dancer.

[Close-up of McTeague's neck from behind. Her hands are clasped tightly around him.

Close-up of Trina, tears running down her cheeks, as she speaks :

TITLE : 'You must be good to me. Very, very good to me, dear — for you are all that I have in the world now.']

Medium close-up of McTeague and Trina kissing, her hands clasped tightly around him. Camera begins to back up as she sits on the bed, and continues to move slowly back through the arch until the curtains can be seen at either side of the screen. Mac approaches and closes the curtains; his feet can just be seen through the slit at the bottom as he returns to Trina. Horizontal barn door down.

[Fade in on the hand sawing wood. Fade out.

Iris in on the Santa Fe Railroad station. 'Der Mommer ', 'der Popper ', Owgooste and 'der Tervins ', loaded with boxes, satchels and valises, are pushing their way through the crowd into the main entrance.

Quick lap dissolve to medium shot of the inside of the station, looking towards the door opening on to the platform. The Sieppes run past the man who takes the tickets. He catches Mr. Sieppe and pushes them back. Mr. Sieppe has to put down four boxes in order to find the tickets. They are in everybody's way. Finally they leave in the direction of the train.

Medium shot of the train. Most of the people have boarded the train, some of them are boarding, and some say goodbye to their friends and relatives. The Sieppes enter the day-coach. The porter at the entrance does not like their looks, he smells that there is no tip coming from that source, and ignores them. 'Mommer ' and 'Popper ' get in first, then realize that the kids are not on yet and need help. They get down and help the kids up. They are in everybody's way. In order to help the kids on, 'Popper ' has to take down the boxes, etc., and put them on the ground. He now hands them up to 'Mommer ', while the kids hang on to her skirts. Suddenly the car is given a terrific push — they are switching the train. 'Der Mommer ' has a big hat box in her hand and it falls off the train and under the wheels. The Sieppes are all screaming and falling all over each other. The car is given another push.

188

Sieppe takes the hat box from underneath and hands it up to 'der Mommer'. 'Der Popper' gets up too.

Close-up of the train whistle.

Close-up of the conductor giving the sign for departure.

Close-up of 'der Mommer' looking at the spring bonnet in the box; it looks like an ice-cream that has been sat upon.

Long shot of the train as it leaves. Iris out.

Iris in on Zerkow's kitchen. Maria is there, with Zerkow sitting across from her at the table. A half-filled bottle of whisky and a broken glass tumbler are on the table.

Medium close-up of Maria and Zerkow. Maria's chin is resting on her fists. Her eyes are wide, gazing into space. She speaks, then stops. Zerkow, hanging on her words, sighs deeply and says :

TITLE : 'I could hear it forever and forever.'

Back to the scene. Maria is still gazing into space. Zerkow thinks.

Close-up of Zerkow as he gets an idea. He develops it in his mind, and looks slowly over to Maria.

Shot from his angle of Maria gazing stupidly into space.

Back to close-up of Zerkow. With a sudden impulse caused by a well-concealed idea he says :

TITLE : 'Maria, will ya marry me? '

Back to close-up of him. He looks anxiously at her.

Close-up from his angle of Maria still gazing into space. She turns slowly and looks at him.

Close-up of Zerkow as he urges her again.

Back to close-up of Maria. There is an almost silly smile around her mouth as she seems to realize what this means. She looks at him, then suddenly gets a more or less serious thought and turns her eyes in the direction of the safe behind the clothes.

Shot from her angle of the lower part of the safe sticking out from underneath the clothes.

Back to close-up as she gives a faint smile and looks back at Zerkow. Then, without moving a muscle, she says :

TITLE : 'Sure! — Why not? '

Medium shot of them both. He grabs hold of her dirty hand, brings his face closer to hers and says : 'Will ya? ' She nods slowly and says : 'Let's have a drink on it.' She grabs the bottle and pours herself a drink, then pushes it over to him. They drink. They put down their glasses and the bottle and he moves his chair closer to her. Grabbing her left wrist with his left hand and putting his right arm on her back, he slaps her cordially on the back and says :

TITLE : ' Now then, Maria, let's have it again.'

Back to the scene. Maria looks at Zerkow as he speaks, very excited :

TITLE : ' Do you think it still exists? '

Back to the scene. Maria shrugs her shoulders, then slowly shakes her head. He gets an idea and says :

TITLE : ' Perhaps it's buried.'

Back to the scene. Maria again shrugs her shoulders and nods her head. He urges her to start. He lets go of her wrist and puts his left hand behind his left ear. Maria starts talking. Iris out.

Fade in on the greedy hands playing with gold. Fade out.]

END OF PART ONE

GREED

Part Two

Fade in :

Title : ' The early months of married life wrought changes. Since her lottery winning Trina feared their good luck might lead to extravagance and her normal instinct for saving became a passion.' [1]

Fade out.

Long shot of a Protestant church. It is Easter Sunday. The service has just ended and people are coming out.

Medium shot of some people leaving the church. Dr. and Mrs. McTeague are among them. He is dressed in a ready-made blue serge suit and is just putting on a straw hat. He looks much more civilized than ever before. She is dressed very neatly and attractively, though simply.

Medium close-up as they approach an old lady flower-seller on the steps of the church. Trina picks two Easter lilies.

[Shot from her angle of the Easter lilies and a cardboard tag reading 10c a piece.]

Close-up of her holding the flowers.

Close-up of the flower-seller smiling.

Medium shot of Trina acting dissatisfied. She exchanges the flowers she is holding for two others.

Back to the scene. She likes them and, without thinking, hands the flowers to Mac and goes to open her purse.

Close-up of Trina opening the purse.

Close-up of the purse. We see lots of dimes, quarters and nickels.

Back to the scene. Trina looks at Mac suspiciously for an instant, then closes the purse quickly and says :

Title : ' I have no small change, Mac.'

Back to the scene as she indicates that he should pay.

Close-up of McTeague.

Back to the scene. Mac fishes around in his pockets, finds he has no small change and gives the saleslady a dollar. He gets the change back.

Medium close-up of Trina looking very self-satisfied.

---

[1] Stroheim's script has a different title :
' The first three years of their married life wrought little change in the fortunes of the McTeagues. Instead of sinking to McTeague's level as she had feared, Trina made McTeague rise to hers.'

Medium close-up of Mac.

Back to Trina, who has the lilies in one hand. She puts her other arm through Mac's, and they walk off happy and contented.

Medium long shot of the church front; people are still pouring out. Ogival-shaped iris out.

[Iris in on the front of McTeague's house; people pass by with Easter lilies and Easter palms. The street is garlanded with bunting and fir branches. American flags and wired electric lights are strung across the street. The McTeagues appear in the foreground. McTeague is carrying the *Sunday Examiner* and the *Chronicle*. As they cross the street, a terribly emaciated horse, worse than Don Quixote's Rosinante, comes clattering down the road. Mrs. McTeague takes her husband's sleeve and tries to pull him forward. He looks up, sees that the horse is too close for them to get across safely and pulls her back.

Medium shot: Marcus Schouler sitting on the horse (taken from a machine ahead of him). He wears a Prince Albert coat, a silk hat, white cotton gloves and a white armband with the word ' Marshal ' on it. There are bicycle straps around the bottom of his pants. Inscribed in black, on one of the ribbons suspended from his lapel, is the word ' Committee '. He also carries a baton with a red-and-white calico covering, and has a medium-sized megaphone hanging around his neck. The horse's tail is braided and interwoven with white streamers, and two fancy streamers hang from each ear.

Back to the McTeagues, who look up and see Marcus. He looks down and recognizes them, then pulls in his horse so sharply that the poor creature almost falls. He wheels the horse around in a regular show-off fashion. He slices the air with his baton, as he gives signals and commands to somebody following him.

Medium close-up of McTeague and Trina. They watch Marcus as he rides on. Mac says:

TITLE : ' Aw — you think you're smart.'

Back to the scene as both of them smile significantly. As they reach the other side of the street, there is a group in front of the house — Mr. and Mrs. Heise, Mr. and Mrs. Ryer and others. The McTeagues join them. McTeague takes off his hat very politely to the ladies — something that he had never done before. They are all very animated and reflect the ' holiday spirit '.

Back to a long shot of Marcus who, still mounted, appears from the left and stops in the middle of the scene. He rears his horse around, then slowly and impressively rides back to the left. Following him are two policemen, who are in turn followed by a banner.

Close-up of the banner: ' Polk Street Improvement Club '.
Back to the scene as the banner is followed by a brass band.
Medium shot of McTeague and the others. They have a few words of conversation. Then the McTeagues go into the house. Mac holds the door open while Trina enters. After they have gone inside, the remaining members of the group poke their heads together and talk about the McTeagues in a way that indicates their liking for the couple, and their awareness of the great change in Dr. McTeague. Iris out.

Iris in on the McTeagues' dining room. McTeague is seated at a table on which there is a neat, white starched tablecloth, and two imitation cut-glass saucers with artichokes in each and a little mayonnaise on the side. He has a napkin poked into his waistcoat (before, he would have tucked it into his collar). Trina enters with a neat, clean apron over her Sunday dress; she carries two plates and a coffee pot. On the plates are little pork sausages, and a bit of mashed potato on the side. Everything is neat, clean and appetizing. Trina puts one plate in front of Mac, takes the other one herself, and starts pouring the coffee. Mac starts eating the mashed potato with his knife. Trina sees him, and lays her hand on his arm to attract his attention. She then speaks to him with a little smile and a rather significant look. As slow as he is, Mac understands. He scrapes the mashed potato off his knife and starts eating with his fork. Trina sits down and starts eating. Then she says:

TITLE: ' Would you believe it? The butcher in the next block charges 2c a pound more now, so I'm buying everything at the other shop six blocks up. He must think we steal the money.'

Back to the scene as she continues speaking very agitatedly. Iris out.
Iris in on the promenade in the Golden Gate Park. People are dressed in their Sunday clothes. Children are playing, and nurses and mothers are out with their baby buggies. Walking arm in arm in bourgeois fashion, the McTeagues pass the bandstand. Trina is enjoying herself very much.
Medium close-up of the McTeagues. Camera moves back on perambulator ahead of them. Trina looks up at Mac and says:

TITLE: ' Isn't this better than drinking your old steam beer? '

Back to the scene as Mac nods. Trina thinks a second, then says:

TITLE: '. . . and it's cheaper too.'

Back to the scene as he laughs a little bit and shakes his head over her incessant references to money, although he can't get sore at her. They walk on. Iris out.

Iris in on a little box-like house with a tiny front yard that is situated on a side street. There are ' To Let ' signs in the window and on the front door, which is open. The owner, an enormous red-faced fellow, is sitting on the front stoop asleep. (He is so fat that his walk seems merely a movement of his feet which pushes his stomach along.) The stoop is littered with pages from the Sunday newspaper; and every moment the breeze picks up a page which then flies up and down the street. McTeague and Trina appear, dressed in the same clothes as in the park. It is now late afternoon.

Medium close-up of Trina and McTeague. Camera moves back again on perambulator as they walk along.

Trina happens to glance towards the house.

The signs saying ' To Let ' are seen from her angle.

Back to medium close-up as she stops and nudges McTeague. He looks up as she points to the house, telling him that it is now empty. It is the very same house that they had admired so often and wished they could have for their own. They see the owner on the stoop.

Seen from their point of view, the owner is sleeping and snoring and the newspaper flying about.

Back to the scene as Trina tells McTeague that she is going to wake up the owner, so that they can look at the house. He agrees and they walk up the steps. The owner wakes up and Trina tells him that they want to see the house. He rises with terrible difficulty.

Medium shot of the entrance of the house. They all go inside.

Medium shot of an empty room as the owner points to it. Trina and McTeague look, nod and turn to another room.

Shot from their angle of the adjoining empty room.

Medium shot of the owner with McTeague and Trina. Trina asks the owner the price. The owner says :

TITLE : ' Thirty-five dollars and water extra.']

TITLE : ' For quite some time Mac had his eye on a little house . . . that they might be by themselves.' [1]

Fade in to a long shot of the house to let. Mac, Trina and the owner are talking outside the front door. Trina and Mac exchange looks. Then Trina talks to the landlord. [He writes down their address, but they do not come to an agreement.]

Medium long shot as they finish talking and start to leave. Camera tilts down with them as they come towards camera, then pans as they

---

[1] This title does not appear in Stroheim's original script.

turn and walk up the street, discussing the house.

Medium close-up of them both as they walk. Camera moves back on a perambulator, tracking in front of them. McTeague says :

Title : 'What d'yer think? '

Back to the scene as Trina puts her chin in the air, and says :

Title : 'No! '[1]

She continues to speak :

Title : 'We can't afford such extravagance.'

Fade out.

[Back to the scene as Mac growls :

Title : 'Sure we can. You talk as though we were paupers. Ain't we got five thousand dollars? '

Back to the scene as Trina immediately flushes and retorts :

---

[1] Stroheim's script has a different title :

'I'm not sure yet. $35 and the water extra . . .'

196

TITLE : ' I don't want you should talk like that. That money's never, never to be touched.'

Back to the scene as McTeague, exasperated, stops and says :

TITLE : '. . . and you've been savun up a good deal beside, in that brass matchbox in the bottom of your trunk. Pretty near $100 I guess.'

Back to the scene as he nods his head in a knowing way. She looks at him and says :

TITLE : ' What are you talking of, Mac? A hundred dollars! I haven't got thirty! '

Back to the scene as McTeague takes her by the arm and says :

TITLE : ' Let's take that little house. That chance might never come again.'

Back to the scene as he continues urging her. Trina thinks and says :

TITLE : '. . . it would be lovely, wouldn't it? — to be all by ourselves? But let's not decide until tomorrow.'

Back to the scene as they continue talking and walking. Iris out.

Iris in on the McTeagues' dining room. It is dusk. McTeague, wearing a flannel bathrobe, is sitting in front of the window. His collar and necktie are off and embroidered carpet slippers adorn his huge feet. One page of the *Examiner* is in his hand and the others are strewn over the floor — Mac is reading.
Medium shot of the kitchen. An old charwoman, Augustine, is washing the dishes. Trina, wearing an apron, stoops down and opens the small icebox. She takes out two bottles of beer, then closes the icebox. She picks up a small tray with two glasses and walks out of the room.
Medium shot of McTeague seated in the armchair. Trina appears carrying the tray with the glasses and the beer. She places the tray on the table, then lights a match which she puts into a coal-shovel, prepared with coffee beans. She opens one bottle of beer, pours out two glasses and hands one to Mac. He points to a column in the newspaper as he looks up at her and says :

TITLE : ' I think that's an outrage.'

Back to Trina, who steps closer and looks over Mac's shoulder at the newspaper article with the headline :

TITLE : ' State Dental Board urges University education as prerequisite for admission to Dental College.'

Back to the scene as Mac explains why he disagrees. Trina sits on his lap with a glass of beer in her hand. They both drink. He starts to wipe his mouth with the back of his hand; she hands him a napkin which she is holding. Iris out.

Iris in on a long shot of Market Street.
Quick lap dissolve to a medium shot of the front of a jewellery store with diamonds and gold jewellery in the window. Mac and Trina appear in the foreground. As they pass the store, Trina looks back over her shoulder at the display window and urges Mac to stop a moment. They stand arm in arm looking in the window.
Shot from their angle of the gold, silver and jewellery.
Medium shot of Mac and Trina seen from inside the store. She points to something in the shop window as if to say : ' That is the one I would like to have if we could afford it.'
Reverse angle shot of them from behind. They turn and walk away from the store. Trina looks back over her shoulder again. Next door there is a millinery shop. As McTeague passes by it, Trina sees a hat that attracts her attention, and draws him back. It is a black picture hat with an enormous yellow paradise feather on it. The small, smart label underneath reads : ' $300.'
Mac and Trina are seen from inside the shop as she says :

TITLE : ' Isn't that a beautiful yellow? But can you imagine anyone paying $300 for a hat? '

Back to Mac as he shrugs his shoulders.
Reverse angle shot as they walk away.
Medium shot of several kids looking through a large telescope on the sidewalk, ranged for the moon. Mac and Trina appear and almost pass by it, but Trina looks up and is attracted by the telescope. She draws McTeague back and tells him that she wants to look through it. He says : ' All right.' The kids leave and Trina gazes through the telescope, telling McTeague that what she sees is ' wonderful '.
Shot from her angle of the moon in iris, coloured gold and yellow.
Back to Trina as she continues to gaze through the telescope.
Iris down on her face looking through the telescope and hold for a second. Then iris out completely.
Iris in on the little house which is ' To Let '. McTeague appears and stops in front on the sidewalk.
Close-up of McTeague looking at the house.

Shot of the house from his angle.

Lap dissolve to a shot of the same house — but now decorated. The 'To Let' signs have gone, and there are curtains at the windows. McTeague, white-haired, is sitting in a comfortable chair in front of the door; Trina, also white-haired, sits next to him. At their feet, six children, three girls and three boys, are playing with wooden Noah's Ark animals. McTeague is smoking his huge porcelain pipe. Trina is knitting a sweater. There are Sunday papers on the floor. One is in McTeague's hand. Behind them stand a couple, apparently their son and daughter-in-law. He is playing a concertina, while she has her arm about his waist and is looking up at him. The gilded tooth is dangling from above the door and the gilt canary cage with the two birds is hanging just above them.

Dissolve to the house as before, with McTeague standing in front. He comes out of his trance and walks up the steps. The owner of the house appears from inside, then both men go into the house. Iris out.

Iris in on the McTeagues' kitchen, where Trina is chopping onions. McTeague enters with his hat still on and walks up to her.

Medium close-up of them both as McTeague speaks : ' Well, Trina, we've got that house, I've taken it.' Trina stops her work and looks up, saying : ' What do you mean?' McTeague explains with gestures that he went over to the house and that he signed the lease. Trina is terribly upset and says :

TITLE : '. . . you mean you signed the paper for the first month's rent?'

Back to McTeague, who nods and says : ' Why, sure — that's business.' Trina says :

TITLE : '. . . and I just found out that there has been water standing in the basement for months — and that we could get it for thirty dollars with the water.'

Back to McTeague, who looks dumbfounded and says :

TITLE : ' Well, we needn't go if it's unhealthy.'

Back to Trina, who gestures very excitedly and replies : ' But you have signed the paper.' She continues speaking :

TITLE : '. . . You've got to pay that first month's rent anyhow. That's thirty-five dollars just thrown away, because I'm not going to move a foot out of here! '

Back to McTeague, who tries to pacify her, saying :

Title : ' Well, it's only thirty-five dollars.'

Back to the scene as Trina puts her hand on her hip and says : ' Only ! Eh? ' Tears come into her eyes. McTeague looks at her in surprise. She slams the chopping bowl down on the table :

Title : ' Well, I won't pay a nickel of it.'

Back to the scene as McTeague says : ' Huh? What? ' Trina repeats : ' I say that you'll find that $35 yourself.' McTeague replies :

Title : ' Why, you got a whole hundred dollars saved up in your matchbox. You pay half and I'll pay half.'

Back to the scene as Trina, furious, slams the table with her fist and says :

Title : '. . . you won't touch my money, I tell you.'

Back to McTeague, who gets a little bit peeved, puts his hands on his hips and looks at her, saying :

Title : ' How does it happen to be yours — I'd like to know? '

Back to the scene as Trina, now beside herself, stamps the floor with her foot.
Close-up of Trina as she again bangs the table with her fist and yells :

Title : ' It's mine ! '

Trina continues to slam the table and yell :

Title : ' It's mine ! '

Back to the same scene.

Title : '. . . every penny of it is mine ! '

Medium shot of them both as Mac says :

Title : ' We'd share the rent there, wouldn't we? Just as we do here? '

Back to the scene as Trina shrugs her shoulders with great affectation and indifference and goes back to chopping the onions. Then, with raised eyebrows, she loftily turns to Mac and, pointing at him, says : ' It's your affair, you settle it with the owner. You got the money.' She feigns calmness, as though the matter were something that no longer concerned her.
Close-up of McTeague. Her manner exasperates him. He is getting sore and says :

200

Title : ' I'll pay my half end and he can come to you for the rest.'

Back to Trina as she puts her hand over her ear to shut out his clamouring.
Close-up of Mac as he looks at her and says with a gesture : ' Aw, you don't try to be smart. Will you pay your half? '
Close-up of Trina as she looks over her shoulder, and says with a grand air : 'You heard what I said.'
Back to close-up of McTeague as he repeats : ' Will you pay? '
Shaking her head violently, she slams the table with her fist : ' No ! '
Close-up of McTeague as he looks at her. Then, sore as a boil, he yells :

Title : ' Miser ! '

Close-up of Trina as she looks at him, speechless.
Back to a close-up of McTeague as he speaks :

Title : ' Miser ! You're worse than old Zerkow ! '

Close-up of Trina, who has tears in her eyes as she says :

Title : ' Haven't you got anything to do, instead of abusing me ? '

Close-up of McTeague as he gestures and again asks : ' Well then, for the last time, will you help me out? '
Medium shot of the scene. Trina starts to cut the heads of a fresh bunch of onions, whistling as she does so. McTeague says : ' Huh? — Huh? Will ya? ' Without looking up at him, Trina remarks :

Title : ' I'd like to have my kitchen to myself, please.'

Back to the scene. McTeague has only enough strength left to shake his head. He cannot make it out. He turns slowly and walks out, banging the door behind him. Iris out.
Iris in on Trina's work-table in the living room near the window. She is carving a little wooden animal.
Close-up of one of her hands holding a nearly-completed figure. Her other hand holds a knife, with which she gives it the finishing touches. She puts the knife down, picks up a paint brush and quickly covers the figure with paint, then throws it into a basket containing other finished animals.
Close-up of Trina. (Camera is on a baby tripod on the table facing her.) She looks in the direction of the dental office and sighs deeply, then stares wide-eyed straight into camera. Her eyes slowly fill with tears.
Medium shot of Trina at the table. She drops her head onto her arms

201

which are resting on the table, and sobs.

Medium close-up of McTeague sitting in the dental chair, smoking his pipe and playing the concertina. His coat and shoes are off and his vest is open. He looks very tired and soon lets the concertina rest on his body as he drops off to sleep.

Medium shot of Trina as she raises her head and looks over towards the dental office. Then she turns and looks in the direction of the trunk underneath her bed in the bedroom.

Shot from her angle of the trunk underneath the bed.

Extreme close-up of Trina's face as she looks up from the trunk towards Mac's office and thinks, gazing in that direction.

Lap dissolve to medium shot of Mac's office. There are no patients. McTeague is working behind the screen on moulds. Trina enters unnoticed by him. She has a big smile on her face and holds something in her hand, which she hides behind her back.

Reverse angle medium close-up of McTeague working behind the screen. Trina's hand comes over the edge of the screen, holding four banknotes (three tens and one five). She slips the notes into his hand. While McTeague is looking at the money in a puzzled way, Trina sneaks up from behind, pulls his head down and kisses him on his bald spot.

Medium shot of them both. Trina is acting embarrassed and he asks her what the money is supposed to be for. She tells him with gestures ' for the house that he had paid on '. He takes it, grins and hugs her in his bear-like fashion as he used to, kissing her until her breath gives out. Lap dissolve to a close-up of Trina, smiling. She rises.

Medium shot of the bedroom. Trina comes in, stoops down, and draws out the trunk from underneath the bed. She listens at the door which leads into the dental office, then takes a key from under the corner of the carpet and quickly unlocks the trunk.

Medium close-up of the trunk. Trina kneels down and reaches into the very bottom of it. She lifts up her bridal dress and removes a brass matchbox filled to overflowing with money of all denominations — and a chamois bag which is very stout. She gets up with the matchbox and bag in her hands.

Medium shot as she rises and sits down on the bed. She listens for a second, then empties the contents of both on the bed cover. She counts the money very carefully and puts her finger to her mouth and thinks.

TITLE : ' A hundred and sixty-five dollars.'

Back to Trina as she picks out a few gold pieces, rubs them between the folds of her apron and breathes on them. She rubs them again, and

then finally takes the three ten-dollar gold pieces and one five and lays them aside. She puts the rest back into the bag and matchbox and quickly covers them both with a cushion. She rises and tiptoes towards the door.

Medium shot as Trina sneaks up to the door and stands listening, the gold in one hand and her other hand at her mouth.

Close-up of Trina, suddenly thoughtful. She opens her hand holding the gold. Her gaze shifts from her hand to the office, then she turns back and looks in the direction of the bag and the matchbox. She looks again at the gold in her hand. Then she decides it is too much and goes back towards the bed.

Medium shot as Trina comes up to the bed and takes the matchbox and bag from underneath the cushion. She puts back two tens and one five, holds the ten-dollar gold piece between her fingers and says to herself, 'That'll be enough.' She replaces the matchbox and the bag under the cushion, and rises. She looks at the gold piece and holds it between her fingers, breathes on it and rubs it for a second, and then examines it.

Close-up of her hand holding the hand-coloured $10 gold piece.

She shakes her head and abruptly sits down on the bed. Once more she removes the matchbox and the bag, spilling some of the contents.

Shot from her angle of the bed, covered with gold and silver pieces, all hand-coloured. She takes out ten silver dollar pieces and puts the ten-dollar gold piece back, then shoves the matchbox and the bag under the cushion. She gets up and walks towards the door.

Medium shot as Trina arrives at the door. She turns the knob and starts to open the door very carefully. She stops, looks down at her hand, which she then opens. Looking first at the ten silver pieces and then back in the direction of McTeague's office, she finally thinks for a second with her hand at her mouth. Trina makes a decision that something is quite unnecessary and foolish. Closing the door just as carefully as she had opened it, without ever having looked through it, she goes back into the bedroom.

Medium shot of the bed as Trina appears. Hurriedly, she takes the matchbox and bag from underneath the cushion and puts the ten silver pieces into the bag. She closes it, ties the string around the top quickly, then takes both the box and the bag and stoops down, putting them back into the trunk. She lets the clothing fall on top of them. Finally, she closes the trunk and carefully locks it, testing the cover to make sure it is locked. She puts the key back underneath the carpet and pushes the trunk underneath the bed, straightens up and breathes deeply, then walks towards the table.

Medium shot as Trina comes up to the table, sits down and starts whistling. Iris out.

Fade in on a pile of gold coins against a black velvet background. Two elongated hands are greedily playing with the coins. Fade out.

Iris in on a puny, homely baby which is lying in a dirty cradle in Zerkow's bedroom. The iris holds there for a second, then enlarges to reveal Maria, lying in bed under a dirty ragged crazy-quilt bed cover. Her hands are thrashing about and her eyes are closed. She speaks in the heat of a fever. Next to her stands Zerkow, in a terribly ragged bathrobe. He straightens the bed cover, then removes the towel from Maria's forehead and wets it in a tiny wash bowl that stands on a chair next to the bed. He rinses the towel and puts it back on her forehead.

Extreme close-up of Zerkow, who weeps as he mumbles :

TITLE : '. . . there were over a hundred pieces and every one of them gold . . .'

Shot from his angle of Maria as she opens her eyes in absolute stupor, and stares at Zerkow although she does not see him. She seems to have a pain in her head, for she raises her hands and holds her head at the temples.

Back to a close-up of Zerkow, as he speaks to her :

TITLE : ' Maria, my girl — don't leave me — do ya hear? '

Back to a close-up of Maria as she groans.

Back to a close-up of Zerkow, who continues :

TITLE : ' — That's all I got — that gold plate worth a fortune. Gold, pure gold, think of it! Can't you remember where it went to? '

Back to close-up of Maria, groaning.

Back to close-up of Zerkow, crying and wringing his hands as he speaks :

TITLE : ' — Tell me at least before you die. Don't cheat me out of it! '

Extreme close-up of Maria, her eyes wide open and feverish as they stare into space but see nothing.

Slow lap dissolve to a strange background covered by weird shadows. The hundred pieces of gold plate are swinging on invisible wires or elastic; each is separately suspended from an invisible vertical wheel. They start swinging, slowly at first, then faster and faster until they circle about in a mad tempo.

Slow lap dissolve to the same background, still with the weird shadows but without the gold plate; fog drifts in until the whole screen is filled. Dissolve in to an extreme close-up of Maria. She seems to be a bit more quiet and restful now; she slowly closes her eyes and dozes off.

Medium shot of the scene including the bed, the cradle and Zerkow. He notices Maria's improvement and wipes the tears from his face with the sleeve of his robe. Then he wets the towel again and puts it back on her forehead.

Close-up of the child in the cradle, crying.

Close-up of Zerkow as he glances at the child with an expression of hatred. He walks over to the cradle and looks down at the wincing, crying child. He then grabs an empty bottle with a nipple, takes a pint of milk and starts filling the bottle with the milk.

Close-up of the two bottles in his hands.

Close-up of Zerkow's face with a miserly expression.

Back to a close-up of the bottles as Zerkow pours half of the milk from the nipple bottle back into the pint bottle.

Back to medium shot as he puts the pint bottle down. He picks up a dirty soup spoon that is lying next to the wash bowl in which he

205

prepared the wet towels, and dips it into the water. He transfers some of the water into the nipple bottle to dilute the milk and make it last longer. He replaces the nipple and gives the bottle to the baby.

Close-up of the baby as he greedily starts to nurse.

Medium shot of Zerkow as he walks over to Maria's bed and sits down. He drops his head in his hands and rests his elbows on his knees. He gazes at Maria.

Extreme close-up of Zerkow as his eyes start to stare into space.

Lap dissolve to a night scene in an old, crumbled-down section of a cemetery lit by a weird light. A few crosses and weeping willow streamers sway to and fro in front of camera. Zerkow is standing in a ditch surrounded by earth thrown up in small mounds. He has a shovel in his hand; a pick lies near by on the ground. He strikes something hard with the shovel. He uncovers a large trunk and quickly opens the unlocked top. Raising his arms towards heaven, he steps back and stares in utter amazement and awe at the contents. He bends down, picks up two objects and looks at them. Then, with an animal-like yell, Zerkow holds them up in the air so that the weird light strikes the two objects — a gold pitcher and a gold bowl. He clasps them to his breast, hugging, kissing and patting them.

Dissolve back to the scene with Zerkow sitting on the bed near the cradle. He comes out of his trance and realizes it was only his imagination; he breaks down on the bed, his body shaking as he sobs. Iris out.

Iris in on the sidewalk in front of the McTeagues' house. (Camera is on the ground on a baby tripod.) Alex, the Irish setter, appears on the run from the right, stops, and looks around. Then the collie approaches from the left. The dogs first plant themselves five feet apart, then move in, each manoeuvring for an attack.
Close-up of the setter, snarling.
Close-up of the collie, the embodiment of fury and unsatisfied hatred.
Back to the two of them as they circle about each other. They stop, wheel about, and circle in the opposite direction. The setter pauses and slowly turns his head away from his enemy. The collie sniffs the air and becomes interested in an old shoe lying in the gutter. They move away from each other.
Medium close-up farther down the sidewalk as the setter appears, turns and barks furiously.
Medium close-up farther up the sidewalk as the collie appears, turns and barks furiously. Iris out.

Iris in on the McTeagues' dining room. Trina and McTeague are eating cod fish. The shovel with the smoking coffee beans rests on the chair. McTeague speaks with his mouth full :

Title : ' What's the matter with a basket picnic over at Schutzen Park next Sunday? The Heises and the Ryers would go too — we could ask Selina — Huh? What d'ya say? '

Back to the scene. At first Trina likes the idea, then she starts thinking and says :

Title : ' I don't know as we can afford it this month, Mac.'

Back to the scene as Mac says : ' Aw, come on.' Trina starts speaking, shaking her head as she says :

Title : ' I got to pay the light bill next week and so many other things.'

Back to the scene as Mac urges her, saying : ' Oh, for God's sake, let's go ! ' Trina thinks a bit, and then says :

Title : ' If you pay half . . . it'll cost three or four dollars at the very least — and mind, right now — the Heises pay their own fare both ways, and everybody gets their own lunch.'

Back to the scene as McTeague says : 'Sure — sure . . . you write Selina and have her join us.' They are both pleased in anticipation of the picnic. Iris out.

Iris in on Mr. and Mrs. Heise and Mr. and Mrs. Ryer standing on the upper deck of the ferry boat as McTeague and Trina approach. They are all laden with baskets. The gangplank is raised.
Long shot of the ferry boat seen from another boat as it starts to leave and moves towards camera.
Medium shot of the three couples in a lively conversation on the upper deck.
Close-up of Trina, laughing, as she says :

TITLE : 'Oh! We are going to have lots of fun — if it's anything I do love, it's a picnic.'

Back to the scene as they all agree with her.
Back to a close-up of Trina, who turns to Mac and says :

TITLE : 'Do you remember our first picnic, Mac?'

Close-up of Mac as he turns to her and says :

TITLE : 'Sure! I'll never forget that liver sausage.'

Back to the scene as Mr. Heise glimpses a familiar figure in the distance and points to him. The others turn and look in that direction.
Close-up of Heise as he says : 'Look who's here.'
Shot from their angle of Marcus Schouler walking up the companion-way. He gapes at them in astonishment for a moment and then runs up to the group.
Shot of Marcus from behind as he approaches the group. He makes great sweeping bows to the three women, shakes hands with Trina, then looks at Heise and says : 'Glad to see you. How do, Mr. Ryer?'
He ignores McTeague, who sits down.
Close-up of Marcus as he speaks :

TITLE : 'Well, by damn, what's up, anyhow?'

Medium shot from his angle of the three women, all speaking at once :

TITLE : 'We're going over to Schutzen Park for a picnic.'

Close-up of Marcus as he says : 'Oh! Is that so?'
Close-up of Trina looking him up and down.
Shot of Marcus from her angle, camera tilting down.
Back to close-up of Trina as she speaks :

Title : ' You look as though you were going somewhere yourself ! '

Close-up of Marcus, who grins and nods :

Title : ' I'm going to see Selina.'

Medium shot of the others from his angle. They all utter surprised exclamations. Trina says :

Title : ' Why, Selina is going with us — we're going to meet her at Schutzen Park.'

Close-up of Marcus, acting vexed and very disappointed. He looks in the direction of McTeague.
Shot from his angle of McTeague sitting quietly. Their eyes meet; McTeague looks away.
Close-up of Mrs. Ryer, who looks at her husband as if for approval, and says :

Title : ' Well, say, why can't Marcus come along with us ? '

Close-up of Mrs. Heise, who says :

Title : ' Why, of course.'

Close-up of the back of Mrs. Heise as Mr. Heise punches her.
Medium close-up of Mr. and Mrs. Heise. She turns towards him for a second and then turns in the direction of Trina and says :

Title : ' Don't you say so, Mrs. McTeague ? '

Close-up of Trina as she turns towards Mrs. Heise and then says :

Title : ' Why, of course, come along with us, if you want to.'

Close-up of Marcus, instantly enthusiastic, who says :

Title : ' You bet I will.'

Back to the scene as he is all enthused and says : ' It's out of sight — it is for a fact.'
Back to a medium shot of the group. Heise says he has an idea. He calls Ryer and Marcus over, and tells them his plan. They agree at once, ' great ! ' He calls Mac, who rises slowly and then walks away towards the left as the women sit down.
Medium shot of the stern of the boat as the four men appear from the right. Heise takes a pint flask from his hip pocket and holds it up. Marcus takes off his hat and bows to the bottle, saying : ' How d'ye do.' Heise removes the cork and passes the bottle round. Each man

takes a swig. Heise looks first at Mac, then at Marcus, and finally says :
' Look here, you two fellas have had a grouch at each other for a long
time. Now what's the matter with your shakin' hands and calling
quits? '

Back to the scene as he looks at McTeague.

Shot from his angle of McTeague, who immediately puts out his great
hand and says : ' I got nothun' against Marcus.'

Back to Heise, who turns from Mac to Marcus.

Shot from his angle of Marcus, who is a little shame-faced and says :
' I guess that's all right.'

Back to Heise, who says : ' That's the idea — that's the idea.'

Medium shot of the four men. Heise grabs Mac and Marcus by their
shoulders and pulls them closer to each other. They shake hands. They
all slap each other on the back. Heise says : ' Let's have another drink
on that.' He takes the flask out again, opens the bottle and hands it to
the first one. Iris out.

Iris in on the front of Zerkow's house. Zerkow comes out with a baby's
coffin under his arm. He is followed by Maria. Camera moves on
perambulator ahead of them. Zerkow shows no signs of mourning or
grief, but Maria is crying. She wipes her tears and seems to hesitate a
moment, apparently looking for something. Zerkow walks off-screen.

Close-up of Maria as she looks around with tear-dimmed eyes.

Shot from her angle of the junk in the yard.

Back to close-up of Maria as she turns until her eyes fall on a dying
geranium in a pot outside the window.

Shot from her angle of the half-dead flower.

Medium shot of Maria. She looks towards the gate.

Shot from her angle of Zerkow walking through the open gate.

Back to the scene as Maria turns quickly, runs over to the window and
grabs the pot. She tears out the plant, which has clods of earth still
attached to the roots.

Close-up of the plant in her hand.

Back to the scene as she quickly hides it under her jacket. Weeping and
drying her tears, she runs towards camera, which is on a perambulator,
moving back ahead of her for a few steps until she goes out of sight.

Long shot from the room of the house opposite, camera tilting down
to show Zerkow as Maria appears through the fence gate. In front of
the gate stand his junk wagon and his emaciated horse. The tin sign,
' Zerkow, Junk Dealer.', is on the wagon. Zerkow is about to toss the
coffin into the back of the junk wagon when Maria realizes his plan
and grabs his arm. With tremendous pleading in her tear-dimmed eyes
she pulls the coffin away from him, pressing it to her body. Zerkow

appears indifferent — as long as he does not have to carry it — to him it is junk. He climbs up on the box, takes the reins and whip, and leaves Maria to climb in as best she can with the baby's coffin in her arms. She finally seats herself and he whips the horse. The junk wagon leaves. Iris out.

Iris in on a medium shot of Old Grannis in his room. He is sewing pamphlets near the wall. He stops for a second and listens, then smiles a bit.

Lap dissolve to a medium shot of Miss Baker's room. Miss Baker is putting two tea cups and saucers on the table near her. Even the second gorum spoon is working today. She fills both cups with tea, and a sweet smile plays on her face as she seats herself in the rocking chair and takes her own cup. She stirs it with the gorum spoon and listens, smiling a bit. She then looks in the direction of the second cup on the table, as if the party on the other side of the wall was going to be her partner at the table. She slowly drinks her tea and smiles dreamily. Iris out.

Iris in on a beautiful lawn under some old trees in Schutzen Park. Mr. and Mrs. Heise, Mr. and Mrs. Ryer, McTeague and Trina, Marcus and Selina are seated amidst the litter from the picnic : ' dead soldiers ', egg shells, chicken bones, apple cores (or orange peel), banana skins, tissue and newspaper. The men have removed their coats and vests as well as their neckties and collars; the women have opened their collars and placed their hats and other accessories on the lawn.

Medium close-up of McTeague, as he picks up a large English walnut and cracks it in the hollow of his arm.

Medium close-up of the other men looking on.

Medium close-up of the women applauding. Everybody is animated. Heise believes his wrists are very strong; he takes Marcus's cane which is stuck in the lawn, holds it with both hands, and invites McTeague to try to twist it out of his hands. McTeague grins from ear to ear. Using only two fingers, he takes hold of the cane and twists it out of Heise's hands with a single movement that nearly sprains the harness-maker's wrists.

Close-up of Trina, who applauds.

Medium shot of the group as McTeague rises; he is all keyed up. Mac sticks out his chest in prizefighter fashion and bows towards the women, who are all smiling. He then grabs hold of Heise; with one hand on the back of his collar and the other hand on the seat of his pants, Mac lifts Heise straight into the air, holds him there a moment, then puts him down like a little baby. All the women applaud. Mac gets swell-headed and his great success turns his head. He grips the arms of the men until they squirm, and slaps Marcus on the back until he gasps for breath.

Close-up of Marcus; he can hardly conceal his hatred.

Close-up of Heise as he says : ' I tell you what — we'll have a tournament.'

Medium shot of the entire group. They all move in closer.

Back to close-up of Heise as he speaks :

TITLE : ' Marcus and I will wrestle, and Doctor and Ryer — and then the winners will wrestle with each other.'

Back to medium shot of the group. The women clap their hands excitedly.

Close-up of Trina as she speaks :

TITLE : ' Better let me hold your money, Mac.'

Back to the scene as Mac gives her his money and his keys. The other men give their valuables to their wives, and the contest begins. Mac starts wrestling with Ryer, whom he throws without even changing his grip. Ryer gets up smiling and shakes hands with Mac as he has seen it done in the prize ring. Next come Marcus and Heise. They struggle together for a few moments until Heise slips and falls back. They topple over together. Marcus slips out from under his opponent; and as they reach the ground he forces down first one of Heise's shoulders and then the other.

Close-up of Heise on the ground as he yells good-naturedly : ' All right — all right — I'm down. Let me get up.'

Back to the scene as Heise rises, points to Mac and Marcus, and says : ' It's up to you and Doc now.' Heise and Ryer draw back a bit to give them room, while the women with Trina in front rise and come forward.

Close-up of Trina, all excited and clapping her hands as she speaks :

TITLE : ' I bet Mac will throw him.'

Close-up of Ryer as he says :

TITLE : ' All ready.'

Medium shot of the entire group. Marcus and the dentist step forward, eyeing each other cautiously. They circle around from right to left, stop, turn, and then circle about from left to right. (Their movements mirror those of the collie and the Irish setter.)

Close-up of McTeague, alert but good-natured.

Close-up of Marcus, his teeth clenched, his eyes glaring.

Back to the scene as the two grab hold of each other. Marcus falls to

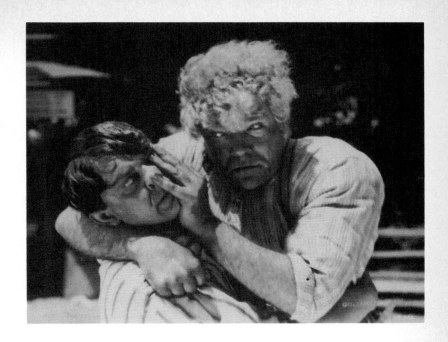

his knees. Mac throws his vast bulk on Marcus's shoulder and thrusts his huge palm against Marcus's face, pushing him backward and downward. Marcus wrenches himself free and falls face down on the ground. McTeague immediately rises.
Close-up of McTeague laughing exultantly as he speaks :

TITLE : ' You're down.'

Back to the scene as Marcus leaps to his feet and says :

TITLE : ' Down nothing, by damn ! My shoulders didn't touch !'

Back to a medium shot of the entire group. McTeague stalks about, swelling with pride. He turns towards the women.
Close-up of McTeague as he speaks :

TITLE : ' Heh, you were down — didn't I throw him, Trina ? '

Close-up of Trina, who applauds and says : ' Of course.'
Back to a close-up of McTeague as he says :

TITLE : ' You can't rattle me.'

Close-up of Marcus, who dances around in rage and says : 'You didn't win; you got to give me another try.'

Medium shot of the group as the other men come crowding up.

Close-up of Heise, who points to Marcus and says : 'He's right.'

Close-up of Ryer, saying : 'You didn't throw him.'

Close-up of Marcus as he speaks :

TITLE : 'Both my shoulders at the same time.'

Close-up of Mac, looking bewildered. He does not understand and, looking from one man to another, says : 'Huh? What? Huh?'

Close-up of Marcus : 'You must rastle me again.'

Close of Mac as he says : 'Sure, I'll rastle you again.'

Close-up of Trina, looking on in some apprehension as she turns slightly towards the other women and says :

TITLE : 'Marcus gets so mad.'

Medium shot of the women. Selina nods and says : 'Yes, but he ain't afraid of anything.'

Close-up of Ryer, as he says : 'All right.'

Medium shot of the group as the match begins. Marcus is very careful. Twice McTeague rushes him and he cleverly steps away. The third time Mac charges him with his head bowed, and Marcus raises himself to his full height and clasps both arms around Mac's neck. Mac reaches for him and accidentally rips away the sleeve of his shirt.

Medium shot of the spectators laughing.

Close-up of Mrs. Ryer as she yells :

TITLE : 'Keep your shirt on.'

Back to a medium shot of the scene. The two men continue grappling at each other, tearing up clods of turf. Suddenly, they fall to the ground with a tremendous thud. As they go down, Marcus writhes in the dentist's grasp like an eel, and lands on his side. McTeague crashes down on top of him like a felled ox.

Close-up of Heise as he says, with a gesture and pantomime : 'Now you got to turn him on his back; he ain't down if you don't.'

Medium close-up of the two men on the ground. Mac digs into Marcus's shoulder with his huge, salient chin. Marcus begins to yield; one shoulder comes down, then the other starts going. Mac applies more pressure and the second shoulder finally comes down.

Close-up of Selina calling out shrilly :

TITLE : 'Ain't Doctor McTeague just that strong!'

214

Close-up of Marcus as he hears her and becomes enraged. He speaks, spitting out words as a snake spits its venom :

Title : ' Damn you ! Get off me ! '

Back to medium close-up of the two men. Marcus twists his head and bites through the lobe of Mac's ear; bright red blood flows all over Mac's face and down his right side.
Medium shot of the scene as the others run over to them. McTeague rises to his feet.

Close-up of McTeague, whose expression is terrible. He bellows once like a hurt beast, then catches Marcus's wrist in both hands and swings him into the air by one arm, like a hammer-thrower swinging his hammer. Marcus's feet flip from the ground; he spins through the air above McTeague's face like a bundle of clothes. Mac lets go of him and Marcus falls to the ground.
Close-up of McTeague in a terrible rage.
Medium close-up of Marcus on the ground as he touches his injured arm with his other hand. A third joint is visible between elbow and wrist.

215

Medium shot of the scene as Heise and Ryer run over and separate the two men.

Close-up of Selina as she turns her head away, covering her face with her hands.

Close-up of Trina wringing her hands and crying in dread : 'Stop them, don't let them fight.'

Back to a medium shot of the scene. Heise clings to Mac and says : 'Don't make a fool of yourself. Listen to me, that's enough.' Trina rushes forward and tries to get hold of Mac :

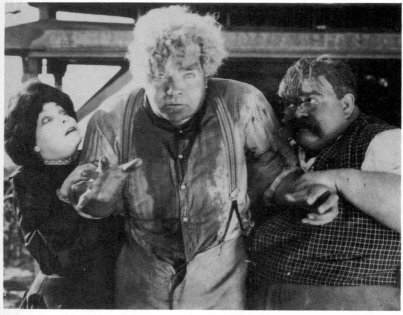

TITLE : ' Mac, dear, listen, it's me, it's Trina, look at me.'

Back to the scene as Heise yells to Ryer to take hold of Mac's other arm.

Close-up of Heise speaking :

TITLE : ' For God's sake, hold up, Doc! Will you? You don't want to kill him, do you? '

Back to the scene. Mrs. Ryer and Mrs. Heise are screaming.

Close-up of Selina giggling with hysteria.

Medium close-up of Marcus as he rises, his arm dangling down at his side. He is terrified, but does not run. With his healthy arm he picks up a jagged stone and stands, ready to defend himself. His injured right arm is terribly swollen, the back of the hand is twisted to where the palm should be, and his face is spotted with Mac's blood and grass stains.

Medium shot of McTeague, covered with blood, being held by Heise, Ryer and Trina. He struggles to tear himself free:

TITLE: 'I'll kill him! Let go of me, will you! I'll kill him!'

Back to the scene. Little by little they manage to pacify Mac. As they let go of him, he turns away and lets his arms fall, then he feels the blood running down, touches his ear with his hand and apparently sees the blood for the first time. Heise goes up to him.
Medium close-up of Heise, McTeague and Trina. Pointing to the bleeding ear, Heise asks: 'What's the best thing to do, Doc?' Mac says: 'Huh? What do ya mean?' Heise repeats the question. Mac does not answer, but stares at the bloodstained bosom of his shirt. Trina speaks:

217

TITLE: 'Mac, tell us the best thing we can do to stop your ear bleeding.'

Back to the scene as Trina and Heise look at him anxiously. McTeague replies:

TITLE: 'Collodium.'

Back to the scene as Heise and Trina both say: 'We haven't got any, we can't get that.' Suddenly, Heise gets an idea and says, 'There is some ice in our lunch basket.' Mac says:

TITLE: 'Ice, sure, ice — that's the word.'

Back to the scene as they rush out of the frame in the direction of the basket.
Medium close-up of Mrs. Heise and Mr. and Mrs. Ryer bandaging Marcus's arm.
Close-up of Selina sitting on the slope of the grass, gasping, sobbing and laughing hysterically.
Medium shot of McTeague, Trina and Mr. Heise. Trina tears a napkin into strips while Heise crushes some of the ice. They make a bandage and start bandaging Mac's head.
Close-up of Selina, who continues to giggle hysterically. With a peal of laughter, she cries out:

TITLE: 'Oh, what a way for our picnic to end!'
Iris out.

Iris in on Zerkow's bedroom. Zerkow is in his nightshirt. He gets into bed and pulls up the covers. Maria is sitting on the bed in a stupor; her chin rests in her hands, her elbows on her knees, as she gazes into space. Zerkow, now under the covers, moves close to her from behind. Propping his chin in his hand and his elbow on the cushion, he says:

TITLE: 'Now then, my girl, let's have it all over again — there were a hundred pieces.'

Back to the scene as Maria turns, looks at him abstractedly and replies:

TITLE: 'I don't know what you're talking about, Zerkow.'

Back to the scene as Zerkow replies: 'I mean the gold plate, the service.' Maria answers:

TITLE: 'There never was no gold plate — no gold service neither. I guess you must have dreamed it.'

Close-up of Zerkow as he looks at her, claws eagerly at his lips with his lean fingers and says : 'Go on, Maria, begin! Begin! The gold plate had . . .'
Close-up of Maria frowning at him as she asks : ' What gold plate? '
Close-up of Zerkow. Staring at her, he sits back and says : 'Your people's gold dishes. You told me about it a hundred times! '
Close-up of Maria as she speaks :

TITLE : ' You're crazy! '

Medium shot of them both. Zerkow gets sore and grabs her wrist, then twists it back and speaks :

TITLE : ' You fool! Don't try to cheat me or I'll do for you! '

Back to the scene as he twists her wrist a little more, pokes his face close to hers and says :

TITLE : ' You know where it is — I believe you got it and are hiding it from me! '

Back to the scene as he rolls his eyes wildly about the room, then lets go of her wrist. He shakes her by the shoulders, and says : ' Where is it? Is it here? Tell me or I'll do for you.' Maria says :

TITLE : ' It ain't here — it ain't anywhere. What gold plate? I don't remember nothun about no gold plate at all.'

Back to scene as Zerkow pushes against her shoulder, now raving mad. He says :

TITLE : ' I'll make you speak yet, I will. . . . '

Back to the scene as Maria replies : ' Aw, shut up! '
Iris out.]

Fade in.

TITLE : ' Marcus's attack was soon a forgotten incident. Mac's moods of wrath always faded in Trina's company.' [1]

Fade out.

Fade in on the McTeagues' bedroom. Mac is seated on the bed in pyjamas. [He takes off his socks, which he puts on the chair.] He gets

---

[1] This title does not appear in Stroheim's script, which had the following :
' Then came the Autumn, all in yellow clad.'

into bed, pulls the covers up and makes himself comfortable. Trina, wearing her nightgown and slippers, sits on the other side of the bed. [As she combs and brushes her marvellous hair, she reads a letter lying on the dresser.

Insert of the letter from her angle : 'Der carpet cleaning and uphol- stery pisness is no good. Der popper has bien obliged to take out a mortgage on der house. He vants to go to New Zealand. Der popper has found a man who vants to go in with somepoty in der ranching pisness, he wrote to Marcus and he toog it up. He is goming down here in der next week. Der tervins haf pin seek with der measles and Owgooste had to go to work. My dear little girl could you lend your poor Mommer $50? ']

Medium close-up of Trina [as she continues brushing her hair]. She turns towards Mac.

Shot from her angle of Mac, half-asleep with his mouth wide open.

Shot from his angle of Trina as she speaks :

TITLE : ' [Say Mac, what do you think.] Mama wants me . . .'

Close-up of Trina speaking :

TITLE : '. . . wants us to send her $50. [She says they're hard up.] '

Shot from her angle of Mac as he looks up, startled, and says : ' Huh? What? '

Back to a shot of Trina from his angle as she repeats what she has said.

Shot from her angle of Mac [first sitting up, then leaning back again on the cushions] as he speaks :

TITLE : ' Well, I guess we can send it, can't we? '

Shot from his angle of Trina, as she puts her little chin in the air and says :

TITLE : ' I wonder if Mommer thinks we're millionaires.'

Shot from her angle of Mac [who sits up again, propping himself up on his elbow] as he replies :

TITLE : ' Trina, you're getting to be a regular stingy, you're getting worse and worse every day.'

Shot from his angle of Trina saying :

TITLE : ' But fifty dollars is fifty dollars . . . [that's two months of our interest].'

Shot from her angle of Mac as he says :

TITLE: 'Well you've got a lot saved up, and besides you still got all o' your $5,000.'

Shot from his angle of Trina, who is very agitated and puts her hands on her hips as she retorts:

TITLE: 'Don't talk that way Mac. That money is never . . . never going to be touched. [I don't believe I've got $50 saved.]'

Back to close-up of Trina.
Shot from her angle of Mac, laughing as he covers up again. [With a gesture, he says: 'Aw, don't kid me.']
Shot from his angle of Trina standing with her back to him. With a slightly sinister look and her finger held thoughtfully to her lip, Trina turns to Mac [and says with a gesture: 'I have not! I have not! You know I haven't!' She continues:

TITLE: 'I can't afford to send her $50.00.']

Close-up of Mac, apparently asleep.
[Shot from her angle of Mac as he says: 'Well, what'll ya do then."
Shot from his angle of her as she speaks:

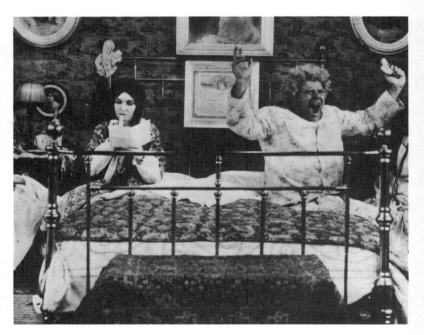

221

TITLE : ' I tell you what we'll do, Mac. We'll send her $25. You send half and I'll send half. How'll that be? '

Shot from her angle of Mac as he nods and says : ' Sure ! '
Back to Trina as she moves closer to Mac, holds out her hand and says : ' Gi' me the money before you forget it.'
Shot from her angle of Mac as he leans over, grabs his pants and then takes out the money. He leans across the bed as Trina sits down on the other side and holds out her hand.
Close-up of Mac as he puts $12.50 into her hand.]
Medium long shot of the scene. Trina is sitting on the bed, looking at Mac.
[She takes the money, walks over to the dresser and puts it in the drawer. Mac lies down again, rolls over on his side, and closes his eyes. Trina finishes braiding her hair and starts putting some cold cream on her face and hands. She walks over to Mac's side of the bed, stoops, looks at him and then at the pants, and then back to him.]
Close-up of Trina as she says : ' Mac? '
Shot from her angle of Mac, sleeping soundly and snoring.
Back to a close-up of Trina. She is smiling.
Medium long shot of the scene. Mac rolls over towards the centre of the bed in his sleep, and Trina sneaks up to the chair at his side of the bed and picks up Mac's pants. She goes through the pockets and removes his money. [She counts it, figures for a second, then keeps some of the money in her hand and puts the rest back into his pocket.]
Close-up of Trina holding the money. She glances at Mac.
Flash of Mac asleep.[1]
Back to medium long shot of Trina tiptoeing back around the bed.
Medium close-up as she puts the money away.

TITLE : ' If Mommer really needs the money so badly she'll write again.'

Medium shot of Trina. She sits, rubbing her hands together like a miser as she puts on cold cream.
Iris down on her hands, hold for a second, then iris out.

---

[1] The following five shots and the title did not appear in Stroheim's original script, which had the following :
' She turns and looks at her hand.
Shot from her angle of the money in her hand : $12.50.
Back to medium shot. Smiling, Trina sneaks over to the dresser and puts the $12.50 into the drawer containing the money Mac gave her. She closes the drawer, then returns to the bed, turns out the light and climbs in. Iris out.'

Fade in on a pile of gold coins against a black velvet background. Two elongated hands are playing greedily with the coins. Fade out.[1]

[Iris in on Zerkow's bedroom. Maria is in bed. On Zerkow's side of the bed the cover is thrown back, and the pillow has an impression in it. Maria turns in her sleep, and her hand accidentally strikes the place where Zerkow's head should be.

Close-up of Maria's hand on Zerkow's pillow, feeling for his head.

Close-up of Maria's half-asleep face as she realizes that Zerkow is not in bed.

Back to a medium shot of the scene, illuminated by the rays of moonlight coming through the small window. Maria sits up in bed, looks around for Zerkow, then realizes he is not there. She leans over and lights the stump of a candle; she listens for a moment, then gets out of bed. Putting a dirty wrapper around her body, Maria takes the candle and sneaks off towards the stairway.

Medium shot of Maria at the top of the stairway. With the candle in her hand, she starts to descend very carefully, on tiptoe.

Medium shot at the bottom of the stairway as Maria appears from above. Shading the candle with her hand, she stops at the bottom and listens into the night. She then turns and starts walking towards the kitchen curtain.

Medium shot of the curtain in the rear that separates the kitchen from the junk shop. Maria appears with the candle, goes to the slit in the curtain and carefully starts to peek through.

Close-up from behind the curtain as Maria's head pokes through.

Shot from her angle of Zerkow. By the light of a lantern, he is breaking up the floorboards in front of the sink with a pickaxe.

Close-up of Zerkow as he stops and says :

TITLE : ' There were more than a hundred pieces and every one of them gold.'

Back to medium shot as he goes back to the digging.

Shot from his angle of the broken boards and the ground beneath.

Back to a close-up of Zerkow as he speaks :

TITLE : ' I'll find it yet — it's hid somewhere in this house.'

Back to a close-up of Maria peeking.

Back to a medium shot from her angle of Zerkow as he looks around disappointedly. He taps the floor in different places, then the walls.

---

[1] This symbolic shot does not appear at this point in Stroheim's script.

Close-up of Zerkow; something in the direction of the curtain seems to attract his attention. He turns suddenly and looks towards Maria.

Shot from his angle of Maria's face peeking through the opening in the curtain.

Back to a close-up of Zerkow as he realizes that Maria is watching him. His expression becomes menacing.

Back to shot from his angle of Maria's face disappearing quickly.

Medium shot of Zerkow as he looks around for something. A horse-whip which he uses on his cart is standing by the curtain. Furious, he grabs the whip and runs off, carrying the lantern in his other hand.

Medium shot from the bottom of the stairway as Maria, frightened to death, runs up the stairs.

Medium shot of Maria appearing at the top of the stairway.

Back to medium shot of the bottom of the stairway as Zerkow runs up the stairs with his whip and the lantern.

Medium shot of Maria at her side of the bed. She blows out the candle, and quickly gets in, covering herself with the bed cover.

Back to medium shot as Zerkow reaches the top of the stairway. He stops and looks over in the direction of Maria.

Shot from his angle of Maria completely hidden under the bed cover.

Medium shot of Zerkow as he approaches her menacingly.

Medium shot of Maria's side of the bed. Zerkow walks over with the whip and tears off the bed cover. His eyes are almost popping out of his head. Maria, pretending that she's just been awakened, sits up and says : ' What do ya want? '

Close-up of Zerkow as he speaks :

TITLE : ' Where is it, you beast! Tell me where it is! '

Close-up from his angle of Maria, who shakes her head and says : ' I don't know.'

Back to Zerkow as he snarls : ' I'll make you speak.' He raises the arm with the whip, and then viciously brings it down onto her.

Back to a close-up of Maria as the whip hits her, and she protects her head with her arms.

Back to flash of Zerkow as he strikes her again, harder.

Back to Maria as the whip hits her arms. Maria says :

TITLE : ' I'd tell you if I knew — but I don't know nothun about it.'

Medium shot of the scene. Zerkow suddenly throws down the whip and takes a large knife from his pants pocket, and quickly opens the blade as he raises the knife.

Close-up of Zerkow with the raised knife, glowering menacingly at

Maria.

Flash of Maria, terrified; she tries to move away.

Medium shot of Zerkow holding Maria, the knife drawn above her throat.

Back to close-up of Zerkow as he says :

TITLE : ' I know you got it hid somewhere. Tell me or I'll do for you ! '

Medium shot of Marcus's room, which is in great confusion. Marcus is in the midst of packing an absurdly inadequate trunk. He is trying to stuff in a pair of cowboy boots; he tries every possible arrangement but the boots simply do not fit.

Close-up of Marcus as he speaks :

TITLE : ' By damn ! I've tried you so — and I've tried you so — and you won't go.'

Back to the scene. He is trying again, and continues :

TITLE : ' Pretty soon, I won't take you at all — you . . .'

Medium shot of the front of Zerkow's fence; lit by the greenish light coming from the street lantern. Maria runs out of the yard. She is barefoot and dressed in her nightgown, with a crazy-quilt around her for warmth. She looks around fearfully for a second, then runs off as fast as she can towards Laguna Street.

Medium shot of McTeague's bedroom. McTeague, wearing pyjamas, is sitting on one side of the bed taking a foot bath. Trina is sitting on the other side dressed in a kimono, and her hair is up in curlers. She holds a nail-file and buffer and is manicuring her nails.

Close-up of Trina as she looks at them critically.

Big close-up from her angle of her nails; they are very beautful.

Medium shot of the top of the stairway as Maria appears on the run, absolutely out of breath. She almost falls over herself. She looks around for a second, not knowing where to turn, then sees Marcus's room and runs towards it.

Medium shot of the hallway outside Marcus's room. Maria runs up and bangs on the door. It is opened from the inside and she quickly slips in.

Medium shot of Maria and Marcus in the room. Maria, beside herself, begs Marcus to lock the door and not let Zerkow get her.

Close-up of Maria, her eyes almost popping out. She is trembling all over with fear. She tells Marcus her story, indicating the length of the knife, and Zerkow's attitude when he raised it ready to kill her.

Medium shot of the top of the stairway as Zerkow, knife still in his hand, comes up the stairs and looks around. He calls Maria.

Medium shot of Maria and Marcus just inside Marcus's room. Maria begs Marcus not to let Zerkow get her. Marcus gestures, ' I'll break him in two — do ya think I'm afraid of his knife? '

Medium shot of the hall outside Marcus's room as Zerkow sneaks up and listens.

Close-up of Zerkow as he yells : ' I know where you are . . . you're in here . . . I'll do for you yet, my girl, come out of there and see if I don't.' Marcus opens the door, stands in the doorway and says : ' I'll do for you myself.'

Close-up of Zerkow as he speaks :

TITLE : ' I want my wife. What's she mean by running into your room? '

Close-up of Maria speaking very excitedly to Marcus : ' Look out, he's got a knife ! '

Close-up of Zerkow as he hears her and says : ' Ah, there you are. Come out of there and come back home.'

Medium shot of the scene as McTeague and Trina appear. They are

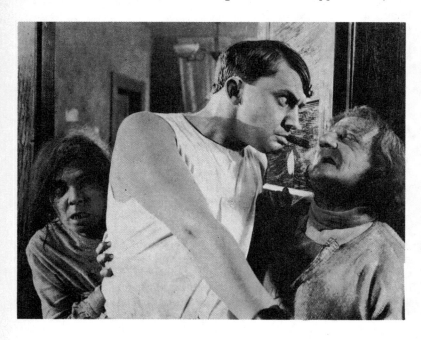

dressed in bathrobes and McTeague is barefoot. They look on with curiosity. Miss Baker and Old Grannis appear from their side. They also wear bathrobes and Miss Baker's hair is in paper curlers.

Close-up of Marcus as he booms : 'Get out of here yourself.'

Back to close-up of Zerkow. He is a little scared of Marcus and answers : 'I'll go, but she's got to come too.'

Back to a close-up of Marcus as he yells : 'Get out of here and put up that knife.'

In medium shot, Marcus wrenches the knife away from Zerkow, then grabs his shoulders, spins him around and kicks him in the seat. Zerkow falls on the floor.

Close-up of Marcus flaming.

Medium shot of the entire group, as Zerkow rises timidly and says : 'I want Maria.' Marcus retorts : 'Get out of here or I'll put you out.' Zerkow runs away.

Close-up of Marcus as he says :

TITLE : 'Huh . . . thinks I'm afraid of his knife . . . I ain't afraid of anybody ! '

Back to the scene as Marcus looks towards McTeague.

Medium shot of the front of the house. Zerkow appears from inside, looks back and then runs off in the direction of his own house.

Medium shot of the group in the hallway outside Marcus's door. Maria comes out into the hall. They all crowd around her, to find out what had happened. Maria begins to explain.

Close-up of Marcus as he asks : 'What did ya tell him about them gold dishes for in the first place ? '

Close-up of Maria, who replies :

TITLE : 'I never told him. I never heard of no gold dishes. I don't know where he got the idea. He must be crazy.'

Back to the scene as they all look at each other.

Medium shot of Zerkow running into his bedroom. He looks wildly about, then gets an idea and runs over to Maria's side of the bed. He lifts up the bed cover, then the sheet and mattress, and finally peers underneath the bed.

Back to a medium shot of the group outside Marcus's door as Maria finishes her story.

Close-up of Maria, who says :

TITLE : 'I guess I'll go back now. I ain't 'fraid of him so long as he ain't got no knife.'

Back to the scene as Marcus tells her to just call him if Zerkow gets 'funny' again. Maria leaves, and the others head back to their own rooms. Marcus enters his room and closes the door. Fade out.

Horizontal barn door in on a man's figure standing in front of a glass door pane with the black lettering : 'State Board of Dentistry'. (We can see only the torso of the man from his shoulders to his waist.) One of his hands holds a cane; the other knocks at the door.
Medium shot of an official seated at a desk inside the office. He hears the knock and says : 'Come in.'
Back to the man outside. The scene is still framed by a horizontal barn door. One hand opens the door and the figure disappears inside; the barn door closes. Iris out.]

Iris in on a medium shot of McTeague's dining room. It is evening and the light is very weak. The window is open and the curtains are blowing in a nice breeze. McTeague is sitting in an armchair with a glass of beer in his hand, and his pipe. Trina cuddles herself down on McTeague's lap and kisses the bald spot on the top of his head.

TITLE : 'Trina's miserly attitude grew steadily through the following months . . . but her brusque outbursts of affection kept her tolerable to the slow-thinking McTeague.' [1]

[Medium close-up of Trina playfully putting her fingers into Mac's ears and eyes. Suddenly she gets very passionate and embraces his thick head and neck with her small arms. She draws his ear closer to her mouth and whispers :

TITLE : 'Do you love me, Mac, dear? Love me Big? BIG?'

Back to the scene as McTeague, puzzled, nods. Trina, dissatisfied, says :

TITLE : 'But I want you to say so!'

Back to the scene as McTeague nods and Trina says :

TITLE : 'Say it then.'

Back to the scene as McTeague says :

TITLE : 'Well, then — I love you.'

Back to the scene as Trina, dissatisfied, insists :

TITLE : 'But you don't say it of your own accord!'

---

[1] This title does not appear in Stroheim's original script.

Back to the scene as McTeague, puzzled, says : 'Well . . . What . . .
I don't understand ! ' Trina kisses him full on the mouth.]
Medium shot as the couple continue to kiss and embrace.
Medium shot of the entrance to the flat. Marcus stands at the door
with a cane in his hand and knocks. (Although he does not wear the
same suit as the man who knocked on the door of the State Board of
Dentistry, the way in which he holds the cane and knocks with the
knuckle of his right middle finger should be enough to identify him as
the same man.)
Close-up of Trina who, startled by the sound, glances in the direction
of the door.
Back to medium shot of Marcus at the door.
Medium shot of McTeague and Trina, both looking embarrassed. Trina
scrambles off McTeague's lap and gestures : 'Put on your coat, Mac,
and smooth your hair.' While she puts the beer bottles away, Mac
quickly puts on his coat and smooths his hair. Trina goes towards the
door and switches on the light.
Medium long shot of Trina as she approaches the door and opens it.
Medium shot of Trina opening the door and uttering an exclamation
of surprise. Marcus, perfectly at ease, stands in the doorway.
Close-up of Marcus speaking : 'Say, can I come in? '
Close-up of Trina, who looks from Marcus to Mac enquiringly.
Close-up of Mac replying : 'Why, I suppose . . . why, of course,
come in.'
Close-ups of Marcus jovial, Trina disturbed, Mac surprised; Trina
opening the door wider, Marcus entering, Marcus's Persian cat sneak-
ing through the open door; Trina inviting Marcus to a seat.
Close-up of Mac as he says : 'Yes, yes, come in; [have some beer.'
With that he bends down and takes a beer bottle and glasses from
underneath the table. Marcus says : 'No, thanks, Doctor.']
Close-up of Trina gesturing to Mac to be careful what he says to
Marcus.
Medium long shot of the entire scene as all three sit down at the table.
Marcus is seated between the couple with Trina slightly behind him.[1]
Medium shot of all three as Marcus speaks :

TITLE : ' Well, bygones is bygones, ain't they Mac? '

---

[1] In the original script Trina was seated beside McTeague and communicated
with him by punching him in the back when Marcus wasn't looking. As shot,
the film has Trina gesturing to Mac behind Marcus's back as they sit at the
table.

Close-up of McTeague replying :

Title : ' Sure.'

Back to close-up of Mac.
Medium close-up of Trina and Marcus as Marcus looks around, taking everything in, and says :

Title : ' Well, how's business, Doc? '[1]

Back to medium close-up of Trina cautioning McTeague behind Marcus's back as he finishes speaking. When Marcus looks at her she acts as if she's merely adjusting her hair.
Back to close-up of Mac. [He smiles good-humouredly and says :

Title : ' Oh, I don't know; we don't complain.']

Medium close-up of Trina and Marcus as Marcus asks :

Title : ' Plenty of money? '

Back to medium close-up of Trina gesturing, ' No,' behind his back.
Close-up of McTeague with a blank look on his face.
Back to medium close-up of Trina and Marcus, who smiles knowingly as he says :

Title : ' Lots to do? '

Medium close-up of Trina and Marcus, who continues :

Title : ' Everything fine, huh? '

Close-up of McTeague.
Back to medium close-up of Trina and Marcus. This time Trina speaks :

Title : ' We've got lots to do . . .'

Back to Trina and Marcus as she concludes :

Title : ' But we haven't got no money.'

Close-up of Mac.
Medium close-up of Trina and Marcus, who says :

Title : ' Well, I'm goin' away. Goin' in ranchin' with an English

---

[1] The original script had the following title after this : ' Well, you two are pretty happy together, ain't you? '

duck.'

[Back to medium close-up of Marcus with Trina, who says: 'Yes, I know.'

TITLE: 'Mama wrote me.']¹

Back to medium shot of the entire scene.
Close-up of Trina asking: 'How long are you going to be gone?'
Back to Marcus as he speaks:

TITLE: 'Coming back? Why? I ain't never coming back.'

Close-up of Trina reacting with surprise.
Close-up of McTeague.
Medium shot of all three as Marcus concludes:

TITLE: 'I came t' say goodbye.'

---

[1] In Stroheim's original script Marcus does not tell Trina where he is going until after this point and the title is slightly different: 'I'm goin' in ranchin' with an English duck, goin' to raise some cattle.'

Back to medium shot of the scene as they continue talking. Fade out.
[1]Iris in on a medium shot of Marcus's cat sitting in McTeague's operating chair and looking up. Iris holds for a second, then opens fully to reveal the bird cage suspended from the ceiling just above the operating chair.
Extreme close-up of the cat with a terrible glint in its eyes.
Shot from its angle of two birds, male and female canaries, cuddled up to each other without seeing the cat.
Back to extreme close-up of the cat's face. Fade out.
[Iris down on one eye, hold for a second, then iris out completely.]
Fade back in to a medium shot of the scene as all three rise from the table. [Marcus says : 'Well, goodbye, Doctor.' He stretches out his hand and McTeague says : 'Goodbye, Marcus.'] The two men shake hands and Marcus speaks :

TITLE : ' I guess we won't never see each other again.'

Back to medium close-up of the two men.
Medium shot of the entire scene as McTeague speaks :

TITLE : 'I guess so.'

Back to the scene. [Marcus says : ' But good luck to you, Doc.']
Then medium close-up of Marcus and Trina as he turns to her, [shakes hands] and says : ' Goodbye.' Marcus moves towards the door.
Close-up of McTeague looking on.
[Medium shot of all three at the door. Marcus opens it and starts to speak.]
Close-up of Marcus which dissolves into an extreme close-up of the cat.
Close-up of the two canaries in their cage.
Extreme close-up of the cat dissolves back into a close-up of Marcus speaking :

TITLE : ' [Goodbye.] Good luck to you both.'

Back to medium shot of the scene as they both exchange farewells. Marcus disappears through the door and closes it behind him. Trina is laughing and playfully nudges Mac in the stomach with her elbow. She mimics Marcus's way of speaking :

TITLE : 'Goodbye ! That's the best thing I ever heard Marcus say.'

Back to medium close-up of Mac holding Trina in his arms. Iris out

---

[1] In the original script, the following brief scene between the cat and the birds occurs at the conclusion of the scene with Marcus.

on their faces.

TITLE : 'So Marcus had left . . . left for good. Never again should they be disturbed by him.' [1]

[Iris in on a medium shot of a patient sitting in the dental chair in McTeague's dental parlour.
Medium shot of the opposite corner of the room where there are three chairs, one of them occupied by another patient.
Medium shot of a letter carrier standing outside McTeague's door with the mail. The postman gets three or four letters together, and shoves them through the letter slit.]
Iris in on a medium shot inside the door as all the letters fall through the slit and land on the floor.
Medium close-up of Trina busily working in the kitchen.
[Close-up of McTeague, who turns as he works and looks towards the door.
Medium close-up of a butcher boy sitting near the door. He picks up the letters and walks towards the office.
Medium shot of McTeague and the patient in the chair. The boy enters and puts the letters on the rack. McTeague thanks him and the boy leaves. McTeague has finished with the patient in the chair. The patient rises and walks away. The next one comes up to the chair and sits down.]
Medium close-up of McTeague getting ready for the next patient. He picks up the three letters and looks at them.
[Close-up of the first envelope, which is from the 'Dental Supply Company'.
Back to Mac as he puts down the letter and takes the next one.
Close-up of the envelope from the 'Milliner'.
Back to Mac as he puts back the second letter and takes the last one.]
Close-up of Mac's hand holding an oblong envelope. Instead of a stamp, the inscription 'Official Business' appears. The printed return address in the left corner reads 'Office State Board of Dentistry' and the envelope is addressed to: 'Mr. McTeague, Polk Street, San Francisco.'
Back to close-up of McTeague as he opens the envelope.
Close-up of the cat sneaking through the open bay window and along the window ledge. With mean eyes it looks up towards the canary bird cage.
Shot from its angle of the bird cage; the two little birds are singing

---

[1] This title does not appear in Stroheim's original script.

233

happily.

Extreme close-up of the cat's face and its mean eyes.

Close-up of Mac reading the letter.[1]

Insert of the letter :

February 10, 1922

John McTeague,
611 Polk St.,
San Francisco.

Dear Sir :

Information has been received at this office that you are engaged in the practice of Dentistry without having in your possession a diploma from a recognized Dental College nor a license issued by the Dental Board of State of California authorizing you to do so.

You are therefore and herewithin enjoined from further practicing dentistry.

It is our duty to inform you that violations of the Dental Practice Act are punishable and subject to criminal prosecution.

Very truly yours,

(signed)

C. J. Rogers

Attorney for Board of

Dental Examiners of California

Extreme close-up of the cat crouching as it eyes the bird cage.

Close-up of the bird cage.

Close-up of the cat running and jumping.

Close-up of the bird cage as the cat pounces and then hangs on the cage, clawing at the birds which flutter about in fright.

Close-up of McTeague with the letter in his hand. He looks up and swats at the cat with the hand holding the letter.

Medium shot of the scene as the cat jumps onto the window sill.

Back to close-up of McTeague as he looks up towards the cage to see if the birds are all right. [He then looks blankly at the letter, not understanding it. He looks from the letter to the waiting patient. He puts down the letter and starts working.

Medium shot of the McTeagues' kitchen. The rays of the midday sun

---

[1] Stroheim's original script had the following insert for the letter :

' As you have never received a diploma from a Dental College, you are in consequence thereof and herewith prohibited and enjoined from further continuing to practice the Dental profession any longer. Legal extract bearing upon the case attached in small type.'

strike the centre of the room, revealing that everything is neat and clean as a whistle. Trina is dressed in a blue calico skirt and a crisp, new pink linen shirt-waist secured by an imitation alligator-skin belt; her enormous tiara of hair is neatly combed and coiled. She is wearing rubber gloves and her sleeves are rolled up as she washes the breakfast dishes.

Close-up of Trina singing happily as she looks up from the basin towards the kitchen shelves.

Shot from her angle of the shelves lined with highly-polished pots and pans that gleam in the sunlight.

Medium shot as she carries on washing the dishes.

Medium shot of Trina as she finishes the dishes. Still singing, she moistens a sponge in the sink, picks up a dry cloth, and goes out towards the dining room.]

Medium shot of the dining room. The sun's rays strike the table, revealing that here, too, everything is clean and neat as a whistle. Trina, still wearing the rubber gloves, starts to wipe the table top with the sponge.

Medium shot of McTeague's office. [McTeague finishes his work; the patient rises and leaves. McTeague turns to the moveable rack on which the mail is lying. He seems very preoccupied.] McTeague takes the open letter and rereads it, then shakes his head and says : ' I don't know . . . I don't know.' He looks in the direction of the door leading into the bedroom and starts walking towards it.

Medium shot of the dining room as Trina, still singing, finishes sponging the table, and then looks up.

Medium shot of McTeague looking confused and stupid as he comes through the archway with the letter and its envelope in his hand.

Medium shot of Trina as Mac appears and she asks : ' What is it, dear? ' McTeague hands her the letter.

Close-up of Trina reading it.

Close-up of her hand holding the sponge. As she reads, her hand squeezes the sponge — water starts dripping out.

Medium shot of Trina and Mac, as she asks : ' What's all this? ' Mac shakes his head and replies : ' I don't know.' Holding the letter in one hand and the sponge in the other, Trina sits down at the table. Mac joins her and Trina spreads the letter out in front of them.

[Medium close-up of them both as Trina speaks :

TITLE : ' Say, Mac, didn't you ever go to a Dental College? '

Back to the scene as McTeague says : ' Huh? What? ' Trina asks :

235

TITLE : ' How did you learn to be a dentist? '

Back to the scene as McTeague tells her. Trina interrupts and repeats :

TITLE : ' But didn't you ever go to a college? '

Back to the scene as McTeague shakes his head and says : ' College? No, I never went — learned from a fella.'
Back to the scene as Trina rolls down her sleeves and fastens the buttons of the cuffs as she says :

TITLE : ' But you know you can't practice unless you're graduated from a college. You haven't the right to call yourself *Doctor*.'

Back to the scene. McTeague stares at her as he says :

TITLE : ' Why — haven't I practiced ten years? — more, nearly twelve? '

Back to the scene as he finishes speaking, and Trina starts to reply :

TITLE : ' . . . But you can't practice unless you've got a diploma.'

Back to the scene as she finishes speaking, and he asks :

TITLE : ' What's that? A diploma? '

Back to the scene as he finishes speaking and she starts to answer :

TITLE : ' I don't know exactly, it's a kind of paper that — that — Oh, Mac, we're ruined.'

Back to the scene as Trina's eyes fill with tears. Mac is very agitated, and cries :

TITLE : ' Ain't I a Dentist? Ain't I a Doctor? Look at my sign and the gold tooth you gave me.']

Close-up of the cat after the birds again.
Close-up of the bird cage.
Back to the scene. [Trina resettles a hairpin at the back of her head and then says : ' Let's read this again.'] They both read the letter. When Trina has finished she says :

TITLE : ' Why it isn't possible ! [What difference does a diploma make if you're a first class dentist?] '

Back to the scene as McTeague shakes his head and declares :

236

Title : ‘ Well I ain’t gonna quit for just a piece of paper.’ [1]

Back to the scene.
Close-up of the door bell in McTeague’s office ringing.
Back to the scene. Mac’s head turns at the sound.
Close-up of the door bell ringing again.
Back to the scene as they both hear the bell. McTeague rises and says :
‘ I got to go back to work.’
[Close-up of Trina. She holds the back of her hand against her lips as
she speaks :

Title : ‘ But you can’t. Don’t you see? Can’t you understand? You’ve
got to stop.’

Back to the scene. Mac does not understand what she is talking about.
Trina continues speaking :

Title : ‘ They’ll arrest you! You’ll go to prison! You can’t work —
we’re ruined! ’

Close-up of Mac as he replies :

Title : ‘ But he’s got an appointment with me.’

Close-up of Trina as she looks at him, thinks for a second, then makes
a resolution and says :]

Title : ‘ Go on Mac! Get all the money before they make you stop.’ [2]

Medium shot of the scene. Mac starts to take the letter with him, but
Trina stops him. He leaves, and she remains seated before the letter,
resting her head on both hands as she reads it over again. Then,
thoughtfully, she puts a finger to her lips.
Extreme close-up of the cat.
Close-up of the bird cage.
Close-up of Trina in soft focus. All at once she snaps her fingers with
a flash of intelligence and says :

Title : ‘ It’s Marcus that’s done it.’

Back to medium close-up of Trina as she stares in the direction of the
dental parlour.

---

[1] Stroheim’s script had a different title here :
  ‘ What was the good? I learned how to operate, wasn’t that enough? ’
[2] Stroheim’s script had a different title here :
  ‘ It ain’t possible they’ll make you stop. Go on Mac! Hurry before he goes.’

Medium shot of Mac working.

Back to medium close-up of Trina. Her eyes fill with tears which soon roll down her cheeks; she breaks down and buries her head in her arms on the table. Fade out.

[Iris in on medium shot of the McTeagues' bedroom from outside the window. It is night and in the background we can see McTeague's face revealed by the moonlight. Trina is standing at the window. She is dressed in her nightgown, a kimono and slippers; her hair hangs down her back in two long braids.

Close-up of Trina's face lit by the moonlight as she stares out of the window.

Close-up of McTeague staring at her.

Reverse angle close-up of Trina turning from the window and asking :

TITLE : 'Didn't you ever go to a Dental College, Mac?'

Close-up of Mac as he shakes his head and answers :

TITLE : 'I learned from the fellow I was apprenticed to. Ain't I got a right to do as I like?'

Back to a close-up of Trina as she says :

TITLE : 'If you know your profession, isn't that enough?'

Back to the scene as McTeague speaks :

TITLE : 'Suppose I go round to the City Hall and see them.'

Back to the scene as he finishes speaking.

Close-up of Trina, who shakes her head and says : 'No, no, don't you do it, Mac,' then continues :

TITLE : 'They'll ask you questions and then they'll find out and you'd be just as bad off as ever.'

Close-up of McTeague as he barks :

TITLE : 'Well, I ain't going to quit for just a piece of paper.'

Medium shot of both of them. Deep in thought, Trina moves away from the window and walks towards him. She passes the foot of the bed, turns and retraces her steps, then stops and turns towards Mac.

Close-up of Trina speaking :

TITLE : 'Oh, Mac, you've got to quit — you can't go on ! We'll both be sent to prison !'

Back to the scene as Trina finishes speaking.
Close-up of McTeague from her angle, staring blankly and slowly nodding his head.
Back to a close-up of Trina from his angle as she laments :

TITLE : ' — and now we're paupers — beggars — '

Back to Trina, who starts crying.
Medium shot as she walks towards Mac's side of the bed and sits heavily at the foot of it, burying her face in her hands.
Close-up of Trina in tears. She says :

TITLE : ' We've got to leave this flat where we've been so happy — and sell all the pretty things — everything.'

Trina starts to cry again; Mac quickly sits up in bed and moves closer to her.
Medium close-up of both of them. Trina is still crying as McTeague speaks :

TITLE : ' We've got your five thousand — and the money you've been savin' up.'

Back to the scene as Trina raises her head and looks inquisitively at Mac as he concludes :

TITLE : ' So we ain't paupers.'

Back to the scene as Trina, now apprehensive, asks : ' What do you mean, Mac? ' He replies :

TITLE : ' Well, we can live on that money until, until, until — '

Back to the scene as he breaks off with an uncertain movement of his shoulders and looks about stupidly. Trina snaps :

TITLE : ' Until what? There ain't never going to be any until! '

Back to the scene as she pauses dramatically and looks at Mac, who stares back at her. She then resumes her speech :

TITLE : ' We've got the interest and what I make with carving — that's about forty a month.'

Back to the scene as she continues speaking. McTeague sinks back into the cushion, turns away from her and looks out again towards the window.
Close-up of Trina as she concludes :

TITLE : 'You'll have to find something else to do.'

Close-up of McTeague, whose glance shifts from the window towards Trina as he asks :

TITLE : 'What will I find to do?'

Medium shot of both of them. Trina shrugs her shoulders. Iris out.]
Fade in.

TITLE : 'Only little by little did the McTeagues understand the calamity that had befallen them.' [1]

[Iris in on McTeague's office seen from outside the bay window towards the door that leads into the bedroom. McTeague is sitting in the operating chair, looking stupidly out of the window. His hands lie idly in his lap. The door in the background opens and Trina enters. She looks towards McTeague, then walks slowly up to him.
Close-up of Trina looking at Mac.
Close-up from her angle of McTeague seen through double veil. His eyes are wide open as he looks out of the window with an unseeing gaze, then turns slowly towards her.]
Medium close-up of both of them, seen through double veil. Trina puts both her arms around Mac's neck and lays his huge head upon her shoulder. He looks up at her and says :

TITLE : '[See? I —] I got everythin' fixed an' ready an' waitin' an' nobody's gonna come anymore.' [2]

[Back to the scene as she pats him on the cheek. He looks up at her and continues speaking :

TITLE : ' — and nobody's ever goin' to come anymore.'

Back to the scene as he throws his arms about her, drawing her closer to him and burying his face on her bosom.
Close-up again through double veil of Trina as she says, tearfully :

TITLE : 'Never mind, dear, it'll all come right in the end and we'll be poor together if we have to.']

Back to the scene. [McTeague looks up at her, then glances at the appointment slate. He points to it. Trina takes it down.] They both

---

[1] Stroheim's script had a different title here :
'And it was only by slow degrees that McTeague abandoned his profession.'
[2] Instead of ' — and nobody's gonna come anymore ', Stroheim's script had
' — and nobody comes ', thus leading into the next title.

look at it together.
Close-up of Trina.
[Close-up of the slate, which reads : Vanovitch, Wed. 2 p.m.

Mrs. Loughhead, Thurs. 9 a.m.
Little Heise, Thurs. at 1.30
Mrs. Watson, Friday
Vanovitch, Saturday at seven

Back to the scene as Trina hands him the little sponge attached to the slate and, in a pitiful way, says : ' Rub it all out.']
Close-up of the slate with her tears dropping on it.
Back to close-up of Trina.
Close-up of the letter from the dental authorities.
Back to the scene as Trina, smiling pitifully through her tears, looks up at Mac and says :

Title : ' That's the way to rub it out — by me crying on it.'

[Back to the scene as she passes her fingers over the tear-blurred writing and washes the slate clean.]
Close-up of the wet slate.
[Back to Trina saying : ' All gone — all gone.']

Close-up of McTeague, who nods stupidly in agreement [and echoes: 'All gone'].

Medium shot from outside the window as McTeague suddenly pulls himself up to his full height of six feet two inches; his enormous fists are raised over his head and block Trina from view. She ducks under his upraised arms and then reappears.

Medium close-up of McTeague and the back of Trina's head. His veins swell and his jaw protrudes. He growls:

Title: 'If I ever meet MARCUS SCHOULER . . .'

Back to close-up of Mac and Trina, who turns, catches her breath and speaks:

Title: 'If you . . . ever . . . do!'

Fade out on medium shot of the scene as Trina continues talking. [Iris in on the McTeagues' dining room door. Trina opens the door and stands there for a moment looking back as McTeague appears. He looks dully at the floor. She says something to him, and they walk away in the direction of the dividing hallway that leads to the toilets.

Medium shot from the top of the stairway as Trina and McTeague appear. She is a little bit ahead of him as they turn towards the right end of the hallway.

Medium shot from behind them as they walk through the open door of a small dingy room.

Reverse shot from inside the room as they enter, looking around, and then pause.

Medium close-up of both of them. Mac continues to inspect the room, while Trina watches him.

Quick pan shot from his angle across the room, ending on the window that leads out onto the roof of the neighbouring house.

Back to a medium shot of both of them. Still looking at Mac, Trina asks: 'Well, what do you think?' Mac glares at her and replies:

Title: 'I ain't going to live here.'

Back to Trina, who looks at him impatiently and states:

Title: 'This is the only thing we can afford.'

Back to the scene. With a sarcastic sneer McTeague says:

Title: 'Afford! You with your five thousand and the three hundred you got saved up talking about afford! You make me sick!'

Close-up of Trina, who stares at Mac and declares : ' Now, Mac, let's have this thing right.'
Close-up of McTeague, who says :

TITLE : ' Let's live decently until we can get a fresh start. We've got the money.'

Close-up of Trina, asking :

TITLE : ' Who's got the money? '

Close-up of McTeague replying : ' We've got it.'
Close-up of Trina as she says : ' We ! '
Close-up of McTeague as he insists :

TITLE : ' What's yours is mine and what's mine is yours, ain't it? '

Close-up of Trina, who rises to her full height and cries : ' No ! it's not ! '
Medium shot of the scene as she stamps her foot and repeats : ' No ! it's not ! '
Close-up of Trina insisting :

TITLE : ' It's all mine ! Mine ! You're not going to touch a penny of my five thousand — not a penny of that little money that I saved ! '

Back to the scene as she thinks for a second and then adds :

TITLE : ' That seventy-five.'

Close-up of McTeague as he sneers and corrects her :

TITLE : ' That two hundred, you mean.'

Back to a close-up of Trina. With raised eyebrows, she flippantly repeats :

TITLE : ' That seventy-five.'

Back to close-up of McTeague sneering and mumbling.
Back to close-up of Trina as she asserts :

TITLE : '. . . and we're just going to live on that forty.'

Back to close-up of McTeague : ' Think I'm going to do that and live in such a room as this? ' He shakes his head.
Back to close-up of Trina, who folds her arms, looks him squarely in the eye and taunts :

TITLE : ' Well, what are you going to do, then? '

Back to close-up of McTeague saying : ' Huh ? '
Back to close-up of Trina as she repeats her question and then adds :

TITLE : '. . . when you earn some money then we'll talk.'

Back to close-up of McTeague, who shakes his head and insists : ' I ain't going to live here.'
Back to close-up of Trina as she says : ' Oh, very well, suit yourself, I'm going to live here.'
Back to close-up of McTeague, who suddenly becomes infuriated. Pointing first to Trina then to himself, he bellows : ' You'll have to live where I tell you to.'
Back to close-up of Trina, who is just as angry as Mac and states :

TITLE : ' Then you'll pay the rent.'

Back to close-up of McTeague as he yells :

TITLE : ' Who's the boss, you or I ? '

Back to close-up of Trina flushing as she cries out : ' Who's got the money I'd like to know.'

Back to close-up of McTeague, now livid, who declares :

TITLE : ' You make me sick — you and your money.'

Back to close-up of Trina, who challenges him angrily :

TITLE : ' Do you know what I'm doing, McTeague ? '

Back to close-up of McTeague as he says : ' No.'

TITLE : ' I am supporting you.'

Back to close-up of McTeague as he mutters : ' Aw shut up, you make me sick.'
Medium shot as Trina quickly walks over to McTeague and stands next to him. He does not move.
Close-up of her foot stamping on the floor three or four times.
Medium close-up of both of them. There are tears in Trina's eyes as she cries :

TITLE : ' You got no right to talk to me that way. I won't have it ! '

Back to the scene as Trina stares at Mac with clenched teeth. McTeague calms down and suddenly gives in :

TITLE : ' Aw, live where you like, then ! '

Back to the scene as Trina looks up, appeased, and asks : ' Well, shall we take this room, then ? ' Disgusted, McTeague replies : ' Aw right, we will take it.' He then adds :

TITLE : ' But why can't you take a little of your money and — and sort of fix it up ? '

Back to the scene as Trina again flares up and yells : ' Not a penny, not a single penny.' McTeague looks at her and then says : ' Aw, I don't care what you do.' He starts to walk away.
Medium shot of both of them as Mac leaves the room.
Medium shot of the front door of McTeague's dental office. Dr. Percy Wilbur appears, looks at the sign and sneers. He opens the door and walks inside.
Shot from inside of the door and the bell on top of it. The dentist looks up at the bell and smiles, then closes the door and looks around. He sneers. The door opens again and McTeague enters.
Close-up of Dr. Wilbur, who bows gracefully to McTeague, says, ' How do,' and then hands McTeague a visiting card from a little pocket folder.
Close-up of McTeague glowering at the dentist as he takes the card and looks at it.

TITLE : ' Dr. Percy Wilbur, Dentist — Polk Street, San Francisco.'

Medium shot of both of them as Dr. Wilbur smiles broadly and says :

TITLE : ' They tell me, Doctor, that you're going out of the profession.'

Back to the scene as both men look towards the door.
Medium shot from their point-of-view as Trina enters, then slows down and looks at the stranger.
Close-up of Dr. Percy bowing gracefully.
Back to shot from their point-of-view of Trina, who apprehensively returns his greeting.
Medium shot of the scene.
Close-up of Dr. Percy as he says :

TITLE : ' I'd like to buy that big golden tooth that you got outside of your window. I don't suppose you'll have any further use for it.'

Back to the scene as Trina shoots a glance at her husband, who begins to glower again.
Back to close-up of Percy asking : ' What do ya say ? '

Close-up of McTeague as he replies :

TITLE : ' I guess not.'

Close-up of Trina annoyed, because Mac is passing up a chance to make some money.
Back to close-up of Dr. Percy as he says :

TITLE : ' What do you say to $10? '

Back to close-up of Trina, her chin in the air, echoing : ' Ten dollars? '
Back to Dr. Percy as he asks : ' Well, what figure do you put on it? '
Close-up of Trina, who thinks for a second and is just about to answer . . .
Close-up of McTeague. He lowers his head and growls : ' You get out of here.'
Medium shot as Dr. Percy says : ' What? ' Pointing to the door, McTeague bellows : ' Get the hell out of here.' As Dr. Percy retreats towards the door, McTeague turns with lowered head and goes for the doctor, who quickly opens the door and runs out. McTeague and Trina follow him into the hallway.
Shot from their point-of-view of the doctor running down the steps. Suddenly his head reappears.
Close-up of Percy calling through the balustrade :

TITLE : ' You don't want to trade anything for a diploma, do you? '

Medium close-up of McTeague and his wife exchanging looks.
Back to a medium shot as McTeague looks at the visiting card which is still in his hand. With a sudden impulse he tears it up and throws the pieces of paper in the air. Then they both slowly walk back towards the office door. Iris out.

Iris in on a cheap, temporary canvas sign above the entrance to McTeague's flat : ' Auction.'
Quick lap dissolve and iris in on a hand holding a gavel and knocking on a small table. Iris enlarges to reveal McTeague's dental office. The curtains and the pictures have been taken down, the bed covers are folded up, the mattress is against the wall and the bed is tied together. The melodeon and all other furnishings from the bedroom and the dining room, as well as the shiny tin pots from the kitchen, are all piled up on the floor. There are people coming and going; men and women with children and market baskets. Funny types of all descriptions are looking around. An Irishman with a big cigar and a derby is ' spieling '; a little Jew who also wears a derby acts as his helper. People are carrying out various things they have bought. Conspicuous

246

among the buyers are : Mr. and Mrs. Ryer who have the chenille portières; Joe Frenna, the bird store woman, the book seller, the restaurant man from downstairs, the palmist, Miss Baker and Mr. Grannis.

Medium close-up of Zerkow and the Irish spieler. Zerkow holds a glass jar containing some gold tape and several nickel-plated instruments. Close-up of them in natural colours.

Back to a medium close-up of Zerkow as he hands the gold tape and the instruments to the Irishman, who then lifts them up and names a price. Nobody wants them. Next to him stands Maria fingering the gold very excitedly.

Medium shot of McTeague and Trina sitting side by side in Miss Baker's room. They are holding hands and listening nervously to the turmoil that comes from the direction of their ' suite '. Next to them stands the giant gold tooth, the concertina and the bird cage.

Medium close-up of them both through single veil. Trina says :

TITLE : ' Mac, you must be reasonable.'

Back to the scene as Mac turns slowly and stares at her. Trina continues :

TITLE : ' The concertina would bring quite a sum and the bird cage is as good as new.'

Back to the scene as McTeague shakes his head and adamantly says : ' No.' Trina speaks and gestures :

TITLE : ' You'll have to do it sooner or later.'

Back to the scene as McTeague again shakes his head and repeats : ' No ! ' They look up towards the door.

Shot from their point-of-view of the open door as Miss Baker enters the room, carrying a little bundle of gay tidies that once hung over the McTeagues' chair backs.

Medium shot of the scene as Miss Baker quickly approaches Mac and Trina.

Close-up of Miss Baker, who holds out the tidies and says :

TITLE : ' I bought them three for a nickel. You don't mind, now do you, Mrs. McTeague? '

Medium close-up of Trina and McTeague from Miss Baker's angle. Trina shakes her head bravely and answers : ' Why, no, of course not, Miss Baker.'

Back to a close-up of Miss Baker saying : 'They'll look very pretty on some of my chairs.'
Medium shot of the three of them as Miss Baker spreads one tidy over the back of a chair for inspection. She turns to Trina and says : 'See? ' Trina nods and says : 'Very pretty.' McTeague nods dully in agreement. Fade out.
Fade in.

Title : ' At last that dreadful day was over.'

Fade out.
Iris in on a medium shot of McTeague, Trina and Miss Baker standing near the door of Miss Baker's room. Miss Baker holds the door ajar and is listening to the sounds in the hallway. McTeague and Trina, holding hands, are also listening.
Medium shot of the hallway in front of McTeague's office as the Irishman who puffs on a cigar and the Jew who smokes a cigarette appear from inside and slam the door behind them. The Irishman slaps the Jew on the back and flashes a big broad smile; the little Jew repeats the gesture. They put their arms around each other and start to walk away.
Back to a medium shot of the group in Miss Baker's room. Miss Baker turns to Mac and Trina and announces : 'They are all gone.'
Medium close-up of the scene. Trina turns to Mac and says : 'Let's go and look — take a last look.' They walk out into the hallway.
Reverse shot in the hallway : McTeague and Trina, followed by Miss Baker, appear in the hallway. Old Grannis walks towards them, carrying a little package. When Miss Baker sees him she hastily retreats into her room. As Old Grannis meets Mac and Trina he points to the package which he carries and indicates that he bought it over at the auction.
Medium close-up of Mac and Trina looking at each other for a second as if to say : 'Did he, too, take advantage of our misfortune? '
Close-up of Old Grannis seen through single veil saying :

Title : ' This was put up — it was of no value but to you — I . . . I ventured to bid it in. I thought perhaps that you wouldn't mind.'

Back to a medium close-up of Mac and Trina, who look from Old Grannis down to the package, then at each other for a second, and finally back to Grannis.
Back to a close-up of Old Grannis as he continues :

Title : ' I bought it for you as a present.'

Back to the scene as Grannis hands the package to Trina. While Trina starts tearing off the wrapping, he runs quickly into his room and closes the door.

Medium close-up of Miss Baker standing close to her slightly ajar door, listening. She has apparently heard everything, for as she leans her head against the door-sash tears run down her cheeks.

Back to a medium shot of McTeague and Trina staring forlornly at the object in their hands.

Close-up from their point of view of the framed photograph of McTeague and Trina in their wedding finery.

Back to medium close-up of Mac and Trina through double veil. Trina's eyes fill again with tears which run down her cheeks as she says :

TITLE : ' Oh, it was good of him.'

Back to the scene as McTeague blows his nose with great care, surreptitiously touching the corner of each eye with the tip of his handkerchief. Trina continues :

TITLE : ' Of course, it wasn't for sale.'

Back to the scene as Trina blows her nose and wipes her eyes. They start walking down the hall.

Medium shot as they go through the door leading to the kitchen.

Reverse shot from the dining room door at the far end of the kitchen as Mac and Trina, who carries the framed photograph, enter the kitchen. Except for a couple of broken bottles, the room is completely empty. Mac and Trina walk towards camera, looking around them sadly.

Reverse shot from behind them as they pass from the kitchen into the dining room.

Medium close-up of Trina and Mac from the dining room. They stand at the kitchen door, look about and then walk into the dining room. Their gaze moves towards the window.

Medium close-up of their sad faces as they recall their wedding day.

Shot of the window from their angle, the walls and the floor. It is the same set we saw when they were first married.

Dissolve in to the wedding scene. The Minister stands behind the little table; McTeague and Trina kneel on either side. Mr. Sieppe is on the left, Mrs. Sieppe is on the right; he has his eyes closed, she is crying. McTeague is putting the wedding ring on Trina's finger. The scene dissolves out and becomes a bare wall and floor.

Back to medium close-up of Mac and Trina looking at each other; she is crying again. They turn and stare in the direction of the spot where Marcus had drunk a toast to their health and happiness at their wedding supper.

Shot from their angle of the empty wall.

Dissolve in to Marcus dressed as he was at the wedding supper, and seated between two other guests. He is smiling broadly and apparently looking straight at Mac and Trina, toasting them.

Dissolve back to medium close-up of Mac and Trina as they look at each other with significant looks, and then turn towards the bedroom.

Shot from their angle of the bedroom through the arch. The only thing in the otherwise bare room is Trina's wedding bouquet. Unsold and forgotten, it hangs in its oval glass frame above the place where the bed had been — a melancholy relic of a vanished happiness.

Quick lap dissolve in to close-up of the wedding bouquet. It goes out of focus.

Medium shot of Mac and Trina seen through double veil. Trina breaks down, sobbing, and puts her arms around McTeague's waist; he lowers his head and nods stupidly, while she sobs. Iris out.

Fade in on a tremendous hand (gilded and hand-coloured) crushing two nude human beings (one male and one female). They are so small that we can see only their heads, shoulders, arms and legs extending from each end of the hand. Their bodies are also hand-coloured flesh colour and the woman has long black hair. Their arms and legs are flailing wildly as they struggle to get free. Then the hand closes with a greedy movement, slowly but surely crushing the life out of the two beings. Their struggles stop and their limbs hang limp. Iris out.[1]

Iris in on Mac and Trina in their new room in the back of the house. Despite its shabbiness, there is still a certain hopeless neatness about the room. Trina is sitting at a little table by the window, working on her wooden figures. Mac stands near her, filling his pipe from a tin labelled 'Mastiff'. His coat and vest are off, his cuffs open. He wears no collar or necktie and his feet are in slippers. He puts the pipe in his mouth and lights it, then walks up and down and takes a couple of

---

[1] In the release print, this symbolic scene follows Trina's murder.

puffs, blowing the smoke into the air. He stops behind Trina; another tin of tobacco rests on the table in front of her.

Medium close-up of both of them as Mac tells Trina that he cannot smoke that tobacco any more. She looks up at him and smiles cynically as she says:

TITLE: 'You used to smoke that all the time.'

Back to the scene as he gets sore and points at her: 'It was you that made me like this one here.' He grabs an empty can of Prince Albert, then angrily hurls it at the corner of the room and spits.

Medium shot of Mac starting to pace the room again.

Close-up of Trina whittling, apparently without any emotion. She still wears her old gloves, although their fingers are now all worn and hang in strips.

Close-up of her hands in the gloves as she puts the knife down to examine the torn fingers of one of the gloves; it is beyond repair.

Flash close-up of Trina sighing.

Back to the scene as she takes off the gloves, rolls them up and throws them to the back of the table. McTeague stops pacing and stands behind Trina.

Medium shot of both of them as he says:

TITLE: 'Say, let's take a ride out to the Park like we used to, huh?'

Back to the scene as Trina looks up from the table and then down again. She picks up her knife and her figures, and returns to her whittling as she announces:

TITLE: 'That means ten cents — and I can't afford it.'

Back to the scene as McTeague says:

TITLE: 'Let's walk there then.'

Back to the scene as Trina shakes her head, points to the figures and says: 'No, I've got to work.' Mac pleads:

TITLE: 'But you've worked morning and afternoon — every day this week.'

Back to the scene as Trina continues to shake her head and again points to the animals: 'No. I got to work.'

Back to medium shot of the scene as McTeague starts to pace again. He puffs on the pipe, then takes it out of his mouth, spits and says:

TITLE: 'Say, let me have some money for a bottle of beer, huh? We

252

haven't had a drop in three weeks.'

Back to the scene as Trina shakes her head and says : 'We can't afford it.' McTeague says : 'But I haven't had a swallow in three weeks.' Trina starts speaking :

TITLE : 'Drink steam beer then — you've got some money left. I gave you four bits day before yesterday.'

Back to the scene as McTeague says :

TITLE : 'But I don't like steam beer any more.'

Back to Trina, now good and sore, who cries :

TITLE : 'You haven't even got a beer income ! You know how much I got for selling everything we had ? '

Back to the scene as Mac shakes his head and says : 'No.' Trina continues :

TITLE : '. . . seventy dollars — and after paying the rent and the grocery bill, I've got fifty left.'

Back to the scene as McTeague shakes his head and says : 'Only fifty? Huh — think of it — only fifty.'
Back to the scene as McTeague paces for a moment, then gets an idea. He slips on his coat, puts on his cap and walks out. As the door bangs, Trina turns and looks, then lays down the knife. She jumps up and runs to the door, opens it a bit and listens outside. She then closes it carefully and runs over to the trunk, which she hurriedly opens, removing the chamois bag from underneath her bridal dress. She takes six gold pieces out of the handkerchief which she had in her bosom. The money is wrapped up in a sheet of paper which she unfolds and looks at :

TITLE : 'Statement, Murphy and Schlavinski, Auctioneers, Second Hand Dealers.

For sale of furniture etc.	$170.00
Less commission for auction	$20.00
Balance	$150.00 '

Back to Trina, who hastily folds the bill and, holding the money in the hollow of her hand, counts it.
Close-up of the hand-coloured gold pieces as Trina puts them into the

chamois bag.

Medium shot of the bar in Joe Frenna's saloon. McTeague appears and goes to the far side of the bar, where the bartender greets him with a pitying expression. McTeague puts down a quarter; the bartender starts pouring steam beer into the tin pitcher.

Back to the McTeagues' room. Trina closes the trunk and puts the key underneath the carpet. She then runs over to the oil stove, lights a match and starts burning the statement.

Medium shot of the exterior of the saloon as McTeague appears with the pitcher wrapped up in a newspaper.

Back to Trina, who is now pouring the ashes from the statement into a bucket. She brushes off her hands, then runs back to the table and starts working. A sound outside attracts her attention. The door opens and McTeague walks into the room holding the pitcher. He takes off his coat and cap, grabs a glass from the shelf, then goes over to the bed and lies down. He fills the glass and drinks, then gets up, takes the concertina down from the shelf above the bed and finally lies back again and starts playing.

Close-up of McTeague. He yawns. Iris out on his face.

Iris in on the window pane of Zerkow's room. Zerkow's face appears from below, presses close to the glass for a moment, then disappears, only to reappear slowly again and gaze into the yard.

Shot from his angle of the junk yard and the back of Maria, who is shovelling some earth into a hole. She steps on top of the mound of earth and stamps on it with her feet. Then, looking around as if she is afraid to be seen, Maria drops the shovel and turns towards the house.

Back to a shot of the window as Zerkow's face disappears quickly.

Medium shot inside Zerkow's room, shooting towards the door. Zerkow ducks behind a pile of junk iron as the door opens and Maria enters and walks upstairs. Zerkow quickly squeezes out from his hiding place, opens the door and goes into the yard.

Medium shot of the yard as Zerkow picks up the shovel. He looks around, makes sure that no one is looking, and starts shovelling.

Close-up of the window on the second floor as Maria appears and accidentally looks down. She sees Zerkow.

Shot from her angle of Zerkow, digging for all he is worth. Suddenly, he finds the body of a dead black cat which he picks up by the tail and then quickly drops. For some reason, he then starts shovelling the earth back on top of it.

Close-up of Maria at the window, laughing diabolically. Iris out.

Iris in on McTeague's room. McTeague is dressed in a soft shirt, but

254

no necktie. Trina wears a blue flannel wrapper and slippers; her hair is carelessly stuck up. They are both sitting silent and sour-faced at the table. A coffee pot, cups and chipped plates with a couple of strips of bacon and bread lie on the table in front of them. McTeague rises, puts on his cap and leaves without saying goodbye. The clock shows seven o'clock. Trina rises and puts the dishes into the sink, where there is already a nice little pile of unwashed dishes from the night before. She then puts a can of condensed milk into a box outside the window which now serves as their refrigerator.

Close-up of Trina stacking the dirty dishes and saving the two or three little bits of bacon and crusts of bread that she and Mac left.

Back to the scene as she goes to the table and starts working. Fade out. Fade in outside a surgical instrument factory. We see McTeague among the men and women who appear and go into the factory.

Medium shot of the workshop as McTeague and others enter. McTeague goes to his place and starts working. Fade out.

Fade in on Trina working. Suddenly she stops, appearing very tired. She looks over in the direction of the trunk, then runs to the door, opens it and looks out. After she closes and locks the door, she goes over to the window and pulls the shade down. Next she goes over to

the trunk, takes the key from under the carpet, and opens it. She takes out the chamois bag and the matchbox, emptying the gold inside them onto the table and piling it up. Taking a rag and some ashes that she has saved in a little box, Trina starts shining the gold pieces with unbelievable delight. She holds each gold piece and after polishing it she looks at it sideways and moves her head from left to right. Finally she gathers all the coins in one heap, rises and draws back to a corner of the room to note the effect. Her head tilted to one side, she returns and lovingly draws the heap towards her, burying her face in it.

Close-up of Trina as she raises her head and looks at the gold with undeniable physical delight.

Shot from her angle of the hand-coloured gold in a large heap.

Back to a close-up of Trina as she drones :

TITLE : ' All mine — and I'm going to get more — more.'

Back to a medium shot as she finishes speaking and plays with the gold. Fade out.

Iris in on Zerkow's place. Zerkow is beating Maria with a horsewhip. She hunches her back to protect her head with her arms, but doesn't resist. He turns the whip around, and biffs her three more good ones with the handle.

Close-up of Zerkow as he strikes her and yells :

TITLE : ' I know you hid them, but I'll make you talk ! '

Close-up of Maria wincing and guarding her head as she says :

TITLE : ' I ain't got nothun' ! '

Back to a medium shot of Zerkow as he drops the whip and takes an ugly knife from his pocket. He grabs Maria's hair, and comes dangerously close with the knife.

Close-up of Maria, who is terrified by the knife. She does some quick thinking and then says :

TITLE : ' If you kill me I'll never tell.'

Back to a close-up of Zerkow. He looks at Maria and then at the knife in his hand. His hand relaxes.

Medium shot of the scene. Zerkow puts the knife away and Maria rises from the floor. Zerkow is shaking all over. Covering his head in his hands, he starts to sob. As he breaks down, he falls on his knees, wrings his hands and begs Maria to tell him. Iris out.

Iris in on McTeague working at the factory. It is noon. Some men take out their lunch boxes and sit down to eat; some take their hats and leave, among them McTeague.

Medium shot of McTeague punching the time clock as he passes the cashier's window. As he starts to leave, the foreman steps up and tells him he is through.

Close-up of McTeague, dumbfounded.

Back to the scene as the foreman tells him to pick up his pay envelope; McTeague nods.

Medium shot of McTeague and the foreman at the cashier's window. The foreman tells the cashier to give Mac his envelope. The cashier has it all ready and gives it to him. McTeague nods, puts it unopened into his pocket and then walks out looking dazed.

Medium shot of Mac outside the factory. He takes out the envelope and looks at it. Then he opens it, counts the money and finally puts it back into his pocket. He walks off slowly towards the left. Fade out.]

TITLE : ' With the stopping of Mac's practice the grind began. Trina sold everything; she worked at toy whittling that her money might remain untouched.' [1]

Medium shot of Trina working at the table by the window.

Close-up of Trina carving the wooden figurines.

Close-up of the pile of wood shavings by her bedroom-slippered foot.

Close-up of the clock on the chair.

Close-up of the unmade bed.

Close-up of a pitcher and basin on the table.

Close-up of a pile of dirty dishes lying in the sink.

Back to medium close-up of Trina working industriously at the table.

Medium shot of McTeague, who appears through the doorway.

Back to medium shot of Trina, who looks up in surprise, then over at the clock.

Close-up of the clock reading five past three.

Medium close-up of Trina.

Medium shot of Mac as he removes his hat, then goes to hang it on the peg. His movements are very slow and deliberate.

Medium shot of Trina as she rises from her chair.

---

[1] This title and the following montage sequence opening the scene did not appear in Stroheim's original script, which had the following :
' Fade in on Trina closing the trunk. She goes back to the table and resumes her work. She suddenly pauses and looks expectantly towards the clock.
Shot from her angle of McTeague entering the room.
Medium shot of both of them as Trina points to the clock. It is only 3 o'clock and she asks him why he is home so early. McTeague replies.'

Medium shot of the scene as Mac sits down on the bed and Trina approaches him.
Medium close-up of the couple as Trina points at the clock.
Close-up of the clock.
Back to medium close-up as Trina asks him why he is home so early. He replies :

TITLE : ' They fired me.'

Back to medium close-up. Trina, wide-eyed with astonishment, first says, ' Fired you? What for?,' then walks up to Mac and shakes him. [McTeague shrugs his shoulders and says : ' I don't know.' Still staring at Mac, Trina sits down.
Close-up of Trina sitting in the chair. She covers her face with her hands, wails, ' What can you do now? ' and continues :]

TITLE : ' Isn't there another surgical instrument factory in town? '

[Close-up of McTeague from her angle as he says : ' Huh? No — I don't know.']
Medium shot of Mac and Trina as he nods and answers :

TITLE : ' Yes . . . There's two more.'

Medium shot of the scene as Trina says : ' Well, you must try them right away — go right there now.' Mac looks up and says : ' Now? ' He shakes his head : ' No, I'll go in the morning.' Trina rises and looks at McTeague with astonishment.
Close-up of Trina, who is very animated. She is insistent and shoves Mac as she cries :

[TITLE : ' You must go this minute ! Not tomorrow.'

Shot from her angle of McTeague as he looks at her stupidly.
Back to Trina, who says :]

TITLE : ' We're losing money every second you sit here . . .'

Back to Trina, still speaking :

TITLE : '. . . and we cannot afford it.'

Medium shot as Trina approaches to get Mac's cap.
Reverse angle shot as she returns with the cap, puts it in Mac's hand, then makes him rise and pushes him towards the door. She orders : ' Now, right now. Don't just sit there.' Like a docile cart-horse he obeys.
Close-up of the couple as they reach the door.

Medium shot of the room in disarray.

Back to close-up as Mac still tries to argue with Trina. They go out of the door.

Medium shot of them in the dimly lit hallway [with the top stairway on the right dividing the hallway on the left. McTeague slowly and unwillingly starts to descend. Suddenly, Trina appears on the run].

Close-up of Trina at the top of the stairs with her hand at her mouth and a wide-eyed, evil look suddenly appearing on her face as she starts to speak.

Close-up of Mac with no expression at all on his face.

Back to close-up of Trina speaking :

TITLE : ' They paid you, didn't they? '

Shot from her angle of Mac, who nods.

Medium shot of Trina arguing with Mac on the landing. She holds out her hand and commands : ' Give it to me.'

[Shot from her angle of Mac, who heaves his shoulders uneasily, shakes his head and says : ' No, I don't want to.']

Close-up of Trina's slippered foot stamping the floor.

Back to medium shot of the scene as Trina insists : ' I've got to have it, I have no more oil for the stove and I must buy some meal tickets.'

Medium close-up of the couple as he says :

TITLE : ' Always money . . . [money].'

Back to close-up of McTeague handing Trina his pay envelope. She tears it open and shakes out the money. Then she goes through all his pockets while he stands there dumbly.

Medium shot of the scene. Finally satisfied, Trina starts to walk away as he descends the stairs.

Medium shot of Mac descending the stairs in the foreground with a blank expression on his face. Trina is sneering as she watches from the background. Suddenly Mac halts on the stairs.

Medium close-up of Trina at the landing above as Mac reappears.

Close-up of McTeague as he starts to speak :

TITLE : ' Better leave me some car fare.'

Back to close-up of Mac.

TITLE : ' It's a long walk.'

Back to close-up of Mac speaking :

TITLE : '. . . an' it's going to rain.'

259

Close-up of Mac as he finishes speaking.
Close-up of Trina as she replies :

Title : ' A big fellow like you 'fraid of a little walk, and it's not going to rain.'

Back to close-up of Trina.
Close-up of Mac reacting.
Medium shot of both of them as he shrugs his shoulders and turns to descend the stairs.
Medium shot of Trina in the corridor. She waits for a second, then runs off towards her room.
Medium long shot in front of the house. Mac comes out.
Medium shot of McTeague's room as Trina enters and locks the door.
Medium long shot of Mac in front of his house as he [looks up at the sky, looks around and sighs,] starts walking off towards the left. At the right we can see Maria pointing him out to two gossiping neighbours.
Medium close-up of Trina, who goes to the trunk and puts the money that she has taken from McTeague into the chamois bag and then smiles as she puts her finger thoughtfully up to her lips. [She closes the trunk quickly and goes back to work.] Fade out.
Fade in on a medium shot of a pair of hands lifting up a dazzling collection of dinner service outlined against a mysterious black background.
Slow lap dissolve into close-up of the same scene. Fade out.[1]

[Medium shot of Maria knocking on the McTeagues' door.
Medium shot of Trina inside the room as she turns and says : ' Come in.' Then she remembers that she has locked the door and so she runs over and unlocks it. Maria enters and Trina asks her to sit down. She sits on the bed with her chin in her hand and starts to tell Trina about her troubles with Zerkow. She describes his crazy digging at night and tells of his whipping her, opening her collar to show Trina the whip marks on her neck and shoulders. Finally she recounts his attempt with the knife. Fade out.

Fade in on another surgical instrument factory with a ' Help Wanted ' sign outside. McTeague appears from the left, looks up at the sign, and then gazes vaguely around. Hesitating, he enters the office.

---

[1] In the release print, these two symbolic shots at the close of this scene have been transposed from a scene between Maria and Zerkow where they appeared in the original script.

Medium shot of the office. McTeague enters and asks the clerk, 'What the chances are for a job.' The clerk looks at him and then shakes his head and says: 'Nothun' doing.' McTeague nods gravely, turns and goes out.

Medium shot of the front of the factory as Mac comes out. He looks around, sighs and walks away. Fade out.

Fade in on medium shot of Trina and Maria in the McTeagues' room. Close-up of Trina as she declares:

TITLE: 'I'd be deathly 'fraid of a man like that.'

Close-up from her angle of Maria, who shakes her head and says:

TITLE: 'He won't kill me. If he would he'd never know where the dishes were — that's what he thinks.'

Back to Trina as she says:

TITLE: 'But you told him about those gold dishes yourself.'

Shot from her angle of Maria, who cries out: 'I? Never! You're a lot of crazy folks!' Fade out.

Fade in on a medium shot of Mac arriving at another surgical instrument factory.

Medium shot of the office as McTeague enters and asks the girl there for a job. She turns to the man in charge and asks him; the man says 'nothing doing'; the girl tells Mac, who merely nods, turns, and walks out.

Medium shot outside the factory as McTeague reappears from inside and looks up at the sky. It starts raining. Mac walks away, his collar turned up and his hands in his pockets. Fade out.

Fade in on Maria and Trina, who are still talking. Close-up of Maria as she says:

TITLE: 'Say, Mrs. McTeague, have you got any tea? Let's make a cup of tea over the stove.'

Close-up of Trina speaking with niggardly apprehension: 'No, haven't got a bit of tea. I surely haven't.' She shakes her head decisively. Fade out.

Fade in on a long shot of a street. It is raining; pouring. Quick lap dissolve in to shot of McTeague walking along, soaking wet. Medium close-up of him taken from a perambulator in front. He is so wet that he doesn't even walk fast any more — there is no use. He mumbles to himself:

TITLE : ' Miser, money — money — and got five thousand.'

Back to the scene as he keeps on walking and mumbling :

TITLE : ' I told her it was going to rain — and not a nickel for car fare.'

Back to the scene as he continues :

TITLE : ' I ain't going to stand it much longer.'

Back to the scene, then fade out.
Fade in on a medium shot of Trina saying 'Goodbye' to Maria.
Maria opens the door and leaves, while Trina goes back to the table.
She thinks for a moment, and then glances towards the stove, then
towards the door. Smiling a bit, she walks over to the stove, lights it,
and puts on a pot of water. She then picks up a tea package, taking
a small pinch of tea with her fingers which she puts in her hand. She
reconsiders, removes some of the tea from her palm and puts the rest
into the pot. Fade out.]
Fade in on a medium long shot of the front of Frenna's saloon. It is
still raining and throughout the following scene people hurry by in the
foreground. McTeague is passing by with lowered head.
Medium shot of Mac with water running off him. He is soaked to the
bone. Heise, who is standing in the doorway, sees Mac, runs over
and pulls him out of the rain into the entrance as he says : ' Hello,
Doc — why, you're soaked through.' He points to Mac's clothes and
continues :

TITLE : ' You oughta taken a car.'

Back to the scene as McTeague says : ' I guess so.'
Medium shot as Heise warns :

TITLE : ' You're goin' to catch your death of cold.'

Back to the scene as he says : ' Come on, let's have a drink.' McTeague
hesitatingly follows Heise.
Interior of the saloon. Camera pans slightly with Heise and McTeague
as they enter and approach the bar.
Medium shot of Mac and Heise at the bar. Mac takes off his hat and
shakes out the water.
Close-up of the bartender.
Medium close-up of Mac and Heise from behind the bar, as Heise
looks around and says :

TITLE : ' [Whisky and gum, twice, Joe.] Two straight, Joe.'

Shot of the bartender from Heise's angle as he looks from Heise towards McTeague and then starts to reach for the bottle. A sign on the wall behind him reads : 'To Trust is to Bust and Bust is Hell.'
Medium close-up of Mac and Heise.
Medium close-up of the bartender.
Close-up of McTeague as he says, 'Whisky? No! I can't drink whisky,' and continues :

TITLE : ' It kind o' disagrees with me.'

Back to close-up of Heise, who replies :

TITLE : ' Aw, Hell ! You'll die . . . if you stand around soaked like that.'

Back to the scene as Heise turns towards Joe again and repeats : ' Two whiskies.'
Medium close-up of Trina in the room shining one of her gold pieces and holding it up admiringly.[1]

TITLE : ' Gold was her master . . .
            a passion with her,
            a mania, a veritable mental disease.'

Back to medium close-up of Trina.
Back to medium shot of the scene in the saloon as the bartender serves the drinks.
Medium shot of Mac and Heise, to the right, from behind the bar. McTeague empties his whisky with one gulp. Heise drinks his slowly, slaps McTeague on the back and says : ' That's the way; it'll do you good.'
[Very much embarrassed, McTeague says :

TITLE : ' I'd ask you to have a drink with me — only — only — you see, I don't believe I got any change.'

Back to the scene as he checks his pockets and shakes his head. Heise slaps him on the back and says, ' That's all right, Doc — want another? Huh? This is my treat. Two more, Joe.'
Medium shot of the scene. Joe takes clean glasses, fills them and puts them on the bar. Heise takes his; Mac hesitates. Heise raises his glass to Mac and starts drinking. McTeague grabs the other glass and drinks his in one gulp.
Medium shot of the scene as Heise pays and they start to leave.

---

[1] This shot of Trina and the accompanying title are not in Stroheim's original script.

Medium shot at the door from outside. Just as the swinging door opens and Mac and Heise start to come out, Ryer enters. He stops them, says 'Hello,' and invites them both to come back to the bar and have one on him.

At first McTeague says, 'No,' but Ryer and Heise convince him that it is good for him and all three go up to the bar.

Medium shot of McTeague, Heise and Ryer at the bar. Ryer orders three whiskies.

Close-up of McTeague as he shakes his head and says :

TITLE : 'No, I'm going home. I've had two glasses of whisky already.'

Medium shot from behind the bar as Ryer slaps Mac on the shoulders and bellows :

TITLE : 'A big strapping chap like you ain't afraid of a little whisky.'

Back to the scene as McTeague speaks :

TITLE : 'Well, I — I — I got to go right afterwards.' Fade out.]

Fade out as Ryer, who is on Mac's left, insists on buying him another drink.

Fade in on medium long shot of McTeague's room.[1] Trina is seated at the table polishing her gold coins.

Close-up of Mac's feet approaching the room along the hallway.

Close-up of Trina reacting with fright to the sound.

Back to close-up of Mac's large feet approaching.

Medium shot of Trina quickly gathering together her gold coins.

Medium close-up of Mac arriving at the door.

Long shot of the room as Trina puts her money in the trunk and locks it.

Close-up of Mac banging angrily at the door as he finds it locked.

Medium shot of Trina in the room, approaching the door.

Long shot of the room as Trina opens the door and Mac enters. He carelessly tosses his hat on its hook; in every respect his appearance and gestures contrast with his arrival earlier in the day. He looks at Trina with a brief but angry glance.

Reverse angle, medium shot of Mac as he goes over to the bed.

Medium shot of Trina watching him suspiciously, a bit surprised at his behaviour.

Medium shot of Mac sitting on the bed and Trina standing near by.

---

[1] The following montage sequence which opens the scene is not found in Stroheim's original script, which merely begins with Trina sitting at the table working as Mac enters the room.

Close-up of Trina looking at him as she says :

TITLE : ' Did you get a place? '

Back to close-up of Trina.
Shot from her angle of Mac, scowling fiercely at his muddy boots.
Close-up of Trina.
Close-up of Mac, who looks up at her angrily.
Medium shot of the scene.
Back to close-up of Mac.
Close-up of Trina asking :

TITLE : ' Did you get caught in the rain? '

Close-up from her angle of Mac as he imitates her : ' Did I? Did I?
Look at me ! ' He continues :

TITLE : ' Wouldn't even gimme a nickel for car fare.'

Back to close-up of Trina protesting :

TITLE : ' But Mac, I didn't know it was going to rain.'

Shot from her angle of Mac, as he puts back his head and laughs
scornfully, his eyes twinkling. He smiles and mimics her tone :

TITLE : ' Aw, no, you didn't know it was going to rain. Didn't I tell
you it was? '

Back to the scene. Mac is furious.
Back to a close-up of Trina, now standing and staring at Mac,
astonished.
[Back to Mac, who looks at her in a mean way and says :

TITLE : ' You're a daisy, you are ! Think I'm going to put up with it
all the time? '

Back to the same close-up of Trina.
Back to Mac as he slaps his thigh with his fist and roars :

TITLE : ' Who's the boss, you or I? '

Back to close-up of Trina as she looks startled, and says :

TITLE : ' Why Mac, I never saw you this way before; you talk like a
different man.']

Back to Mac, who savagely slaps his thigh again and says :

TITLE : [' I am a different man.] You ain't gonna make small of me

265

all the time.'

Back to close-up of Mac.
Back to Trina. She tries to change the subject and asks :

TITLE : ' Did you get a place? '

Back to close-up of Trina.
Medium shot from her angle of McTeague as he jumps up briskly and comes towards her.
Medium shot of Trina and Mac standing directly in front of their wedding photograph, which hangs on the wall behind them.
Medium close-up of them both as McTeague speaks :

TITLE : ' Gi'me back the money I gave you [as I was going away].'

Back to the scene as Trina says : ' I can't.'

TITLE : ' I paid the grocery bill with it.'

Back to the scene as Mac says :

TITLE : ' I don't believe you.'

Close-up of Trina, who convincingly feigns innocence and sincerity as she says :

TITLE : ' Why, Mac, do you think I'd lie to you? '

[Back to the scene as he looks at her.]
Close-up of Trina as she looks at him like an innocent little thing. [She continues to speak : ' Do you think I'd lower myself to do that? ']
Back to close-up of Trina and McTeague as he says : ' The next time I'll keep it myself.' Trina touches him on the arm and repeats :

TITLE : ' Did you get a place? '

Back to the scene as McTeague starts to turn his back on her. But Trina holds him by the sleeve and asks : ' Tell me, Mac, please — did you? ' Mac turns around and thrusts his face close to hers.
Medium close-up of both of them. Mac's heavy jaw protrudes and his little eyes twinkle meanly as he yells : ' No! No! Do ya hear? No! ' Trina cowers before him. Then, suddenly, she begins to sob, sits down in the chair, putting her head in her hand as she cries.
Medium shot of Mac as he looks around the room with a cynical smile.
Shot from his angle of the unmade bed.
Back to medium shot of Mac.
Shot from his angle of the sink full of dirty dishes.

266

Back to medium shot of Mac.
Close-up of the two birds fighting in their cage.
Back to Mac as he says :

Title : ' Ain't that fine? '

Close-up of Mac as he adds :

Title : ' Ain't it lovely? '

Close-up of Trina, who looks up, still sobbing, and says : ' It isn't my fault.'
[Close-up of McTeague as he says : ' It is, too . . .' Then continues :

Title : '. . . we could live like Christians. You got more than five thousand dollars and you're so damn stingy that you'd rather live in a stinking rat hole . . .'

Back to the scene as Mac points at the room and continues speaking :

Title : '. . . before you'd part with a nickel of it. I'm sick and tired of the whole business.']

Close-up from his angle of Trina turning towards him. Although there are tears running down her cheeks, she is sore and retorts :

Title : ' I won't have you yell at me like that.' [1]

Back to close-up of McTeague, now purple with rage. [He yells : ' What? Get into a worse hole than this? We'll just see about that! ' He rises slowly.] Without taking his eyes off Trina, he slowly comes at her with lowered head.
Close-up of both of their faces. Trina doesn't give an inch.
Extreme close-up of Mac's face looming even closer.
Back to close-up as he pokes his face closer to hers. Spitting every word into her face like a snake, he orders :

Title : ' You're going to do just as I tell you after this —Trina McTeague! '

Back to the scene. On the wall behind them we can see their marriage licence hanging. Trina gets a whiff of Mac's breath. Waving her hand between their faces, she says : ' You've been drinking whisky.' Mac smiles cynically and replies :

---

[1] Stroheim's script had a different title : ' And now that you're out of a job we can't afford to live even in this rat hole.'

TITLE : 'Yes, I've been drinking whisky. [What've ya got to say about it?] '

Back to the scene as Trina starts to sob, covering her face with her hands. McTeague catches her wrists in one palm and pulls them down. Trina's face is streaming with tears; her adorable little chin is upraised and quivering. McTeague growls : 'Let's hear what you got to say.' Sobbing, Trina shakes her head [and answers : ' Nothing.' McTeague snarls : ' Then stop that noise.'

TITLE : ' Stop it ! Ya hear me? ']

Close-up of McTeague.
Close-up of Trina.
Back to the scene as Mac yells : ' Stop it.' He raises his open hand and bellows : ' Stop ! ' Trina looks at him fearfully.
Close-up of Mac's angry face.
Close-up of Trina watching him fearfully; she looks from his face to his hand.
Shot from her angle of McTeague's terribly large open hand, which suddenly contracts into a fist.
[Back to close-up of Trina. She is terrified and chokes back her sobs.]
Back to the scene as McTeague says, ' That's more like it,' and shoves her onto the bed. Trina rises immediately while Mac continues :

TITLE : ' I'm beat out and I don't want to be bothered ! '

Back to the scene as Trina nods and answers : ' Yes.' McTeague turns and snarls, then hits Trina, shoving her out of the way. He takes off his jacket and flops on the bed with his boots still on.[1]
[Close-up of Trina as she cranes her neck and looks at Mac. She goes to the table, sits down, stretches her arms out in front of her and buries her head in them. She cries and sobs as though her heart would break. Close-up of the window pane with sheets of water pouring down.]
Close-up of the canary cage. The two birds are fighting.
[Close-up of McTeague's face, his mouth wide open, snoring to beat the band.]
Close-up of Trina seated at the table. She raises her head, thinks for a moment, then glances over at Mac, and finally looks off into space and muses :

TITLE : ' I wonder where he got the money . . . to buy the whisky? '

---

[1] Stroheim's script had the following : ' Mac takes off his coat and shirt, slips his boots from his big feet, then stretches out on the bed and rolls over towards the wall.'

Close-up of Trina with her finger held up to her lip. Iris down on her finger, hold for a moment, then iris out.

[Medium shot as Trina rises, goes over to the bed and picks up Mac's coat which had fallen to the floor. She goes through his pockets, but does not find anything. Then she sneaks over to the bed and, with her eyes on Mac, very carefully goes through the pockets of his pants. Again she finds nothing.

Close-up of Trina looking thoughtful, with her finger on her lip.

TITLE : ' I wonder if he's got any money he don't tell me about. I'll have to look out for that.'

Back to the scene, then iris out.

Iris in on Old Grannis's room, where Grannis is showing a stranger his book-binding apparatus. The stranger is very interested and compliments Old Grannis on his invention as he shakes hands with him. Grannis walks him to the door, bows him out and closes the door. Then he goes back to the little table and sits down. Fingering his chin, he thinks and listens at the wall with a little smile.

Quick lap dissolve to medium shot of Miss Baker's room. Miss Baker has a tea cup in her hand. A second cup, saucer and spoon are laid out at the place across from her. She listens at the wall and smiles a bit. Iris out.

Fade in.

TITLE : ' As time went on, McTeague's idleness became habitual.'

Fade out.

Fade in on a street where a huge dredger works at an excavation site. McTeague saunters along, his hands in his pockets, a pipe in his mouth; he stops at the rail and watches.

Close-up of McTeague as he lazily looks on and puffs at his pipe.

Shot from his angle of an unusually active scene : a crane and a dredger are in operation; there are men digging, drillers working, and workmen running back and forth with lumber.

Back to a close-up of McTeague, who takes his pipe out of his mouth and spits elaborately.

Back to the scene as he slowly saunters away. Fade out.

Fade in on Mac's room. In the background we can see the dirty dishes in the sink. Trina is sitting at the table, all her money piled neatly in front of her.

Close-up of Trina as she says :

TITLE : ' Four hundred and fifty. How I've slaved and saved for you! '

Back to the scene as she looks lovingly at the money, embracing it with her arms saying :

Title : ' No one shall ever, ever get you ! '

Back to the scene as she plunges her small fingers into the pile of money and murmurs to it affectionately. Fade out.
Fade in on a long shot of the beach at the Golden Gate. Several rocky points jut up in the background. Mac appears, and lies down on the beach. Bracing himself on his elbow, he looks out over the ocean.
Close-up of McTeague, pipe in mouth, as he gazes at the ocean.
Shot from his angle of the endless waves. Iris out.
Iris in on a medium shot of the hallway outside Miss Baker's room. Trina appears in her blue flannel wrapper and raps on the door. Nobody answers. Old Grannis's door stands a little ajar. He comes out a little way in the hall and they greet each other. He tells her very politely that Miss Baker has gone out.
Medium close-up of both of them as Trina speaks :

Title : ' Don't you go to your Dog Hospital any more, Mr. Grannis? '

Back to the scene as Grannis shakes his head and replies :

Title : ' I've given it up.'

Back to the scene as Trina says : ' Given it up? ' Old Grannis nods and explains :

Title : ' You see, I'm about to sell the patent of my contrivance for binding books . . .'

Back to the scene. Trina looks astonished; Grannis strokes his chin thoughtfully and says : ' It's quite a sum, in fact — yes, quite a sum.'
Back to the scene as Trina good-naturedly says : ' Why, isn't that fine.'

Title : ' Is it a good price? '

Back to Grannis, who nods and says :

Title : ' I never dreamed of having so much money.'

Back to Trina, thinking. Then she speaks decisively :

Title : ' Now, Mr. Grannis, I want to give you a good piece of advice.'

Back to the scene. He listens very politely as she continues speaking :

Title : ' Here are you and Miss Baker, that have been in love with each other for . . .'

Back to the scene as Old Grannis interrupts her, terribly upset. Rubbing his chin, he says :

TITLE : ' Oh, Mrs. McTeague — that subject — if you would please — Miss Baker is such an estimable lady ! '

Back to the scene as Trina says : ' Oh fiddlesticks.' He can hardly believe his ears ; she continues talking :

TITLE : ' You two are in love with each other, and have been living here side by side year in and year out and never said a word.'

Back to the scene. Old Grannis is terribly upset ; his hand twitches, he is rubbing his chin. Trina smiles and continues :

TITLE : ' As soon as she comes home, I want you should go right in and tell her you've come into money, and you want her to marry you.'

Back to the scene as Old Grannis, alarmed and perturbed, replies : ' It's impossible — it's quite out of the question.'

TITLE : ' I wouldn't presume.'

Back to the scene as Trina says :

TITLE : ' Well do you love her or not ? '

Back to the scene as Grannis fidgets all over and says :

TITLE : ' I . . . I . . . you must excuse me, it's a matter so personal . . . so . . . I . . . I . . . Oh — yes I love her — Oh, yes, indeed ! '

Back to the scene as Trina smiles and says :

TITLE : ' Well then, she loves you — she told me so.'

Back to the scene. He is dumbfounded. She tells him to do just as she advised, to go right into Miss Baker's room and have it over when she comes home and not to say another word. With that, Trina abruptly says, ' Goodbye,' and walks away, leaving Old Grannis standing there, his hands trembling.

Close-up of Old Grannis as he speaks :

TITLE : ' She said she . . . she . . . she . . . told her . . . she said that . . . that . . .'

Back to the scene as he turns and enters his room, then closes the door. Medium shot inside the room as Grannis closes the door. He walks over to the armchair and draws it closer to the wall. Iris out.

271

Fade in on a street scene. Heise stands in front of his harness shop talking to Ryer as McTeague comes along. It is dusk and the street lights are already on.

Medium close-up as Heise and Ryer greet Mac and ask him where he has been. He points in the direction. They suggest a drink at Frenna's; he hesitates for a second, looks in the direction of his flat and then agrees. Heise turns to Mrs. Heise, who stands in the doorway of the shop, and tells her to watch the store. The three men walk away towards Frenna's.

Medium shot of the exterior of Frenna's saloon as the three arrive and go inside.

Medium shot of the interior of the bar as the three men enter. The bartender immediately pushes a bottle of whisky and three glasses towards them. Fade out.]

TITLE : ' As time went on, Mac's idleness became habitual. His dislike for Trina increased with every day of her persistent stinginess.' [1]

Fade in on medium long shot of the interior of Frenna's saloon. The bartender can be seen behind the bar, with Heise, McTeague and Ryer drinking in the foreground.

Medium close-up of the three men at the bar. Mac says : ' I'll get some money and come back.'

Back to the scene as Mac goes to leave. Fade out.

Fade in on medium long shot of McTeague's room. Trina is in bed sleeping.

Close-up of Mac suddenly entering.

Close-up of Trina sitting up in bed in alarm.

Close-up of Mac rapidly approaching her.

Medium shot as he grabs her brutally and pulls her up on the bed.

Medium close-up of Mac talking angrily; she is frightened.

Close-up of the trunk with the clock and other objects on it.

Back to medium close-up of Mac arguing with her and twisting her arm. He smiles evilly as he says :

TITLE : ' You with all that money . . . an' me with nothin'. Come 'n ! '

Back to the scene. He grabs her hand and brings it towards his mouth to bite her fingers.

Close-up of Trina in pain and very frightened.

---

[1] This title and the following scene do not appear at this point in Stroheim's original script. But it incorporates material originally appearing in other scenes, which are either no longer in the released print or were not shot.

Close-up of the angry McTeague.

Close-up of Trina agreeing to his demand.

Close-up of Mac.

Back to the scene as Trina bends over and gets some money for him from under the mattress of the bed. Mac looks at it in disgust and says : ‘ One dollar. Is that all? ’

Medium close-up as Mac resumes torturing her and mimics her reply, ‘ I haven't got any more.’ She gets him some more money from the drawer of the table.

Close-up of Mac looking in the drawer as Trina looks on.

Medium long shot as Mac throws the drawer away and takes the money which Trina gives him.

Close-up of Mac smiling evilly as he grabs her hand again. She asks him :

Title : ‘ Don't you love me any more, Mac? ’

Back to the scene. He is laughing as he replies :

Title : ‘ Sure I do.’

Back to the scene as he hits her soundly, and she falls on the bed.
Close-up of Mac looking at her.
Close-up of Trina hiding in the bed.
Close-up of Mac satisfied.
Medium long shot of Mac crossing the room and disappearing through the doorway.
Fade out on long shot of the room.
[Fade in on McTeague's room, where Trina is cooking something on the stove. She has put plates, knives and forks on the table, and is now apparently waiting for her 'lord and master' to come home to dinner. She looks at the clock; it's seven o'clock. She sits down at the work-table and resumes her work. She still wears the blue wrapper and her hair looks worse than ever; the floor is covered by whittlings and the room is filled with smoke from the stove. Suddenly, the door opens and Mac enters. He throws his cap on the hook and takes off his coat. Trina rises and serves his food. Mac sits down and starts eating. She goes back to the table and resumes her work, crunching on a piece of bread.
Close-up of McTeague stuffing the steaming mashed potato into his mouth. He looks over at Trina.

Shot from his angle of Trina working to beat the band. She throws a finished figure into the basket, takes a bite from the small piece of bread that lies next to her, and then picks up a chunk of wood.
Back to close-up of McTeague; he gets sore and bellows :

TITLE : ' Stop working.'

Shot from his angle of Trina as she turns and looks at him in surprise.
Shot from her angle of McTeague as he continues yelling : ' Stop it, I tell you.'
Back to Trina, as she looks at Mac in utter amazement, and asks : ' But why? '
Back to McTeague as he yells :

TITLE : ' Put 'em away or I'll pinch you.'

Shot from his angle of Trina, who defiantly turns away and resumes her work.
Medium shot of the scene. With lowered head, McTeague rises, marches over to the work-table and slaps Trina's face.
Close-up of McTeague as he says :

TITLE : ' I won't have you work.'

Back to the scene as he takes the knife and the brushes from Trina and forces her to sit idle. As he walks away, she starts to sob and buries her head in her hands. He looks over at her; she is sobbing. He gets sore. Banging down the chair, he rises and goes over to Trina; he pinches her arm.
Medium shot of the couple. She cries, then screams. McTeague grins, pinches her again and says : ' Give me a little money.' Trina shakes her head and says :

TITLE : ' I haven't a cent.'

Back to the scene. McTeague pinches her again and she cries : ' Mac, will you stop it ! I won't have you pinch me that way ! ' Ignoring her comment, McTeague calmly says, ' Hurry up,' and nips the flesh on her shoulder between his thumb and forefinger. Trina wrenches free and, caressing her shoulder, says : ' You've no idea how that hurts, Mac. Stop ! ' He growls : ' Give me some money then.' Trina takes a dollar out of her skirt pocket, telling him that it is all she has. McTeague grins and speaks :

TITLE : ' One more, just for luck.'

Back to the scene as Trina starts crying and says :

275

TITLE : ' How can you hurt a woman so? '

Back to the scene as McTeague grins and taunts :

TITLE : ' That's right, cry. I never saw such a little fool.'

Medium shot of both of them as Mac takes his coat and cap and walks out of the room, slamming the door behind him.
Close-up of Trina as she raises her head and looks in the direction of the door. She sees it is closed and cries :

TITLE : ' A whole dollar and I eat bread.'

Back to Trina, who rises and turns out the light. The moonlight coming through the window illuminates the scene as she throws herself down on top of the bed, buries her head in the cushion and cries.
Medium shot of McTeague entering Frenna's saloon.
Shot from the bar towards the private booth as McTeague enters. Heise, Ryer and others are there and greet him as he sits down. Heise pushes his glass and a bottle over to Mac, who fills it. Fade out as Mac starts drinking.
Iris in on a clock showing midnight.
Lap dissolve in to McTeague's room. The door opens and McTeague enters; he goes over to the bed, sits down and takes off his shoes.
Medium close-up of McTeague sitting on the bed as the shoes fall to the floor. He belches slightly.
Close-up of Trina as she turns her face towards Mac and watches him; she is still lying on top of the bed dressed in the wrapper.
Back to a medium shot of McTeague, now undressed, as he slips underneath the bed cover.
Close-up of Trina as she whispers : ' Mac.'
Close-up of McTeague as he opens his eyes, turns a bit and says : ' Huh? '
Close-up of Trina, who says :

TITLE : ' Mac, do you love me? ' '

Back to a close-up of Mac, who turns away without answering, then closes his eyes and yawns.
Back to a close-up of Trina as she speaks :

TITLE : ' Don't you love me any more, Mac? '

Back to close-up of Mac as he turns and mutters : ' Shut up and let me sleep.'
Back to Trina as she implores :

276

Title : ' Just tell me that you love me.'

Back to the scene as she tenderly stretches out her hand to caress him.
Back to a close-up of Mac as Trina's hand reaches out and caresses his hair; suddenly, he seizes her hand.
Back to a close-up of Trina, who screams and then quickly covers her mouth with her other hand.
Back to McTeague, who brutally pushes her hand away.
Back to close-up of Trina. She holds the injured hand and tenderly caresses the finger tips. They seem to hurt terribly, for she moans and groans.
Medium shot of the scene illuminated only by faint moonlight. McTeague turns, raises himself a bit, gives her a tremendous whack, then lies back and turns his back to her.
Close-up of Trina crying and caressing her finger tips.
Close-up of the bird cage; the birds are fighting, and feathers fly about.
Iris out.
Fade in.

Title : ' This brutality in some strange inexplicable way aroused in Trina a morbid, unwholesome love of submission.'

Fade out.
Vertical barn door in on the exterior of the McTeagues' flat. Trina, dressed in her blue wrapper, her hair mussy, comes out of the door and trots slowly away towards the right.
Long shot of the alley as Trina appears from the left and runs up, her slippers clip-clapping with every step.
Medium shot in front of Zerkow's gate. At the right-hand side of the gate a man is sharpening a wicked-looking knife on a grindstone. Trina appears, glances at the man, then opens the gate and enters the yard.
Medium shot of the front of Zerkow's house as Trina appears and presses the bell. When it does not ring, she looks up.
Close-up of the bell-wire. It is broken.
Back to the scene as Trina walks inside.
Medium shot inside the house as Trina enters, goes to the stairway and looks around. She yells up the stairs : ' Maria ! ' Apparently she gets no answer, since she next looks towards the curtained partition and then walks off towards camera.
Medium shot towards the curtained partition. A light burning behind it throws a very clear shadow on the curtain of Maria, apparently asleep in a chair. Trina disappears through the slit in the curtain. Trina's shadow stops, then curiously and suspiciously approaches closer

277

to the shadow of Maria. She touches Maria with her hand to wake her up. The shadow of Maria's body falls from the chair to the ground. Trina screams and makes a terrified gesture with her arms as she backs up towards the curtain. She turns again and runs terrified towards camera and on past it.

Medium close-up shooting through the window as Trina appears from behind the curtain. She pauses and looks about in absolute terror, running her fingers through her hair. She does not know what to do, but finally runs out of the house.

Long shot of the scene, angled down from a rooftop on the opposite side of the alley. Trina runs out of the door.

Medium shot from across the street towards the gate as Trina runs through the gate and looks about wildly.

Medium shot up the alley with Trina on the right and a butcher's cart opposite her on the left. The butcher boy has one foot on the wheel and is just climbing up. In the foreground, a wild game peddler with a brace of ducks in his hand is walking in the middle of the street towards Trina with his back to camera.

Close-up of Trina as she frantically waves at the butcher boy.

Shot from her angle of the butcher boy, who stares at her and then swings himself into his seat and drives off, looking back.

Medium shot from across the street towards Trina as the game peddler passes, looking at Trina suspiciously. She realizes that he too would run away and so does not call him. The peddler walks on.

Close-up of Trina who puts her hands to her head; she looks about as if trying to concentrate, and then runs off.

Shot from Laguna Street towards the alley. Still terrified, Trina is running towards camera.

Medium shot of Heise's Harness Shop. He is standing in the doorway, dusting some of the leather things on the sidewalk when Trina appears at a run.

Medium close-up of both of them. Trina touches him on the shoulder and pulls him away by the sleeve; he turns to her, startled and terribly frightened. Trina puts her hand to her throat as if swallowing something that is choking her and tells him: 'Maria has been killed, Zerkow's wife, I found her, come quick!' Heise says: 'Get out, you're joking.' She replies: 'No, come, I found her, she's dead.'

Medium shot as they run off towards the left.

Medium shot towards the alley. The two appear from the left and approach at a run.

Medium shot from across the street towards Zerkow's house. The wild game peddler, a man wearing a broad-brimmed hat and a woman with her skirts tucked up and a scrubbing brush in her hand stand gossiping outside the gate. Trina and Heise run up to the house from the right. As they pass the gate and enter the yard, the wild game peddler asks them if there is anything wrong.

Shot from Zerkow's doorway towards Laguna Street. Two men who have just passed Heise and Trina stop and turn around to watch them.

Shot from Zerkow's doorway of the house opposite. A woman with a towel wrapped around her head raises the window and calls down to the woman with the game peddler.

Medium shot of the entrance to Zerkow's as Heise and Trina rush through the door.

Shot from inside as they enter on the run. Heise turns to Trina and asks: 'Where?' She points to the kitchen in the back. They both run towards it.

Medium shot from the sink towards the curtain. Heise and Trina enter, stop and look over to the ground.

Shot from their angle of Maria lying face downward on the floor.

Back to the scene as Heise says:

Title: 'By God, he's done for her in good shape this time — he always

279

said he would.

Back to the scene as Heise says that they must get a policeman. He drags Trina away; she has been standing there immobile, strangely fascinated.

Shot from the curtain towards the door. The game peddler, the man with the broad-brimmed hat, the scrubwoman and three other men are standing in the front room. With excited faces, they watch Heise and Trina leave; then, filled with morbid curiosity, the group advances towards the curtain in terrible awe.

Long shot angled down from the roof top as Heise and Trina run out of the house. The alley in front of Zerkow's house is packed solid with curious people. Heise and Trina dash through the gate and try to force their way through the crowd. Two policemen elbow their way through the crowd towards the gate. With them is a plainclothes policeman who disperses the mob. As the two uniformed officers run into the yard, a third officer arrives. Heise and Trina tell him that a murder has been committed. He runs out towards Laguna Street. Heise, Trina and the two other policemen go into the yard.

Shot from inside the yard towards the door. The policeman, Trina and Heise are running through the yard towards camera. One 'blue coat' starts clearing out the people who have accumulated in the yard.

Medium shot focussed on the curtain as Heise, Trina and the policeman arrive. They go through the curtain into the kitchen. We can see their silhouettes on the curtain as they look at the body. The policeman is the only one that goes nearer. Their shadows get smaller as they come back to the curtain. They come out of the kitchen and walk away towards the camera.

Medium shot as they arrive at the door and go out into the yard.

Long shot from Zerkow's roof of the yard and the street. An ambulance drives up; a doctor and an orderly jump off the wagon and enter the yard. One policeman is keeping back the crowd on the street, a second policeman stands in the yard. All the windows in the house opposite are packed with people looking down, and many others look over the fence. Heise, Trina and the third policeman walk towards the gate. When they reach the middle of the yard, they meet the doctor and the orderly. The policeman tells the doctor that Maria is dead; the doctor and the orderly turn to go back to the ambulance.

Shot from the roof of the house opposite Zerkow's. Trina and Heise are still in the yard and the policeman stands in front of the doorway. McTeague appears, looks around dumbfounded; then sees Trina and walks quickly over. With gestures, she excitedly tells him what has

280

happened. Slow iris out.

Iris in on McTeague's room. Trina is sitting on her side of the bed in a nightgown, her hair all down.

Close-up of Trina, gazing wide-eyed into space as she says :

TITLE : ' — And all this on account of a set of gold dishes that never existed.'

Back to the scene as Trina shudders and gets into bed. Iris out.

Iris in on the ferry tower; the clock reads five minutes past midnight. Dissolve out and in to a wharf on the waterfront. Several longshoremen and two policemen are lifting a dripping body onto the wharf.

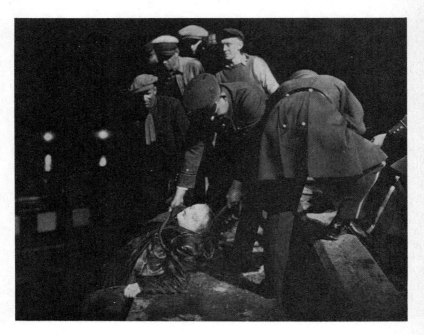

Close-up of the corpse's hand clutching a gunny sack.

Back to the scene as the policemen unsuccessfully try to pry the gunny sack out of the stiff hand. Finally, they take a knife, cut the sack off, and empty the contents on the wharf.

Close-up of a great quantity of rusty tin pans, dishes, brass knives and forks. Iris down on the tin dishes, hold for a second, and then iris out completely.

Iris in on McTeague's room. Trina is in bed asleep. McTeague is sitting on his side in his underwear, taking off his socks. Trina awakens with a shrill scream, trying to push somebody away from her. McTeague turns, looks at her and says: 'Huh? What? What is it?'
Close-up of Trina, who sits up with a terrified expression on her face and speaks:

TITLE: 'Oh, Mac, I had such an awful dream. Maria was chasing me — I couldn't run. Oh, I'm so frightened.'

Close-up of McTeague as he mutters:

TITLE: 'Aw, you and your dreams.'

Back to the scene as he continues: 'Shut up . . .' and adds:

TITLE: '. . . or I'll give you a dressing down.'

Back to the scene. Trina lies back in bed and sobs; he continues to undress. Iris out.
Iris in on a cheque from a book store. It is made out to Chas. W. Grannis for $500 and dated May 1, 1922. Iris enlarges to reveal Old

Grannis sitting in his cushioned armchair, holding the cheque. It is dusk; the book-binding machine is gone. Grannis listens a moment, then looks at the table on which the binding apparatus had stood; it is empty. A vast regret wells up within him.

Close-up of Grannis's hand with tears falling on it; the other hand wipes them off with an old-fashioned silk handkerchief.

Back to medium shot as he leans his face in his hands.

Medium shot of Miss Baker having tea in her room. There is a tea cup in her hand, and a second one stands on the table next to her. She listens at the wall, then looks at the second tea cup, then back to the wall. With a sudden resolve she rises, fills the second tea cup and walks towards the door.

Medium shot of Miss Baker going out of the door with the tea cup.

Medium shot of Miss Baker rapping timidly on Grannis's door.

Medium shot of Grannis as the door opens and he looks up, startled.

Close-up of Grannis staring towards the door.

Shot from his angle of Miss Baker carrying her cup of tea and holding it out to him.

Close-up of Miss Baker as she says :

TITLE : ' I thought you would like to have a cup.'

Shot from her angle of Old Grannis, whose hands drop to the arms of his chair as he leans forward a little and looks at her blankly.

Close-up of Miss Baker. She repeats that she has made some tea and that she thought he would like to have a cup. She is trembling so much that half of the tea has been spilt.

Close-up of Grannis, still silent, bending forward with wide eyes, and clutching the arms of his chair.

Close-up of Miss Baker as she splutters :

TITLE : ' Oh, I didn't mean . . . I didn't know it would seem like this . . . I only meant to be kind and bring you some tea.'

Close-up of Grannis, whose eyes get wider and fill with tears.

Back to the scene as Miss Baker continues speaking, tears in her eyes :

TITLE : '. . . And now it seems so improper — unladylike — you can never think well of me — I'll go.'

Back to the scene as Old Grannis cries : ' Stop.'

Shot from his angle. Miss Baker had already turned to go, but now turns back and looks at him over her shoulder; her eyes very wide open, tears running down her cheeks.

Medium close-up from her angle of Old Grannis rising to his feet as he says :

Title : ' I didn't know it was you at first — I couldn't believe you would be so good — so kind to me.'

Back to the scene as he walks up to Miss Baker.
Medium shot of Miss Baker at the door. Grannis appears and says :

Title : ' Oh, you are kind ! I — I — you have — have made me very happy.'

Back to the scene. Tears run down both their cheeks. Grannis reaches out and takes the tray from Miss Baker's hands, then turns and walks back into the room to set it upon the table. But the piles of pamphlets are in the way, and since he holds the tray with both hands, he can't make room for it. Embarrassed, he pauses for a moment, then turns and looks at Miss Baker and says : ' Won't you, please? '
Shot from his angle of Miss Baker saying : ' Wait, I'll help you,' as she comes into the room.
Medium shot of the scene. She moves the pamphlets to one side; Old Grannis puts down the tray and thanks her.
Medium close-up of both of them as Miss Baker splutters :

Title : ' Now . . . now . . . now I will go back.'

Back to the scene as Old Grannis protests : ' No, don't go, please,' and continues :

Title : ' Don't go, please — I've been so lonely tonight — and last night too — all this year — all my life.'

Back to the scene as Miss Baker speaks :

Title : ' I — I've forgotten the sugar.'

Back to the scene as Grannis quickly responds :

Title : ' I never use it.'

Back to the scene as Miss Baker says :

Title : ' But it's cold and I've spilled it . . . '

Back to the scene as Old Grannis says that it does not matter, and draws up his armchair for her. She says that she should not : ' This is so . . .' But she sits down, resting her elbows on the table and hiding her face in her hands. She then looks up, glances about, and comments :

TITLE : ' I thought you were binding your books tonight.'

Back to the scene as Old Grannis draws up a chair and sits down. He shakes his head and explains : ' I've sold my apparatus.' Miss Baker looks astonished and says : ' — And you're not going to bind books any more? ' Grannis sadly shakes his head. Miss Baker speaks :

TITLE : ' I used to hear you — '

Back to the scene as Grannis remarks : ' Yes, I heard you too.' He points to the chair, saying : ' I used to work here,' and continues :

TITLE : '. . . And didn't you sit close to the partition on the other side too? '

Back to the scene as Miss Baker, very much embarrassed, replies :

TITLE : ' I — I don't know where I sat.'

Back to the scene as Old Grannis shyly puts out his hand and takes hers which lies in her lap. He bends forward and, putting his face close to hers, asks : ' Didn't you sit close to the partition on your side? ' Miss Baker answers hesitatingly :

TITLE : ' No — I don't know — perhaps — sometimes.'

Back to the scene. Old Grannis looks a little bit disappointed and she adds with a little gasp :

TITLE : ' Oh yes, oh yes, I often did.'

Back to the scene as Old Grannis puts his arms about her, and kisses her faded cheeks. They sit there in the grey evening, holding hands.
Shot from the window into the street. A street car passes, a garbage wagon goes by in the opposite direction, an Italian organ-grinder stands on the sidewalk with two small monkeys that jump up and down while some kids stand watching.
Quick lap dissolve to the monkeys kissing each other.
Dissolve back to a close-up of Grannis's left hand held by both of Miss Baker's, while his right hand pats her left. Iris out.
Iris in on a sign reading : ' Rooms to let.' Iris enlarges to reveal Trina standing in front of Zerkow's gate, her finger held thoughtfully to her lips. She stares across the cleared junk yard towards the house. McTeague appears from the left, sees Trina and stops.
Medium close-up. Mac asks Trina what she is doing there. Pointing to the house, she answers : ' Now we've found a place to move to.' McTeague cries : ' What? In that dirty house? '

285

TITLE : 'Where you found Maria?'

Back to the scene as Trina says :

TITLE : 'I can't afford that room in the flat any more, now that you can't get any work to do.'

Back to the scene as Mac protests :

TITLE : 'But there's where Zerkow killed Maria. And you wake up and squeal in the night just thinking of it.'

Back to the scene as Trina says : 'I know, it will be bad at first.' She adds :

TITLE : 'But I'll get used to it and it's just half again as cheap.'

Back to the scene as she says resolutely : 'I'm going to take it!' McTeague fumes :

TITLE : '— And I have to live in that dirty rat hole, just so's you can save money.'

Back to the scene as Trina retorts :

TITLE : 'Find work to do and then we'll talk.'

Back to the scene as they look at each other. Suddenly Mac mutters : 'All right,' and starts to walk away.
Medium shot of the scene. He continues on his way as Trina stares after him in surprise. For a moment she is a bit troubled but soon overcomes her doubts, opens the gate and walks in. Iris out.

Fade in.

TITLE : 'The McTeagues now began to sink rapidly lower and lower.'

Fade out.
Iris in on the McTeagues' second floor room in Zerkow's house. Mac is asleep; Trina is washing over the washtub and washboard. She wears the torn blue wrapper and torn blue slippers and her hair is worse than ever. She is washing carelessly. The room is in a terrible condition and there are whittlings underneath the work table. Mac awakens and stretches his arms. Yawning, he looks towards the window.
Shot from his angle of the window, with the rain whipping against it.
Close-up of Mac as he says : 'Damned rain.'
Medium close-up of Trina at the washtub. Without turning, without even looking up, she says : 'It's been raining all night.' McTeague

286

speaks :

Title : ' Well, I'll go anyhow. The fish will bite all the better for the rain.'

Back to Trina as she stops washing, and with one hand on her hip turns towards Mac and says :

Title : ' Look here, why don't you bring some of your fish home sometime ? '

Medium close-up of Mac putting his socks on. Hearing Trina's words, he stops and stares at her. His face takes on a mean expression and his eyes twinkle as he says with a sarcastic laugh :

Title : ' Huh ! So we could have 'em for breakfast. Might save you a nickel, mightn't it ? '

Back to Trina as she says :

Title : ' Well ? And if it did ? '

Back to Mac as he buttons the last button on his pants and grumbles :

Title : ' Aw, shut up.'

Back to Trina, who turns disgustedly and goes back to her washing.
Medium shot of Mac as he calls over to Trina to get his breakfast.
Back to a medium close-up of Trina. She takes her hands out of the tub and dries them on her apron.
Close-up of her hands; her nails are blue and purple, two fingers are bound with small linen strips tied up with thread and another with a little piece of tape.
Back to medium close-up of Trina sighing, apparently in pain, as she dries her fingers. She walks in a slovenly manner over to the stove, takes the coffee pot and pours Mac a cup of coffee. She takes a chipped plate with three strips of bacon and a bit of mashed potato on it, puts it down on the table in front of Mac and returns to her washing. Mac sits down alone.
Medium shot of Trina back at the washtub as she resumes her washing.
Close-up of Mac as he looks at the plate; he is unwashed and un-combed and he don't give a damn.
Shot from his angle of the three lonesome strips of bacon shrivelled up on the plate.
Back to a close-up of McTeague; he makes a disgusted face and looks up towards the window.

Shot from his angle of the dripping laundry hanging from a clothes line in the window. It is raining and everything has a dull, hopeless look.

Back to a close-up of Mac as he turns to the right.

Shot from his angle of the right half of the room with the unmade, filthy bed, etc.

Back to a close-up of Mac as he turns towards the left.

Shot from his angle of the left side of the room. Trina is wringing out a pair of Mac's flannel underwear.

Back to a close-up of Mac, who looks disgusted. He gazes from Trina towards the trunk.

Shot from his angle of the trunk.

Back to Mac. He has a mean expression on his face as he speaks :

TITLE : 'Living in this hole and feedin' me this, you ought to soon have another thousand saved up.'

Close-up of Trina as she turns and looks searchingly at him and says : ' A thousand? Huh ! '

TITLE : ' — Not a hundred and fifty, not a hundred . . .'

Back to a close-up of Mac as he grins sarcastically; his glance falls on some object on the floor.

Shot from his angle of the gold tooth, which Trina is using as a table for dirty dishes.

Back to Mac as he gets an idea. He looks in the direction of Trina, then back at the tooth, and finally at the banged-up alarm clock.

Shot from his angle of the clock. It reads 9:30.

Back to a medium shot of the scene as Mac rises, puts on his cap and coat, without even buttoning the collar of his shirt, walks over to the tooth, and takes the dirty dishes off and lifts it up.

Close-up of Trina, who turns and asks : ' What are you going to do? '

Close-up of Mac with the tooth under his arm as he turns and growls :

TITLE : ' None of your damn business.'

Back to Trina as she resumes washing, and Mac leaves with the tooth. Fade out.

Fade in on the intersection of Laguna and Hayes Street. It is raining — raining — raining, and the street is deserted. Mac appears and crosses Hayes Street from the corner of Laguna with the gold tooth under his arm. A stray dog runs behind him. When he reaches the centre of the street Mac turns for a second, looking upward towards the old window, the very window where that tooth had hung and shone so attractively in the sunlight. He turns back and starts to walk on. Fade out.

Fade in on the door to a very nice dental office. A sign on the door reads : 'Dr. Wilbur Percy, Dentist, Ordinations, nine to twelve, two to four, Enter Without Knocking.' Mac appears with the tooth under his arm, puts it down on the floor and knocks before opening the door. Interior of the dental office. Mac walks inside without the tooth. 'Gray House' sits in front of the lit fireplace, a large mirror hangs over the mantel, and there are violets in a glass bowl on a polished table. Dr. Percy, wearing a white coat and looking very doctorish, is working on a patient. He sees Mac, looks up at him and enquires : 'What can I do for you this morning, Mister McTeague? Something wrong with the teeth? '

Shot from his angle of Mac as he replies : ' No.'

Close-up of Mac, who continues :

TITLE : ' I want to sell you my sign — that big tooth of French gilt — you know? That you made an offer for once? '

Shot from his angle of Dr. Percy shaking his head as he says : ' I don't want that now.'

TITLE : ' Big signs are vulgar.'

Back to Mac, from Percy's angle. He stares down at the floor, horribly embarrassed, not knowing whether to stay or to go.

Close-up of Dr. Percy as he speaks :

TITLE : ' But if it will help you out any — I'll — well, I'll give you five dollars for it.'

Back to a medium shot of Mac as he says : ' All right.' He turns, opens the door, and walks out to get the tooth.

Shot of Percy, who starts to work on the patient, and then looks up towards the door.

Shot from his angle of Mac as he enters with the tooth, which he puts down on the floor, embarrassed.

Shot from his angle as Dr. Percy approaches.

Medium shot of Mac and Dr. Percy, who extracts his wallet which is filled with money. He pulls out a $10 bill and asks : ' Got any change? ' Embarrassed, Mac says : ' No.' The dentist smiles sarcastically, puts the $10 bill back and says : ' Oh, I got one.' He extracts a $5 bill and gives it to Mac, who thanks him, turns, opens the door and goes out. Iris down on Percy grinning as he puts his wallet back. He looks down at

the tooth. Iris out completely.

Fade in on Trina whittling at the table in Mac's room. Mac enters and throws his cap on the hook.

Close-up of Trina as she looks up and asks :

TITLE : ' How much did you get? '

Close-up of Mac as he turns, glares at her and says : ' None of your business.'

Back to the scene. Mac fumbles in his trousers pockets, takes out a dollar, walks over to Trina and declares :

TITLE : ' Listen here, I'm sick and tired of bacon and mashed potato.'

Back to the scene as he throws the dollar on the table and continues speaking :

TITLE : ' — Get a steak or chops or something.'

Back to the scene as Trina looks dumbfounded and protests :

TITLE : ' Why, Mac, we can't afford to. Let me put that money away against a rainy day.'

Back to the scene as Mac thrusts his face close to hers and says threateningly : ' You do as I tell you ! ' Trina pleads with him : ' Please, Mac dear.' He ignores her and continues :

TITLE : ' Hurry, now ! I'll bite your fingers again, pretty soon.'

Back to the scene as she continues pleading. Mac comes still closer and snatches at her hand; Trina winces and shrinks back, saying : ' All right ! ' She takes the dollar and goes towards the door.
Medium shot as she takes her shawl from the hook and leaves. Fade out.]

TITLE : ' As Trina's greed grew, Mac's ambition waned . . . and died. They sank lower and lower that Trina might still save from her meagre earnings.' [1]

Long shot of Mac sitting disconsolately on the side of the bed with his head in his hands. The McTeagues' wedding portrait hangs on the wall near him.
Close-up of Mac turning to look at the picture.
Close-up of the torn wedding picture.
Close-up of Mac turning back. (The picture reminds him of the wedding dinner.)
Fade in on the ' Semite Market ', a small butcher's shop on a side street. The rain is still pouring down. Trina arrives on the run, closes her umbrella and goes into the shop.
Medium shot of Trina arriving at the meat counter. [Two cats jump from the meat onto the ground.] The butcher appears and asks her what she wants, pointing out the selection of meat and indicating the cost.
[Medium close-up of the butcher and Trina. Trina says : ' I want fifteen cents' worth o' mutton chops.' The butcher says with a gesture : ' They're two for a quarter.'] Trina shakes her head and says : ' Ain't you got some cheaper? '
Close-up of Trina, thoughtful, with her finger to her lips.
Back to the scene as the butcher looks at her for a moment and then takes a barrel of meat from underneath the counter, saying :

TITLE : ' That's three days old. It's hardly fit for dogs.'

---

[1] This title and the following shots of Mac do not appear in Stroheim's original script.

Back to the scene as he offers the barrel, then goes off to the right.

Medium close-up of Trina poking about in the barrel and grimacing at the bad smell. She selects two chops.

Back to the scene as Trina nods to the butcher, who reappears and wraps up the two chops; she pays him.

[Close-up of the butcher's hand receiving the $1 from Trina.

Back to the scene as he throws the $1 into the cash register and rings up the sale.]

Close-up of the cash register recording '15c'.

Back to the scene as he hands over the change and she walks out.

Medium close-up of Trina outside the shop. She stops for a second. [Close-up of her hands.] She is holding the 85c change in one hand. After hesitating for a moment, she transfers 60c into her right skirt pocket and keeps only a quarter in her left pocket.

Back to the scene in long shot as she opens her umbrella and runs off. Fade out.

Fade in on the McTeagues' room. Trina enters, shakes off the rain and removes her shawl.

Close-up of Mac, who is still sitting on the bed. [He is smoking and putting on his big buckled shoes.]

Back to medium shot of Trina as she approaches the stove with the package of meat.
Back to close-up of Mac watching her closely.
Medium shot of Trina opening the package, lighting a gas burner and getting a frying pan.
Close-up of Mac watching with a dazed look on his face.
Medium shot of Trina putting the chops in the pan and starting to cook them.
Close-up of Mac, who looks down at Trina's trunk.
Close-up of the trunk.
Back to close-up of Mac.
Medium shot of Trina cooking.
Medium close-up of Mac, who rises. [He turns towards her, holding out his hand.]
Medium shot of Trina at the stove as Mac approaches and demands :

TITLE : ' Where's my change? '

Back to medium shot as Trina turns, acting as if she had forgotten all about it. She gives Mac the quarter. He looks at it and says : [' Is that all? ']

TITLE : ' Two bits o' a dollar? '

Close-up of Trina, who acts unusually excited about the high cost of living and says : [' If you got to have meat, you got to pay for it.' He believes her.]

TITLE : ' Do you think I'd cheat you? '

Close-up of Mac holding one hand to the back of his head and looking a bit bewildered.
Back to medium shot of the scene as Mac goes over to sit down. Fade out.

[Iris in on several carpenters at work on the partition wall between Grannis's and Miss Baker's rooms. They have broken through the wall and are putting in a door. Boards, tools and wood shavings litter the room. Grannis and Miss Baker are standing in the bay window near the goldfish. Their arms are around each other's waists and she is leaning her false curls against her new husband's shoulder. They are looking on in ecstasy. Slowly their gaze moves from the wall towards the window.
Medium close-up of them holding hands and looking lovingly at each

other. They turn and look out through the window into the street.

Shot from their angle of the window and the dreary street outside; it is pouring with rain.

Lap dissolve in to a scene from the same angle, taken in natural colours. Through the window we can see a gorgeous apple and peach orchard in bloom. Mr. and Mrs. Grannis, dressed in their Sunday finery, walk arm in arm towards camera. They stop for a second, imbibe the scent of the blossoms, sigh happily and look at each other. He points to the bench next to them and they sit down holding hands. Lap dissolve out.

Dissolve in to the original medium shot with Mr. and Mrs. Grannis standing in the room by the window. They look at each other, smiling happily.

Medium close-up of both of them as he takes her left hand and looks at it, fingers the thin gold band and then kisses it. As he bows his head to kiss the ring, she lowers hers and kisses him on the head. In the background we can see the carpenters sawing a board for the door. Iris down on the saw, hold for a second, then iris out completely.]

TITLE : 'Mac's meal was eaten and finished in silence. For the first time in his life he had thoughts.'[1]

[Iris in on McTeague's room. He rises and wipes his mouth with the back of his hand, then takes his overcoat, slips it on, and picks up his hat and fishing tackle.

Close-up of McTeague as he looks at Trina and announces :

TITLE : 'I'm going to be gone all day.']

Medium shot of the scene. Trina is clearing the table. Mac puts a piece of bread in his pocket, gets his fishing gear and rod, and goes towards the door. He stops and turns.

Close-up of Mac as he says :

TITLE : 'So long —'

Shot from his angle of Trina, who looks over at Mac, very much surprised by his amiability.

Medium shot of the scene as she puts down the dishes and walks up to him.

Medium close-up of Trina and Mac. She puts her arms around his neck and says :

---

[1] This title does not appear in Stroheim's original script.

TITLE : 'Kiss me goodbye, Mac — [You do love me a little yet, don't you?] '

Back to medium close-up of them. He looks at her dully as she continues speaking; she grabs his hair to pull his face down to hers and gives him a big kiss on the mouth. Then she thoughtfully puts her finger to her mouth and says :[1]

TITLE : 'Why don't you bring some of your fish home sometimes? '

Back to the scene as Mac nods disgustedly and growls :

TITLE : 'It might save you a nickel.'

Back to medium close-up of the couple as Mac looks back into the

---

[1] The following exchange about the fish is transposed in the film from its original place in the script. Stroheim's script has the following at this point :
TITLE : 'We'll be happy again some day — It's hard times now, but we'll pull out.'
Back to the scene as he nods vaguely. She continues speaking :
TITLE : ' — You'll find something to do pretty soon.'
Back to the scene as Mac says : 'I guess so,' and allows her to kiss him.

room at Trina's trunk.

Close-up of the trunk.

Back to medium close-up of Mac as he continues to gaze around the room.

Close-up of the bird cage; the two canaries are jumping up and down.

Back to the scene as Mac looks up at the cage, stares at the birds, and then says :

TITLE : ' I think I'll take them birds of mine along.'

Back to the scene as Trina glances at him and asks :

TITLE : ' Sell 'em? '

Back to the scene. He looks at her for a second, a crafty look in his eyes. Mac keeps his thoughts to himself and says : ' Yes, sell 'em.' Trina cautions : ' But don't you let that bird store woman cheat you.'

TITLE : ' — You ought to make her give you five dollars for them.'

Back to the scene as Mac nods and goes to get the bird cage.

Close-up of Trina, who is still speaking :

TITLE : '. . . Maybe six dollars.' [1]

Medium shot of the bird cage by the window. Outside, we can see the rain pouring down. Mac appears and wraps the cage in an old newspaper.

Close-up of Trina watching him.

Medium shot of Mac walking back towards Trina with the cage in one hand and his fishing line in the other.

Medium close-up of Mac, who again stops for a second and says :

TITLE : ' Well, so long — [so long].'

Medium close-up of Trina smiling at Mac as she says :

TITLE : ' Goodbye, Mac.'

Back to the scene. Trina watches as Mac goes to the door and leaves.

Close-up of Trina with her finger to her lips.

Medium shot at the foot of the steps. Mac appears, carrying the bird cage and fishing tackle. He starts walking towards the door, stops for a second, looks back once more and all around, then exits.

Medium shot of the front of the house. On the wall next to the door are the words : ' All kinds of junk — rags — sacks — iron.' Mac

---

[1] This title does not appear in Stroheim's script.

appears, carrying the bird cage and the fishing tackle. He looks up towards the house and then walks away.

Medium shot of Mac's room. Trina is sitting on the floor next to the open trunk, gazing at a couple of gold pieces and murmuring :

TITLE : 'How I've slaved and starved for you.' [1]

Fade out.

[She polishes the coins until they gleam, then she closes the trunk and looks at it for a moment. Finally, after she has put the key under the carpet, Trina rises and goes over to the work table.

Medium shot of the work table as Trina sits down and starts whittling.

Close-up of Trina; her fingers seem to hurt her. She stops for a second and looks at them.

Close-up of her fingers; they are blue and lacerated, the nails are blue and purple.

Back to the scene as she gazes into space for a second, and then, with a deep sigh, resumes her work. Fade out.

---

[1] This title is transposed in the film from its original place in an earlier scene.

Fade in on the points of some rocks near the ocean. It is foggy and a fine rain falls. Mac is sitting on the rocks, fishing and looking stupidly into the water; the bird cage wrapped in newspaper lies beside him. Close-up of Mac, who is mumbling to himself.

Title : ' I ain't going to stand it much longer — '

Shot from behind Mac with the ocean in the background. He is slowly shaking his head. Suddenly Mac feels a tug on the rod and starts taking in his line. Iris down on his head, hold for a second, then pan to the stretch of water where Mac's line is sunk as a fish appears dangling on the end of the line. Iris out completely.

Iris in on an alarm clock; it shows seven o'clock. Iris enlarges to reveal Trina, who is still whittling. She turns, looks at the clock and then rises. She cannot understand why Mac is so late. She goes over to the door, opens it, and listens. Disappointed, she closes the door, walks over to the oil stove and lights the fire. She puts the remainder of the mashed potatoes still on the plate and three strips of bacon into the frying pan. Fade out.

Fade in on the point of rocks at the ocean. It is growing dark; waves crash up against the rocks. Mac has gone. Iris down on the place where Mac had been sitting, hold for a second, and then iris out.

Iris in on the clock : eight o'clock. Iris enlarges to show Trina working at the table. She glances over at the clock; she cannot understand where Mac is. She rises, puts her shawl over her head and hurries from the room.

Lap dissolve to a shot of Zerkow's yard. Trina appears through the gate and looks up and down the alley. Lap dissolve as she walks off towards the right.

Medium shot of Heise closing up his harness shop. Trina appears and they greet each other. She asks him if he has seen Mac; Heise shakes his head : 'No.' Trina suggests that Mac may be at Frenna's saloon. When Heise agrees, she begs him to go in and see. They both leave towards the right, while Mrs. Heise finishes closing the door.

Quick lap dissolve to the entrance of Frenna's saloon as Heise and Trina arrive. Heise goes in while Trina stays outside.

Medium shot inside the saloon as Heise enters and asks the bartender if Mac is there or has been there. The bartender replies : 'No,' and Heise leaves.

Back to the front of the saloon as Heise appears from inside and tells Trina that Mac is not in the saloon and that the bartender hasn't seen him. Trina is worried; she thanks Heise and hurries away. Heise looks after her for a second, scratches his head, and then goes back into the saloon.

Medium shot of the end of the alley leading to Zerkow's hut. A Salvation Army band is passing as Trina appears. The rain has stopped, but the pavement is still wet.

Close-up of Trina as she pauses to watch the band, which has stopped at the entrance to the alley.

Quick lap dissolve to large close-up of the big drum with a stick hitting it in slow march tempo (let run for six feet).

Back to a medium shot of Trina; she turns and walks on.

Back to a close-up of the drum, with the hand drumming in the same tempo. Fade out.

Medium shot outside McTeague's room. It is almost dark. Trina appears on the run, listens at the door for a moment and then opens it. The room is dark.

Medium shot of the inside of the room shooting towards the door. Trina walks in and closes the door behind her.

Close-up of Trina, one sore finger raised to her lips, as she says : ' Isn't this funny.' She looks in the direction of the clock.

Shot from her angle of the clock : half-past eight.

Back to a close-up of Trina; a great fear seizes her. Dissolve out.

Dissolve in to a rocky section of the beach (not the one where Mac was fishing). Mac is standing on the rocks, trying to haul in a fish. He leans over quite a bit, loses his balance and falls into the ocean. The water closes over him.

Lap dissolve back to Trina. She disperses the vision and says : ' No — Mac can take care of himself.'

Medium shot, low camera set-up, from inside the room and shooting towards the door on the ground floor of Zerkow's house. The door opens. We can see a pair of legs and shoes entering, but it is too dark to identify them. The door slams shut.

Back to Trina as she hears the bang. She sighs with relief, quickly opens the door and calls down : ' Is that you, Mac? ' There is no answer.

Back to the scene. Trina is quite frightened. She stamps her foot, puts her shawl over her head, and leaves the room. Fade out.

Fade in.

TITLE : ' Night drew her sable curtain down and pinned it with a star.'

Fade out.

Long shot in front of Mac's former flat. The solitary figure of Trina is seen walking slowly down towards Hayes Street. She stops and looks back, then glances towards Frenna's. Finally, she turns and walks on.

299

Medium shot at the corner of the street, underneath the bay window, as Trina appears. She looks up and down the street, but sees no one. A policeman with a night stick in his hand passes her with his flat-footed walk; he turns casually and looks after her for a second, then walks on. Trina looks up towards the bay window; there is a rusty iron rod projecting out and writing on the window says : ' To Let.'
Close-up of Trina looking up.
Shot from her angle of the protruding iron rod.
Lap dissolve in to the same scene, but with the gold tooth hanging from the rod. Lap dissolve out.
Back to close-up of Trina as she turns and looks down Laguna Street.
Shot from her angle of the gold tooth as it hangs, brightly illuminated, from the bay window in the next block.
Back to a close-up of Trina as she speaks :

TITLE : ' Life isn't so gay — but I wouldn't mind anything if only Mac was home all right.'

Medium shot from behind her as a street car stops farther down the street. Trina bends forward to see if Mac is going to get off it. But only two people descend : a man and a woman, apparently sweethearts. The man kisses the girl, who reciprocates, and they start to cross the street.
Back to medium shot of Trina, who has been watching the couple. As the street car continues on its way, she starts walking again, very disappointed.
Medium shot from ahead of Trina (from perambulator). She walks into the light of a street lantern in front of the door to her former home. All at once an idea comes to Trina; a terrible idea, even more terrible than the thought of her husband's death. Raising her sore fingers to her lips, she cries : ' Oh no, oh no. It isn't true, but suppose . . .' A terrible fear seizes her and starts to run off.
Medium shot in front of Zerkow's fence as Trina runs up. She hesitates for a second, then looks up and again cries : ' No ! No ! It isn't possible, but suppose — suppose — ' The terror returns and she opens the gate and runs into the yard.
Medium shot of the front of the house as Trina dashes inside.
Medium shot of the top of the stairs in front of her door. Trina runs up, all out of breath. For some reason or other she hesitates in the hallway, afraid to open the door; but finally she goes in, pauses, and with trembling fingers lights the lamp.
Close-up as she slowly turns, her sore fingers up to her mouth, and looks at her trunk.

Shot from her angle of the trunk; the lock is broken.

Close-up of Trina as she moans: ' No — no — no — , it isn't true, it isn't true ! '

Medium shot as she drops on her knees in front of the trunk and tosses back the lid. Plunging her hands down into the corner underneath her wedding dress, she finds the brass matchbox and the chamois bag; she lifts them up.

Close-up of the matchbox and the chamois bag — they are empty.

Back to the scene as Trina flings herself full length upon the floor, burying her face in her arms and rolling her head from side to side.

Close-up of Trina lying on the floor. Tears roll down her cheeks, her hair is undone; and she sobs as she screams :

TITLE : ' Oh, if you'll only come back — you can have all the money — half of it — '

Back to a close-up as she thinks for a second, then corrects herself as she continues :

TITLE : ' Oh, give me back my money — I've worked so hard for you — for them — and now, I'm a beggar.'

Back to the scene. Trina's grief is terrible. She repeatedly digs her nails into her skull, clutching and tearing at the heavy coils of her hair. Then she strikes her forehead with clenched fists, while her body shakes from head to foot. Finally, she beats her head upon the floor with all her strength, and screams :

TITLE : ' — Gone for good — gone and never coming back — gone with my gold pieces.'

Fade out.
Fade in.

TITLE : ' Gold — what can it not do and undo.'

Fade out.

Fade in on Trina in bed. On one side stand Miss Baker (now Mrs. Grannis) and Mr. Grannis — on the other side the doctor, and the landlady a little farther to the left. The doctor washes the bloodstains off Trina's forehead with sterilized cotton and paints the wound with iodine; he listens to her heart with a stethoscope.

Close-up of Trina. Her eyes are closed and her breath is coming in short gasps. She slowly opens her eyes.

Medium close-up of Mr. and Mrs. Grannis. Mrs. Grannis is crying, and points to the trunk, telling him all about it. They both look over.

Shot from their point of view of the trunk. Trina's things are strewn all over the floor, including the empty matchbox and bag, but dominating everything else is her white silk wedding dress, which hangs more than half out of the trunk.

Back to the scene as the Grannises look at each other. As the doctor puts the stethoscope aside and feels Trina's pulse, his eyes fall on the fingers of her right hand. He takes them up quickly and looks sharply at them.

Close-up of her hand; on two fingers, a deep red glow extends from the fingertips down to the second knuckle.

Back to the scene as the doctor whistles and speaks :

TITLE : ' We'll have to have those fingers amputated beyond a doubt, or else the entire hand — or even worse.'

Close-up of Trina; tears run down her cheeks as she looks at the doctor. She has heard everything, and moans :

TITLE : ' — And my work — '

Back to the scene. The doctor turns to the landlady; Mrs. Grannis kneels down next to Trina, pats her hand and her head, and cries. Iris down on Trina looking over at the table.

Shot from her angle of a carton on the table with the label ' Non-poisonous paints ' in iris. Iris out completely.]

Fade in.

TITLE : ' Mac never returned after that day . . . so Trina took employment as a scrubwoman.' [1]

[Iris in on a hand with only two fingers which are holding a scrubbing brush, scrubbing a floor. Iris enlarges as camera tilts and moves back on perambulator to reveal Trina.]

Medium shot of Trina, scrubbing a floor. She has aged considerably, and has a suffering expression engrained on her face. She finishes scrubbing, rises and picks up her bucket and brush [and sand, and wipes her forehead]. Then she stands still and rests for a second.

Long shot of exterior of a building : ' Lester Memorial Kindergarten.' A street car passes on the street.

Back to medium shot of Trina still standing in the same position.

Long shot inside the building as Trina goes towards the main room,

---

[1] This title does not appear in Stroheim's script, which instead has the following :
TITLE : ' One can hold a scrubbing brush with two good fingers and the stumps of two others, even if both joints of the thumb are gone, but it takes considerable practice to get used to it.'

where we see some children who have arrived and are now playing. [The teacher arrives, meets Trina in the hall and thanks her.
Medium shot of Trina as she nods dully to the teacher, who stops, opens her bag and gives Trina a cheque. Trina takes it, thanks her, and then follows the teacher into the main room.]
Medium shot of the main room as Trina passes through. Some of the children follow her towards the right.
Medium shot of a closed double door on the right which leads to the cloakroom. The kids open it, run in and hang up their hats and caps. A black cat jumps off the coat rack and runs out. Trina enters and puts the bucket and the brush on the floor. [She looks at the cheque.]
Medium shot of Trina, who closes the double doors and then continues on towards her room at the back of the school.[1]
Medium shot of some kids running around and bumping into each other as they play.
Back to medium shot of Trina arriving at her room. Fade out.
[Close-up of Trina as she looks at the cheque and something resembling a smile comes into her face. She has an idea.
Medium shot as she hurries out of the cloakroom.
Shot from behind Trina through the main school room as she appears through the doorway and turns to the left.
Shot from the opposite side of the street as Trina leaves the school house, walks through the gate, turns to the right and ducks into the Chinese laundry.
Medium shot of Trina inside the Chinese laundry. A Chinaman appears and says: 'Hello.' She shows him the cheque. He looks at it casually for amusement, then nods, gives her a paint brush and Chinese ink, and points to the place on the back of the cheque where she should endorse it. She looks for a second at her right hand, then takes the brush in her left hand and signs the cheque while the Chinaman goes to a closet in the back of the laundry. He takes out a cashbox, then brings it back to the counter and spills the contents on the table. He starts to give her paper money, but she refuses to take it. Then as he starts to count out the amount in silver coins, Trina spots a twenty-dollar gold piece and a ten-dollar gold piece. Pointing to them, she says: 'Gi' me that.' He replies: 'Allee light,' and gives her the gold in exchange for the cheque. He says: 'Goodbye,' and she goes out.
Medium shot through the window of the Chinese laundry as Trina appears through the doorway and turns to the left.

---

[1] This and the following two shots do not appear in Stroheim's script, in which the scene continues as will be seen below.

Shot from the kindergarten porch towards the gate in the street. Trina arrives from the right, hurries through the gate, runs up the steps and turns to the left.

Shot of the main school room as Trina passes by. In the background we can see the teacher, with a pencil in her hand, directing the kids in singing.

Medium shot outside Trina's room. She unlocks the door with a key from her pocket.

Medium shot of the room as Trina enters and locks the door behind her. She runs over to the trunk under the bed and pulls it out. We can see the repaired lock and the marks of the iron where it was broken open. She takes the keys from the string around her neck, unlocks the trunk and takes out the chamois bag, which is almost empty. After pulling down the shades and turning on the electric light, she empties the contents of the bag on the bed cover, and counts the money.

Close-up from her angle of $48 : one twenty-dollar gold piece, two ten-dollar gold pieces, one five-dollar gold piece and three silver pieces (all hand-coloured).

Back to the scene. Trina gazes at the money with great pleasure, distressed only by the paltry number of coins. She kisses the gold pieces, polishes them with her apron and then puts them back in the chamois bag. She feels the bag and realizes how slender it is.

Close-up of Trina, remembering how nice and full and heavy the bag once was. She gazes into space and laments :

TITLE : ' I could have forgiven him if he had only gone away and left me my money — '

Back to the scene as she looks at the stumps of her fingers, and continues :

TITLE : ' — Even this.'

Back to Trina as her eyes narrow and her mouth hardens. She clenches her left hand and says :

TITLE : ' — But now — I'll — never — forgive — him — as — long — as — I — live.'

Back to the scene as she suddenly gets an idea.

Medium shot in front of the bed as Trina kneels down, reaches under the bed and takes out a dusty parcel tied up in newspaper. She breaks the string; it is McTeague's concertina. She thinks for a second, then picks up the concertina and lays it on the bed. She then takes the bag and quickly puts it back in the trunk. She sees the wedding dress, looks at it, holds it up and thinks for a moment, then folds and wraps it up in a piece of newspaper. Very carefully she locks the trunk and pushes it underneath the bed. Finally, she takes her hat and jacket, covers the concertina with the newspaper and goes out, carrying the concertina and the wedding dress under her arm.

Medium shot of the front of the kindergarten as Trina walks by towards the right. Fade out.

Iris in on McTeague's hand placing a twenty-dollar gold piece on the bar. The bartender's hand appears and takes the coin.

Long shot of the bar-room, which is on the waterfront. The bartender rings up the bill, and then goes back to McTeague and leaves the change (two quarters) on the bar. Mac is standing at the bar, half-cockeyed, with a dozen men around him. They all slap him on the back and drink to him. He looks around and fumbles in his pocket, then takes out the last five-dollar piece and plonks it on the bar. He makes it clear that it is his last one— his pockets are empty. The men comment: 'What the hell do you care?' Mac says: 'Let's have another drink. What'll it be?' The bartender takes their orders and starts to fix the drinks. Iris out on Mac stupefied.

Fade in on Trina's room. Trina enters, closes the door and locks it. She goes over to the bed and takes off her hat and coat. Then, holding a new five-dollar gold piece in her hand, she unlocks the trunk and takes out the bag.

Close-up of Trina as she looks at the coin, smiling.

Close-up of her hand holding the five-dollar gold piece (hand-coloured). Back to the scene as she kisses it, opens the bag and puts the coin inside. She shakes the bag, then throws the contents on the bed cover and plays with the coins. Finally, she removes a piece of paper from the trunk and reads it.

Flash insert of the receipt from Oelbermann for $4,800.

Back to the scene as she refills the bag, very aware of how thin it is; she gets the brass matchbox and opens it. It is empty.

Close-up of Trina thinking.

Lap dissolve to a locked safe with the name 'Rudolph Oelbermann' on it.

Lap dissolve to a shot of the safe, open with piles of gold in one section. There is a light on them and they gleam.

Quick lap dissolve back to Trina's face. She looks back at the bag and then gets an idea. She puts the bag and box back into the trunk, locks it and pushes it under the bed. Then she takes her hat and coat and puts them on as she hurriedly unlocks the door and runs out. Fade out.

Iris in on the exterior of the waterfront saloon. McTeague comes out alone. He stops and reaches into his pocket for his tobacco tin. He takes it out and pours some out, but it is empty. He throws it away with a curse and fumbles in his pockets; they are all empty. Two of the men who had been drinking with him come out of the saloon. Mac sees them, walks up to the men and asks : ' Have you got some tobacco? ' They say : ' No,' and walk on while Mac stands there. He makes a step towards the bar, then retraces it and looks around. His glance falls on the sidewalk.

Shot from his angle of a half-burned cigar which somebody has crushed on the sidewalk.

Back to the scene as he picks it up, breaks it, puts it in his pipe and lights it. He puffs, spits, looks around for a moment and then walks away. Iris out.

Iris in on Oelbermann's office. Trina is sitting opposite Oelbermann at his desk.

Medium close-up of them as Oelbermann speaks :

TITLE : ' — This will reduce the amount of your interest by just half.'

Back to the scene as Trina says : ' Yes, I know — I thought of that.' Oelbermann continues :

TITLE : ' This isn't business-like at all — to draw so much without notice.'

Back to the scene as Trina nods and says : ' Yes, I know, but you see — ' Oelbermann interrupts :

TITLE : ' I'd prefer if you would draw it all at once now, today, and be done with it.'

Back to the scene as he asks : ' Shall I draw you a cheque? ' Trina says : ' No, no,' refusing with characteristic apprehension. ' No, I'll leave it with you. Just half — what I ask for.' He writes her a cheque, gives it to her and asks for her old receipt. When she hands it to him, he writes down : ' Cash $2400.00, Balance $2400.00,' blots the receipt and then gives it back to her. She thanks him and leaves the office.

Medium shot of Trina passing through Oelbermann's store. In the background a girl with a basket stands at the counter, pouring out wooden figures like those Trina used to make. Trina stops for a second, looks first at the figures and then at her mutilated hands. She sighs and walks out.

Medium shot of the front of the store. Trina appears from inside the store; she unfolds the cheque and stares at it.

Close-up of Trina looking thoughtfully at the cheque and visualizing the whole $4800 in gold, her breath becoming short. Slowly, she turns around and re-enters the store.

Medium shot of Oelbermann writing in the office. Trina enters, and stands trembling at the corner of Oelbermann's desk.

Close-up of Oelbermann. He looks up, startled.

Close-up of Trina as she tries to get her voice. She speaks :

TITLE : ' Yes — all right — I'll — you can give me all the money.'

Back to a close-up of Oelbermann, who looks at her and thinks for a second.

Back to a medium shot as he takes his cheque book and writes another cheque.

Close-up of Trina watching him, her eyes glistening. Iris down on her face.

Iris in on the pay teller's window; the cashier's hand is piling up 240 twenty-dollar gold pieces. As he counts out the last three, the iris enlarges to reveal Trina watching him with glistening eyes. A special officer on the other side watches her. The bank teller puts the money in a canvas sack, and hands it to Trina.

Close-up of Trina as she takes the sack with her mutilated hand. She looks around furtively, puts the sack under her jacket, and starts to walk out. Iris out.]

Fade in.

TITLE : ' — And with all her gold she was alone — a solitary, abandoned woman — [lost in the eddies of the great city's tide — the tide that always ebbs].'

Fade out.

Fade in to a long shot of the deserted street outside the kindergarten. It is night and a street lamp lights the scene. A light in Trina's window shines through a crack in the shade and a dim light comes from the Chinese laundry next door.

Quick lap dissolve to medium shot of the interior of Trina's room. The bed is open; Trina is standing in her petticoat and shirt in front of the bed, pouring the gold pieces from the chamois bag onto the sheets with mad delight. She spreads the coins out on the bed, takes a cushion away, looks around, then drops her petticoat and stands only in her long shirt. [She looks towards the light, runs over to the door and tries it, then runs back.

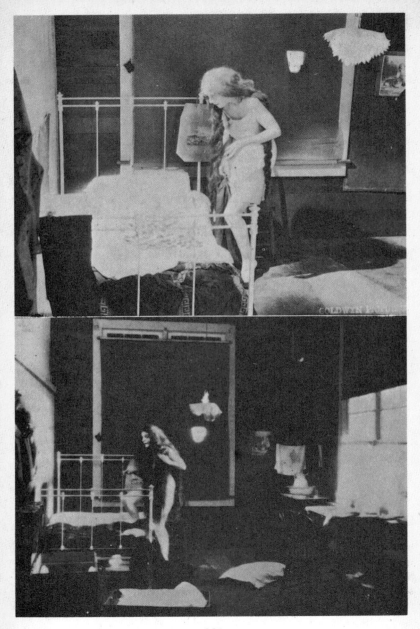

Close-up of her shoulders as her hands gather the shirt and pull it over her head; she drops it and turns out the light.

Long shot of the room lit by one thin streak of light as her nude body gets into bed.

Close-up of Trina in bed. Her hands pour gold pieces over her nude shoulders; she is experiencing a physical delight and smiles a bit. Iris out.

Iris in on the clock just striking midnight.

Lap dissolve to a long shot of the deserted kindergarten. Mac enters from the right carrying the bird cage covered with paper. He looks around.]

Medium close-up of Mac bending over a trash can; he holds a torn photograph and looks over towards the school house.

Close-up of McTeague's wedding picture, torn in two, showing Mac in a formal suit.

Back to medium close-up of Mac bending over.

Close-up of the torn bit of photo with Trina in her wedding dress.

Back to medium close-up of Mac as he looks up at the school.

Long shot of the street and the school as Mac approaches the gate; he is carrying the bird cage.

Medium close-up of Trina just settling herself more comfortably as she lies in bed.

Medium shot of Mac approaching Trina's window.

Close-up of Trina in bed.

Medium shot of Mac just outside the window.

Close-up of Mac. He listens a moment, then knocks on the window.

Medium close-up of Trina in bed; she sits up, terribly frightened, and listens.

Back to medium close-up of Mac knocking.

Medium close-up of Trina, who [grabs the sheet and puts it over her head, then] rises from the bed.

Medium close-up of Mac at the window.

Medium shot of Trina covering the gold coins with the bed cover.

Medium close-up of Mac.

Medium close-up of Trina wrapping a blanket around her as she goes towards the window.

Medium close-up of Trina at the window. She raises the shade a bit and looks out. The moonlight pours in as she sees Mac and draws back in fright.

Shot from her angle of Mac motioning to her to raise the sash.

Back to medium shot of the scene as Mac gestures to her to open the window. She obeys reluctantly, then cautiously locks the partially open

309

window.

Close-up from her angle of Mac as he steps closer and says :

TITLE : 'Say, Trina — let me in, will ya? [I'm starvin' — I haven't slept in a Christian bed for two weeks.] '

Shot from his angle of Trina as she whispers : 'No, I won't let you in.' Medium shot over her shoulder of Mac as he says : 'But Trina, I tell you I'm starving.'
[Shot from his angle of Trina retorting :

TITLE : 'A man can't starve with $450, I guess.']

Shot from her angle of McTeague saying :
TITLE : 'Trina, I ain't had nothin' to eat since yesterday mornin'.' [1]

Shot from his angle of Trina as she shakes her head and speaks :

TITLE : 'I'll see you starve before you get any more of my money.'

---

[1] This title does not appear in Stroheim's script, which instead has the following :
TITLE : 'Well, I've spent them — but you can't see me starve, Trina, no matter what's happened.'

Shot from her angle of Mac as he steps back a pace and says : 'What did you say? Huh? '
[Shot from his angle of Trina as she declares : 'I won't give you any money, never again — not a cent! '
Shot from her angle of Mac imploring :

TITLE : 'Trina, I ain't had a thing to eat since yesterday morning — that's God's truth.'

Back to a shot from his angle of Trina as she shakes her head.
Back to Mac as he argues :

TITLE : 'Even if I did get off with your money — you can't see me starve, can ya? And walk the streets because I ain't got no place to sleep? '

Back to Trina as she shakes her head.
Back to Mac as he says :

TITLE : 'Well then — gi'me a dollar — gi'me a half dollar — say, gi'me a dime and I can get a cup of coffee.'

Back to Trina as she shakes her head.
Shot from her angle of Mac as he pauses.] He looks up at her with curious intentness, nonplussed, and exclaims :

TITLE : ' [You must be crazy, Trina,] I wouldn't let a dog go hungry.'

Back to a shot through the window of Trina reacting to his outburst.
Medium close-up from inside of their faces at the window. Trina holds out her mutilated hand and says :

TITLE : 'Not if he'd bitten you? '

Back to close-up of Trina.
Medium close-up of both of them as Mac stares at Trina's hand, then looks up at her in silence. [Finally, he speaks :

TITLE : 'Then will ya gi'me something to eat? ']

Back to Trina as she cries : 'No! ' and shakes her head.
Back to Mac. He raises one enormous, lean fist, then growls and threatens :

TITLE : 'If I had hold of you . . . [I'd make you dance — and I will yet!] '

Back to close-up of Mac, furious.

Medium close-up of the scene as Mac turns and starts to walk away.
Medium close-up of Mac as he stamps off.
Medium shot of Trina, her two fingers held to her lips. With frightened gestures of both hands, she realizes what she has done.
[Close-up of Trina. She leans over the window.
Medium shot from outside as she looks out and calls : ' Mac, oh Mac.' No answer.
Medium shot from the inside of the room. Trina draws her head back, closes the window and starts crying; then she goes over to the bed and turns out the light.
Medium shot of the front of the bed as she takes the cover off; the whole bed is filled with gold pieces. Seeing them, Trina remembers what she has done by refusing her husband a dime for something to eat. She breaks down at the bed and cries.
Close-up of Trina as she speaks :

TITLE : ' — But he stole my money — I couldn't forgive anyone that — No, not even my mother.'

Back to the scene as she shakes her head decisively. Iris out.

Fade in on the Civic Center Park, with a bench and street lantern. Mac apears, tired, disheartened and sore. He sits down on the bench and puts the bird cage down next to him.
Close-up of Mac as he speaks :

TITLE : ' Five thousand and she wouldn't gi'me a dime to get a cup of coffee with.'

Back to the scene. Mac's expression becomes mean, his jaw goes forward and he mumbles, clenching his fists :

TITLE : ' Oh ! If I once get my hands on you — '

Back to the scene as he clutches at the darkness in front of him. A policeman appears, approaches Mac slowly, looks at him, and then says : ' Move on.' Mac glances up, takes the cage, rises and walks off. The policeman looks after him, then sits down himself. Fade out.
Fade in.

TITLE : ' — That night he walked the streets until morning — '

Fade out.
Fade in on Kearny Street. It is morning and there is general traffic.
Quick lap dissolve to the front of a piano store where three men are

loading a piano onto a truck. Mac appears, carrying the bird cage; he stops and watches. The man carrying the front part of the piano is a big, heavy-set Negro.

Close-up of a banana peel on the sidewalk as the Negro steps on it.

Back to the scene as he slips and falls, and the piano lands on top of his leg. Alarmed, Mac rushes up. He looks around for a second, sees a big coloured woman standing by, and quickly puts the bird cage in her arms.

Close-up of the coloured woman holding the bird cage in her hands and looking dumbfounded.

Back to the scene. Mac lifts the front of the piano; other people drag the Negro out from under it. Mac is holding the front part of the piano all by himself. Suddenly he decides to put it on the truck. Mac tries to get the attention of the two men at the back of the piano, but they are watching their fellow-worker being carried out. So he himself goes to the rear and pushes it on the truck. The foreman has witnessed this and looks at Mac with interest; Mac stands aside, dully looking on.

Medium close-up of the foreman as he talks to Mac and asks him if he wants a job. Mac looks at him, looks at the piano, then says: 'Yes.' The foreman asks him to come inside. Mac remembers his bird cage and turns back.

Back to the scene as Mac takes the cage from the coloured woman. The foreman looks at it in astonishment, then leads the way inside. Mac follows. The ambulance passes by them. Fade out.

Fade in.

TITLE: 'McTeague's enormous strength, useless all his life, stood him in good stead at last.'

Fade out.

Iris in on the store room of the piano store, where Mac and three other men are lifting pianos onto two piano trucks. He shows tremendous strength — more than the three other men together. One of the other men is not doing his work the way Mac wants him to do it. In a bullying way, Mac tells him about it. The man mutters resentfully: 'Aw, go hang yourself.'

Medium close-up of Mac and the other man. Mac stares at him for a second and then, with the force of a piston leaping from its cylinder, he punches the fellow in the jaw.

Back to the scene as the guy topples over, rubs his jaw and then gets up. Mac turns as if nothing had happened and the other two men smile a little, while the man who was hit gets up and comes up to Mac from behind.

313

Close-up of the man who was hit; he looks at Mac in an astonished way and taps him on the sleeve.

Medium shot of the scene as Mac turns around with his fist ready. But the other fellow says : 'Oh, no — let me look at that.' He gingerly takes Mac's fist, looks at it and feels it; Mac looks on dully, unable to figure out what the other guy wants. The fellow who was hit opens his own hand and holds it out as if to say : ' Put it there, kid, some fist! ' Mac shakes hands with the guy, who says : ' Let's have a drink on that.' His hand goes to his hip.

Close-up of the man's face, which is filled with terrible consternation. He looks first towards Mac and then towards the other two fellows.

Back to a medium shot of the scene. Glancing again at Mac and the other fellows, he takes an empty, broken flask out of his overalls. He throws the flask in a corner as one of the other two guys takes out his own flask filled with moonshine, looks around to make sure nobody is looking and comes over to Mac. He takes off the cork and offers it to Mac.

Close-up of Mac as he takes the flask, says : ' Here goes,' and drinks.

Medium shot of all four men. Mac is still holding the flask to his mouth; they look at him in great astonishment. When he finally lowers the flask, it's half-empty. He gives it back. They all stare at him in great wonder. Fade out.

Fade in on a tiny room, papered with newspaper and cutouts from the *Police Gazette*. The bird cage is hanging up in a corner. Mac enters, exhausted, and sits down on the bed. He takes off his shoes and coat, produces a pint flask of moonshine from his pocket and takes a good swig. He looks at the bird cage.

Close-up of the bird cage; the two birds are having a row.

Close-up of Mac watching them. He takes another swig and then puts the bottle down on the bed. He thinks a moment and looks up. His eyes twinkle meanly as he speaks :

TITLE : ' — Five thousand and she wouldn't give me a dime — '

Back to the scene as Mac clenches his fists and growls :

TITLE : ' Oh — if I get my hands on you — '

Back to the scene as he clutches at the air in front of him, then takes the bottle and downs another shot.

Medium shot as he lies back on the bed. Iris out.

Fade in.

TITLE : ' This day shall change all griefs and quarrels into love.'

314

Fade out.

Iris in on half a dozen ladies decorating a Christmas tree which is standing in the main room of the kindergarten. Trina is helping. Fade out.

Iris in on a holly wreath in the window of the piano store. Iris enlarges to reveal the front of the store lit by a flood of light. Holiday shoppers crowd the sidewalk; some carry packages, others hold small Christmas trees. A Salvation Army man dressed as Santa Claus is ringing a bell and asking for contributions.

Quick lap dissolve in to a shot of the interior of the store. With bent knees, Mac and his co-workers walk past the counter on which musical instruments are being piled up from a large box. Mac looks around, sees that no one is looking, and stops his fellow-workers. He takes a pint flask out of his pocket, gives them a drink and then takes one himself.

Close-up of Mac taking a swig. He lowers the bottle and wipes his mouth with the back of his hand. He is just about to put it back when he turns towards the counter and sees something that looks very familiar to him.

Shot from his angle of a clerk sorting three or four concertinas and a couple of flutes.

Back to a close-up of Mac, as he steps up a bit closer.

Close-up of his concertina.

Back to a close-up of Mac as he recognizes his concertina.

Back to a medium shot of the scene. His fellow-workers urge him to get back to work; he does not pay any attention to them. He walks over to the counter, takes the concertina and stares at it.

Medium close-up of the clerk and Mac. Pointing to the concertina, Mac says : ' Say, where did this come from ? ' The clerk replies : ' Why, let's see,' then looks at the tag on the concertina and says :

TITLE : ' We got that from a second-hand store up on Pacific Street.'

Back to the scene as Mac looks at the clerk and then announces : ' Well, it's mine.' The clerk says :

TITLE : ' It's yours for $11.'

Back to the scene as Mac insists : ' It's mine and I'm going to take it.' The clerk says : ' Aw, Mac, what do ya mean ? ' Mac answers :

TITLE : ' I mean it was stolen from me — you got no right to it.'

Back to the scene as the clerk raises one shoulder and puts the concertina up on the shelf, saying : 'You talk to the boss about it, it's none of my affair — you want to buy it? — $11.' Mac gets an idea, takes out his old dilapidated pocket book, removes four single-dollar bills from it, and counts them out. With a gesture of his fingers, the clerk says : 'Ten,' then sticks up his thumb which means one more, that is eleven. Mac fumbles some in his pockets, but cannot find any more money.

Extreme close-up of Mac. He looks at the clerk, looks down at the money, looks up towards the concertina, and then thinks. He gets an idea about where he can get the rest to pay for his concertina, and with sudden decision says :

TITLE : 'I'll give it to ya tomorrow.'

Back to the scene as the clerk replies : 'All right,' points to the concertina and says : 'It's up there.' Mac starts to walk off, pauses to look back at the concertina and then thoughtfully walks on, taking his flask out and gulping a swig as he walks away from camera. Fade out.

Fade in on the main room of the kindergarten. Everything is decorated, but the floor is littered with pine needles and scraps of paper, etc. Five of the ladies are leaving, the sixth is talking to Trina.

Medium close-up of both of them as the lady says :

TITLE : 'Now, if you'll tidy up here, Mrs. McTeague — I think that will be all.'

Back to the scene as she opens her pocket book, gives Trina a silver dollar and says : 'Merry Christmas.' Trina thanks the woman and wishes her the same.

Back to medium shot as Trina walks the lady to the door. Trina goes back into the room and then walks towards the right.

Medium shot of Trina's room. Trina enters and runs over to the trunk. She opens it and puts the dollar into the matchbox, then closes and locks the trunk and shoves it under the bed. She rises, looks around, and then goes over to the oil stove. She starts the fire and puts the coffee on. Fade out.

Fade in on long shot of Market Street, brightly illuminated and bustling with Christmas activity.

Quick lap dissolve to Mac walking on a sidewalk near a little alley. Half a dozen people with packages and small Christmas trees, etc., pass by. Mac looks around and then steps into the alley.

Medium shot as Mac appears in the alley. A man and a girl are kissing each other. Embarrassed, they break apart and walk away. Mac moves

into the place where they were standing and takes out his flask.
Close-up of the flask, which is two-thirds empty. Mac takes one swig,
makes a face and shakes himself. He holds the open bottle and allows
the first drink to settle as he mutters to himself :

Title : ' — And I got to work like a dray horse, while she sits at home
by her stove and counts her money — and then sells my concertina! '

Back to the scene as he curses and takes another swig. He corks the
bottle, puts it back into his pocket and walks on. Fade out.]
Fade in on medium shot of Trina with her skirts pinned up scrubbing
the floor of the room just opposite the main entrance.[1] A black cat is
sitting near her. Trina stops for a moment, wipes her damp forehead
with the back of her mutilated hand, and then resumes her work.
[Quick lap dissolve to long shot of the front of the kindergarten. A
light is shining through the windows of the school, and a little tree
which is decorated and illuminated can be seen. A man passes by
carrying a rocking horse, two balloons and two other packages. A
couple of late delivery wagons pass by. Then Mac appears from the
right and stops at the lamp-post.
Close-up of Mac as he looks up and down the street and then stares
at the school house.
Back to the scene as a policeman slowly passes by and turns to look
over his shoulder at Mac. The policeman turns and walks on. Mac
looks after him and then quickly goes through the gate to the school
house.]
Close-up of the black cat in the school room; it is suddenly frightened
by something and runs off.
Shot from behind Trina towards the entrance. Trina continues scrubbing the floor; steam rises from the bucket beside her.
Close-up of Mac's head in silhouette seen through the doorway.
[Back to the scene as the cat runs towards the cloakroom on the left
and through the double door, which is ajar, as Mac swings the front
door open.
Close-up of Mac. With one sweeping glance he surveys the room and
floor. Then he concentrates his attention on Trina and his eyes reduce
to little pinheads.]
Shot from behind Trina, kneeling. She sits back on her heels and
brings the back of her dripping hand to her mouth in a frightened
way. She is paralysed with fear as the door swings open with force and
Mac enters.

---

[1] In Stroheim's script, this shot starts with an iris in on Trina's hand holding a
scrubbing brush; the iris then enlarges and camera moves back to show Trina.

Medium shot of the scene. Never looking away from Trina, Mac slowly walks towards her with lowered head and clenched fists.

Medium close-up of Trina. She wants to scream but has lost her voice. With the greatest effort she rises. [Camera pans up with her and comes closer until her face fills the entire screen.]

Medium shot of the scene showing Trina and Mac surrounded by Christmas decorations.

Shot from her angle of Mac's face in close-up coming nearer.

Back to extreme close-up of Trina as she cries out, terrified :

TITLE : ' Mac — listen — oh don't — I'll scream — I'll do anything ! I'll give you some money.'

Back to close-up of Mac, as he looks at her and growls :

TITLE : ' I want that five thousand.'

[Back to close-up of Trina as she shakes her head and protests : ' I haven't got it — it isn't here.' She points towards the door and says : ' Uncle Oelbermann's got it.'

Back to Mac as he looks at her and bellows :

Title : 'That's a lie — Oelbermann told me that you got it.'

Back to a close-up of Trina as she shakes her head and cries : 'No! That's a lie — that's not true.'
Back to a close-up of Mac, who says : 'You had it long enough, now I want it — do ya hear?'
Back to Trina as she replies :

Title : 'Mac, I can't give you that money.'

Back to Mac as he speaks : 'Yes you will — every nickel of it.'
Back to Trina as she shakes her head and says : 'No, no, I won't give it to you.'
Back to the scene as Mac orders : 'Give me that money.'
Back to Trina as she shakes her head and says : 'No.'
Back to Mac as he threatens :

Title : 'For the last time — will you give me that money?']

Back to Trina as she cries : 'No! No!'
Medium shot of both of them in front of the double door leading into the cloakroom. Trina has regained her wits and with unbelievable rapidity darts past him and squeezes through the open door.
Medium close-up on the other side of the door as she locks the door from inside and then, terrifically frightened, looks around for something to put in front of the door. There is nothing.
Medium close-up of Trina, inside.
Medium close-up of Mac, outside, banging on the door.
Back to Trina, terrified.
Back to Mac, who throws his weight against the door.
Medium shot of the school room as Mac, with one move, bursts through the locked door. As the door opens, Trina tries to brush past him but Mac grabs and twirls her around and they disappear into the dark cloakroom.
Long shot of the exterior of the school; two policemen saunter up and stand on the sidewalk.
Back to medium shot of Mac and Trina; he hits her once; she staggers back into the darkness and he follows her with clenched fists. Camera keeps on grinding at the open door with the dark room behind for at least twenty feet. Right after Mac and Trina have twirled into the room the black cat runs out frightened towards camera.
Long shot of the two policemen outside the school.
Back to medium shot of the dark cloakroom. Mac can be seen indistinctly, striking Trina repeatedly as she continues to fight back.

319

Back to long shot of the exterior and the two policemen.

Back to medium shot of the scene as Mac backs out, his face scratched and his cheek bleeding. He turns and looks about, takes one step towards camera and steps on one of Trina's shoes. He viciously kicks it in the direction of the cloakroom, and then he goes off to the right towards Trina's room.

Medium shot of Trina's room. The door flies open and Mac enters. [He strikes a match, then sees the light globe and turns on the lamp.] He looks around and sees the trunk by the bed. (The letters 'TS' can be seen painted on the side.)

Medium shot from the school room towards the open door of the cloakroom as the black cat runs inside. Just then Mac reappears and closes the double door behind him.

Medium long shot of the front of the kindergarten. The two policemen stand talking right outside the gate. (One of them is the policeman who had seen Mac outside.)

Medium shot of the school room towards the double door. Mac comes out with the canvas sack. He puts it into the top of his pants and buttons his coat over it; then he turns and closes the door. He starts to walk off towards the right, hesitates a moment, then goes and takes a last look at Trina's motionless body before he walks off.

Medium long shot of the front of the kindergarten; the two policemen are just saying goodnight to each other.

Medium shot of Mac just emerging from the building.

Back to medium long shot of the school as one policeman walks off to the right while the other goes off to the left. Just then Mac appears from inside the school house, opens the gate and looks up and down the street.

Medium shot of the overcast sky.

Close-up of Mac as he adjusts the bag of money hidden in his pants, looks at his injured hand, and then buttons up his jacket and wipes the blood off his hands onto his jacket.

Back to medium close-up of Mac as he looks up towards the sky and mumbles :

TITLE : ' I bet it'll rain tomorrow.'

Back to shot of Mac.

Long shot of school exterior as Mac goes off towards the right. Fade out.

Fade in on a tremendous hand crushing two nude human beings, etc. Fade out.[1]

---

[1] This symbolic shot has been transposed from an earlier scene.

[Iris in on the church bell of old St. Patrick's ringing for Christmas midnight. Iris out.

Iris in on Mac's room. He's got a blanket with a miner's hitch over his shoulder, a candle in one hand, and the other hand on the door knob. His eyes fall on the covered bird cage. With the candle still in his hand, Mac walks towards it and takes off the towel.

Close-up of the cage : only the male is living; the female lies dead on the floor of the cage.

Close-up of Mac as he looks at it without realizing the irony of the female bird's death.

Back to the scene as he opens the door very gently, takes out the dead bird, looks at it for a second, thinks, then puts it on the table. He closes the door, thinks again, looks first towards the door of the room, then underneath the bed. He goes over and takes a couple of sacks from under the bed, covers the cage, picks it up and walks out of the room. Iris out.

Iris in on a ferry boat. Mac appears with the bird cage in his hand and the blanket on his back and jumps on board just as the ferry boat leaves. Slow iris out.

Iris in on people boarding the overland train. Mac is among them, carrying his bird cage and his blanket. Iris out.

Iris in on the front of the kindergarten as kids dressed in Sunday clothes arrive.

Medium shot of six or eight kids assembled in front of the kindergarten door. A couple of new ones arrive; one starts fiddling with the handle of the door. As the child plays with it, the door opens. The child cries : 'Oh, look here.' Playful and laughing, they all walk through the open door.

Medium shot of the main school room shooting towards the main entrance. The kids enter, laughing, and move towards the left of camera in the direction of the cloakroom. A little coloured girl points to something at the bottom of the door; they all look.

Shot from their angle of the cloakroom. The black cat sits in front of the closed door, sniffing through the crack. The kids tiptoe up to the door. As the tallest of the little girls opens the door, the cat slinks in swiftly. Each kid wants to be the first one inside; they all storm in, practically at the same time. They hang their coats and caps up. Suddenly, the little coloured girl points to something in the corner, apparently behind the door. They all look and then, with indescribable fear, run out screaming, falling over each other as they try to get out as quickly as possible. Iris out.

321

Fade in on a long shot from the top of a hill of the 'S'-shaped American River and a highway at the bottom. We can see a sign board reading 'To Iowa Hill', with an arrow pointing to the left, and an automobile stage turning around a sharp curve.

Quick lap dissolve to Mac sitting in the moving stage, holding the canary cage on his lap and smoking his pipe. He seems to be engrossed in the surrounding countryside. He turns and looks at various trails of trees and mountains.

Long shot from the road behind the stage as it goes around the bend. Fade out.

Fade in on a long shot of the main street in Iowa Hill. The stage arrives from camera and stops. Mac and the others get off.

Quick lap dissolve to a medium shot of Mac with the blanket roll and the bird cage as he passes a house which used to be a bar and now serves as a school. He is about to pass an alley on his way towards the house and the grocery store when he stops, retraces two or three steps, and looks towards the right into a gulch.

Close-up of Mac as he smiles, remembering, and then nods gravely and raises his right ear as if he is listening for something.

Quick lap dissolve in to the stamps working at the mills.

Lap dissolve back to a medium shot of Mac as he leaves towards the right.

Medium shot of the stage driver and the grocer looking after him and laughing about the bird cage.

Medium long shot from behind Mac as he descends the valley. Fade out.

Fade in.

TITLE : 'Straight as a homing pigeon following a blind and unreasoned instinct, Mac returned to the Big Dipper Mine.'

Fade out.

Iris in on long shot of the road that leads to the Big Dipper Mine camp. A solitary figure, with blanket roll on one side and the bird cage in his hand, Mac walks towards camera.

Close-up of Mac as he looks at the camp.

Shot from his angle of the mill working.

Back to medium shot of Mac. Hearing the noise of the stamps, he feels at home. He nods, satisfied, and starts to walk down towards the camp. Fade out.

Lap dissolve in to the front of the office building as Mac appears. He nods as he looks at the building, then drops his blanket roll on a lumber pile, knocks at the open door and enters the building.

Quick lap dissolve to three men and a great dane puppy inside the office. The foreman, in muddy overalls, comes forward.

Medium close-up of Mac and the foreman. Mac asks: What's the show for a job?' The foreman asks: 'Have you been a miner already?' When Mac says: 'Yes,' the foreman adds:

TITLE: 'How long since you mine?'

Back to the scene as Mac instinctively lies and replies:

TITLE: 'Oh, year or two.'

Back to the scene as the foreman says: 'Show your hands.' Mac holds out his hard, calloused palms. The foreman says: 'I want a chuck tender on the night shift, can you do it?' Mac nods and answers: 'I'll go on tonight. I can tend a chuck.'

Back to the scene as the foreman goes over, takes a card, then comes back ready to write something down and asks:

TITLE: 'What's your name?'

Close-up of Mac as he starts. He wasn't prepared for this. He says: 'Huh? What?'

Close-up of the foreman, who repeats: 'What's the name?'

Back to a close-up of Mac as he looks quickly from the foreman over to the wall.

Shot from his angle of the railroad calendar with the heading 'Burlington Railroad', which hangs from the desk.

Back to a close-up of Mac as he says:

TITLE: 'Burlington.'

Back to the scene as the foreman writes down the name, gives the card to Mac and tells him to be at the mill at six o'clock. Fade out on Mac leaving.

Fade in.

TITLE: 'McTeague picked up his life again exactly where he had left it the day when his mother had sent him away.'

Fade out.

Iris in on the acetylene light on Mac's cap. Iris enlarges as camera moves back on perambulator to reveal Mac assisting at the burly drill. He changes the drill, putting in a longer one; other miners are working nearby and sweating. Iris out on the drill.

Fade in.

TITLE : ' The second week McTeague's shift worked in the day time and slept at night.'

Fade out.

Iris in on Mac sleeping on his belly, breathing heavily but regularly. He suddenly awakens and sits up, looking about from side to side. An alarm clock hanging on the wall next to the lantern reads 3:30. He mutters : ' What was it? I wonder what it was? ' Then he rises, lights his acetylene lamp and carefully walks out.

Long shot of the interior of the bunk house. Mac carefully goes about the room, throwing the light into the dark corners and peering under all the beds, including his own. Then he goes to the door and starts to walk out.

Medium shot in front of the bunk house. Mac appears, listens, and again mutters : ' I wonder what it was.'

TITLE : ' There was something — Why did I wake up? '

Back to the scene as he listens again, looks around, then finally goes back into the house.

Medium shot of the interior of the bunk house as he arrives back at his bed, muttering to himself : ' There was something.' He looks at the bird in the cage hanging from the wall at his bedside. Finally he tries to overcome his feeling and goes back to bed. Just as he is lying down, he sits up again as if electrocuted, and speaks :

TITLE : ' There is something now — '

Close-up of Mac listening with wide eyes piercing the darkness, as he says :

TITLE : ' I don't know what it is.'

Back to a close-up of him as he turns from one side to the other in rapid succession as if afraid of someone standing behind him. He speaks :

TITLE : ' I don't hear anything — and I don't see anything — but I feel something, right now.'

Back to a close-up as he says : ' I wonder — I don't know.' He goes back to bed. Iris out on his face, awake, listening, his eyes piercing the darkness.

Fade in.

324

Title : 'From this time on there was a change. McTeague grew restless, uneasy, suspicious of something, he could not say what, that annoyed him incessantly.'

Fade out.
Iris in on the bird cage. Iris enlarges and camera moves back on perambulator to reveal Mac again asleep in bed, but fully dressed with his cap on. He again sits up suddenly, listens, peers into the darkness and says :

Title : 'Here it is again — '

Back to the scene as he rises, dumbfounded. He is almost scared. He takes the lantern and walks out.
Medium shot outside the bunk house. Mac appears with the lantern and looks around, moving the lantern up and down as if to light up the surroundings. Then he listens out into the night with his head bent forward. Fade out.
Fade in.

Title : 'What strange sixth sense — what animal cunning — what brute instinct clamoured for recognition and obedience? '

Fade out.
Iris in on the interior of the bunk house. Taking care that he is not disturbing his room mates, Mac very carefully puts the blanket roll — which is already wrapped — up on his shoulder, takes the bird cage and, looking about, tiptoes out.
Medium shot outside the front of the bunk house, lit by moonlight. Mac appears from inside the house with the blanket roll. He closes the door, listens and walks away. Fade out.

Iris in on a day shot of a sheriff and two deputies driving in a Dodge up to the office of the mining camp. The barrels of their Winchester rifles stick out of the car. The cashier and foreman are talking at the fence. As the car pulls up, they turn. As the sheriff gets out, they come up to the car and say : 'Hello.' The sheriff knows them and quickly introduces the two deputies from San Francisco. He asks if a man by the name of McTeague was there; they reply : 'Don't know him.' With gestures, he explains that the man was carrying a bird cage. The cashier and the foreman look at each other and say : 'Yes.'

Title : 'He's been gone for two days.'

Back to the scene as the sheriff asks : 'You don't know where? ' They

325

shake their heads. Iris down on the sheriff's head as he takes off his hat and scratches his head. Iris out completely.

Medium long shot of McTeague as he starts to walk towards a hotel in the distance. Fade out.

Fade in on a shot outside the Hotel Keeler as Mac approaches. A number of saddle horses are tied to trees and fences. A man, Cribbens, is standing at the entrance watching Mac walk up to the hotel.

Medium close-up of McTeague and Cribbens. McTeague quickly turns, and looks over his shoulder at Cribbens as if afraid of something. Cribbens turns and nods in a friendly way; McTeague nods back and enters the hotel. Cribbens slowly follows. Fade out.

Fade in on Cribbens and several other men in the bar-room. Mac enters, walks over to the bar and stands next to Cribbens. He orders himself some beer and starts drinking.

Close-up of one big, burly, bearded fellow who bangs the bar and announces to the others :

TITLE : ' There's gold in them damn Panamint Mountains — I'm telling you ! '

Back to the scene as the remark triggers great controversy among the men.

Medium close-up of Cribbens and McTeague. Cribbens glances questioningly at McTeague, looks him up and down, and asks :

TITLE : ' Were you thinking of prospecting ? '

Back to the scene as McTeague says : ' I don't know.'

TITLE : ' I've been a miner all right.'

Back to the scene as Cribbens continues :

TITLE : ' — Well, I'm going to have a look around — what's your name ? '

Close-up of Mac as he says : ' Huh ? ' and then replies :

TITLE : ' My name's Carter.'

Back to the scene as Cribbens says :

TITLE : ' Well, my name is Cribbens.'

Back to the scene as the two men solemnly shake hands. Cribbens takes out some ' Battle Axe ', bites off a chew and says :

TITLE : 'If you ain't got nothing else to do you might come along with me and see if we can't find a contact, or copper sulphate or something — Even if we don't find colour, we may find silver bearing galena.'

Back to the scene as the two keep on talking. Cribbens suggests that they sit down at the little table. McTeague takes his little bottle and his glass. Cribbens does the same.
Medium shot at the small table as McTeague and Cribbens sit down. Medium close-up of both of them. Banging the table with his fist, Cribbens speaks :

TITLE : 'Gi' me a long distinct contact and sedimentary and igneous rocks and I'll sink a shaft without ever seeing colour.'

Back to the scene as McTeague puts his huge chin in the air, and says :

TITLE : 'Gold is where you find it.'

Close-up of Cribbens, who tucks the corners of his moustache into his mouth and sucks the tobacco juice off of it. He thinks for a second, then abruptly spits out the ends of his moustache and says :

TITLE : 'Say, Carter, let's make a go of this — you got a little cash, I suppose — fifty dollars or so?'

Close-up of Mac as he stammers : 'Huh? Yes, — I — I —'
Back to the scene as Cribbens says : 'Well, I got about $50. We'll go partners — what do ya say?' McTeague looks at him, thinks for a second, then says : 'Sure.' Cribbens adds :

TITLE : 'Well, it's a go then — huh?'

Back to the scene as Mac holds out his hand and answers :

TITLE : 'That's the word.'

Back to the scene. They drink with profound gaiety. Fade out.
Iris in on the front of the livery stable as Cribbens, Mac and the stable owner appear from inside. Cribbens has a saddle horse; Mac has a mule and a burro that is loaded with shovels, picks, etc.
Medium close-up of Mac, who has his blanket roll open on the ground and the sack with the money in his hand. He pays the owner.
Close-up of Cribbens looking at the sack. He sees the money, whistles in amazement and speaks :

TITLE : '— And me asking you if you had fifty — you carry your mine around with you, don't ya?'

Close-up of the livery stable man. He looks at the sack, then at Cribbens, then at Mac, and laughs.

Close-up of McTeague, who glances from Cribbens to the livery stable man and says:

TITLE: 'I guess so — I just sold a claim I had up in Eldorado County — '

Back to the scene. Mac hands the money to the livery stable man, puts the sack back on the blanket, then quickly rolls up the blanket and puts it on the mule.

Close-up of Cribbens looking at the mule.

Shot from his angle of the bird cage hanging on the mule.

Back to Cribbens, who asks:

TITLE: 'Say, why in thunder don't you leave that fool canary behind?'

Shot from his angle of Mac, who looks at Cribbens and then gazes down at the bird cage.

Back to Cribbens as he concludes:

TITLE: ' — And it will surely die — '

Back to McTeague, who shakes his head and answers: 'I've had it too long.'

Back to the scene. Cribbens and the livery stable man laugh and shake their heads. Mac and Cribbens mount, wave to the livery stable man and ride off.

Iris down on the livery stable man looking after them, still smiling. Hold for a second as he shakes his head, and then iris out completely. Fade in.

TITLE: 'A new life began for McTeague.'

Fade out.

Fade in on a long shot of Panamint Valley filled with cattle. In the distance we can see the tiny figures of McTeague and Cribbens with their outfit. Some mounted cowboys pass them, giving a high sign and looking back at them as they ride on. Mac and the rest of the party slowly advance. Fade out.

Fade in on Mac, Cribbens, the horse, the mule and the burro on the summit of a hill. Behind them lies Panamint Valley; in front of them, as far as the eye can see, stretches the desert.

Medium close-up of Cribbens and Mac. Cribbens points with his arm along the Eastern slope of the Panamint Range below them, and speaks :

TITLE : 'Gold Gulch.'

Back to the scene as McTeague looks from the eastern slope out to the desert.
Shot from his angle of the desert as far as the eye can see.
Close-up of McTeague, amazed and uncomfortable. He turns towards Cribbens and asks, 'What do you call that desert out yonder?'
Close-up of Cribbens as he looks towards the desert and then back to Mac. He answers :

TITLE : 'That? That's Death Valley.'

Back to close-up of McTeague. He looks towards the desert as he repeats the words, 'Death Valley'.
Resume on them both as Cribbens says :

TITLE : 'First thing we got to do now is find water — it's pretty rare around here.'

Back to the scene as McTeague looks at him, then nods gravely and says :

TITLE : 'Water — that's the word.'

Resume on them both as they continue to ride down the hill. Fade out.
Iris in on the mule's head. It snorts, pushing its nose into the air and blowing twice through its nostrils. Iris enlarges to reveal Cribbens and McTeague mounted on the mule and the horse. Cribbens says, 'Smells it, the son-of-a-gun. Let him have the reins.' McTeague loosens the reins and they move on. Fade out.
Fade in as they arrive at another part of the canyon. The mule heads straight for the water. Cribbens says to Mac, 'Didn't I tell you?' They both dismount and look at the water.
Shot from their angle of a thin stream of brackish water filtering over a ledge of rock. Cribbens says, 'This is where we'll camp.'
Close-up of Cribbens as he takes the saddle off the horse and turns towards Mac. He speaks :

TITLE : 'We'll have to picket them — there's some loco-weed around here — if they get to eatun that, they'll sure go plumb crazy.'

Back to the scene as Mac nods and they start to picket their animals.

Fade out.

Iris in on McTeague and Cribbens camped where we left them the night before; their animals are picketed nearby. They have lit a little fire, on which they are making coffee. The two men rise and look about.

Close-up of Cribbens who has noticed something.

Shot from his angle of the remains of an abandoned prospector's camp; charred ashes, one or two tins, one or two miner's pans and a broken pick.

Medium shot, as Cribbens turns to Mac, pointing at the evidence of the previous camp. He speaks :

TITLE : 'Don't it make you sick — us mushheads going over ground that's been covered already.'

Resume on the two men as Mac nods in agreement. Cribbens indicates with gestures, 'We better pack up right now', and adds :

TITLE : 'We'd better move to the south.'

Back to the scene as Mac nods again. They start packing up. Fade out.

Fade in on McTeague and Cribbens leading their animals down the side of a gulch.

Close-up of Cribbens as he suddenly spots something and cries, 'Wait a second!' He points and Mac comes up to him : they both look.

Close-up of Cribbens, staring.

Shot from his angle of a rock formation : grano-diorite on slate.

Cribbens speaks as he points to it :

TITLE : 'That's grano-diorite on slate — God! If we could only find the quartz between the two now.'

Close-up of Mac as he looks ahead and then turns back to Cribbens, saying, 'Look on ahead there.'

TITLE : '. . . ain't that quartz?'

Resume on medium shot of the two men. Cribbens puts his hand over Mac's mouth and looks in the direction McTeague is pointing. Then he yells out :

TITLE : 'By God, pardner — By God!'

Medium shot of the scene. Cribbens bends down and examines the rock, then asks Mac to give him the hammer quickly. Mac gets the pick off the burro. Cribbens tells him to get to work hacking some chunks out of the rock, while he gets down on his hands and knees to do the same.

Close-up of Cribbens now terribly excited. He says :

TITLE : 'Got you this time — you son of a gun. — By God ! '

Resume on medium shot of the scene. Cribbens urges Mac to work faster. Suddenly he draws his revolver and throws it towards McTeague, saying :

TITLE : 'Take the gun and look around pardner — this here's our claim.'

Back to the scene as McTeague takes the gun and looks round, puzzled and dumb-founded, while Cribbens puts the chunks into his hat and runs over to their animals. He dumps the quartz fragments into a pan which he has taken from the mule. McTeague grinds the lumps into an iron mortar, while Cribbens sets up the tiny scales and gets out the spoons. He then announces, 'That's fine enough ', and asks McTeague to give him some water. Then he scoops up a spoonful of the mortar and begins to spoon. They are both on their hands and knees, heads close together.

Close-up of Cribbens with the spoon; his hand shakes. He says he cannot do it, for he is too excited. He gives the spoon to McTeague, who takes it and begins rocking it gently in his huge fingers.

Medium close-up of Cribbens and McTeague. Cribbens excitedly whispers :

TITLE : 'Don't see it yet ! '

Back to the scene as he sucks both ends of his moustache into his mouth in anticipation.

Large close-up of the horned spoon with quartz sediment dwindling by degrees, leaving a thin streak of gold (hand-coloured). Cribbens says, ' We got it, pardner.' They look at each other, and then Cribbens gets up with a great leap.

Medium shot of the scene as Cribbens finishes jumping up and down and starts yelling. He is almost crazy with excitement. ' We got it, we struck it, pardner, we got it ! ' He adds :

TITLE : ' We're millionaires ! '

Resume on the scene as he snatches up his revolver and with inconceivable rapidity fires it five times. Then he puts out his hand and shakes McTeague's vigorously. Suddenly he stops, thinks of something and says :

TITLE : ' Say, what'll we call her? '

Back to the scene as McTeague shakes his head and says, ' I don't know — I don't know.' Cribbens slaps McTeague on the back and says, ' I got it.'

TITLE : ' Last Chance.'

Resume on them as Mac nods reflectively. They start to stake out the ground. Fade out.]

TITLE : ' McTeague had been missing from San Francisco weeks, when — '[1]

[Square-shaped iris in on a ' Wanted ' notice, just being tacked up; we can see two hands, a hammer and a tack.]
Close-up of the notice headed by McTeague's wedding photograph. The caption reads :

---

[1] This title does not appear in Stroheim's original script.

332

Reward of $100, for the arrest and apprehension of a man by the name of McTeague who has committed murder in San Francisco and has been traced as far as Western portion of Inyo County. He is believed at this time to be hiding in either the Pinto or Panamint Hills in the vicinity of Keeler.

[The square-shaped iris enlarges as the camera moves back on perambulator, revealing the Wells Fargo office at Modoc, with the sign on the door. The scene includes a general group of cowboys, mounted and dismounted, a couple of buggies and a couple of old Fords.]

Medium long shot of the scene. There are people in front of the grocery store looking at another copy of the notice. [A cowboy rides up in backview, so that we do not see his face. He moves close to the notice.]

Close-up of Marcus. He is wearing cowboy's gear, and it is he who is reading the notice.

Close-up of the section of the notice mentioning the reward for Mac's capture.

Medium shot of the scene. Marcus has finished reading. He turns round, gesturing threateningly, and muttering, 'Damn you, damn you,' then quickly he remounts his horse and rides off.

Long shot of Marcus riding away. Fade out.

[Iris in on a camp fire : Cribbens and McTeague are finishing their supper. They are camping right on their stake-out claim. McTeague has a Winchester rifle across his knees.

Close-up of McTeague, thinking he hears a noise. 'What's that?'

Close-up of Cribbens, looking up.

Medium close-up of the two men. McTeague grabs his Winchester. He gets up. In a second Cribbens has whipped out his revolver and has stepped up to his side.

Medium close-up of the two men. Then Cribbens speaks :

TITLE : 'What is it? See anybody?'

Resume on the two men peering into the night. McTeague shakes his head, and Cribbens asks him :

TITLE : 'Hear anything?'

Back to the scene as McTeague again shakes his head and Cribbens asks him, 'What is it then?' McTeague shrugs his shoulders and says :

TITLE : 'I don't know — there is something.'

Back to the scene. Cribbens asks 'What?' McTeague says :

TITLE : 'Didn't you notice?'

Resume on the two men. Cribbens, who is mystified, repeats, 'What?' But McTeague only shrugs his shoulders, saying, 'I don't know, something or other.' He releases the hammer of the rifle and says: 'I guess it wasn't anything.' Cribbens asks him again for an explanation.
Close-up of McTeague shrugging his shoulders, as he says:

TITLE: 'I had an idea that all — it came all of a sudden — something — I don't know what —'

Resume on the two men. Cribbens tells him, 'Aw, I guess you imagined something.' McTeague nods, 'Yes, I guess so'. Then they roll themselves up in their blankets and lie down again. Iris out.
Iris in on the street in Keeler. A number of saddle-horses are hitched in front of a hotel. The sign reads 'Hotel Keeler'.]
Quick lap dissolve to long shot of the interior of the pool [bar] room of the hotel, shooting from above. The sheriff and posse are assembled there and the sheriff is just swearing them all in.
Medium long shot of the front of the hotel as Marcus rides up.
Medium close-up from behind, as he jumps from his exhausted horse, which is full of lather, its flanks beating.
Medium shot as Marcus enters the hotel on the run.
Close-up of his face.
Shot of the interior of the pool room as Marcus comes in and looks round. He asks the sheriff whether they are going to pursue McTeague. The sheriff nods, and Marcus offers his assistance.
[Close-up of the sheriff. He looks at Marcus, saying:

TITLE: 'Got enough men already — too many.'

Resume on the scene. The sheriff points at the bunch of men. Marcus looks at them.
Resume on the sheriff. He continues:

TITLE: 'It's too hard to find water for so many men and horses.'

Close-up of Marcus, quivering with excitement and anger, as he replies:

TITLE: 'But none of you fellows have ever seen 'um.'

Back to the scene. Marcus looks round at the others as if expecting some applause from them. But they just press closer to get a better look.]
Resume on medium close-up of the sheriff speaking to Marcus, who replies with wild gestures, 'I know him well — I can identify 'um.'
[Back to a general shot of the pool room. Marcus turns to the other

334

men.

Resume on close-up of Marcus, who continues :

TITLE : ' . . . and his wife — the one he killed — is a cousin o' mine.']

Back to long shot as the others get more interested.
Medium close-up of the sheriff and Marcus who adds :

TITLE : ' — and that five thousand he got away with . . . belongs to me [by rights.] '

Long shot of the scene, including the bar. Marcus bellows, ' I'm going along, do ya hear? ' He raises his fists, shouting, ' I'm going along, I tell you.'
Resume on the sheriff and Marcus who yells again :

TITLE : ' There ain't a man o' you big enough to stop me from going — [any two of you].'

Back to close-up of the sheriff, who looks at Marcus with a smile, saying :

TITLE : ' Lord love you — come along then. He's been reported heading for Death Valley.'

Long shot of the room, shot from a high angle. The sheriff slaps Marcus on the shoulder. Fade out.[1]
[Marcus slowly calms down.
Iris out on Marcus telling them all about it.
Iris in on McTeague and Cribbens stretched out on the ground wrapped up in their blankets. The fire has burned down to a mere glimmering of ashes. McTeague suddenly sits up.
Close-up of McTeague as he listens out into the night, and tries to penetrate it with his eyes.
Resume on medium shot as he rises and looks about.
Close-up of Mac as he murmurs :

TITLE : ' Go now, and leave the claim — leave a fortune ! No, by God ! I won't ! '

Back to the scene as Mac raises his Winchester to his shoulder and aims it into space. Then slowly he lets the rifle down and walks off. Fade out.

---

[1] The scene which begins with the title ' That night desolation lay still around Mac ' is inserted at this point in the release print (see page 340).

Iris in on a nearby hill-top. Mac is standing there with the rifle cradled in his arm, looking back over his shoulder in the direction from which they had come.

Close-up of Mac as he shakes his huge head and says:

TITLE: 'Aw, show yourself, will you.'

Resume on Mac as he brings the rifle up to his shoulder and covers point after point along the range of hills to the west, until he faces the camera and says:

TITLE: 'Come on — I ain't afraid of you.'

Back to scene. Suddenly he hears something. He listens in the direction of the sound, but does not hear any more. He continues to gaze out over the country, his rifle at the ready. Iris down on his face, hold there for a second, then iris out completely.]

Medium shot of the posse mounting up in the foreground in front of the Keeler Hotel. Among the many members of the group we can see Marcus holding two canteens, and standing near the sheriff. The sheriff gives the sign and they all ride off. The camera tracks up ahead of them on the perambulator, as the posse canters forward. Slow fade out.

[Fade in on the camp site. McTeague has his mule packed and ready; the canary cage is attached to the pommel and he has Cribbens's Winchester.

Close-up of McTeague who looks around, and listens, compelled by some mysterious fear. He takes the bridle and walks off, leading the mule. Fade out.

Fade in.

TITLE: ' — then the sun looked o'er the shoulder of the world.'

Fade out.

Fade in on a brief shot of a sunrise in natural colour. Fade out.

Fade in on Mac and the mule walking along in the early morning light. Mac stops and takes the gunny sack off the cage, dampens it from his canteen and puts it back. He is about to start again, when he looks back at the mine he has just left. He thinks for a moment, and mutters to himself, 'What a fool I am, leave a million behind.' Then he exclaims savagely:

TITLE: 'No by God! I'm going back.'

Back to the scene as Mac turns the mule around and he starts walking back to the camp.

Shot from perambulator ahead of McTeague as he treads on, his pace getting slower with every step. Suddenly he stops, hesitating. He clenches his fists and gnashes his teeth; then he cries aloud, shaking his head, 'I can't — I can't.' He turns the mule quickly around.

Medium long shot as he retraces his steps. He looks over his shoulder, and then he hits the mule to make him go faster. Fade out.

Fade in on a long shot of Panamint Valley, the same shot as was used when McTeague and Cribbens met the cowboys. In the far distance we can see the posse cantering along. Fade out.

Iris in on the foot of Panamint Range with the desert stretching ahead as far as the eye can see. McTeague appears and stops, looking round.

Close-up of Mac as he wipes the sweat from his face. He looks up towards the sun.

Shot from his angle of the sun shining right into the lens of the camera.

Back to close-up as he says, 'If it gets much hotter, I don't know.' He shakes his head, and wipes his eyelids.

Back to the scene. Suddenly the mule kicks, squeals and lashes out. It runs a few steps, halts, then squeals again. Mac runs after it and

337

finally catches it. He speaks.

TITLE : ' He's eatun some of that loco-weed.'

Back to the scene as Mac pats the mule. He washes out its mouth with water from the canteen, and starts to walk on. Fade out.
Iris in on Cribbens' camp. Cribbens awakens and sits up. He looks over to where Mac had been lying, then looks round and rises quickly, seeing that the mule has gone too. He runs over to the supplies and sees some of them have gone as well.
Close-up of Cribbens. He is dumb-founded. He calls, ' Carter, Oh, Carter! ', using his hand as a megaphone. Then he listens but there is not a sound.
Medium shot as he sits down, paralysed. He does not know what to think. Iris out on his blank-looking face.
Fade in.

TITLE : ' The sun was a disc of molten brass — swimming in the burned-out blue of the sky.' Fade out.]

TITLE : ' The fugitive.'[1]

Long shot of Mac with the mule at the foot of the mountain, headed toward the desert.
Medium shot of Mac and the mule plodding along.
Close-up of Mac and the mule.
Back to another long shot of them walking towards the desert. Fade out.
Fade in on a shot of the sun shining directly into the camera lens, as it just appears over the mountain rock.
[Quick lap dissolve to long shot of McTeague tramping along towards the camera.]
He stops and wipes the sweat from his face and shakes his head. He strips off his woollen shirt, hangs it over the saddle and unbuttons his undershirt. He ties his handkerchief loosely about his neck. Then he takes a rest leaning against the mule and looking up at the sun.
Shot of the sun shining directly into the camera.
Back to medium close-up of Mac. [Fade out.]
[Fade in.

---

[1] This title did not appear in Stroheim's original script. In the release version of *Greed* this short sequence of Mac as the fugitive was inserted before Marcus joins the sheriff's posse, but it has been included here in its original position for the sake of continuity.

TITLE : '—a silence, vast illimitable silence, enfolded him like an immeasurable tide.' Fade out.]

Slow pan across the horizon.
Resume on medium shot of Mac with the mule, as he says :

TITLE : 'If it gets much hotter, I don't know —'

Extreme long shot of the posse, tiny in the distance.
Long shot of Mac and the mule walking along. Then they stop.
Shot of McTeague leaning against the mule again. He is breathing heavily, wiping the perspiration from his face. Suddenly he hears something.
Medium shot of Mac listening. Then he realises what it is and looks down at the ground.
Close-up of twelve rattles, shaking.
Medium shot of Mac and the mule, which shies away.
Another close-up of the rattlesnake.
Back to a close-up of McTeague. He searches the ground, then he spots it.
Shot from his angle of the round coil of the snake, with its slowly-waving clover-shaped head and erect whirring tail.
Close-up of the mule shying.
Close-up of Mac looking steadily at the snake.
[Close-up of the snake's head.
Resume on McTeague still staring at it.]
Close-up of two Gila monsters crawling by.
Shot from McTeague's angle of the snake slithering away after them.
Resume on McTeague as he shakes his head and says, 'God . . . what a country.'
[Close-up of McTeague. His tongue is getting dry and he takes the canteen and has a drink. He washes out the mule's mouth and then lifts up the dried gunny sack over the bird cage.
Close-up of the bird cage. He fills the little water container and then wets the gunny sack. Then he goes on again.]
Pan with Mac and the mule in long shot as they travel on.
Resume on extreme long shot of the posse.
Extreme long shot of Mac and the mule. Fade out.
[Fade in.

TITLE : 'Fiercer and fiercer grew the heat under the remorseless scorch of the sun, until it finally set in a cloudless glory of red gold.'

Fade out.

339

Fade in on a shot of the sunset, including Mac and the mule walking along. Mac stops and wipes himself off. He looks about. He takes the saddle off the mule, unloads the birdcage and his gear and spreads the blanket on the ground. Then he takes a drink of water.
Fade in.

TITLE : ' Never in McTeague's life had sleep seemed so sweet to him.'

Fade out.]
Fade in.

TITLE ; ' That night desolation lay still around Mac. Every nerve cried aloud for rest, yet every instinct seemed goading him to hurry on.'[1]

Fade out.
Long shot of the desert. Mac is asleep and the mule stands nearby.
Iris in on Mac's sleeping face. He suddenly sits up, wide awake, alert, listening, his eyes piercing the darkness. The mule stands in the background.
Medium close-up as he rises with the Winchester in his arm. He looks round quickly and furtively.
Close-up of McTeague as he yells out in frenzy :

TITLE : ' Damn you, come on, will you — and have it out ! '

Resume on Mac in medium shot as he brings the rifle to his shoulder and covers bush after bush. Suddenly the rifle discharges.
Close-up of Mac. He lowers the rifle hastily, cursing himself. ' You fool — you've done it now — they could hear that miles away.'
Medium shot of Mac as he stands listening intently, the rifle smoking in his hands.
Close-up of him listening. [Mac turns quickly, rolls up the blanket and saddles his mule.
Close-up of McTeague as he puts his outfit together, and speaks :

TITLE : ' Hurry on, you fool — you've done it — they ain't far off now.'

Resume on Mac. He is ready to go and he starts to reload the gun.]
Medium close-up of McTeague as he looks at the gun.
Close-up from his angle of the empty magazine.
Back to medium shot as he claps his hand to his side, feeling rapidly for a cartridge.
[Close-up of McTeague as he realises that he has no cartridges with him.]

---

[1] This title did not appear in Stroheim's original script.

Long shot of Mac as he throws the rifle away with a terrible curse.
[He takes the canteen and fills it from a mud hole. He takes a few steps towards the camera, then stops.
Close-up of McTeague as he thinks, gets an idea and says :

Title : ' You don't dare come out here after me.'

Resume on McTeague as he walks out of shot to the right of the camera.] Fade out.
[Fade in on Cribbens's camp. Cribbens is sitting at the fire. The sheriff's posse arrives and dismounts.
Medium shot of Cribbens with his drawn revolver. He thinks they are going to swipe his claim, until he recognizes the sheriff and his deputies. They ask him about the man with the canary cage, and he replies, ' Yes ', adding :

Title : ' He disappeared last night.'

Close-up of Marcus, sore as a boil.
Resume on medium shot as Cribbens explains that they have struck a deposit, and points to it. The sheriff looks at his watch, then gives orders to camp.
Close-up of Marcus looking off into the valley.
Iris down on his face filled with indescribable hate. The camera holds for a second, then iris out completely.
Iris in on McTeague's feet and the mule's hoofs cracking the sun-baked flakes of alkali, white as snow as they walk.]
Long shot of Mac and the mule travelling along.
Extreme long shot of the posse in the distance.
Resume on Mac and the mule who have halted for a moment.

Title : ' And for days on Mac went . . . chasing the receding horizon that always fled before him.'[1]

Fade out.
Fade in on McTeague and the mule dragging themselves along, nothing in sight but alkali. [The mule stops and lies down with his jaws wide open. McTeague takes a handful of water and wipes out its mouth and again sprinkles the flour sacks on the birdcage.
Close-up of McTeague who speaks :

Title : ' I got to get out of here — I ain't got any too much water.'

[1] This title did not appear in Stroheim's original script, which had the following : ' Once more the dawn flamed and glowed like a brazier and the sun rose, a vast, red-hot coal floating in fire.'

Back to the scene as he urges the mule on. Fade out.]
Fade in on medium long shot of McTeague and the mule approaching a tree and a few bushes in the distance.

TITLE : 'The last waterhole.'[1]

Back to the scene as Mac and the mule arrive at the waterhole.
Medium close-up of Mac lying prone on the ground beside the hole.
Medium shot of Mac filling a pan of water for the mule, then filling his canteen and giving water to the bird.
Extreme long shot of the posse in the distance.
Medium shot of the place where McTeague had stopped the night before and fired his rifle, then changed his direction. The sheriff's posse rides up and stops. They look at the footprints and can hardly believe their eyes. They all remain mounted throughout this scene.
[Close-up of the sheriff who speaks :

TITLE : 'It ain't reason — what in thunder is he up to — cutting out into Death Valley at this time of the year.'

Resume on a general shot of the posse, as a discussion begins about their next movements.
Close-up of the sheriff as he speaks.

TITLE : 'I don't figure on going into that alkali sink with no eight men and horses.'

Close-up of Marcus protesting.]
Medium close-up of the sheriff as he speaks to Marcus.

TITLE : 'It's impossible to cross Death Valley. There ain't enough water for one man an' his mount — let alone eight.'

Back to medium close-up of the sheriff concluding his statement.
Medium shot of the posse. Marcus protests with all the strength of his lungs against abandoning the trail now that they have found it.
Medium shot of Mac just leaving the waterhole with the mule.
Cut back to the posse in medium shot.
Medium close-up of the sheriff. He decides what to do.

TITLE : 'We got to [make a] circle around the valley [and head him off at Gold Mountain.]'

Back to medium close-up of Marcus and the sheriff. Marcus says ' I

---

[1] This title did not appear in Stroheim's original script.

won't give up.' He points out :

Title : ' Like hell I will! I ain't sworn in. [I ain't under no orders.]

Close-up of Marcus speaking :

Title : ' I'll do as I please.'

Resume on the sheriff with Marcus. The sheriff replies :

Title : ' Go on then — you damn fool, but I ain't got nothun to do with it. If you catch him put these bracelets on him and bring him in.'

Medium shot of the posse. The sheriff takes a pair of handcuffs out of his pocket and tosses them over to Marcus who catches them and puts them in his pocket. He is as sore as a boil. [He mounts his horse.] Extreme long shot as Marcus rides away, following Mac's footprints. The men in the posse watch him go off towards Death Valley.
[The sheriff gives the sign to go on and they all ride towards the camera.]
Fade in.

Title : ' Mac was headed for the very heart of Death Valley . . . that horrible wilderness of which even beasts were afraid.'[1]

Fade out.
Pan with McTeague's feet and the mule's legs in medium close-up as they drag over the cracked ground. [Mac stops, clears away the hot surface alkali and spreads out his blanket. The mule lays down. He takes off the saddle and looks at the canteen, shaking it. There is not any too much in it. He does not drink but also lays down. Fade out. Fade in on Marcus riding for all he is worth. Fade out.
Fade in.

Title : ' Again the red hot day burned up over the horizon.'

Fade out.]
Fade in on a long shot of the sun rising.
Long shot of Mac and the mule in the distance.
Medium shot of Mac standing next to his mule all packed and ready to go. The sweat is running down his face; he looks up at the sun.
[Shot from his angle of the sun shining right into the camera.
Resume on close-up of Mac.] He speaks :

---

[1] This title did not appear in Stroheim's original script, which had the following : ' The sun set once more — night came on — the stars burned slowly into the cool dark purple of the sky.'

Title : ' It's going to be worse than ever today.'

Resume on Mac and the mule in medium shot.
Long shot of them as they trudge on. Fade out.
Fade in on a long shot of Marcus riding up to the water hole.
Close-up of the horrified reaction on his face. [The horse gives out and collapses.]
Medium close-up of the water hole : it has dried up.
Resume on Marcus's horrified expression.
Medium close-up of Marcus drinking from his canteen as he sits on his horse. Fade out.
Fade in on a long shot of Mac and the mule stopping. Mac clears away the hot surface and spreads out his blanket.
Long shot of Marcus standing beside his dying horse, cursing.
Close-up of Marcus swearing. He takes a can of beans and the canteen off the saddle and takes a drink.
Shot of the sun from his angle shining directly into the lens.
Resume on medium close-up of Marcus wiping the sweat from his brow, then he continues on foot leaving the dead horse behind.
Medium long shot of Mac just lying down with the mule standing nearby.
Long shot of Marcus walking. He stops.
Medium shot of him looking down.
Close-up from his angle of a footprint in the ground.
Back to medium long shot of Marcus.
Another shot of the sun shining relentlessly down.
Medium shot of Marcus. He is raging with thirst. He takes his canteen, gulps a mouthful of water, then realises that it is now empty. He throws the canteen away with a curse, then says :

Title : ' By damn, if he ain't got no water with 'um I'll be in a bad way — [I will for a fact].'

Medium shot of Marcus as he scratches himself.
Long shot of Marcus as he staggers on over the desert.

Title : ' But hatred and the greed for gold kept Marcus up . . .and closer and closer he came.'[1]

Fade in on long shot, with McTeague asleep in the foreground. Marcus sneaks up stealthily from the background with a pistol, walking

---

[1] This title did not appear in Stroheim's original script

at first, then crouching and finally arriving on his hands and knees.
Medium shot of Mac sitting up. He looks about but does not see
anything at first. Then he recognises Marcus and does not move.
Close-up of Marcus, yelling, ' Hands up ! '
Close-up of McTeague reacting with surprise and raising his hands.
Resume on Marcus aiming the gun.
Medium close-up of the two men as Marcus repeats, ' Hands up. [I'll
give you three to do it in — '

TITLE : ' One — '

Resume on Marcus counting :

TITLE : ' Two — '

Back to a shot of Mac from Marcus's angle, putting his hands above
his head.]
Medium shot of them both getting up. Marcus goes up to Mac with
the pistol at the ready, searches him, going through all his pockets.
But Mac has nothing, not even a knife. Marcus asks :

TITLE : ' What did you do with that five thousand ? '

Medium shot of the two men with the mule nearby. Mac replies :

TITLE : ' It's on the mule.'

[Shot from his angle of the mule standing at some distance.
Back to a close-up of Marcus as he turns from the mule towards Mac
and says :

TITLE : ' That canvas sack? '

Close-up of Mac as he says, ' Yes ', and nods.
Close-up of Marcus, saying :

TITLE : ' Got it at last.']

Medium close-up of Mac looking sullenly at Marcus.
A shot of the sun beating down.
Resume on the two men as Marcus asks :

TITLE : ' Got any water? '

Back to the scene as Mac nods in the direction of the mule. Marcus
turns and moves towards the mule, about to reach for the bridle rein,
but the mule squeals, turns up its head and gallops off a little distance.
Medium shot of the mule standing in the white desert.
Close-up of Marcus, swearing.
Close-up of McTeague as he says :

TITLE : ' He ate some loco-weed.'

Long shot of the scene. For a moment Marcus hesitates, then tries
to run after the mule. He realises that McTeague might try to get
away. He stops and thinks for a second, then realises that Mac cannot
get away. He runs on after the mule, the revolver in his hand, shouting
and cursing.
Shot of the mule pursued by Marcus. Marcus stops and waves to
McTeague.
Shot from his angle of McTeague coming slowly towards Marcus.]
Medium shot of Mac and Marcus, who asks :

TITLE : ' Is all the water we got on the saddle? '

Resume on Marcus and Mac looking at the mule.
Long shot of the mule from their point of view.
Medium close-up of them both. [Marcus says :

TITLE : ' If he should keep on running . . . ']

Mac says :

TITLE : 'He ate some loco-weed. We'd better finish him . . . t'ain't right to let him suffer.'

[Back to the scene as a great fear comes over Mac. He says :

TITLE : 'We can catch him all right.'

Resume on them both as Marcus reassuringly answers :

TITLE : 'Oh, I guess we can catch him— '

Medium shot of them both. Marcus lays down the hammer of his revolver and slides it back into his holster.
Shot of the mule running with Mac and Marcus in pursuit. The mule stops and blows through its nostrils.
Medium close-up of Marcus and McTeague. Marcus is panting and says : 'He's clean crazy.' Mac says with a gesture, 'We ought to come on him quiet.' Marcus gestures, 'I'll sneak on him quiet, you stay here.'
Medium long shot of Marcus as he goes forward a step at a time. He is almost within arm's reach of the bridle when the mule shies and gallops away again. Marcus dances with rage, shaking his fists and swearing. Then the mule stops again.
Medium close-up of Marcus as McTeague comes up. Marcus says :

TITLE : 'We've got to follow him.'

McTeague nods gravely as Marcus explains :

TITLE : 'There's no water within seventy miles of here.'

Medium long shot as they start after the mule again, almost catching him again, but he runs away out of reach.
Medium close-up of Marcus and McTeague. Marcus says, 'There ain't no use.'
Back to the scene as he draws his revolver and cocks it.
McTeague says :

TITLE : 'Steady now, it won't do to shoot through the canteen.']

Resume on them as Marcus says, 'Leave that to me.'
Long shot of the mule galloping along.
Medium long shot of Mac and Marcus who is about twenty yards from the mule. He makes a rest with his forearm.
Cut back to the mule in long shot.
Medium close-up of Mac and Marcus. The latter fires towards camera.
[Close-up of McTeague as he looks towards the mule and yells, 'You got him, no, shoot him again.']

347

Medium long shot of the mule trailing one foreleg. Marcus fires as he runs; the mule pitches forwards then rolls sideways on his left side where the canteen is slung. Its legs kick out in one final movement.

Medium shot of the dead mule on the ground. Marcus and McTeague run up to it.

Medium close-up of Marcus who snatches the battered canteen from under the body. He looks at it closely.

Close-up of the busted canteen, not a drip in it.

Close-up of Marcus as he looks from the canteen up towards Mac.

Close-up of McTeague as he looks from the canteen to Marcus.

Medium shot of them both. They are looking at each other, then they look down at the ground.

Shot from their angle of the last drop of water being absorbed into the alkali.

[Back to close-up of Marcus. He says :

TITLE : ' We are dead men.'

Close-up of McTeague as he looks at Marcus, then out towards the desert.

Shot from his angle of the desert.

Quick pan across the sun shining right into the camera.

Resume on McTeague. He is looking up at the sun. Then he turns to Marcus and says :

TITLE : ' Where's the nearest water? ']

Medium close-up of them both. Marcus replies :

TITLE : ' There ain't no water within a hundred miles of here.'

Quick long shot of the two men standing by the dead mule in the middle of the desert.

Medium close-up of them both as McTeague repeats stupidly : ' A hundred miles ', and Marcus continues :

TITLE : ' We . . . are . . . dead . . . men.' [I tell you we're done for — by damn — we ain't ever going to get out of here.']

Resume on them both. McTeague repeats, ' Done for — yes — we're done for.' Marcus asks sharply, ' What are we going to do now? '
[Mac says :

TITLE : ' Well, let's be moving along somewhere.'

Marcus looks at him and asks :

TITLE : ' What's the good of moving on? '

Mac replies :

TITLE : ' What's the good of stopping here? '

Mac wipes his forehead with the back of his hand, and Marcus wipes
himself with a handkerchief.
Close-up of McTeague trying to swallow and saying :

TITLE : ' I never was so thirsty — I can hear my tongue rubbing
against the roof of my mouth.'

Close-up of Marcus as he says, ' Well, we can't stop here. We got
to go somewhere.']
Medium shot of the sun shining directly into the lens.
Medium shot of both men standing hopelessly in the desert.
Close-up of Mac nodding slowly.
Close-up of Marcus as he looks around, then at McTeague [and says :

TITLE : ' Anything we want to take along with us from the mule? ']

Close-up of the canvas bag which has split open with twenty dollar
gold pieces spilling out.
Back to medium close-up of them both. The two men look at each
other and both get the same idea. McTeague takes a step forward and
says : ' I guess . . . '

TITLE : ' . . . even if we're done for, I'll take some of my truck along.'

Marcus very aggressively says : ' Hold on ', and puts one of his hands
against Mac's chest.

TITLE : ' I ain't so sure 'bout who that money belongs to.'

Mac replies, ' Well I am.' They look at each other with ancient hate.
Mac speaks :

TITLE : ' —an' don't try and load that gun either.'

Large close-up of McTeague : his eyes draw to fine twinkling points.
Close-up of his fists knotting themselves like wooden mallets.
Back to medium close-up of Mac as he moves one step nearer to
Marcus, then another.
Close-up of Marcus as he drags the handcuffs from his pocket with his
left hand while holding the revolver like a club in his right. He speaks :

TITLE : [' You soldiered me out of that money once, and played me for a sucker — it's my turn now.] Don't lay your fingers on that sack.'

Medium shot of them both. Marcus bars McTeague's way.

Long shot of the two men. Suddenly they grapple; in another instant they are rolling and struggling on the white ground.

The camera pans to follow the movement of the fight. [Mac thrusts Marcus backwards until he trips and falls over the body of the dead mule. The birdcage breaks from the saddle and rolls out on the ground.]

Close-up of Marcus's hand holding the revolver like a club. McTeague's hand takes it from him.

Close-up of McTeague's left wrist being caught by the handcuffs, as he hits Marcus.

Back to the scene in medium long shot as they fight on. McTeague strikes blindly with the gun. Clouds of dust envelop the two men.

[Close-up of McTeague panting; he looks down to his enemy on the ground.]

Shot from his angle of Marcus on the ground, lying still and bloody. [He suddenly regains his energy.]

Close-up of Marcus, who becomes motionless.

Medium shot of them both. McTeague hits him for the last time and pauses. He tries to rise but feels a pull on his left wrist.

Close-up of the two wrists handcuffed together.

Close-up of McTeague reacting.

Medium long shot of the scene.

Close-up of McTeague looking down.

Close-up from his angle of Marcus's dead body.

Back to close-up of McTeague. He turns and looks at the canvas bag on the saddle of the dead mule.

Shot from his angle of the canvas bag with gold pieces falling out to the sand.

Resume on McTeague. [He looks once more at the handcuffs and at the body.]

Close-up of the empty canteen.

Medium long shot of scene: he sits down cumbersomely and looks around stupidly.

Medium close-up of Mac.

Medium close-up of Marcus's corpse.

[Shot of the desert from Mac's angle.]

Close-up of the dead Marcus.
Back to McTeague as he looks at the bird cage.
Close-up of the bird cage.
Medium long shot of Mac. He fetches the bird cage and places it on Marcus's stomach.
Medium close-up of Mac. He reaches into the cage to catch the bird. It uses its last ounce of strength in endeavouring to escape his grasp.
Close-up of the little bird held in Mac's bloody fingers.
Medium shot of Mac looking round.
Extreme close-up of the bird.
Medium close-up of Mac. He kisses the bird and tosses it into the air.
Close-up of the bird as it lands dead on the empty canteen.
Close-up of Mac. He sits back on his haunches nodding gravely.
Close-up of the bag with the coins spilling out.
Medium close-up of Mac sitting on the ground.
Long shot of the desolate group.
Extreme long shot of Mac with Marcus's dead body and the dead mule seen as tiny figures in the white landscape with the sun shining down on them.
[Back to McTeague nodding gravely.
Fade out.
Fade in.

TITLE : 'O cursed lust of gold!
when for thy sake
the fool throws up his interest in both worlds.
First, starved in this, then damn'd in that to come.'

Fade out.]

THE END